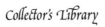

Collector's Library

❀

CLASSIC CRIME STORIES

CLASSIC CRIME STORIES

❀

Selected and Introduced by
DAVID STUART DAVIES

Collector's Library

This edition published in 2014 by
Collector's Library
an imprint of CRW Publishing Limited
69 Gloucester Crescent, London NW1 7EG

ISBN 978 1 909621 17 6

Typeset in Great Britain by Antony Gray
Printed and bound in China by Imago

Contents

Introduction

Most stories feature a crime. Take, for instance, a sweeping saga such as *Gone with the Wind*, or the Dickens classic *Great Expectations*, or modern best-sellers like the Harry Potter series. There is some unpleasant criminal activity in all of them. And yet they are not crime stories *per se*. The unlawful acts are incidental to the main thrust of the plot. In these tales, the murder or the felony are the sparks that help to ignite the plot and keep it burning effectively, but they are not the main focus of the narrative.

In this special bespoke collection each story concerns itself specifically with some unlawful act. This becomes the *raison d'être* of the tale. And tales they are: beautifully constructed miniatures that are lean, sinewy and superbly contrived to engage the reader. Each has a sharp and surprising plot which is unfolded with aplomb. The majority of these stories come from what is often regarded as the golden age of crime fiction, which had its beginnings in the late nineteenth century and flourished in the twentieth until the outbreak of the Second World War. It was a period of real elegance in fiction. In every one of these sweetmeats of literary endeavour there is style, finesse and a wonderful manipulation of the English language. These short tales are not only entertaining because of their content, but also because of the beauty of their construction and delivery.

Most of the stories in this collection have been

plucked from the pages of the long-forgotten periodicals which once filled the shelves of news-agents and railway bookstalls and were eagerly consumed by readers in that far off age before the television and other electronic devices dominated the realm of home entertainment. These publications attracted the greatest of writers and thus it was a time when the short-story format was not only popular but reached a high standard of literary excellence. While it is true that the majority of authors in this collection focused their art on crime fiction, writers were often drawn from other genres to dabble in the dark world that lies on the wrong side of the law. Here we have tales by Robert Louis Stevenson, Guy de Maupassant, Arnold Bennett and W. W. Jacobs, who reveal so much flair for their subject matter that it is a pity they did not write more narratives in this vein.

Many of the tales selected for this volume feature puzzles which require the sharp brain and ingenious deductive reasoning of a uniquely talented individual who is able to unravel the mystery: the literary detective. Many consider Sherlock Holmes to be the godfather of fictional sleuths and in many ways he is, but there were keen-eyed, sharp-nosed investigators before Holmes appeared on the scene, including Poe's Auguste Dupin, Dickens's canny Sergeant Bucket from *Bleak House* and the quick-witted and cunning Sergeant Cuff from Wilkie Collins's *The Moonstone*. However, it is fair to say that Holmes started the vogue for the charismatic, idiosyncratic private detective, a figure that developed and dominated the golden age of crime fiction. From the seeds sown by Holmes grew Peter Wimsey, Hercule Poirot,

Campion and many others. While all these characters owe a debt to Conan Doyle for inventing the great Sherlock, their creators placed their own individual stamp on their sleuths, gracing them with talents, peculiarities and foibles peculiar to them. We have a fair selection of such fellows sprinkled about this collection. Of these, Dr Gideon Fell ('The Wrong Problem') and Dr Thorndyke ('The Echo of Mutiny' & 'The Moabite Cipher') deserve special mention.

Doctor Gideon Fell, an amateur detective, was created by John Dickson Carr, an American who spent most of his adult life in England; Fell is an Englishman who lives in a London suburb and is described as a corpulent man with a moustache who wears a cape and a shovel hat and walks with the aid of two canes. Fell is frequently called upon by the police, whom he frustrates in the usual manner of most fictional detectives by refusing to share his deductions until he has arrived at a complete solution to the problem. He is supposed by many to be based upon G. K. Chesterton, whom in physical appearance and personality Doctor Fell closely resembles. Carr's genius was in conceiving and then explaining apparently impossible crimes. His ingenuity remains unsurpassed – as you will see when you read his contribution to this collection.

Dr John Evelyn Thorndyke is the brainchild of R. Austin Freeman, who described him as an expert in 'medical jurisprudence'. Originally a doctor, Thorndyke turned to the bar and became one of the first forensic-scientist detectives. Freeman's stories present the reader with challenging intellectual puzzles. His solutions are based on his method of collecting all possible data however insignificant and drawing inferences from his findings before looking at any of the protagonists and their possible motives. Indeed, Freeman, it is said, conducted all experiments mentioned in the stories himself. It is this method which gave rise to one of Freeman's most ingenious innovations, 'the inverted detective story', where the criminal act is described first and the reader's interest lies predominantly in Thorndyke's subsequent unravelling of it. This technique is used in 'The Echo of Mutiny'; while the more traditional whodunnit puzzle is found in 'The Moabite Cipher'. The great Raymond Chandler once wrote of Freeman: '[He] is a wonderful performer. He has no equal in the genre.'

While some of the other authors whose tales I have chosen for this crime-fiction cocktail will be familiar to those with an interest in the genre – G. K. Chesterton, Ernest Bramah, Edgar Wallace, M. P. Shiel and others – there are a sprinkling of forgotten names whose stories still sparkle after the dust has been blown off them. For example, A. J. Alan, J. J. Bell and J. S. Fletcher fall into this category. Therefore, while some giants and popular scribes of the genre like Doyle and Carr are well represented in this volume, as they should be, there are unexpected delights provided by less familiar names.

It is a shame that today the short story has become the Cinderella of fiction. This collection of crime stories seeks to open the door once more on that fascinating period where brief doses of mystery, murder and mayhem provide an exquisite divertissement from the mundanities of everyday life.

About the Authors

R. Austin Freeman (1862–1943)

In creating Dr John Evelyn Thorndyke, Richard Austin Freeman was able to use his own knowledge and experience as a physician and trained scientist in conjuring up problems and their fascinating solutions for his detective. There was a great deal of the author in his character. Freeman, like Thorndyke, was a stickler for accuracy and thoroughness: he would test out the various murderous devices he created for his tales before he would allow himself to publish the stories depicting their use. Like Holmes, Thorndyke shares his lodgings – a combined home and laboratory at 5A King's Bench Walk in London's Inner Temple – with a doctor, in this case his chronicler, Christopher Jervis. Thorndyke made his debut in the novel *The Red Thumb Mark* (1907) and appeared regularly thereafter in short stories and novels until *The Jacob Street Mystery* in 1942, a year before his author's death.

G. K. Chesterton (1874–1936)

Gilbert Keith Chesterton is now chiefly remembered for his detective stories featuring the deceptively simple-minded cleric, Father Brown. Ironically, rather like Conan Doyle, he viewed his crime-fiction tales as an easy means to supplement his income from his political and religious writings, which he regarded as being more worthy and important. Father Brown was created by Chesterton in tribute to his friend Father John O'Connor who inspired him and late in life baptised him into the Catholic faith. The pleasure of the Father Brown stories lies not solely in the unravelling of a conundrum, but also in the touches of sly humour and the author's wonderful manipulation of the English language. In 'The Hammer of God', the contrast between the horrendous murder and the gentle way the mild-mannered priest solves the mystery adds an element of quiet comic irony to the narrative.

W. W. Jacobs (1863–1943)

William Wymark Jacobs was the master of the short story. While many of his tales were humorous, his masterpiece was the grisly and gripping 'The Monkey's Paw'. However, 'The Well', the story on offer in this collection, has dark qualities of its own. The author leads the reader to reach various conclusions in this story of blackmail and murder in such a subtle and suggestive way that it creates its own form of mystery and suspense. The objectivity of the style also imbues the story with a sense of impending tragedy.

Maurice Le Blanc (1864–1941)

Le Blanc was a French playwright, short-story writer and novelist, most famous for creating the popular rogue Arsene Lupin, the 'Prince of Thieves'. Lupin swaggered through a thirty-five-year career that made him internationally famous. Le Blanc often had his tongue in his cheek, his plots being parodies of crime fiction, and on occasion he even had his hero lock horns with Britain's brightest detective Holmlock

Shears (also sometimes referred to as Herlock Sholmes). Lupin also had a film career both in silent and talking pictures. John Barrymore portrayed the likeable scoundrel in MGM's *Arsene Lupin* (1932). His colourful character brought Le Blanc wealth and fame and eventually the Legion of Honour. In our story, 'The Lady with the Hatchet', Lupin has adopted the identity of Prince Renine (as he often did) in order to solve a neat little puzzle concerning the mysterious disappearance of five women.

Edgar Wallace (1875–1932)

Wallace was one of the most prolific British writers of adventure stories and crime fiction of all time. In his short life he wrote one hundred and seventy-three books and numerous short stories, thus earning himself the title the 'king of thrillers'. He first found success with his novel *The Four Just Men*: the book became a best-seller and firmly established him as a popular author. He died in the United States *en route* to Hollywood to work on the screenplay *King Kong*. Although he received a screen credit, he did no actual work on the film. 'The Treasure Hunt' features the activities of Mr J. G. Reeder, the mild-mannered but brilliant sleuth who works for the Director of Public Prosecutions.

Max Pemberton (1863–1950)

Sir Max Pemberton was a popular British novelist, working mainly in the adventure and mystery genres. Between 1896 and 1906 he edited *Cassell's Magazine*, a publication based on the *Strand* and containing many excellent short stories and serialised novels. Pemberton was responsible for publishing the early works of R. Austin Freeman and William Le Queux, whose stories also feature in this volume. His novel *The Iron Pirate*, which had a great success in the early 1890s, launched his own writing career. He founded the London School of Journalism in 1920. 'The Ripening Rubies' is one of Pemberton's famous jewel mysteries; written with great style, it captures the elegance of London society at a time when it is being targeted by a cunning jewel thief.

William Le Queux (1864–1927)

Le Queux was a prolific writer, penning over one hundred and fifty novels, and yet he is largely forgotten today. He mainly wrote in the genres of mystery, thriller and espionage. His most successful works were the invasion fantasies *The Great War in England in 1897* (1894) and *The Invasion of 1910*. The luridly titled 'The Purple Death' presents a fascinating mystery concerning three dead bodies found on a boat in the Channel, each one of them bright purple in the face. The various expert members of the Crime Club are called upon to investigate.

A. J. Alan (1883–1941)

A. J. Alan was the pseudonym of Leslie Harrison Lambert, an English magician, intelligence officer, short-story writer and radio broadcaster. He was unique in that he came to be published after he read his own stories on the BBC radio. He broadcast 'My Adventure in Jermyn Street' on 31 January 1924. Following his immediate success, he quickly became one of the most popular broadcasting personalities of the time. He went to considerable trouble over the writing of his stories, taking a couple of months for each one and only broadcasting about five times a year. He carefully cultivated an apparently extemporary, conversational style which made his stories seem like anecdotes concerning strange events that had happened to him. The endings were whimsical and unexpected. 'My Adventure at Chislehurst' is typical of a light-hearted style which masks a clever and cunning construction.

John Dickson Carr (1906–1977)

Carr was an American writer, many years resident in Britain, who published a great number of crime stories under a range of pen names as well as under his own. Carter Dickson, Carr Dickson and Roger Fairbairn were three of the names he used. He focused on complex, plot-driven stories in which the puzzle was paramount, and he was the master of the locked-room mystery. Carr's two major detectives, Dr Fell and Sir Henry Merrivale, are superficially similar. Both are large, blustery, upper-class, eccentric Englishmen somewhere between middle-aged and elderly. It is Fell who features in our chosen tale 'The Wrong Problem', in which he hears the story of two gruesome and baffling murders and exposes the culprit and method. It is a wonderfully atmospheric and subtle piece.

Robert Louis Stevenson (1850–1894)

This Scottish author, famous for this rousing tales of adventure such as *Treasure Island* and *Kidnapped*, also wrote a number of ghost tales and detective mysteries, among them the gothic-horror masterpiece *Dr Jekyll and Mr Hyde*. Indeed, grisly stories had an irresistible appeal for him and he once planned a collection of picturesque murder cases, beginning with 'The Red Barn'. Although the book never materialised, 'Markheim' may well have fitted into such a volume. It is a remarkable nightmare of a tale revealing great psychological perception concerning the mind and guilt of a murderer. The air of unreality that Stevenson evokes effectively contributes to the horror of the story.

Arthur Conan Doyle (1859–1930)

To any reader of crime fiction, Conan Doyle needs no introduction. He is well known as the creator of Sherlock Holmes, a character based partly on Dr Joseph Bell, Doyle's tutor at Edinburgh University, and showing traces of several literary influences, but springing mainly from the author's own rich imagination. Holmes was both an armchair detective and a man of action – 'Come, Watson, the game is afoot.' No classic crime collection would be complete without a Holmes tale. I have chosen 'The Man with the Twisted Lip', which shows the detective in great form and has one of the most unusual openings of any Holmes story. The main plot was suggested to Doyle by the account of a newspaper reporter taking on the role of a beggar on the streets of London in order to write about the experience for his newspaper.

J. J. Bell (1871–1934)

Glasgow-born John Joy Bell, known professionally as J. J. Bell, was a journalist and author. After becoming a journalist, Bell worked for the *Glasgow Evening Times*, and as a sub-editor on the *Scots Pictorial*. His tales described the life of working-class Glaswegians, and were often written in the vernacular. He created the character of 'Macgreegor' for his *Evening Times* readers, and the stories were so popular that they were published in book form and later made into a film. His short stories can be a little over-sentimental, but this is not the case with 'The Message on the Sundial', which puzzles the reader as to how the culprit will be exposed.

Ernest Bramah (1868–1942)

Born in Manchester as Ernest Bramah Smith, he found his way into journalism after an unsuccessful attempt to become a farmer, and from there into writing fiction. He was extremely reticent about his personal life and a rumour circulated that he was a well-known literary figure hiding behind a pseudonym. Bramah did little to dispel this notion. He created Max Carrados, the first blind detective. Blinded in his youth, Carrados was sanguine about his disability: 'A new world to explore, new experiences, new powers awakening; strange new perceptions; life in the fourth dimension.' The stories are clever, and while at times the plots strain credibility concerning Carrados's abilities, they are told with verve and humour. 'Who Killed Charlie Winpole?' concerns the death of a young boy by poisoning and the plight of a wrongly accused man. Max Carrados unfastens the knot of this complicated case with aplomb.

Arnold Bennett (1867–1931)

Bennett was a great English novelist, dramatist and journalist whose major works describe life in 'the Potteries' – the 'Five Towns' of north Staffordshire, where he lived as a boy. However, he did also have a liking for mystery fiction. His novel *The Grand*

Babylon Hotel (1902), for example, contains much pure detection. 'The Murder of the Mandarin' is taken from Bennett's 1907 collection of short stories, *The Grim Smile of the Five Towns*, four of which feature Vera Cheswardine, a wealthy young bride who constantly overspends her allowance. This is a light-hearted and whimsical tale and is great fun.

Sheridan Le Fanu (1814–1873)

Le Fanu was an Irish writer of gothic tales and mystery novels. He was the leading ghost-story writer of the nineteenth century and was central to the development of the genre in the Victorian era. His best known works are *Uncle Silas*, the vampire classic *Carmilla* and *The House by the Churchyard*. His short stories always had a mystery element presented in a rather frightening way. This is certainly true of 'The Murdered Cousin', which is a highly melodramatic tale of avarice, mystifying murder and intrigue.

M. P. Shiel (1865–1947)

Matthew Phipps Shiel was a prolific British writer of West Indian descent. His legal surname remained 'Shiell' though he adopted the shorter version as a *de facto* pen name. He moved to England in 1885, and after working as a teacher and translator, he broke into the fiction market with a series of short stories published in the *Strand* and other magazines. His early literary reputation was based on two collections of short stories *Prince Zaleski* (1895) and *Shapes in the Fire* (1896), which are considered by some critics to be the most flamboyant works of the English decadent movement. 'The Race of Orven', which features the mystical detective Zaleski, is a strange tale of murder and burglary. The style is rich, esoteric and poetic. This is quite the most unusual tale in this collection.

J. S. Fletcher (1863–1935)

Joseph Smith Fletcher, a Yorkshireman, born in Halifax, was a prolific writer in the mode of Edgar Wallace, turning out over 120 books in the crime field alone. Despite this remarkable output, he is hardly remembered today, which is a shame for he certainly had a flair for intriguing the reader from the first page. This he does in 'From Behind the Barrier', which concerns a man from the narrator's past returning to beg for help with a life-threatening dilemma.

Guy de Maupassant (1850–1893)

Regarded as the French master of the short story, Maupassant was, as a young man, encouraged by the novelist Gustave Flaubert to take up writing, for which he had a natural talent. His creative life lasted only a relatively short length of time – eleven years of intensive work – and yet in that period he produced over three hundred short stories and six novels. His subject matter was the trials and tribulations of ordinary people presented in a realistic and objective fashion. 'Vendetta', typical of this style, is a grim tale of revenge recounted almost in documentary mode, which heightens the suspense and tension leading to its uncompromisingly dark denouement.

Headon Hill (1857–1924)

Headon Hill, actually Francis Edward Grainger, worked under his real name as a freelance journalist for various magazines and newspapers. For his own literary works, mostly mystery novels, he used the pseudonym Headon Hill, possibly chosen with the beauty spot overlooking Alum Bay on the Isle of Wight in mind, and created a sharp-witted private investigator with the exotic name of Sebastian Zambra, who appeared in a number of short stories which were published in *The Million* and similar magazines. Zambra, who was very much in the Sherlock Holmes mould, features in 'The Sapient Monkey', a clever little tale of sleight of hand involving a simian accomplice.

About the Editor

David Stuart Davies is an author, playwright and editor. His fiction includes six novels featuring his wartime detective Johnny Hawke and six Sherlock Holmes novels – the latest being *Sherlock Holmes and the Devil's Promise* (2014). He has also penned a series of dark, gritty crime novels set in Yorkshire in the 1980s. The first, *Brothers in Blood*, appeared in 2013 and the second, *Innocent Blood*, in 2015. He is a committee member of the Crime Writers' Association and edits their monthly publication *Red Herrings*; he is also a Fellow of the Royal Literary Fund.

David Stuart Davies is regarded as an authority on Sherlock Holmes and is the author of two Holmes plays, *Sherlock Holmes: The Last Act* and *Sherlock Holmes: The Death and Life*, which are available on audio CD. He has written the Afterwords for all the Collector's Library Holmes volumes, as well as those for many of their other titles.

CLASSIC CRIME STORIES

The Echo of a Mutiny

R. AUSTIN FREEMAN

PART ONE
Death on the Girdler

Popular belief ascribes to infants and the lower animals certain occult powers of divining character denied to the reasoning faculties of the human adult; and is apt to accept their judgement as finally overriding the pronouncements of mere experience.

Whether this belief rests upon any foundation other than the universal love of paradox it is unnecessary to enquire. It is very generally entertained, especially by ladies of a certain social status; and by Mrs Thomas Solly it was loyally maintained as an article of faith.

'Yes,' she moralised, 'it's surprisin' how they know, the little children and the dumb animals. But they do. There's no deceivin' them. They can tell the gold from the dross in a moment, they can, and they reads the human heart like a book. Wonderful, I call it. I suppose it's instinct.'

Having delivered herself of this priceless gem of philosophic thought, she thrust her arms elbow-deep into the foaming washtub and glanced admiringly at her lodger as he sat in the doorway, supporting on one knee an obese infant of eighteen months and on the other a fine tabby cat.

James Brown was an elderly seafaring man, small

and slight in build and in manner suave, insinuating and perhaps a trifle sly. But he had all the sailor's love of children and animals, and the sailor's knack of making himself acceptable to them, for, as he sat with an empty pipe wobbling in the grasp of his toothless gums, the baby beamed with humid smiles, and the cat, rolled into a fluffy ball and purring like a stocking-loom, worked its fingers ecstatically as if it were trying on a new pair of gloves.

'It must be mortal lonely out at the lighthouse,' Mrs Solly resumed. 'Only three men and never a neighbour to speak to; and, Lord! what a muddle they must be in with no woman to look after them and keep 'em tidy. But you won't be overworked, Mr Brown, in these long days; daylight till past nine o'clock. I don't know what you'll do to pass the time.'

'Oh, I shall find plenty to do, I expect,' said Brown, 'what with cleanin' the lamps and glasses and paintin' up the ironwork. And that reminds me,' he added, looking round at the clock, 'that time's getting on. High water at half-past ten, and here it's gone eight o'clock.'

Mrs Solly, acting on the hint, began rapidly to fish out the washed garments and wring them out into the form of short ropes. Then, having dried her hands on her apron, she relieved Brown of the protesting baby.

'Your room will be ready for you, Mr Brown,' said she, 'when your turn comes for a spell ashore; and main glad me and Tom will be to see you back.'

'Thank you, Mrs Solly, ma'am,' answered Brown, tenderly placing the cat on the floor; 'you won't be more glad than what I will.' He shook hands warmly with his landlady, kissed the baby, chucked the cat under the chin, and, picking up his little chest by its becket, swung it on to his shoulder and strode out of the cottage.

His way lay across the marshes, and, like the ships in the offing, he shaped his course by the twin towers of Reculver that stood up grotesquely on the rim of the land; and as he trod the springy turf, Tom Solly's fleecy charges looked up at him with vacant stares and valedictory bleatings. Once, at a dyke-gate, he paused to look back at the fair Kentish landscape: at the grey tower of St Nicholas-at-Wade peeping above the trees and the faraway mill at Sarre, whirling slowly in the summer breeze; and, above all, at the solitary cottage where, for a brief spell in his stormy life, he had known the homely joys of domesticity and peace. Well, that was over for the present, and the lighthouse loomed ahead. With a half-sigh he passed through the gate and walked on towards Reculver.

Outside the whitewashed cottages with their official black chimneys a petty-officer of the coastguard was adjusting the halyards of the flagstaff. He looked round as Brown approached, and hailed him cheerily.

'Here you are, then,' said he, 'all figged out in your new togs, too. But we're in a bit of a difficulty, d'ye see. We've got to pull up to Whitstable this morning, so I can't send a man out with you and I can't spare a boat.'

'Have I got to swim out, then?' asked Brown.

The coastguard grinned. 'Not in them new clothes, mate,' he answered. 'No, but there's old Willett's boat; he isn't using her today; he's going over to Minster to see his daughter, and he'll let us have the loan of the boat. But there's no one to go with you, and I'm responsible to Willett.'

'Well, what about it?' asked Brown, with the deep-sea sailor's (usually misplaced) confidence in his power to handle a sailing-boat. 'D'ye think I can't manage a tub of a boat? Me what's used the sea since I was a kid of ten?'

'Yes,' said the coastguard; 'but who's to bring her back?'

'Why, the man that I'm going to relieve,' answered Brown. 'He don't want to swim no more than what I do.'

The coastguard reflected with his telescope pointed at a passing barge. 'Well, I suppose it'll be all right,' he concluded; 'but it's a pity they couldn't send the tender round. However, if you undertake to send the boat back, we'll get her afloat. It's time you were off.'

He strolled away to the back of the cottages, whence he presently returned with two of his mates, and the four men proceeded along the shore to where Willett's boat lay just above high-water mark.

The *Emily* was a beamy craft of the type locally known as a 'half-share skiff', solidly built of oak, with varnished planking and fitted with main and mizzen lugs. She was a good handful for four men, and, as she slid over the soft chalk rocks with a hollow rumble, the coastguards debated the advisability of lifting out the bags of shingle with which she was ballasted. However, she was at length dragged down, ballast and all, to the water's edge, and then, while Brown stepped the main mast, the petty-officer gave him his directions. 'What you've got to do,' said he, 'is to make use of the flood-tide. Keep her nose nor'-

east, and with this trickle of nor'-westerly breeze you ought to make the lighthouse in one board. Anyhow don't let her get east of the lighthouse, or, when the ebb sets in, you'll be in a fix.'

To these admonitions Brown listened with jaunty indifference as he hoisted the sails and watched the incoming tide creep over the level shore. Then the boat lifted on the gentle swell. Putting out an oar, he gave a vigorous shove off that sent the boat, with a final scrape, clear of the beach, and then, having dropped the rudder on to its pintles, he seated himself and calmly belayed the main-sheet.

'There he goes,' growled the coastguard; 'makin' fast his sheet. They will do it' (he invariably did it himself), 'and that's how accidents happen. I hope old Willett'll see his boat back all right.'

He stood for some time watching the dwindling boat as it sidled across the smooth water; then he turned and followed his mates towards the station.

Out on the south-western edge of the Girdler Sand, just inside the two-fathom line, the spindle-shanked lighthouse stood a-straddle on its long screw-piles like some uncouth red-bodied wading bird. It was now nearly half flood-tide. The highest shoals were long since covered, and the lighthouse rose above the smooth sea as solitary as a slaver becalmed in the 'middle passage'.

On the gallery outside the lantern were two men, the entire staff of the building, of whom one sat huddled in a chair with his left leg propped up with pillows on another, while his companion rested a telescope on the rail and peered at the faint grey line of the distant land and the two tiny points that marked the twin spires of Reculver.

'I don't see any signs of the boat, Harry,' said he.

The other man groaned. 'I shall lose the tide,' he complained, 'and then there's another day gone.'

'They can pull you down to Birchington and put you in the train,' said the first man.

'I don't want no trains,' growled the invalid. 'The boat'll be bad enough. I suppose there's nothing coming our way, Tom?'

Tom turned his face eastward and shaded his eyes. 'There's a brig coming across the tide from the north,' he said. 'Looks like a collier.' He pointed his telescope at the approaching vessel, and added: 'She's got two new cloths in her upper fore topsail, one on each leech.'

The other man sat up eagerly. 'What's her trysail like, Tom?' he asked.

'Can't see it,' replied Tom. 'Yes, I can, now: it's tanned. Why, that'll be the old *Utopia*, Harry; she's the only brig I know that's got a tanned trysail.'

'Look here, Tom,' exclaimed the other, 'if that's the *Utopia*, she's going to my home and I'm going aboard of her. Captain Mockett'll give me a passage, I know.'

'You oughtn't to go until you're relieved, you know, Barnett,' said Tom doubtfully; 'it's against regulations to leave your station.'

'Regulations be blowed!' exclaimed Barnett. 'My leg's more to me than the regulations. I don't want to be a cripple all my life. Besides, I'm no good here, and this new chap, Brown, will be coming out presently. You run up the signal, Tom, like a good comrade, and hail the brig.'

'Well, it's your look-out,' said Tom, 'and I don't mind saying that if I was in your place I should cut off home and see a doctor, if I got the chance.' He sauntered off to the flag-locker, and, selecting the two code-flags, deliberately toggled them on to the halyards. Then, as the brig swept up within range, he hoisted the little balls of bunting to the flagstaff-head and jerked the halyards, when the two flags blew out making the signal 'Need assistance'.

Promptly a coal-soiled answering pennant soared to the brig's main-truck; less promptly the collier went about, and, turning her nose down stream, slowly drifted stern-forwards towards the lighthouse. Then a boat slid out through her gangway, and a couple of men plied the oars vigorously.

'Lighthouse ahoy!' roared one of them, as the boat came within hail. 'What's amiss?'

'Harry Barnett has broke his leg,' shouted the lighthouse keeper, 'and he wants to know if Captain Mockett will give him a passage to Whitstable.'

The boat turned back to the brig, and after a brief and bellowed consultation, once more pulled towards the lighthouse.

'Skipper says yus,' roared the sailor, when he was within earshot, 'and he says look alive, 'cause he don't want to miss his tide.'

The injured man heaved a sigh of relief. 'That's good news,' said he, 'though, how the blazes I'm going to get down the ladder is more than I can tell. What do you say, Jeffreys?'

'I say you'd better let me lower you with the tackle,' replied Jeffreys. 'You can sit in the bight of a rope and I'll give you a line to steady yourself with.'

'Ah, that'll do, Tom,' said Barnett; 'but, for the Lord's sake, pay out the fall-rope gently.'

The arrangements were made so quickly that by

the time the boat was fast alongside everything was in readiness, and a minute later the injured man, dangling like a gigantic spider from the end of the tackle, slowly descended, cursing volubly to the accompaniment of the creaking of the blocks. His chest and kitbag followed, and, as soon as these were unhooked from the tackle, the boat pulled off to the brig, which was now slowly creeping stern-foremost past the lighthouse. The sick man was hoisted up the side, his chest handed up after him, and then the brig was put on her course due south across the Kentish Flats.

Jeffreys stood on the gallery watching the receding vessel and listening to the voices of her crew as they grew small and weak in the increasing distance. Now that his gruff companion was gone, a strange loneliness had fallen on the lighthouse. The last of the homeward-bound ships had long since passed up the Princes Channel and left the calm sea desolate and blank. The distant buoys, showing as tiny black dots on the glassy surface, and the spindly shapes of the beacons which stood up from invisible shoals, but emphasised the solitude of the empty sea, and the tolling of the bell buoy on the Shivering Sand, stealing faintly down the wind, sounded weird and mournful. The day's work was already done. The lenses were polished, the lamps had been trimmed, and the little motor that worked the foghorn had been cleaned and oiled. There were several odd jobs, it is true, waiting to be done, as there always are in a lighthouse; but, just now, Jeffreys was not in a working humour. A new comrade was coming into his life today, a stranger with whom he was to be shut up alone, night and day, for a month on end, and whose temper

34

and tastes and habits might mean for him pleasant companionship or jangling and discord without end. Who was this man Brown? What had he been? and what was he like? These were the questions that passed, naturally enough, through the lighthouse keeper's mind and distracted him from his usual thoughts and occupations.

Presently a speck on the landward horizon caught his eye. He snatched up the telescope eagerly to inspect it. Yes, it was a boat; but not the coastguard's cutter, for which he was looking. Evidently a fisherman's boat and with only one man in it. He laid down the telescope with a sigh of disappointment, and, filling his pipe, leaned on the rail with a dreamy eye bent on the faint grey line of the land.

Three long years had he spent in this dreary solitude, so repugnant to his active, restless nature: three blank, interminable years, with nothing to look back on but the endless succession of summer calms, stormy nights and the chilly fogs of winter, when the unseen steamers hooted from the void and the fog-horn bellowed its hoarse warning.

Why had he come to this Godforsaken spot? and why did he stay, when the wide world called to him? And then memory painted him a picture on which his mind's eye had often looked before and which once again arose before him, shutting out the vision of the calm sea and the distant land. It was a brightly coloured picture. It showed a cloudless sky brooding over the deep blue tropic sea: and in the middle of the picture, seesawing gently on the quiet swell, a white-painted barque.

Her sails were clewed up untidily, her swinging yards jerked at the slack braces and her untended wheel

35

revolved to and fro to the oscillations of the rudder.

She was not a derelict, for more than a dozen men were on her deck; but the men were all drunk and mostly asleep, and there was never an officer among them.

Then he saw the interior of one of her cabins. The chart-rack, the telltale compass and the chronometers marked it as the captain's cabin. In it were four men, and two of them lay dead on the deck. Of the other two, one was a small, cunning-faced man, who was, at the moment, kneeling beside one of the corpses to wipe a knife upon its coat. The fourth man was himself.

Again, he saw the two murderers stealing off in a quarter-boat, as the barque with her drunken crew drifted towards the spouting surf of a river-bar. He saw the ship melt away in the surf like an icicle in the sunshine; and, later, two shipwrecked mariners, picked up in an open boat and set ashore at an American port.

That was why he was here. Because he was a murderer. The other scoundrel, Amos Todd, had turned Queen's Evidence and denounced him, and he had barely managed to escape. Since then he had hidden himself from the great world, and here he must continue to hide, not from the law – for his person was unknown now that his shipmates were dead – but from the partner of his crime. It was the fear of Todd that had changed him from Jeffrey Rorke to Tom Jeffreys and had sent him to the Girdler, a prisoner for life. Todd might die – might even now be dead – but he would never hear of it: would never hear the news of his release.

He roused himself and once more pointed his telescope at the distant boat. She was considerably nearer now and seemed to be heading out towards the lighthouse. Perhaps the man in her was bringing a message; at any rate, there was no sign of the coastguard's cutter.

He went in, and, betaking himself to the kitchen, busied himself with a few simple preparations for dinner. But there was nothing to cook, for there remained the cold meat from yesterday's cooking, which he would make sufficient, with some biscuit in place of potatoes. He felt restless and unstrung; the solitude irked him, and the everlasting wash of the water among the piles jarred on his nerves.

When he went out again into the gallery the ebb-tide had set in strongly and the boat was little more than a mile distant; and now, through the glass, he could see that the man in her wore the uniform cap of the Trinity House. Then the man must be his future comrade, Brown; but this was very extraordinary. What were they to do with the boat? There was no one to take her back.

The breeze was dying away. As he watched the boat, he saw the man lower the sail and take to his oars; and something of hurry in the way the man pulled over the gathering tide caused Jeffreys to look round the horizon. And then, for the first time, he noticed a bank of fog creeping up from the east and already so near that the beacon on the East Girdler had faded out of sight. He hastened in to start the little motor that compressed the air for the foghorn and waited awhile to see that the mechanism was running properly. Then, as the deck vibrated to the roar of the horn, he went out once more into the gallery.

The fog was now all round the lighthouse and the boat was hidden from view. He listened intently. The enclosing wall of vapour seemed to have shut out sound as well as vision. At intervals the horn bellowed its note of warning, and then all was still save the murmur of the water among the piles below, and, infinitely faint and far away, the mournful tolling of the bell on the Shivering Sand.

At length there came to his ear the muffled sound of oars working in the holes; then, at the very edge of the circle of grey water that was visible, the boat appeared through the fog, pale and spectral, with a shadowy figure pulling furiously. The horn emitted a hoarse growl; the man looked round, perceived the lighthouse and altered his course towards it.

Jeffreys descended the iron stairway, and, walking along the lower gallery, stood at the head of the ladder earnestly watching the approaching stranger. Already he was tired of being alone. The yearning for human companionship had been growing ever since Barnett left. But what sort of comrade was this stranger who was coming into his life? And coming to occupy so dominant a place in it.

The boat swept down swiftly athwart the hurrying tide. Nearer it came and yet nearer: and still Jeffreys could catch no glimpse of his new comrade's face. At length it came fairly alongside and bumped against the fender-posts; the stranger whisked in an oar and grabbed a rung of the ladder, and Jeffreys dropped a coil of rope into the boat. And still the man's face was hidden.

Jeffreys leaned out over the ladder and watched him anxiously, as he made fast the rope, unhooked the sail from the traveller and unstepped the mast.

When he had set all in order, the stranger picked up a small chest, and, swinging it over his shoulder, stepped on to the ladder. Slowly, by reason of his encumbrance, he mounted, rung by rung, with never an upward glance, and Jeffreys gazed down at the top of his head with growing curiosity. At last he reached the top of the ladder and Jeffreys stooped to lend him a hand. Then, for the first time, he looked up, and Jeffreys started back with a blanched face.

'God Almighty!' he gasped. 'It's Amos Todd!'

As the newcomer stepped on the gallery, the fog-horn emitted a roar like that of some hungry monster. Jeffreys turned abruptly without a word, and walked to the stairs, followed by Todd, and the two men ascended with never a sound but the hollow clank of their footsteps on the iron plates. Silently Jeffreys stalked into the living-room and, as his companion followed, he turned and motioned to the latter to set down his chest.

'You ain't much of a talker, mate,' said Todd, looking round the room in some surprise; 'ain't you going to say "good-morning"? We're going to be good comrades, I hope. I'm Jim Brown, the new hand, I am; what might your name be?'

Jeffreys turned on him suddenly and led him to the window. 'Look at me carefully, Amos Todd,' he said sternly, 'and then ask yourself what my name is.'

At the sound of his voice Todd looked up with a start and turned pale as death. 'It can't be,' he whispered, 'it can't be Jeff Rorke!'

The other man laughed harshly, and leaning forward, said in a low voice: 'Hast thou found me, O mine enemy!'

'Don't say that!' exclaimed Todd. 'Don't call me

39

your enemy, Jeff. Lord knows but I'm glad to see you, though I'd never have known you without your beard and with that grey hair. I've been to blame, Jeff, and I know it; but it ain't no use raking up old grudges. Let bygones be bygones, Jeff, and let us be pals as we used to be.' He wiped his face with his handkerchief and watched his companion apprehensively.

'Sit down,' said Rorke, pointing to a shabby rep-covered armchair; 'sit down and tell me what you've done with all that money. You've blued it all, I suppose, or you wouldn't be here.'

'Robbed, Jeff,' answered Todd; 'robbed of every penny. Ah! that was an unfortunate affair, that job on board the old *Sea-flower*. But it's over and done with and we'd best forget it. They're all dead but us, Jeff, so we're safe enough so long as we keep our mouths shut; all at the bottom of the sea – and the best place for 'em too.'

'Yes,' Rorke replied fiercely, 'that's the best place for your shipmates when they know too much; at the bottom of the sea or swinging at the end of a rope.' He paced up and down the little room with rapid strides, and each time that he approached Todd's chair the latter shrank back with an expression of alarm.

'Don't sit there staring at me,' said Rorke. 'Why don't you smoke or do something?'

Todd hastily produced a pipe from his pocket, and having filled it from a moleskin pouch, stuck it in his mouth while he searched for a match. Apparently he carried his matches loose in his pocket, for he presently brought one forth – a red-headed match, which, when he struck it on the wall, lighted with a pale-blue flame. He applied it to his pipe, sucking in his cheeks while he kept his eyes fixed on his companion. Rorke, meanwhile, halted in his walk to cut some shavings from a cake of hard tobacco with a large clasp-knife; and, as he stood, he gazed with frowning abstraction at Todd.

'This pipe's stopped,' said the latter, sucking ineffectually at the mouthpiece. 'Have you got such a thing as a piece of wire, Jeff?'

'No, I haven't,' replied Rorke; 'not up here. I'll get a bit from the store presently. Here, take this pipe till you can clean your own: I've got another in the rack there.' The sailor's natural hospitality overcoming for the moment his animosity, he thrust the pipe that he had just filled towards Todd, who took it with a mumbled 'Thank you' and an anxious eye on the open knife. On the wall beside the chair was a roughly carved pipe-rack containing several pipes, one of which Rorke lifted out; and, as he leaned over the chair to reach it, Todd's face went several shades paler.

'Well, Jeff,' he said, after a pause, while Rorke cut a fresh 'fill' of tobacco, 'are we going to be pals same as what we used to be?'

Rorke's animosity lighted up afresh. 'Am I going to be pals with the man that tried to swear away my life?' he said sternly; and after a pause he added: 'That wants thinking about, that does; and meantime I must go and look at the engine.'

When Rorke had gone the new hand sat, with the two pipes in his hands, reflecting deeply. Abstractedly he stuck the fresh pipe into his mouth, and, dropping the stopped one into the rack, felt for a match. Still with an air of abstraction he lit the pipe, and having smoked for a minute or two, rose from the chair and began softly to creep across the room, looking about him and listening intently. At the door he paused to look out into the fog, and then, having again listened attentively, he stepped on tiptoe out on to the gallery and along towards the stairway. Of a sudden the voice of Rorke brought him up with a start.

'Hallo, Todd! where are you off to?'

'I'm just going down to make the boat secure,' was the reply.

'Never you mind about the boat,' said Rorke. 'I'll see to her.'

'Right-o, Jeff,' said Todd, still edging towards the stairway. 'But, I say, mate, where's the other man – the man that I'm to relieve?'

'There ain't any other man,' replied Rorke; 'he went off aboard a collier.'

Todd's face suddenly became grey and haggard. 'Then there's no one here but us two!' he gasped; and then, with an effort to conceal his fear, he asked: 'But who's going to take the boat back?'

'We'll see about that presently,' replied Rorke; 'you get along in and unpack your chest.'

He came out on the gallery as he spoke, with a lowering frown on his face. Todd cast a terrified glance at him, and then turned and ran for his life towards the stairway.

'Come back!' roared Rorke, springing forward along the gallery; but Todd's feet were already clattering down the iron steps. By the time Rorke reached the head of the stairs, the fugitive was near the bottom; but here, in his haste, he stumbled, barely saving himself by the handrail, and when he recovered his balance Rorke was upon him. Todd darted to the head of the ladder, but, as he grasped the stanchion, his pursuer seized him by the collar. In a moment he had turned with his hand under his coat. There was a quick blow, a loud curse from Rorke, an answering yell from Todd, and a knife fell spinning through the air and dropped into the fore-peak of the boat below.

'You murderous little devil!' said Rorke in an ominously quiet voice, with his bleeding hand gripping his captive by the throat. 'Handy with your knife as ever, eh? So you were off to give information, were you?'

'No, I wasn't, Jeff,' replied Todd in a choking voice; 'I wasn't, s'elp me, God. Let go, Jeff. I didn't mean no harm. I was only – ' With a sudden wrench he freed one hand and struck out frantically at his captor's face. But Rorke warded off the blow, and, grasping the other wrist, gave a violent push and let go. Todd staggered backwards a few paces along the staging, bringing up at the extreme edge; and here, for a sensible time, he stood with wide-open mouth and starting eyeballs, swaying and clutching wildly at the air. Then, with a shrill scream, he toppled backwards and fell, striking a pile in his descent and rebounding into the water.

In spite of the audible thump of his head on the pile, he was not stunned, for when he rose to the surface, he struck out vigorously, uttering short, stifled cries for help. Rorke watched him with set teeth and quickened breath, but made no move. Smaller and still smaller grew the head with its little circle of ripples, swept away on the swift ebb-tide, and fainter the bubbling cries that came across the smooth water. At length as the small black spot began to fade in the fog, the drowning man, with a final effort, raised his head clear of the surface and sent a last, despairing shriek towards the lighthouse. The foghorn sent back an answering bellow; the head sank below the surface and was seen no more; and in the dreadful stillness that settled down upon the sea there sounded faint and far away the muffled tolling of a bell.

Rorke stood for some minutes immovable, wrapped in thought. Presently the distant hoot of a steamer's whistle aroused him. The ebb-tide shipping was beginning to come down and the fog might lift at any moment; and there was the boat still alongside. She must be disposed of at once. No one had seen her arrive and no one must see her made fast to the lighthouse. Once get rid of the boat and all traces of Todd's visit would be destroyed. He ran down the ladder and stepped into the boat. It was simple. She was heavily ballasted, and would go down if she filled.

He shifted some of the bags of shingle, and, lifting the bottom boards, pulled out the plug. Instantly a large jet of water spouted up into the bottom. Rorke looked at it critically, and, deciding that it would fill her in a few minutes, replaced the bottom boards; and having secured the mast and sail with a few turns of the sheet round a thwart, to prevent them from floating away, he cast off the mooring-rope and stepped on the ladder.

As the released boat began to move away on the tide, he ran up and mounted to the upper gallery to watch her disappearance. Suddenly he remembered Todd's chest. It was still in the room below. With a hurried glance around into the fog, he ran down to the room, and snatching up the chest, carried it out on the lower gallery. After another nervous glance around to assure himself that no craft was in sight, he heaved the chest over the handrail, and, when it fell with a loud splash into the sea, he waited to watch it float away after its owner and the sunken boat. But it never rose; and presently he returned to the upper gallery.

The fog was thinning perceptibly now, and the boat remained plainly visible as she drifted away. But she sank more slowly than he had expected, and presently as she drifted farther away, he fetched the telescope and peered at her with growing anxiety. It would be unfortunate if anyone saw her; if she should be picked up here, with her plug out, it would be disastrous.

He was beginning to be really alarmed. Through the glass he could see that the boat was now rolling in a sluggish, waterlogged fashion, but she still showed some inches of free-board, and the fog was thinning every moment.

Presently the blast of a steamer's whistle sounded close at hand. He looked round hurriedly and, seeing nothing, again pointed the telescope eagerly at the dwindling boat. Suddenly he gave a gasp of relief. The boat had rolled gunwale under; had staggered back for a moment and then rolled again, slowly, finally, with the water pouring in over the submerged gunwale.

In a few more seconds she had vanished. Rorke lowered the telescope and took a deep breath. Now he was safe. The boat had sunk unseen. But he was better than safe: he was free. His evil spirit, the standing menace of his life, was gone, and the wide world, the world of life, of action, of pleasure, called to him.

In a few minutes the fog lifted. The sun shone brightly on the red-funnelled cattle-boat whose whistle had startled him just now, the summer blue came back to sky and sea, and the land peeped once more over the edge of the horizon.

He went in, whistling cheerfully, and stopped the motor; returned to coil away the rope that he had thrown to Todd; and, when he had hoisted a signal for assistance, he went in once more to eat his solitary meal in peace and gladness.

PART TWO
The Singing Bone

(*Related by Christopher Jervis*, MD)

To every kind of scientific work a certain amount of manual labour naturally appertains, labour that cannot be performed by the scientist himself, since art is long but life is short. A chemical analysis involves a laborious 'clean up' of apparatus and laboratory, for which the chemist has no time; the preparation of a skeleton – the maceration, bleaching, 'assembling', and riveting together of bones – must be carried out by someone whose time is not too precious. And so with other scientific activities. Behind the man of science with his outfit of knowledge is the indispensable mechanic with his outfit of manual skill.

Thorndyke's laboratory assistant, Polton, was a fine example of the latter type, deft, resourceful, ingenious and untiring. He was somewhat of an inventive genius, too; and it was one of his inventions that connected us with the singular case that I am about to record.

Though by trade a watchmaker, Polton was, by choice, an optician. Optical apparatus was the passion

46

of his life; and when, one day, he produced for our inspection an improved prism for increasing the efficiency of gas-buoys, Thorndyke at once brought the invention to the notice of a friend at the Trinity House.

As a consequence, we three – Thorndyke, Polton and I – found ourselves early on a fine July morning making our way down Middle Temple Lane bound for the Temple Pier. A small oil-launch lay alongside the pontoon, and, as we made our appearance, a red-faced, white-whiskered gentleman stood up in the cockpit.

'Here's a delightful morning, doctor,' he sang out in a fine, brassy, resonant, seafaring voice; 'sort of day for a trip to the lower river, hey? Hallo, Polton! Coming down to take the bread out of our mouths, are you? Ha, ha!' The cheery laugh rang out over the river and mingled with the throb of the engine as the launch moved off from the pier.

Captain Grumpass was one of the Elder Brethren of the Trinity House. Formerly a client of Thorndyke's he had subsided, as Thorndyke's clients were apt to do, into the position of a personal friend, and his hearty regard included our invaluable assistant.

'Nice state of things,' continued the captain, with a chuckle, 'when a body of nautical experts have got to be taught their business by a parcel of lawyers or doctors, what? I suppose trade's slack and "Satan findeth mischief still", hey, Polton?'

'There isn't much doing on the civil side, sir,' replied Polton, with a quaint, crinkly smile, 'but the criminals are still going strong.'

'Ha! mystery department still flourishing, what? And, by Jove! talking of mysteries, doctor, our people have got a queer problem to work out; something quite in your line – quite. Yes, and, by the Lord Moses, since I've got you here, why shouldn't I suck your brains?'

'Exactly,' said Thorndyke. 'Why shouldn't you?'

'Well, then, I will,' said the captain, 'so here goes. All hands to the pump!' He lit a cigar, and, after a few preliminary puffs, began: 'The mystery, shortly stated, is this: one of our lighthousemen has disappeared – vanished off the face of the earth and left no trace. He may have bolted, he may have been drowned accidentally or he may have been murdered. But I'd rather give you the particulars in order. At the end of last week a barge brought into Ramsgate a letter from the screw-pile lighthouse on the Girdler. There are only two men there, and it seems that one of them, a man named Barnett, had broken his leg, and he asked that the tender should be sent to bring him ashore. Well, it happened that the local tender, the *Warden*, was up on the slip in Ramsgate Harbour, having a scrape down, and wouldn't be available for a day or two, so, as the case was urgent, the officer at Ramsgate sent a letter to the lighthouse by one of the pleasure steamers saying that the man should be relieved by boat on the following morning, which was Saturday. He also wrote to a new hand who had just been taken on, a man named James Brown, who was lodging near Reculver, waiting his turn, telling him to go out on Saturday morning in the coastguard's boat; and he sent a third letter to the coastguard at Reculver asking him to take Brown out to the lighthouse and bring Barnett ashore. Well, between them, they made a fine muddle of it. The coastguard couldn't spare either a boat or a man, so they borrowed a fisherman's boat, and in this the man Brown started off alone, like an idiot, on the chance that Barnett would be able to sail the boat back in spite of his broken leg.

'Meanwhile Barnett, who is a Whitstable man, had signalled a collier bound for his native town, and got taken off; so that the other keeper, Thomas Jeffreys, was left alone until Brown should turn up.

'But Brown never did turn up. The coastguard helped him to put off and saw him well out to sea, and the keeper, Jeffreys, saw a sailing-boat with one man in her making for the lighthouse. Then a bank of fog came up and hit the boat, and when the fog cleared she was nowhere to be seen. Man and boat had vanished and left no sign.'

'He may have been run down,' Thorndyke suggested.

'He may,' agreed the captain, 'but no accident has been reported. The coastguards think he may have capsized in a squall – they saw him make the sheet fast. But there weren't any squalls; the weather was quite calm.'

'Was he all right and well when he put off?' enquired Thorndyke.

'Yes,' replied the captain, 'the coastguards' report is highly circumstantial; in fact, it's full of silly details that have no bearing on anything. This is what they say.' He pulled out an official letter and read: ' "When last seen, the missing man was seated in the boat's stern to windward of the helm. He had belayed the sheet. He was holding a pipe and tobacco-pouch in his hands and steering with his elbow. He was filling the pipe from the tobacco-pouch." There! "He was holding the pipe in his hand," mark you! not with his toes; and he was filling it from a tobacco-pouch, whereas you'd have expected him to fill it from a coal scuttle or a feeding-bottle. Bah!' The captain rammed the letter back in his pocket and puffed scornfully at his cigar.

'You are hardly fair to the coastguard,' said Thorndyke, laughing at the captain's vehemence. 'The duty of a witness is to give all the facts, not a judicious selection.'

'But, my dear sir,' said Captain Grumpass, 'what the deuce can it matter what the poor devil filled his pipe from?'

'Who can say?' answered Thorndyke. 'It may turn out to be a highly material fact. One never knows beforehand. The value of a particular fact depends on its relation to the rest of the evidence.'

'I suppose it does,' grunted the captain; and he continued to smoke in reflective silence until we opened Blackwall Point, when he suddenly stood up.

'There's a steam trawler alongside our wharf,' he announced. 'Now what the deuce can she be doing there?' He scanned the little steamer attentively, and continued: 'They seem to be landing something, too. Just pass me those glasses, Polton. Why, hang me! it's a dead body! But why on earth are they landing it on our wharf? They must have known you were coming, doctor.'

As the launch swept alongside the wharf, the captain sprang up lightly and approached the group gathered round the body. 'What's this?' he asked. 'Why have they brought this thing here?'

The master of the trawler, who had superintended the landing, proceeded to explain.

'It's one of your men, sir,' said he. 'We saw the body lying on the edge of the South Shingles Sand, close to the beacon, as we passed at low water, so we put off the boat and fetched it aboard. As there was nothing to identify the man by, I had a look in his pockets and found this letter.'

He handed the captain an official envelope addressed to: 'Mr J. Brown, co Mr Solly, Shepherd, Reculver, Kent'.

'Why, this is the man we were speaking about, doctor,' exclaimed Captain Grumpass. 'What a very singular coincidence. But what are we to do with the body?'

'You will have to write to the coroner,' replied Thorndyke. 'By the way, did you turn out all the pockets?' he asked, turning to the skipper of the trawler.

'No, sir,' was the reply. 'I found the letter in the first pocket that I felt in, so I didn't examine any of the others. Is there anything more that you want to know, sir?'

'Nothing but your name and address, for the coroner,' replied Thorndyke, and the skipper, having given this information and expressed the hope that the coroner would not keep him 'hanging about', returned to his vessel and pursued his way to Billingsgate.

'I wonder if you would mind having a look at the body of this poor devil, while Polton is showing us his contraptions,' said Captain Grumpass.

'I can't do much without a coroner's order,' replied Thorndyke; 'but if it will give you any satisfaction, Jervis and I will make a preliminary inspection with pleasure.'

'I should be glad if you would,' said the captain. 'We should like to know that the poor beggar met his end fairly.'

The body was accordingly moved to a shed, and, as Polton was led away, carrying the black bag that contained his precious model, we entered the shed and commenced our investigation.

The deceased was a small, elderly man, decently dressed in a somewhat nautical fashion. He appeared to have been dead only two or three days, and the body, unlike the majority of seaborne corpses, was uninjured by fish or crabs. There were no fractured bones or other gross injuries, and no wounds, excepting a ragged tear in the scalp at the back of the head.

'The general appearance of the body,' said Thorndyke, when he had noted these particulars, 'suggests death by drowning, though, of course, we can't give a definite opinion until a post mortem has been made.'

'You don't attach any significance to that scalp-wound, then?' I asked.

'As a cause of death? No. It was obviously inflicted during life, but it seems to have been an oblique blow that spent its force on the scalp, leaving the skull uninjured. But it is very significant in another way.'

'In what way?' I asked.

Thorndyke took out his pocket-case and extracted a pair of forceps. 'Consider the circumstances,' said he. 'This man put off from the shore to go to the lighthouse, but never arrived there. The question is, where did he arrive?' As he spoke he stooped over the corpse and turned back the hair round the wound with the beak of the forceps. 'Look at those white objects among the hair, Jervis, and inside the wound. They tell us something, I think.'

I examined, through my lens, the chalky fragments

to which he pointed. 'These seem to be bits of shells and the tubes of some marine worm,' I said.

'Yes,' he answered; 'the broken shells are evidently those of the acorn barnacle, and the other fragments are mostly pieces of the tubes of the common serpula. The inference that these objects suggest is an important one. It is that this wound was produced by some body encrusted by acorn barnacles and serpula; that is to say, by a body that is periodically submerged. Now, what can that body be, and how can the deceased have knocked his head against it?'

'It might be the stem of a ship that ran him down,' I suggested.

'I don't think you would find many serpulae on the stem of a ship,' said Thorndyke. 'The combination rather suggests some stationary object between tide-marks, such as a beacon. But one doesn't see how a man could knock his head against a beacon, while, on the other hand, there are no other stationary objects out in the estuary to knock against except buoys, and a buoy presents a flat surface that could hardly have produced this wound. By the way, we may as well see what there is in his pockets, though it is not likely that robbery had anything to do with his death.'

'No,' I agreed, 'and I see his watch is in his pocket; quite a good silver one,' I added, taking it out. 'It has stopped at 12.13.'

'That may be important,' said Thorndyke, making a note of the fact; 'but we had better examine the pockets one at a time, and put the things back when we have looked at them.'

The first pocket that we turned out was the left hip-pocket of the monkey jacket. This was apparently the one that the skipper had rifled, for we found in it two letters, both bearing the crest of the Trinity House. These, of course, we returned without reading, and then passed on to the right pocket. The contents of this were commonplace enough, consisting of a briar pipe, a moleskin pouch and a number of loose matches.

'Rather a casual proceeding, this,' I remarked, 'to carry matches loose in the pocket, and a pipe with them, too.'

'Yes,' agreed Thorndyke; 'especially with these very inflammable matches. You notice that the sticks had been coated at the upper end with sulphur before the red phosphorous heads were put on. They would light with a touch, and would be very difficult to extinguish; which, no doubt, is the reason that this type of match is so popular among seamen, who have to light their pipes in all sorts of weather.' As he spoke he picked up the pipe and looked at it reflectively, turning it over in his hand and peering into the bowl. Suddenly he glanced from the pipe to the dead man's face and then, with the forceps, turned back the lips to look into the mouth.

'Let us see what tobacco he smokes,' said he.

I opened the sodden pouch and displayed a mass of dark, fine-cut tobacco. 'It looks like shag,' I said.

'Yes, it is shag,' he replied; 'and now we will see what is in the pipe. It has been only half-smoked out.' He dug out the 'dottle' with his pocketknife on to a sheet of paper, and we both inspected it. Clearly it was not shag, for it consisted of coarsely cut shreds and was nearly black.

'Shavings from a cake of "hard",' was my verdict, and Thorndyke agreed as he shot the fragments back into the pipe.

The other pockets yielded nothing of interest, except a pocketknife, which Thorndyke opened and examined closely. There was not much money, though as much as one would expect, and enough to exclude the idea of robbery.

'Is there a sheath-knife on that strap?' Thorndyke asked, pointing to a narrow leather belt. I turned back the jacket and looked.

'There is a sheath,' I said, 'but no knife. It must have dropped out.'

'That is rather odd,' said Thorndyke. 'A sailor's sheath-knife takes a deal of shaking out as a rule. It is intended to be used in working on the rigging when the man is aloft, so that he can get it out with one hand while he is holding on with the other. It has to be and usually is very secure, for the sheath holds half the handle as well as the blade. What makes one notice the matter in this case is that the man, as you see, carried a pocketknife; and, as this would serve all the ordinary purposes of a knife, it seems to suggest that the sheath-knife was carried for defensive purposes: as a weapon, in fact. However, we can't get much further in the case without a post mortem, and here comes the captain.'

Captain Grumpass entered the shed and looked down commiseratingly at the dead seaman.

'Is there anything, doctor, that throws any light on the man's disappearance?' he asked.

'There are one or two curious features in the case,' Thorndyke replied; 'but, oddly enough, the only really important point arises out of that statement of the coastguard's, concerning which you were so scornful.'

'You don't say so!' exclaimed the captain.

'Yes,' said Thorndyke; 'the coastguard states that

when last seen deceased was filling his pipe from his tobacco-pouch. Now his pouch contains shag; but the pipe in his pocket contains hard cut.'

'Is there no cake tobacco in any of the pockets?'

'Not a fragment. Of course, it is possible that he might have had a piece and used it up to fill the pipe; but there is no trace of any on the blade of his pocket-knife, and you know how this juicy black cake stains a knife-blade. His sheath-knife is missing, but he would hardly have used that to shred tobacco when he had a pocketknife.'

'No,' assented the captain; 'but are you sure he hadn't a second pipe?'

'There was only one pipe,' replied Thorndyke, 'and that was not his own.'

'Not his own!' exclaimed the captain, halting by a huge, chequered buoy, to stare at my colleague. 'How do you know it was not his own?'

'By the appearance of the vulcanite mouthpiece,' said Thorndyke. 'It showed deep tooth-marks; in fact, it was nearly bitten through. Now a man who bites through his pipe usually presents certain definite physical peculiarities, among which is, necessarily, a fairly good set of teeth. But the dead man had not a tooth in his head.'

The captain cogitated a while, and then remarked: 'I don't quite see the bearing of this.'

'Don't you?' said Thorndyke. 'It seems to me highly suggestive. Here is a man who, when last seen, was filling his pipe with a particular kind of tobacco. He is picked up dead, and his pipe contains a totally different kind of tobacco. Where did that tobacco come from? The obvious suggestion is that he had met someone.'

'Yes, it does look like it,' agreed the captain.

'Then,' continued Thorndyke, 'there is the fact that his sheath-knife is missing. That may mean nothing, but we have to bear it in mind. And there is another curious circumstance: there is a wound on the back of the head caused by a heavy bump against some body that was covered with acorn barnacles and marine worms. Now there are no piers or stages out in the open estuary. The question is, what could he have struck?'

'Oh, there is nothing in that,' said the captain. 'When a body has been washing about in a tide-way for close on three days – '

'But this is not a question of a body,' Thorndyke interrupted. 'The wound was made during life.'

'The deuce it was!' exclaimed the captain. 'Well, all I can suggest is that he must have fouled one of the beacons in the fog, stove in his boat and bumped his head, though, I must admit, that's rather a lame explanation.' He stood for a minute gazing at his toes with a cogitative frown and then looked up at Thorndyke.

'I have an idea,' he said. 'From what you say, this matter wants looking into pretty carefully. Now, I am going down on the tender today to make enquiries on the spot. What do you say to coming with me as adviser – as a matter of business, of course – you and Dr Jervis? I shall start about eleven; we shall be at the lighthouse by three o'clock, and you can get back to town tonight, if you want to. What do you say?'

'There's nothing to hinder us,' I put in eagerly, for even at Bugsby's Hole the river looked very alluring on this summer morning.

'Very well,' said Thorndyke, 'we will come. Jervis is

57

evidently hankering for a sea-trip, and so am I, for that matter.'

'It's a business engagement, you know,' the captain stipulated.

'Nothing of the kind,' said Thorndyke; 'it's unmitigated pleasure; the pleasure of the voyage and your high well-born society.'

'I didn't mean that,' grumbled the captain, 'but, if you are coming as guests, send your man for your night gear and let us bring you back tomorrow evening.'

'We won't disturb Polton,' said my colleague; 'we can take the train from Blackwall and fetch our things ourselves. Eleven o'clock, you said?'

'Thereabouts,' said Captain Grumpass; 'but don't put yourselves out.'

The means of communication in London have reached an almost undesirable state of perfection. With the aid of the snorting train and the tinkling, two-wheeled 'gondola', we crossed and recrossed the town with such celerity that it was barely eleven when we reappeared on Trinity Wharf with a joint Gladstone and Thorndyke's little green case.

The tender had hauled out of Bow Creek, and now lay alongside the wharf with a great striped can buoy dangling from her derrick, and Captain Grumpass stood at the gangway, his jolly, red face beaming with pleasure. The buoy was safely stowed forward, the derrick hauled up to the mast, the loose shrouds rehooked to the screw-lanyards, and the steamer, with four jubilant hoots, swung round and shoved her sharp nose against the incoming tide.

For near upon four hours the ever-widening stream of the 'London River' unfolded its moving panorama.

The smoke and smell of Woolwich Reach gave place to lucid air made soft by the summer haze; the grey huddle of factories fell away and green levels of cattle-spotted marsh stretched away to the high land bordering the river valley. Venerable training ships displayed their chequered hulls by the wooded shore, and whispered of the days of oak and hemp, when the tall three-decker, comely and majestic, with her soaring heights of canvas, like towers of ivory, had not yet given place to the mud-coloured saucepans that fly the white ensign nowadays and devour the substance of the British taxpayer: when a sailor was a sailor and not a mere seafaring mechanic. Sturdily breasting the flood-tide, the tender threaded her way through the endless procession of shipping; barges, billy-boys, schooners, brigs; lumpish black-seamen, blue-funnelled China tramps, rickety Baltic barques with twirling windmills, gigantic liners, staggering under a mountain of top-hamper. Erith, Purfleet, Greenhithe, Grays greeted us and passed astern. The chimneys of Northfleet, the clustering roofs of Gravesend, the populous anchorage and the lurking batteries, were left behind, and, as we swung out of the Lower Hope, the wide expanse of sea reach spread out before us like a great sheet of blue-shot satin.

About half-past twelve the ebb overtook us and helped us on our way, as we could see by the speed with which the distant land slid past, and the freshening of the air as we passed through it.

But sky and sea were hushed in a summer calm. Balls of fleecy cloud hung aloft, motionless in the soft blue; the barges drifted on the tide with drooping sails, and a big, striped bell buoy – surmounted by a staff and cage and labelled, 'Shivering Sand' – sat dreaming in the sun above its motionless reflection, to rouse for a moment as it met our wash, nod its cage drowsily, utter a solemn ding-dong, and fall asleep again.

It was shortly after passing the buoy that the gaunt shape of a screw-pile lighthouse began to loom up ahead, its dull-red paint turned to vermilion by the early afternoon sun. As we drew nearer, the name Girdler, painted in huge, white letters, became visible, and two men could be seen in the gallery around the lantern, inspecting us through a telescope.

'Shall you be long at the lighthouse, sir?' the master of the tender enquired of Captain Grumpass; 'because we're going down to the North-East Pan Sand to fix this new buoy and take up the old one.'

'Then you'd better put us off at the lighthouse and come back for us when you've finished the job,' was the reply. 'I don't know how long we shall be.'

The tender was brought to, a boat lowered, and a couple of hands pulled us across the intervening space of water.

'It will be a dirty climb for you in your shore-going clothes,' the captain remarked – he was as spruce as a new pin himself, 'but the stuff will all wipe off.' We looked up at the skeleton shape. The falling tide had exposed some fifteen feet of the piles, and piles and ladder alike were swathed in sea-grass and encrusted with barnacles and worm-tubes. But we were not such town-sparrows as the captain seemed to think, for we both followed his lead without difficulty up the slippery ladder, Thorndyke clinging tenaciously to his little green case, from which he refused to be separated even for an instant.

'These gentlemen and I,' said the captain, as we

stepped on the stage at the head of the ladder, 'have come to make enquiries about the missing man, James Brown. Which of you is Jeffreys?'

'I am, sir,' replied a tall, powerful, square-jawed, beetle-browed man, whose left hand was tied up in a rough bandage.

'What have you been doing to your hand?' asked the captain.

'I cut it while I was peeling some potatoes,' was the reply. 'It isn't much of a cut, sir.'

'Well, Jeffreys,' said the captain, 'Brown's body has been picked up and I want particulars for the inquest. You'll be summoned as a witness, I suppose, so come in and tell us all you know.'

We entered the living-room and seated ourselves at the table. The captain opened a massive pocket-book, while Thorndyke, in his attentive, inquisitive fashion, looked about the odd, cabin-like room as if making a mental inventory of its contents.

Jeffreys' statement added nothing to what we already knew. He had seen a boat with one man in it making for the lighthouse. Then the fog had drifted up and he had lost sight of the boat. He started the foghorn and kept a bright look-out, but the boat never arrived. And that was all he knew. He supposed that the man must have missed the lighthouse and been carried away on the ebb-tide, which was running strongly at the time.

'What time was it when you last saw the boat?' Thorndyke asked.

'About half-past eleven,' replied Jeffreys.

'What was the man like?' asked the captain.

'I don't know, sir; he was rowing, and his back was towards me.'

'Had he any kitbag or chest with him?' asked Thorndyke.

'He'd got his chest with him,' said Jeffreys.

'What sort of chest was it?' enquired Thorndyke.

'A small chest, painted green, with rope beckets.'

'Was it corded?'

'It had a single cord round, to hold the lid down.'

'Where was it stowed?'

'In the stern-sheets, sir.'

'How far off was the boat when you last saw it?'

'About half a mile.'

'Half a mile!' exclaimed the captain. 'Why, how the deuce could you see that chest half a mile away?'

The man reddened and cast a look of angry suspicion at Thorndyke. 'I was watching the boat through the glass, sir,' he replied sulkily.

'I see,' said Captain Grumpass. 'Well, that will do, Jeffreys. We shall have to arrange for you to attend the inquest. Tell Smith I want to see him.'

The examination concluded, Thorndyke and I moved our chairs to the window, which looked out over the sea to the east. But it was not the sea or the passing ships that engaged my colleague's attention. On the wall, beside the window, hung a rudely carved pipe-rack containing five pipes. Thorndyke had noted it when we entered the room, and now, as we talked, I observed him regarding it from time to time with speculative interest.

'You men seem to be inveterate smokers,' he remarked to the keeper, Smith, when the captain had concluded the arrangements for the 'shift'.

'Well, we do like our bit of 'baccy, sir, and that's a fact,' answered Smith. 'You see, sir,' he continued, 'it's a lonely life, and tobacco's cheap out here.'

'How is that?' asked Thorndyke.

'Why, we get it given to us. The small craft from foreign, especially the Dutchmen, generally heave us a cake or two when they pass close. We're not ashore, you see, so there's no duty to pay.'

'So you don't trouble the tobacconists much? Don't go in for cut tobacco?'

'No, sir; we'd have to buy it, and then the cut stuff wouldn't keep. No, it's hard tack to eat out here and hard tobacco to smoke.'

'I see you've got a pipe-rack, too, quite a stylish affair.'

'Yes,' said Smith, 'I made it in my off-time. Keeps the place tidy and looks more ship-shape than letting the pipes lay about anywhere.'

'Someone seems to have neglected his pipe,' said Thorndyke, pointing to one at the end of the rack which was coated with green mildew.

'Yes; that's Parsons, my mate. He must have left it when he went off near a month ago. Pipes do go mouldy in the damp air out here.'

'How soon does a pipe go mouldy if it is left untouched?' Thorndyke asked.

'It's according to the weather,' said Smith. 'When it's warm and damp they'll begin to go in about a week. Now here's Barnett's pipe that he's left behind – the man that broke his leg, you know, sir – it's just beginning to spot a little. He couldn't have used it for a day or two before he went.'

'And are all these other pipes yours?'

'No, sir. This here one is mine. The end one is Jeffreys', and I suppose the middle one is his too, but I don't know it.'

'You're a demon for pipes, doctor,' said the captain,

strolling up at this moment; 'you seem to make a special study of them.'

' "The proper study of mankind is man", ' replied Thorndyke, as the keeper retired, 'and "man" includes those objects on which his personality is impressed. Now a pipe is a very personal thing. Look at that row in the rack. Each has its own physiognomy which, in a measure, reflects the peculiarities of the owner. There is Jeffreys' pipe at the end, for instance. The mouthpiece is nearly bitten through, the bowl scraped to a shell and scored inside and the brim battered and chipped. The whole thing speaks of rude strength and rough handling. He chews the stem as he smokes, he scrapes the bowl violently, and he bangs the ashes out with unnecessary force. And the man fits the pipe exactly: powerful, square-jawed and, I should say, violent on occasion.'

'Yes, he looks a tough customer, does Jeffreys,' agreed the captain.

'Then,' continued Thorndyke, 'there is Smith's pipe, next to it; "coked" up until the cavity is nearly filled and burnt all round the edge; a talker's pipe, constantly going out and being relit. But the one that interests me most is the middle one.'

'Didn't Smith say that was Jeffreys' too?' I said.

'Yes,' replied Thorndyke, 'but he must be mistaken. It is the very opposite of Jeffreys' pipe in every respect. To begin with, although it is an old pipe, there is not a sign of any tooth-mark on the mouthpiece. It is the only one in the rack that is quite unmarked. Then the brim is quite uninjured: it has been handled gently, and the silver band is jet-black, whereas the band on Jeffreys' pipe is quite bright.'

'I hadn't noticed that it had a band,' said the captain. 'What has made it so black?'

Thorndyke lifted the pipe out of the rack and looked at it closely. 'Silver sulphide,' said he, 'the sulphur no doubt derived from something carried in the pocket.'

'I see,' said Captain Grumpass, smothering a yawn and gazing out of the window at the distant tender. 'Incidentally it's full of tobacco. What moral do you draw from that?'

Thorndyke turned the pipe over and looked closely at the mouthpiece. 'The moral is,' he replied, 'that you should see that your pipe is clear before you fill it.' He pointed to the mouthpiece, the bore of which was completely stopped up with fine fluff.

'An excellent moral too,' said the captain, rising with another yawn. 'If you'll excuse me a minute I'll just go and see what the tender is up to. She seems to be crossing to the East Girdler.' He reached the telescope down from its brackets and went out on to the gallery.

As the captain retreated, Thorndyke opened his pocketknife, and, sticking the blade into the bowl of the pipe, turned the tobacco out into his hand.

'Shag, by Jove!' I exclaimed.

'Yes,' he answered, poking it back into the bowl. 'Didn't you expect it to be shag?'

'I don't know that I expected anything,' I admitted. 'The silver band was occupying my attention.'

'Yes, that is an interesting point,' said Thorndyke, 'but let us see what the obstruction consists of.' He opened the green case, and, taking out a dissecting needle, neatly extracted a little ball of fluff from the bore of the pipe. Laying this on a glass slide, he teased it out in a drop of glycerine and put on a cover-glass while I set up the microscope.

'Better put the pipe back in the rack,' he said, as he laid the slide on the stage of the instrument. I did so and then turned, with no little excitement, to watch him as he examined the specimen. After a brief inspection he rose and waved his hand towards the microscope.

'Take a look at it, Jervis,' he said.

I applied my eye to the instrument, and, moving the slide about, identified the constituents of the little mass of fluff. The ubiquitous cotton fibre was, of course, in evidence, and a few fibres of wool, but the most remarkable objects were two or three hairs – very minute hairs of a definite zigzag shape and having a flat expansion near the free end like the blade of a paddle.

'These are the hairs of some small animal,' I said; 'not a mouse or rat or any rodent, I should say. Some small insectivorous animal, I fancy. Yes! Of course! They are the hairs of a mole.' I stood up, and, as the importance of the discovery flashed on me, I looked at my colleague in silence.

'Yes,' he said, 'they are unmistakable; and they furnish the keystone of the argument.'

'You think that this is really the dead man's pipe, then?' I said.

'According to the law of multiple evidence,' he replied, 'it is practically a certainty. Consider the facts in sequence. Since there is no sign of mildew on it, this pipe can have been here only a short time, and must belong either to Barnett, Smith, Jeffreys or Brown. It is an old pipe, but it has no tooth-marks on it. Therefore it has been used by a man who has no teeth. But Barnett, Smith and Jeffreys all have teeth and mark their pipes, whereas Brown has no teeth. The tobacco in it is shag. But these three men do not smoke shag, whereas Brown had shag in his pouch. The silver band is encrusted with sulphide; and Brown carried sulphur-tipped matches loose in his pocket with his pipe. We find hairs of a mole in the bore of the pipe; and Brown carried a moleskin pouch in the pocket in which he appears to have carried his pipe. Finally, Brown's pocket contained a pipe which was obviously not his and which closely resembled that of Jeffreys; it contained tobacco similar to that which Jeffreys smokes and different from that in Brown's pouch. It appears to me quite conclusive, especially when we add to this evidence the other items that are in our possession.'

'What items are they?' I asked.

'First there is the fact that the dead man had knocked his head heavily against some periodically submerged body covered with acorn barnacles and serpulae. Now the piles of this lighthouse answer to the description exactly, and there are no other bodies in the neighbourhood that do: for even the beacons are too large to have produced that kind of wound. Then the dead man's sheath-knife is missing, and Jeffreys has a knife-wound on his hand. You must admit that the circumstantial evidence is overwhelming.'

At this moment the captain bustled into the room with the telescope in his hand. 'The tender is coming up towing a strange boat,' he said. 'I expect it's the missing one, and, if it is, we may learn something. You'd better pack up your traps and get ready to go on board.'

We packed the green case and went out into the gallery, where the two keepers were watching the approaching tender; Smith frankly curious and interested, Jeffreys restless, fidgety and noticeably pale. As the steamer came opposite the lighthouse, three men dropped into the boat and pulled across, and one of them – the mate of the tender – came climbing up the ladder.

'Is that the missing boat?' the captain sang out.

'Yes, sir,' answered the officer, stepping on to the staging and wiping his hands on the reverse aspect of his trousers, 'we saw her lying on the dry patch of the East Girdler. There's been some hanky-panky in this job, sir.'

'Foul play, you think, hey?'

'Not a doubt of it, sir. The plug was out and lying loose in the bottom, and we found a sheath-knife sticking into the kelson forward among the coils of the painter. It was stuck in hard as if it had dropped from a height.'

'That's odd,' said the captain. 'As to the plug, it might have got out by accident.'

'But it hadn't sir,' said the mate. 'The ballast-bags had been shifted along to get the bottom boards up. Besides, sir, a seaman wouldn't let the boat fill; he'd have put the plug back and baled out.'

'That's true,' replied Captain Grumpass; 'and certainly the presence of the knife looks fishy. But where the deuce could it have dropped from, out in the open sea? Knives don't drop from the clouds – fortunately. What do you say, doctor?'

'I should say that it is Brown's own knife, and that it probably fell from this staging.'

Jeffreys turned swiftly, crimson with wrath. 'What

d'ye mean?' he demanded. 'Haven't I said that the boat never came here?'

'You have,' replied Thorndyke; 'but if that is so, how do you explain the fact that your pipe was found in the dead man's pocket and that the dead man's pipe is at this moment in your pipe-rack?'

The crimson flush on Jeffreys' face faded as quickly as it had come. 'I don't know what you're talking about,' he faltered.

'I'll tell you,' said Thorndyke. 'I will relate what happened and you shall check my statements. Brown brought his boat alongside and came up into the living-room, bringing his chest with him. He filled his pipe and tried to light it, but it was stopped and wouldn't draw. Then you lent him a pipe of yours and filled it for him. Soon afterwards you came out on this staging and quarrelled. Brown defended himself with his knife, which dropped from his hand into the boat. You pushed him off the staging and he fell, knocking his head on one of the piles. Then you took the plug out of the boat and sent her adrift to sink, and you flung the chest into the sea. This happened about ten minutes past twelve. Am I right?'

Jeffreys stood staring at Thorndyke, the picture of amazement and consternation; but he uttered no word in reply. 'Am I right?' Thorndyke repeated. 'Strike me blind!' muttered Jeffreys. 'Was you here, then? You talk as if you had been. Anyhow,' he continued, recovering somewhat, 'you seem to know all about it. But you're wrong about one thing. There was no quarrel. This chap, Brown, didn't take to me and he didn't mean to stay out here. He was going to put off and go ashore again and I wouldn't let him. Then he hit out at me with his knife and I knocked it out of his hand and he staggered backwards and went overboard.'

'And did you try to pick him up?' asked the captain.

'How could I,' demanded Jeffreys, 'with the tide racing down and me alone on the station? I'd never have got back.'

'But what about the boat, Jeffreys? Why did you scuttle her?'

'The fact is,' replied Jeffreys, 'I got in a funk, and I thought the simplest plan was to send her to the cellar and know nothing about it. But I never shoved him over. It was an accident, sir; I swear it!'

'Well, that sounds a reasonable explanation,' said the captain. 'What do you say, doctor?'

'Perfectly reasonable,' replied Thorndyke, 'and, as to its truth, that is no affair of ours.'

'No. But I shall have to take you off, Jeffreys, and hand you over to the police. You understand that?'

'Yes, sir, I understand,' answered Jeffreys.

'That was a queer case, that affair on the Girdler,' remarked Captain Grumpass, when he was spending an evening with us some six months later. 'A pretty easy let off for Jeffreys, too – eighteen months, wasn't it?'

'Yes, it was a very queer case indeed,' said Thorndyke. 'There was something behind that "accident", I should say. Those men had probably met before.'

'So I thought,' agreed the captain. 'But the queerest part of it to me was the way you nosed it all out. I've had a deep respect for briar pipes since then. It was a remarkable case,' he continued. 'The way in which you made that pipe tell the story of the murder seems to me like sheer enchantment.'

'Yes,' said I, 'it spoke like the magic pipe – only that wasn't a tobacco-pipe – in the German folk-story of the "Singing Bone". Do you remember it? A peasant found the bone of a murdered man and fashioned it into a pipe. But when he tried to play on it, it burst into a song of its own:

> My brother slew me and buried my bones
> Beneath the sand and under the stones.'

'A pretty story,' said Thorndyke, 'and one with an excellent moral. The inanimate things around us have each of them a song to sing to us if we are but ready with attentive ears.'

The Moabite Cipher

R. AUSTIN FREEMAN

A large and motley crowd lined the pavements of Oxford Street as Thorndyke and I made our way leisurely eastward. Floral decorations and drooping bunting announced one of those functions inaugurated from time to time by a benevolent Government for the entertainment of fashionable loungers and the relief of distressed pickpockets. For a Russian Grand Duke, who had torn himself away, amidst valedictory explosions, from a loving if too demonstrative people, was to pass anon on his way to the Guildhall; and a British Prince, heroically indiscreet, was expected to occupy a seat in the ducal carriage.

Near Rathbone Place Thorndyke halted and drew my attention to a smart-looking man who stood lounging in a doorway, cigarette in hand.

'Our old friend Inspector Badger,' said Thorndyke. 'He seems mightily interested in that gentleman in the light overcoat. How d'ye do, Badger?' for at this moment the detective caught his eye and bowed. 'Who is your friend?'

'That's what I want to know, sir,' replied the inspector. 'I've been shadowing him for the last half-hour, but I can't make him out, though I believe I've seen him somewhere. He don't look like a foreigner, but he has got something bulky in his pocket, so I must keep him in sight until the Duke is safely past.

I wish,' he added gloomily, 'these beastly Russians would stop at home. They give us no end of trouble.'

'Are you expecting any – occurrences, then?' asked Thorndyke.

'Bless you, sir,' exclaimed Badger, 'the whole route is lined with plain-clothes men. You see, it is known that several desperate characters followed the Duke to England, and there are a good many exiles living here who would like to have a rap at him. Hallo! What's he up to now?'

The man in the light overcoat had suddenly caught the inspector's too enquiring eye, and forthwith dived into the crowd at the edge of the pavement. In his haste he trod heavily on the foot of a big, rough-looking man, by whom he was in a moment hustled out into the road with such violence that he fell sprawling face downwards. It was an unlucky moment. A mounted constable was just then backing in upon the crowd, and before he could gather the meaning of the shout that arose from the bystanders, his horse had set down one hind-hoof firmly on the prostrate man's back.

The inspector signalled to a constable, who forthwith made a way for us through the crowd; but even as we approached the injured man, he rose stiffly and looked round with a pale, vacant face.

'Are you hurt?' Thorndyke asked gently, with an earnest look into the frightened, wondering eyes.

'No, sir,' was the reply; 'only I feel queer – sinking – just here.'

He laid a trembling hand on his chest, and Thorndyke, still eyeing him anxiously, said in a low voice to the inspector: 'Cab or ambulance, as quickly as you can.'

A cab was led round from Newman Street, and the injured man put into it. Thorndyke, Badger, and I entered, and we drove off up Rathbone Place. As we proceeded, our patient's face grew more and more ashen, drawn, and anxious; his breathing was shallow and uneven, and his teeth chattered slightly. The cab swung round into Goodge Street, and then – suddenly, in the twinkling of an eye – there came a change. The eyelids and jaw relaxed, the eyes became filmy, and the whole form subsided into the corner in a shrunken heap, with the strange gelatinous limpness of a body that is dead as a whole, while its tissues are still alive.

'God save us! The man's dead!' exclaimed the inspector in a shocked voice – for even policemen have their feelings. He sat staring at the corpse, as it nodded gently with the jolting of the cab, until we drew up inside the courtyard of the Middlesex Hospital, when he got out briskly, with suddenly renewed cheerfulness, to help the porter to place the body on the wheeled couch.

'We shall know who he is now, at any rate,' said he, as we followed the couch to the casualty-room. Thorndyke nodded unsympathetically. The medical instinct in him was for the moment stronger than the legal.

The house-surgeon leaned over the couch, and made a rapid examination as he listened to our account of the accident. Then he straightened himself up and looked at Thorndyke.

'Internal haemorrhage, I expect,' said he. 'At any rate, he's dead, poor beggar! – as dead as Nebuchadnezzar. Ah! here comes a bobby; it's his affair now.'

A sergeant came into the room, breathing quickly,

and looked in surprise from the corpse to the inspector. But the latter, without loss of time, proceeded to turn out the dead man's pockets, commencing with the bulky object that had first attracted his attention; which proved to be a brown-paper parcel tied up with red tape.

'Porkpie, begad!' he exclaimed with a crestfallen air as he cut the tape and opened the package. 'You had better go through his other pockets, sergeant.'

The small heap of odds and ends that resulted from this process tended, with a single exception, to throw little light on the man's identity; the exception being a letter, sealed, but not stamped, addressed in an exceedingly illiterate hand to Mr Adolf Schönberg, 213 Greek Street, Soho.

'He was going to leave it by hand, I expect,' observed the inspector, with a wistful glance at the sealed envelope. 'I think I'll take it round myself, and you had better come with me, sergeant.'

He slipped the letter into his pocket, and, leaving the sergeant to take possession of the other effects, made his way out of the building.

'I suppose, doctor,' said he, as we crossed into Berners Street, 'you are not coming our way! Don't want to see Mr Schönberg, h'm?'

Thorndyke reflected for a moment. 'Well, it isn't very far, and we may as well see the end of the incident. Yes; let us go together.'

No. 213, Greek Street, was one of those houses that irresistibly suggest to the observer the idea of a church organ, either jamb of the doorway being adorned with a row of brass bell-handles corresponding to the stop-knobs.

These the sergeant examined with the air of an

expert musician, and having, as it were, gauged the capacity of the instrument, selected the middle knob on the right-hand side and pulled it briskly; whereupon a first-floor window was thrown up and a head protruded. But it afforded us a momentary glimpse only, for, having caught the sergeant's up-turned eye, it retired with surprising precipitancy, and before we had time to speculate on the apparition, the street-door was opened and a man emerged. He was about to close the door after him when the inspector interposed.

'Does Mr Adolf Schönberg live here?'

The new-comer, a very typical Jew of the red-haired type, surveyed us thoughtfully through his gold-rimmed spectacles as he repeated the name.

'Schönberg – Schönberg? Ah, yes! I know. He lives on the third-floor. I saw him go up a short time ago. Third-floor back'; and indicating the open door with a wave of the hand, he raised his hat and passed into the street.

'I suppose we had better go up,' said the inspector, with a dubious glance at the row of bell-pulls. He accordingly started up the stairs, and we all followed in his wake.

There were two doors at the back on the third-floor, but as the one was open, displaying an un-occupied bedroom, the inspector rapped smartly on the other. It flew open almost immediately, and a fierce-looking little man confronted us with a hostile stare.

'Well?' said he.

'Mr Adolf Schönberg?' enquired the inspector.

'Well? What about him?' snapped our new acquaintance.

'I wished to have a few words with him,' said Badger.

'Then what the deuce do you come banging at *my* door for?' demanded the other.

'Why, doesn't he live here?'

'No. First-floor front,' replied our friend, preparing to close the door.

'Pardon me,' said Thorndyke, 'but what is Mr Schönberglike? I mean – '

'Like?' interrupted the resident. 'He's like a blooming Sheeny, with a carroty beard and gold gig-lamps!' and, having presented this impressionist sketch, he brought the interview to a definite close by slamming the door and turning the key.

With a wrathful exclamation, the inspector turned towards the stairs, down which the sergeant was already clattering in hot haste, and made his way back to the ground-floor, followed, as before, by Thorndyke and me. On the doorstep we found the sergeant breathlessly interrogating a smartly dressed youth, whom I had seen alight from a hansom as we entered the house, and who now stood with a note-book tucked under his arm, sharpening a pencil with deliberate care.

'Mr James saw him come out, sir,' said the sergeant. 'He turned up towards the Square.'

'Did he seem to hurry?' asked the inspector.

'Rather,' replied the reporter. 'As soon as you were inside, he went off like a lamplighter. You won't catch him now.'

'We don't want to catch him,' the detective rejoined gruffly; then, backing out of earshot of the eager pressman, he said in a lower tone: 'That was Mr Schönberg, beyond a doubt, and it is clear that he has some reason for making himself scarce; so I shall consider myself justified in opening that note.'

He suited the action to the word, and, having cut the envelope open with official neatness, drew out the enclosure.

'My hat!' he exclaimed, as his eye fell upon the contents. 'What in creation is this? It isn't shorthand, but what the deuce is it?'

He handed the document to Thorndyke, who, having held it up to the light and felt the paper critically, proceeded to examine it with keen interest. It consisted of a single half-sheet of thin notepaper, both sides of which were covered with strange, crabbed characters, written with a brownish-black ink in continuous lines, without any spaces to indicate the divisions into words; and, but for the modern material which bore the writing, it might have been a portion of some ancient manuscript or forgotten codex.

'What do you make of it, doctor?' enquired the inspector anxiously, after a pause, during which Thorndyke had scrutinised the strange writing with knitted brows.

'Not a great deal,' replied Thorndyke. 'The character is the Moabite or Phoenician – primitive Semitic, in fact – and reads from right to left. The language I take to be Hebrew. At any rate, I can find no Greek words, and I see here a group of letters which *may* form one of the few Hebrew words that I know – the word *badim*, "lies".' But you had better get it deciphered by an expert.'

'If it is Hebrew,' said Badger, 'we can manage it all right. There are plenty of Jews at our disposal.'

'You had much better take the paper to the British

Museum,' said Thorndyke, 'and submit it to the keeper of the Phoenician antiquities for decipherment.'

Inspector Badger smiled a foxy smile as he deposited the paper in his pocketbook. 'We'll see what we can make of it ourselves first,' he said; 'but many thanks for your advice, all the same, doctor. No, Mr James, I can't give you any information at present; you had better apply at the hospital.'

'I suspect,' said Thorndyke, as we took our way homewards, 'that Mr James has collected enough material for his purpose already. He must have followed us from the hospital, and I have no doubt that he has his report, with "full details", mentally arranged at this moment. And I am not sure that he didn't get a peep at the mysterious paper, in spite of the inspector's precautions.'

'By the way,' I said, 'what do you make of the document?'

'A cipher, most probably,' he replied. 'It is written in the primitive Semitic alphabet, which, as you know, is practically identical with primitive Greek. It is written from right to left, like the Phoenician, Hebrew, and Moabite, as well as the earliest Greek, inscriptions. The paper is common cream-laid note-paper, and the ink is ordinary indelible Chinese ink, such as is used by draughtsmen. Those are the facts, and without further study of the document itself, they don't carry us very far.'

'Why do you think it is a cipher rather than a document in straightforward Hebrew?'

'Because it is obviously a secret message of some kind. Now, every educated Jew knows more or less Hebrew, and, although he is able to read and write only the modern square Hebrew character, it is so easy to transpose one alphabet into another that the mere language would afford no security. Therefore, I expect that, when the experts translate this document, the translation or transliteration will be a mere farrago of unintelligible nonsense. But we shall see, and meanwhile the facts that we have offer several interesting suggestions which are well worth consideration.'

'As, for instance – ?'

'Now, my dear Jervis,' said Thorndyke, shaking an admonitory forefinger at me, 'don't, I pray you, give way to mental indolence. You have these few facts that I have mentioned. Consider them separately and collectively, and in their relation to the circumstances. Don't attempt to suck my brain when you have an excellent brain of your own to suck.'

On the following morning the papers fully justified my colleague's opinion of Mr James. All the events which had occurred, as well as a number that had not, were given in the fullest and most vivid detail, a lengthy reference being made to the paper 'found on the person of the dead anarchist', and 'written in a private shorthand or cryptogram'.

The report concluded with the gratifying – though untrue – statement that 'in this intricate and important case, the police have wisely secured the assistance of Dr John Thorndyke, to whose acute intellect and vast experience the portentous cryptogram will doubtless soon deliver up its secret.'

'Very flattering,' laughed Thorndyke, to whom I read the extract on his return from the hospital, 'but a little awkward if it should induce our friends to deposit a few trifling mementoes in the form of nitro-compounds on our main staircase or in the cellars. By the way, I met Superintendent Miller on London Bridge. The "cryptogram", as Mr James calls it, has set Scotland Yard in a mighty ferment.'

'Naturally. What have they done in the matter?'

'They adopted my suggestion, after all, finding that they could make nothing of it themselves, and took it to the British Museum. The Museum people referred them to Professor Poppelbaum, the great palaeographer, to whom they accordingly submitted it.'

'Did he express any opinion about it?'

'Yes, provisionally. After a brief examination, he found it to consist of a number of Hebrew words sandwiched between apparently meaningless groups of letters. He furnished the Superintendent off-hand with a translation of the words, and Miller forthwith struck off a number of hectograph copies of it, which he has distributed among the senior officials of his department; so that at present' – here Thorndyke gave vent to a soft chuckle – 'Scotland Yard is engaged in a sort of missing word – or, rather, missing sense – competition. Miller invited me to join in the sport, and to that end presented me with one of the hectograph copies on which to exercise my wits, together with a photograph of the document.'

'And shall you?' I asked.

'Not I,' he replied, laughing. 'In the first place, I have not been formally consulted, and consequently am a passive, though interested, spectator. In the second place, I have a theory of my own which I shall test if the occasion arises. But if you would like to take part in the competition, I am authorised to show you the photograph and the translation. I will pass them on to you, and I wish you joy of them.'

He handed me the photograph and a sheet of paper

that he had just taken from his pocketbook, and watched me with grim amusement as I read out the first few lines.

'Woe, city, lies, robbery, prey, noise, whip, rattling, wheel, horse, chariot, day, darkness, gloominess, clouds, darkness, morning, mountain, people, strong, fire, them, flame.'

'It doesn't look very promising at first sight,' I remarked. 'What is the Professor's theory?'

'His theory – provisionally, of course – is that the words form the message, and the groups of letters represent mere filled-up spaces between the words.'

'But surely,' I protested, 'that would be a very transparent device.'

Thorndyke laughed. 'There is a childlike simplicity about it,' said he, 'that is highly attractive – but discouraging. It is much more probable that the words are dummies, and that the letters contain the message. Or, again, the solution may lie in an entirely different direction. But listen! Is that cab coming here?'

It was. It drew up opposite our chambers, and a few moments later a brisk step ascending the stairs heralded a smart rat-tat at our door. Flinging open the latter, I found myself confronted by a well-dressed stranger, who, after a quick glance at me, peered inquisitively over my shoulder into the room.

'I am relieved, Dr Jervis,' said he, 'to find you and Dr Thorndyke at home, as I have come on somewhat urgent professional business. My name,' he continued, entering in response to my invitation, 'is Barton, but you don't know me, though I know you both by sight. I have come to ask you if one of you – or, better still, both – could come tonight and see my brother.'

'That,' said Thorndyke, 'depends on the circumstances and on the whereabouts of your brother.'

'The circumstances,' said Mr Barton, 'are, in my opinion, highly suspicious, and I will place them before you – of course, in strict confidence.'

Thorndyke nodded and indicated a chair.

'My brother,' continued Mr Barton, taking the proffered seat, 'has recently married for the second time. His age is fifty-five, and that of his wife twenty-six, and I may say that the marriage has been – well, by no means a success. Now, within the last fortnight, my brother has been attacked by a mysterious and extremely painful affection of the stomach, to which his doctor seems unable to give a name. It has resisted all treatment hitherto. Day by day the pain and distress increase, and I feel that, unless something decisive is done, the end cannot be far off.'

'Is the pain worse after taking food?' enquired Thorndyke.

'That's just it!' exclaimed our visitor. 'I see what is in your mind, and it has been in mine, too; so much so that I have tried repeatedly to obtain samples of the food that he is taking. And this morning I succeeded.' Here he took from his pocket a wide-mouthed bottle, which, disengaging from its paper wrappings, he laid on the table. 'When I called, he was taking his breakfast of arrowroot, which he complained had a gritty taste, supposed by his wife to be due to the sugar. Now I had provided myself with this bottle, and, during the absence of his wife, I managed unobserved to convey a portion of the arrowroot that he had left into it, and I should be greatly obliged if you would examine it and tell me if this arrowroot contains anything that it should not.'

He pushed the bottle across to Thorndyke, who carried it to the window, and, extracting a small quantity of the contents with a glass rod, examined the pasty mass with the aid of a lens; then, lifting the bell-glass cover from the microscope, which stood on its table by the window, he smeared a small quantity of the suspected matter on to a glass slip, and placed it on the stage of the instrument.

'I observe a number of crystalline particles in this,' he said, after a brief inspection, 'which have the appearance of arsenious acid.'

'Ah!' ejaculated Mr Barton, 'just what I feared. But are you certain?'

'No,' replied Thorndyke; 'but the matter is easily tested.'

He pressed the button of the bell that communicated with the laboratory, a summons that brought the laboratory assistant from his lair with characteristic promptitude.

'Will you please prepare a Marsh's apparatus, Polton,' said Thorndyke.

'I have a couple ready, sir,' replied Polton.

'Then pour the acid into one and bring it to me, with a tile.'

As his familiar vanished silently, Thorndyke turned to Mr Barton.

'Supposing we find arsenic in this arrowroot, as we probably shall, what do you want us to do?'

'I want you to come and see my brother,' replied our client.

'Why not take a note from me to his doctor?'

'No, no; I want you to come – I should like you both to come – and put a stop at once to this dreadful business. Consider! It's a matter of life and death. You won't refuse! I beg you not to refuse me your help in these terrible circumstances.'

'Well,' said Thorndyke, as his assistant reappeared, 'let us first see what the test has to tell us.'

Polton advanced to the table, on which he deposited a small flask, the contents of which were in a state of brisk effervescence, a bottle labelled 'calcium hypochlorite', and a white porcelain tile. The flask was fitted with a safety-funnel and a glass tube drawn out to a fine jet, to which Polton cautiously applied a lighted match. Instantly there sprang from the jet a tiny, pale violet flame. Thorndyke now took the tile, and held it in the flame for a few seconds, when the appearance of the surface remained unchanged save for a small circle of condensed moisture. His next proceeding was to thin the arrowroot with distilled water until it was quite fluid, and then pour a small quantity into the funnel. It ran slowly down the tube into the flask, with the bubbling contents of which it became speedily mixed. Almost immediately a change began to appear in the character of the flame, which from a pale violet turned gradually to a sickly blue, while above it hung a faint cloud of white smoke. Once more Thorndyke held the tile above the jet, but this time, no sooner had the pallid flame touched the cold surface of the porcelain, than there appeared on the latter a glistening black stain.

'That is pretty conclusive,' observed Thorndyke, lifting the stopper out of the reagent bottle, 'but we will apply the final test.' He dropped a few drops of the hypochlorite solution on to the tile, and immediately the black stain faded away and vanished. 'We can now answer your question, Mr Barton,' said he, replacing the stopper as he turned to our client. 'The specimen that you brought us certainly contains arsenic, and in very considerable quantities.'

'Then,' exclaimed Mr Barton, starting from his chair, 'you will come and help me to rescue my brother from this dreadful peril. Don't refuse me, Dr Thorndyke, for mercy's sake, don't refuse.'

Thorndyke reflected for a moment.

'Before we decide,' said he, 'we must see what engagements we have.'

With a quick, significant glance at me, he walked into the office, whither I followed in some bewilderment, for I knew that we had no engagements for the evening.

'Now, Jervis,' said Thorndyke, as he closed the office door, 'what are we to do?'

'We must go, I suppose,' I replied. 'It seems a pretty urgent case.'

'It does,' he agreed. 'Of course, the man may be telling the truth, after all.'

'You don't think he is, then?'

'No. It is a plausible tale, but there is too much arsenic in that arrowroot. Still, I think I ought to go. It is an ordinary professional risk. But there is no reason why you should put your head into the noose.'

'Thank you,' said I, somewhat huffily. 'I don't see what risk there is, but if any exists I claim the right to share it.'

'Very well,' he answered with a smile, 'we will both go. I think we can take care of ourselves.'

He re-entered the sitting-room, and announced his decision to Mr Barton, whose relief and gratitude were quite pathetic.

'But,' said Thorndyke, 'you have not yet told us where your brother lives.'

'Rexford,' was the reply – 'Rexford, in Essex. It is an out-of-the-way place, but if we catch the seven-fifteen train from Liverpool Street, we shall be there in an hour and a half.'

'And as to the return? You know the trains, I suppose?'

'Oh yes,' replied our client; 'I will see that you don't miss your train back.'

'Then I will be with you in a minute,' said Thorndyke; and, taking the still-bubbling flask, he retired to the laboratory, whence he returned in a few minutes carrying his hat and overcoat.

The cab which had brought our client was still

waiting, and we were soon rattling through the streets towards the station, where we arrived in time to furnish ourselves with dinner-baskets and select our compartment at leisure.

During the early part of the journey our companion was in excellent spirits. He despatched the cold fowl from the basket and quaffed the rather indifferent claret with as much relish as if he had not had a single relation in the world, and after dinner he became genial to the verge of hilarity. But, as time went on, there crept into his manner a certain anxious restlessness. He became silent and preoccupied, and several times furtively consulted his watch.

'The train is confoundedly late!' he exclaimed irritably. 'Seven minutes behind time already!'

'A few minutes more or less are not of much consequence,' said Thorndyke.

'No, of course not; but still – Ah, thank Heaven, here we are!'

He thrust his head out of the off-side window, and gazed eagerly down the line; then, leaping to his feet, he bustled out on to the platform while the train was still moving.

Even as we alighted a warning bell rang furiously on the up-platform, and as Mr Barton hurried us through the empty booking-office to the outside of the station, the rumble of the approaching train could be heard above the noise made by our own train moving off.

'My carriage doesn't seem to have arrived yet,' exclaimed Mr Barton, looking anxiously up the station approach. 'If you will wait here a moment, I will go and make enquiries.'

He darted back into the booking-office and through

it on to the platform, just as the up-train roared into
the station. Thorndyke followed him with quick but
stealthy steps, and, peering out of the booking-office
door, watched his proceedings; then he turned and
beckoned to me.

'There he goes,' said he, pointing to an iron foot-
bridge that spanned the line; and, as I looked, I saw,
clearly defined against the dim night sky, a flying
figure racing towards the 'up' side.

It was hardly two-thirds across when the guard's
whistle sang out its shrill warning.

'Quick, Jervis,' exclaimed Thorndyke; 'she's off!'

He leaped down on to the line, whither I followed
instantly, and, crossing the rails, we clambered up
together on to the footboard opposite an empty first-
class compartment. Thorndyke's magazine knife,
containing, among other implements, a railway-key,
was already in his hand. The door was speedily
unlocked, and, as we entered, Thorndyke ran through
and looked out on to the platform.

'Just in time!' he exclaimed. 'He is in one of the
forward compartments.'

He relocked the door, and, seating himself,
proceeded to fill his pipe.

'And now,' said I, as the train moved out of the
station, 'perhaps you will explain this little comedy.'

'With pleasure,' he replied, 'if it needs any explanation. But you can hardly have forgotten Mr
James's flattering remarks in his report of the Greek
Street incident, clearly giving the impression that the
mysterious document was in my possession. When I
read that, I knew I must look out for some attempt to
recover it, though I hardly expected such prompt-
ness. Still, when Mr Barton called without credentials

or appointment, I viewed him with some suspicion. That suspicion deepened when he wanted us both to come. It deepened further when I found an impossible quantity of arsenic in his sample, and it gave place to certainty when, having allowed him to select the trains by which we were to travel, I went up to the laboratory and examined the timetable; for I then found that the last train for London left Rexford ten minutes after we were due to arrive. Obviously this was a plan to get us both safely out of the way while he and some of his friends ransacked our chambers for the missing document.'

'I see; and that accounts for his extraordinary anxiety at the lateness of the train. But why did you come, if you knew it was a "plant"?'

'My dear fellow,' said Thorndyke, 'I never miss an interesting experience if I can help it. There are possibilities in this, too, don't you see?'

'But supposing his friends have broken into our chambers already?'

'That contingency has been provided for; but I think they will wait for Mr Barton – and us.'

Our train, being the last one up, stopped at every station, and crawled slothfully in the intervals, so that it was past eleven o'clock when we reached Liverpool Street. Here we got out cautiously, and, mingling with the crowd, followed the unconscious Barton up the platform, through the barrier, and out into the street. He seemed in no special hurry, for, after pausing to light a cigar, he set off at an easy pace up New Broad Street.

Thorndyke hailed a hansom, and, motioning me to enter, directed the cabman to drive to Clifford's Inn Passage.

'Sit well back,' said he, as we rattled away up New Broad Street. 'We shall be passing our gay deceiver presently – in fact, there he is, a living, walking illustration of the folly of underrating the intelligence of one's adversary.'

At Clifford's Inn Passage we dismissed the cab, and, retiring into the shadow of the dark, narrow alley, kept an eye on the gate of Inner Temple Lane. In about twenty minutes we observed our friend approaching on the south side of Fleet Street. He halted at the gate, plied the knocker, and after a brief parley with the night-porter vanished through the wicket. We waited yet five minutes more, and then, having given him time to get clear of the entrance, we crossed the road.

The porter looked at us with some surprise. 'There's a gentleman just gone down to your chambers, sir,' said he. 'He told me you were expecting him.'

'Quite right,' said Thorndyke, with a dry smile, 'I was. Good-night.'

We slunk down the lane, past the church, and through the gloomy cloisters, giving a wide berth to all lamps and lighted entries, until, emerging into Paper Buildings, we crossed at the darkest part to King's Bench Walk, where Thorndyke made straight for the chambers of our friend Anstey, which were two doors above our own.

'Why are we coming here?' I asked, as we ascended the stairs.

But the question needed no answer when we reached the landing, for through the open door of our friend's chambers I could see in the darkened room Anstey himself with two uniformed constables and a couple of plain-clothes men.

'There has been no signal yet, sir,' said one of the

latter, whom I recognised as a detective-sergeant of our division.

'No,' said Thorndyke, 'but the MC has arrived. He came in five minutes before us.'

'Then,' exclaimed Anstey, 'the ball will open shortly, ladies and gents. The boards are waxed, the fiddlers are tuning up, and – '

'Not quite so loud, if you please, sir,' said the sergeant. 'I think there is somebody coming up Crown Office Row.'

The ball had, in fact, opened. As we peered cautiously out of the open window, keeping well back in the darkened room, a stealthy figure crept out of the shadow, crossed the road, and stole noiselessly into the entry of Thorndyke's chambers. It was quickly followed by a second figure, and then by a third, in which I recognised our elusive client.

'Now listen for the signal,' said Thorndyke. 'They won't waste time. Confound that clock!'

The soft-voiced bell of the Inner Temple clock, mingling with the harsher tones of St Dunstan's and the Law Courts, slowly tolled out the hour of midnight; and as the last reverberations were dying away, some metallic object, apparently a coin, dropped with a sharp clink on to the pavement under our window.

At the sound the watchers simultaneously sprang to their feet.

'You two go first,' said the sergeant, addressing the uniformed men, who thereupon stole noiselessly, in their rubber-soled boots, down the stone stairs and along the pavement. The rest of us followed, with less attention to silence, and as we ran up to Thorndyke's chambers, we were aware of quick but stealthy footsteps on the stairs above.

'They've been at work, you see,' whispered one of the constables, flashing his lantern on to the iron-bound outer door of our sitting-room, on which the marks of a large jemmy were plainly visible.

The sergeant nodded grimly, and, bidding the constables to remain on the landing, led the way upwards.

As we ascended, faint rustlings continued to be audible from above, and on the second-floor landing we met a man descending briskly, but without hurry, from the third. It was Mr Barton, and I could not but admire the composure with which he passed the two detectives. But suddenly his glance fell on Thorndyke, and his composure vanished. With a wild stare of incredulous horror, he halted as if petrified; then he broke away and raced furiously down the stairs, and a moment later a muffled shout and the sound of a scuffle told us that he had received a check. On the next flight we met two more men, who, more hurried and less self-possessed, endeavoured to push past; but the sergeant barred the way.

'Why, bless me!' exclaimed the latter, 'it's Moakey; and isn't that Tom Harris?'

'It's all right, sergeant,' said Moakey plaintively, striving to escape from the officer's grip. 'We've come to the wrong house, that's all.'

The sergeant smiled indulgently. 'I know,' he replied. 'But you're always coming to the wrong house, Moakey; and now you're just coming along with me to the right house.'

He slipped his hand inside his captive's coat, and adroitly fished out a large, folding jemmy; whereupon the discomfited burglar abandoned all further protest.

On our return to the first-floor, we found Mr Barton sulkily awaiting us, handcuffed to one of the constables, and watched by Polton with pensive disapproval.

'I needn't trouble you tonight, doctor,' said the sergeant, as he marshalled his little troop of captors and captives. 'You'll hear from us in the morning. Good-night, sir.'

The melancholy procession moved off down the stairs, and we retired into our chambers with Anstey to smoke a last pipe.

'A capable man, that Barton,' observed Thorndyke – 'ready, plausible, and ingenious, but spoilt by prolonged contact with fools. I wonder if the police will perceive the significance of this little affair.'

'They will be more acute than I am if they do,' said I.

'Naturally,' interposed Anstey, who loved to 'cheek' his revered senior, 'because there isn't any. It's only Thorndyke's bounce. He is really in a deuce of a fog himself.'

However this may have been, the police were a good deal puzzled by the incident, for, on the following morning, we received a visit from no less a person than Superintendent Miller, of Scotland Yard.

'This is a queer business,' said he, coming to the point at once – 'this burglary, I mean. Why should they want to crack your place, right here in the Temple, too? You've got nothing of value here, have you? No "hard stuff", as they call it, for instance?'

'Not so much as a silver teaspoon,' replied Thorndyke, who had a conscientious objection to plate of all kinds.

'It's odd,' said the superintendent, 'deuced odd.

When we got your note, we thought these anarchist idiots had mixed you up with the case – you saw the papers, I suppose – and wanted to go through your rooms for some reason. We thought we had our hands on the gang, instead of which we find a party of common crooks that we're sick of the sight of. I tell you, sir, it's annoying when you think you've hooked a salmon, to bring up a blooming eel.'

'It must be a great disappointment,' Thorndyke agreed, suppressing a smile.

'It is,' said the detective. 'Not but what we're glad enough to get these beggars, especially Halkett, or Barton, as he calls himself – a mighty slippery customer is Halkett, and mischievous, too – but we're not wanting any disappointments just now. There was that big jewel job in Piccadilly, Taplin and Horne's; I don't mind telling you that we've not got the ghost of a clue. Then there's this anarchist affair. We're all in the dark there, too.'

'But what about the cipher?' asked Thorndyke.

'Oh, hang the cipher!' exclaimed the detective irritably. 'This Professor Poppelbaum may be a very learned man, but he doesn't help us much. He says the document is in Hebrew, and he has translated it into Double Dutch. Just listen to this!' He dragged out of his pocket a bundle of papers, and, dabbing down a photograph of the document before Thorndyke, commenced to read the Professor's report. ' "The document is written in the characters of the well-known inscription of Mesha, King of Moab" (who the devil's he? Never heard of him. Well known, indeed!) "The language is Hebrew, and the words are separated by groups of letters, which are meaningless, and obviously introduced to mislead and confuse

96

the reader. The words themselves are not strictly consecutive, but, by the interpellation of certain other words, a series of intelligible sentences is obtained, the meaning of which is not very clear, but is no doubt allegorical. The method of decipherment is shown in the accompanying tables, and the full rendering suggested on the enclosed sheet. It is to be noted that the writer of this document was apparently quite unacquainted with the Hebrew language, as appears from the absence of any grammatical construction." That's the Professor's report, doctor, and here are the tables showing how he worked it out. It makes my head spin to look at 'em.'

He handed to Thorndyke a bundle of ruled sheets, which my colleague examined attentively for a while, and then passed on to me.

'This is very systematic and thorough,' said he. 'But now let us see the final result at which he arrives.'

'It may be all very systematic,' growled the superintendent, sorting out his papers, 'but I tell you, sir, it's all BOSH!' The latter word he jerked out viciously, as he slapped down on the table the final product of the Professor's labours. 'There,' he continued, 'that's what he calls the "full rendering", and I reckon it'll make your hair curl. It might be a message from Bedlam.'

Thorndyke took up the first sheet, and as he compared the constructed renderings with the literal translation, the ghost of a smile stole across his usually immovable countenance.

'The meaning is certainly a little obscure,' he observed, 'though the reconstruction is highly ingenious; and, moreover, I think the Professor is probably right. That is to say, the words which he has supplied are probably the omitted parts of the passages from which the words of the cryptogram were taken. What do you think, Jervis?'

	Space	Word	Space	Word	Space	Word
Moabite	Y7	५7Δ9	Δ7	470	7Δ	7Y4
Hebrew		כזבים		עיר		אוי
Translation		LIES		CITY		WOE
Moabite	57	644	6 Y7	74X	ⴄエ	6エ7
Hebrew		קלק		טרח		גזל
Translation		NOISE		PREY		ROBBERY
Moabite	w4	57Y&	44	woq	70⧺	XYW
Hebrew		אופן		רעש		שוט
Translation		WHEEL		RATTLING		WHIP
Moabite	Y7	7YƷ	Δ7	39474	74X	⧺Y⧺
Hebrew		יום		מרכבה		סוס
Translation		DAY		CHARIOT		HORSE

The Professor's Analysis
Handwritten: Analysis of the cipher with translation into modern square Hebrew characters + a translation into English. NB. The cipher reads from right to left.

He handed me the two papers, of which one gave the actual words of the cryptogram, and the other a suggested reconstruction, with omitted words supplied. The first read:

'Woe — city — lies — robbery — prey — noise — whip — rattling — wheel — horse — chariot — day — darkness — gloominess — cloud — darkness — morning — mountain — people — strong — fire — them — flame.'

Turning to the second paper, I read out the suggested rendering: ' "Woe to the bloody city! It is full of lies and robbery; the prey departeth not. The noise of a whip, and the noise of the rattling of the wheels, and of the prancing horses, and of the jumping chariots.

' "A day of darkness and of gloominess, a day of clouds, and of thick darkness, as the morning spread upon the mountains, a great people and a strong.

' "A fire devoureth before them, and behind them a flame burneth." '

Here the first sheet ended, and, as I laid it down, Thorndyke looked at me enquiringly.

'There is a good deal of reconstruction in proportion to the original matter,' I objected. 'The Professor has "supplied" more than three-quarters of the final rendering.'

'Exactly,' burst in the superintendent; 'it's all Professor and no cryptogram.'

'Still, I think the reading is correct,' said Thorndyke. 'As far as it goes, that is.'

'Good Lord!' exclaimed the dismayed detective. 'Do you mean to tell me, sir, that that balderdash is the real meaning of the thing?'

'I don't say that,' replied Thorndyke. 'I say it is correct as far as it goes; but I doubt its being the solution of the cryptogram.'

'Have you been studying that photograph that I gave you?' demanded Miller, with sudden eagerness.

'I have looked at it,' said Thorndyke evasively, 'but I should like to examine the original if you have it with you.'

'I have,' said the detective. 'Professor Poppelbaum sent it back with the solution. You can have a look at it, though I can't leave it with you without special authority.'

He drew the document from his pocketbook and

handed it to Thorndyke, who took it over to the window and scrutinised it closely. From the window he drifted into the adjacent office, closing the door after him; and presently the sound of a faint explosion told me that he had lighted the gas-fire.

'Of course,' said Miller, taking up the translation again, 'this gibberish is the sort of stuff you might expect from a parcel of crack-brained anarchists; but it doesn't seem to mean anything.'

'Not to us,' I agreed; 'but the phrases may have some pre-arranged significance. And then there are the letters between the words. It is possible that they may really form a cipher.'

'I suggested that to the Professor,' said Miller, 'but he wouldn't hear of it. He is sure they are only dummies.'

'I think he is probably mistaken, and so, I fancy, does my colleague. But we shall hear what he has to say presently.'

'Oh, I know what he will say,' growled Miller. 'He will put the thing under the microscope, and tell us who made the paper, and what the ink is composed of, and then we shall be just where we were.' The superintendent was evidently deeply depressed.

We sat for some time pondering in silence on the vague sentences of the Professor's translation, until, at length, Thorndyke reappeared, holding the document in his hand. He laid it quietly on the table by the officer, and then enquired: 'Is this an official consultation?'

'Certainly,' replied Miller. 'I was authorised to consult you respecting the translation, but nothing was said about the original. Still, if you want it for further study, I will get it for you.'

'No, thank you,' said Thorndyke. 'I have finished with it. My theory turned out to be correct.'

'Your theory!' exclaimed the superintendent, eagerly. 'Do you mean to say – ?'

'And, as you are consulting me officially, I may as well give you this.'

He held out a sheet of paper, which the detective took from him and began to read.

'What is this?' he asked, looking up at Thorndyke with a puzzled frown. 'Where did it come from?'

'It is the solution of the cryptogram,' replied Thorndyke.

The detective reread the contents of the paper, and, with the frown of perplexity deepening, once more gazed at my colleague.

'This is a joke, sir; you are fooling me,' he said sulkily.

'Nothing of the kind,' answered Thorndyke. 'That is the genuine solution.'

'But it's impossible!' exclaimed Miller. 'Just look at it, Dr Jervis.'

I took the paper from his hand, and, as I glanced at it, I had no difficulty in understanding his surprise. It bore a short inscription in printed capitals, thus:

THE PICKERDILLEY STUF IS UP THE CHIMBLY 416 WARDOUR ST 2ND FLUR BACK IT WAS HID BECOS OF OLD MOAKEYS JOOD MOAKEY IS A BLITER.

'Then that fellow wasn't an anarchist at all?' I exclaimed.

'No,' said Miller. 'He was one of Moakey's gang. We suspected Moakey of being mixed up with that job, but we couldn't fix it on him. By Jove!' he added, slapping his thigh, 'if this is right, and I can lay my hands on the loot! Can you lend me a bag, doctor? I'm off to Wardour Street this very moment.'

We furnished him with an empty suitcase, and, from the window, watched him making for Mitre Court at a smart double.

'I wonder if he will find the booty,' said Thorndyke. 'It just depends on whether the hiding-place was known to more than one of the gang. Well, it has been a quaint case, and instructive, too. I suspect our friend Barton and the evasive Schönberg were the collaborators who produced that curiosity of literature.'

'May I ask how you deciphered the thing?' I said. 'It didn't appear to take long.'

'It didn't. It was merely a matter of testing a hypothesis; and you ought not to have to ask that question,' he added, with mock severity, 'seeing that you had what turn out to have been all the necessary facts, two days ago. But I will prepare a document and demonstrate to you tomorrow morning.'

'So Miller was successful in his quest,' said Thorndyke, as we smoked our morning pipes after breakfast. 'The "entire swag", as he calls it, was "up the chimbly", undisturbed.'

He handed me a note which had been left, with the empty suitcase, by a messenger, shortly before, and I was about to read it when an agitated knock was heard at our door. The visitor, whom I admitted, was a rather haggard and dishevelled elderly gentleman, who, as he entered, peered inquisitively through his concave spectacles from one of us to the other.

'Allow me to introduce myself, gentlemen,' said he. 'I am Professor Poppelbaum.'

Thorndyke bowed and offered a chair.

'I called yesterday afternoon,' our visitor continued, 'at Scotland Yard, where I heard of your
remarkable decipherment and of the convincing
proof of its correctness. Thereupon I borrowed
the cryptogram, and have spent the entire night in
studying it, but I cannot connect your solution with
any of the characters. I wonder if you would do me
the great favour of enlightening me as to your method
of decipherment, and so save me further sleepless
nights? You may rely on my discretion.'

'Have you the document with you?' asked Thorndyke.

The Professor produced it from his pocketbook,
and passed it to my colleague.

'You observe, Professor,' said the latter, 'that this is
a laid paper, and has no watermark?'

'Yes, I noticed that.'

'And that the writing is in indelible Chinese ink?'

'Yes, yes,' said the savant impatiently; 'but it is the
inscription that interests me, not the paper and ink.'

'Precisely,' said Thorndyke. 'Now, it was the ink
that interested me when I caught a glimpse of the
document three days ago. "Why," I asked myself,
"should anyone use this troublesome medium" – for
this appears to be stick ink – "when good writing ink
is to be had?" What advantages has Chinese ink over
writing ink? It has several advantages as a drawing
ink, but for writing purposes it has only one: it is
quite unaffected by wet. The obvious inference, then,
was that this document was, for some reason, likely
to be exposed to wet. But this inference instantly
suggested another, which I was yesterday able to put
to the test – thus.'

He filled a tumbler with water, and, rolling up the document, dropped it in. Immediately there began to appear on it a new set of characters of a curious grey colour. In a few seconds Thorndyke lifted out the wet paper, and held it up to the light, and now there was plainly visible an inscription in transparent lettering, like a very distinct watermark. It was in printed capitals, written across the other writing, and read:

THE PICKERDILLEY STUF IS UP THE CHIMBLY 416 WARDOUR ST 2ND FLOUR BACK IT WAS HID BECOS OF OLD MOAKEYS JOOD MOAKEY IS A BLITER.

The Professor regarded the inscription with profound disfavour.

'How do you suppose this was done?' he asked gloomily.

'I will show you,' said Thorndyke. 'I have prepared a piece of paper to demonstrate the process to Dr Jervis. It is exceedingly simple.'

He fetched from the office a small plate of glass, and a photographic dish in which a piece of thin notepaper was soaking in water.

'This paper,' said Thorndyke, lifting it out and laying it on the glass, 'has been soaking all night, and is now quite pulpy.'

He spread a dry sheet of paper over the wet one, and on the former wrote heavily with a hard pencil, 'Moakey is a bliter.' On lifting the upper sheet, the writing was seen to be transferred in a deep grey to the wet paper, and when the latter was held up to the light the inscription stood out clear and transparent as if written with oil.

'When this dries,' said Thorndyke, 'the writing will

completely disappear, but it will reappear whenever the paper is again wetted.'

The Professor nodded.

'Very ingenious,' said he – 'a sort of artificial palimpsest, in fact. But I do not understand how that illiterate man could have written in the difficult Moabite script.'

'He did not,' said Thorndyke. 'The "cryptogram" was probably written by one of the leaders of the gang, who, no doubt, supplied copies to the other members to use instead of blank paper for secret communications. The object of the Moabite writing was evidently to divert attention from the paper itself, in case the communication fell into the wrong hands, and I must say it seems to have answered its purpose very well.'

The Professor started, stung by the sudden recollection of his labours.

'Yes,' he snorted; 'but I am a scholar, sir, not a policeman. Every man to his trade.'

He snatched up his hat, and with a curt 'Good-morning,' flung out of the room in dudgeon.

Thorndyke laughed softly.

'Poor Professor!' he murmured. 'Our playful friend Barton has much to answer for.'

The Hammer of God

G. K. CHESTERTON

The little village of Bohun Beacon was perched on a hill so steep that the tall spire of its church seemed only like the peak of a small mountain. At the foot of the church stood a smithy, generally red with fires and always littered with hammers and scraps of iron; opposite to this, over a rude cross of cobbled paths, was the Blue Boar, the only inn of the place. It was upon this crossway, in the lifting of a leaden and silver daybreak, that two brothers met in the street and spoke; though one was beginning the day and the other finishing it. The Revd and Hon. Wilfred Bohun was very devout, and was making his way to some austere exercises of prayer or contemplation at dawn. Colonel the Hon. Norman Bohun, his elder brother, was by no means devout, and was sitting in evening dress on the bench outside the Blue Boar, drinking what the philosophic observer was free to regard either as his last glass on Tuesday or his first on Wednesday. The colonel was not particular.

The Bohuns were one of the very few aristocratic families really dating from the Middle Ages, and their pennon had actually seen Palestine. But it is a great mistake to suppose that such houses stand high in chivalric traditions. Few except the poor preserve traditions. Aristocrats live not in traditions but in fashions. The Bohuns had been Mohocks under

Queen Anne and Mashers under Queen Victoria. But, like more than one of the really ancient houses, they had rotted in the last two centuries into mere drunkards and dandy degenerates, till there had even come a whisper of insanity. Certainly there was something hardly human about the colonel's wolfish pursuit of pleasure, and his chronic resolution not to go home till morning had a touch of the hideous charity of insomnia. He was a tall, fine animal, elderly, but with hair startlingly yellow. He would have looked merely blond and leonine, but his blue eyes were sunk so deep in his face that they looked black. They were a little too close together. He had very long yellow moustaches: on each side of them a fold or furrow from nostril to jaw, so that a sneer seemed to cut into his face. Over his evening clothes he wore a curiously pale yellow coat that looked more like a very light dressing gown than an overcoat, and on the back of his head was stuck an extraordinary broad-brimmed hat of a bright green colour, evidently some oriental curiosity caught up at random. He was proud of appearing in such incongruous attires – proud of the fact that he always made them look congruous.

His brother the curate had also the yellow hair and the elegance, but he was buttoned up to the chin in black, and his face was clean-shaven, cultivated and a little nervous. He seemed to live for nothing but his religion; but there were some who said (notably the blacksmith, who was a Presbyterian) that it was a love of Gothic architecture rather than of God, and that his haunting of the church like a ghost was only another and purer turn of the almost morbid thirst for beauty which sent his brother raging after women and wine. This charge was doubtful, while the man's practical piety was indubitable. Indeed, the charge was mostly an ignorant misunderstanding of the love of solitude and secret prayer, and was founded on his being often found kneeling, not before the altar, but in peculiar places, in the crypts or gallery, or even in the belfry. He was at the moment about to enter the church through the yard of the smithy, but stopped and frowned a little as he saw his brother's cavernous eyes staring in the same direction. On the hypothesis that the colonel was interested in the church he did not waste any speculations. There only remained the blacksmith's shop, and though the blacksmith was a Puritan and none of his people, Wilfred Bohun had heard some scandals about a beautiful and rather celebrated wife. He flung a suspicious look across the shed, and the colonel stood up laughing to speak to him.

'Good-morning, Wilfred,' he said. 'Like a good landlord I am watching sleeplessly over my people. I am going to call on the blacksmith.'

Wilfred looked at the ground and said: 'The blacksmith is out. He is over at Greenford.'

'I know,' answered the other with silent laughter; 'that is why I am calling on him.'

'Norman,' said the cleric, with his eye on a pebble in the road, 'are you ever afraid of thunderbolts?'

'What do you mean?' asked the colonel. 'Is your hobby meteorology?'

'I mean,' said Wilfred, without looking up, 'do you ever think that God might strike you in the street?'

'I beg your pardon,' said the colonel; 'I see your hobby is folklore.'

'I know your hobby is blasphemy,' retorted the religious man, stung in the one live place of his nature.

'But if you do not fear God, you have good reason to fear man.'

The elder raised his eyebrows politely. 'Fear man?' he said.

'Barnes the blacksmith is the biggest and strongest man for forty miles round,' said the clergyman sternly. 'I know you are no coward or weakling, but he could throw you over the wall.'

This struck home, being true, and the lowering line by mouth and nostril darkened and deepened. For a moment he stood with the heavy sneer on his face. But in an instant Colonel Bohun had recovered his own cruel good humour and laughed, showing two doglike front teeth under his yellow moustache. 'In that case, my dear Wilfred,' he said quite carelessly, 'it was wise for the last of the Bohuns to come out partially in armour.'

And he took off the queer round hat covered with green, showing that it was lined within with steel. Wilfred recognised it indeed as a light Japanese or Chinese helmet torn down from a trophy that hung in the old family hall.

'It was the first to hand,' explained his brother airily; 'always the nearest hat – and the nearest woman.'

'The blacksmith is away at Greenford,' said Wilfred quietly; 'the time of his return is unsettled.'

And with that he turned and went into the church with bowed head, crossing himself like one who wishes to be quit of an unclean spirit. He was anxious to forget such grossness in the cool twilight of his tall Gothic cloisters; but on that morning it was fated that his still round of religious exercises should be everywhere arrested by small shocks. As he entered the church, hitherto always empty at that hour, a kneeling figure rose hastily to its feet and came towards the full daylight of the doorway. When the curate saw it he stood still with surprise. For the early worshipper was none other than the village idiot, a nephew of the blacksmith, one who neither would nor could care for the church or for anything else. He was always called 'Mad Joe', and seemed to have no other name; he was a dark, strong, slouching lad, with a heavy white face, dark straight hair, and a mouth always open. As he passed the priest, his moon-calf countenance gave no hint of what he had been doing or thinking of. He had never been known to pray before. What sort of prayers was he saying now? Extraordinary prayers surely.

Wilfred Bohun stood rooted to the spot long enough to see the idiot go out into the sunshine, and even to see his dissolute brother hail him with a sort of avuncular jocularity. The last thing he saw was the colonel throwing pennies at the open mouth of Joe, with the serious appearance of trying to hit it.

This ugly sunlight picture of the stupidity and cruelty of the earth sent the ascetic finally to his prayers for purification and new thoughts. He went up to a pew in the gallery, which brought him under a coloured window which he loved and which always quieted his spirit; a blue window with an angel carrying lilies. There he began to think less about the half-wit, with his livid face and mouth like a fish. He began to think less of his evil brother, pacing like a lean lion in his horrible hunger. He sank deeper and deeper into those cold and sweet colours of silver blossoms and sapphire sky.

In this place half an hour afterwards he was found by Gibbs, the village cobbler, who had been sent for him in some haste. He got to his feet with promptitude, for he knew that no small matter would have brought Gibbs into such a place at all. The cobbler was, as in many villages, an atheist, and his appearance in church was a shade more extraordinary than Mad Joe's. It was a morning of theological enigmas.

'What is it?' asked Wilfred Bohun rather stiffly, but putting out a trembling hand for his hat.

The atheist spoke in a tone that, coming from him, was quite startlingly respectful, and even, as it were, huskily sympathetic.

'You must excuse me, sir,' he said in a hoarse whisper, 'but we didn't think it right not to let you know at once. I'm afraid a rather dreadful thing has happened, sir. I'm afraid your brother – '

Wilfred clenched his frail hands. 'What devilry has he done now?' he cried in involuntary passion.

'Why, sir,' said the cobbler, coughing, 'I'm afraid he's done nothing, and won't do anything. I'm afraid he's done for. You had really better come down, sir.'

The curate followed the cobbler down a short winding stair which brought them out at an entrance rather higher than the street. Bohun saw the tragedy in one glance, flat underneath him like a plan. In the yard of the smithy were standing five or six men, mostly in black, one in an inspector's uniform. They included the doctor, the Presbyterian minister, and the priest from the Roman Catholic chapel to which the blacksmith's wife belonged. The latter was speaking to her, indeed, very rapidly, in an undertone, as she, a magnificent woman with red-gold hair, was sobbing blindly on a bench. Between these two groups, and just clear of the main heap of hammers, lay a man in evening dress, spread-eagled and flat on his face. From the height above Wilfred could have sworn to every item of his costume and appearance, down to the Bohun rings upon his fingers; but the skull was only a hideous splash, like a star of blackness and blood.

Wilfred Bohun gave but one glance, and ran down the steps into the yard. The doctor, who was the family physician, saluted him, but he scarcely took any notice. He could only stammer out: 'My brother is dead. What does it mean? What is this horrible mystery?' There was an unhappy silence; and then the cobbler, the most outspoken man present, answered: 'Plenty of horror, sir,' he said, 'but not much mystery.'

'What do you mean?' asked Wilfred, with a white face.

'It's plain enough,' answered Gibbs. 'There is only one man for forty miles round that could have struck such a blow as that, and he's the man that had most reason to.'

'We must not prejudge anything,' put in the doctor, a tall, black-bearded man, rather nervously; 'but it is competent for me to corroborate what Mr Gibbs says about the nature of the blow, sir; it is an incredible blow. Mr Gibbs says that only one man in this district could have done it. I should have said myself that nobody could have done it.'

A shudder of superstition went through the slight figure of the curate. 'I can hardly understand,' he said.

'Mr Bohun,' said the doctor in a low voice, 'metaphors literally fail me. It is inadequate to say that the skull was smashed to bits like an eggshell. Fragments of bone were driven into the body and the ground like bullets into a mud wall. It was the hand of a giant.'

He was silent a moment, looking grimly through his glasses; then he added: 'The thing has one advantage – that it clears most people of suspicion at one stroke. If you or I or any normally made man in the country were accused of this crime, we should be acquitted as an infant would be acquitted of stealing the Nelson Column.'

'That's what I say,' repeated the cobbler obstinately, 'there's only one man that could have done it, and he's the man that would have done it. Where's Simeon Barnes, the blacksmith?'

'He's over at Greenford,' faltered the curate.

'More likely over in France,' muttered the cobbler.

'No; he is in neither of those places,' said a small and colourless voice, which came from the little Roman priest who had joined the group. 'As a matter of fact, he is coming up the road at this moment.'

The little priest was not an interesting man to look at, having stubbly brown hair and a round and stolid face. But if he had been as splendid as Apollo no one would have looked at him at that moment. Everyone turned round and peered at the pathway which wound across the plain below, along which was indeed walking, at his own huge stride and with a hammer on his shoulder, Simeon the smith. He was a bony and gigantic man, with deep, dark, sinister eyes and a dark chin beard. He was walking and talking quietly with two other men; and though he was never specially cheerful, he seemed quite at his ease.

'My God!' cried the atheistic cobbler; 'and there's the hammer he did it with.'

'No,' said the inspector, a sensible-looking man

with a sandy moustache, speaking for the first time. 'There's the hammer he did it with, over there by the church wall. We have left it and the body exactly as they are.'

All glanced round, and the short priest went across and looked down in silence at the tool where it lay. It was one of the smallest and the lightest of the hammers, and would not have caught the eye among the rest; but on the iron edge of it were blood and yellow hair.

After a silence the short priest spoke without looking up, and there was a new note in his dull voice. 'Mr Gibbs was hardly right,' he said, 'in saying that there is no mystery. There is at least the mystery of why so big a man should attempt so big a blow with so little a hammer.'

'Oh, never mind that,' cried Gibbs, in a fever. 'What are we to do with Simeon Barnes?'

'Leave him alone,' said the priest quietly. 'He is coming here of himself. I know these two men with him. They are very good fellows from Greenford, and they have come over about the Presbyterian chapel.'

Even as he spoke the tall smith swung round the corner of the church and strode into his own yard. Then he stood there quite still, and the hammer fell from his hand. The inspector, who had preserved impenetrable propriety, immediately went up to him.

'I won't ask you, Mr Barnes,' he said, 'whether you know anything about what has happened here. You are not bound to say. I hope you don't know, and that you will be able to prove it. But I must go through the form of arresting you in the King's name for the murder of Colonel Norman Bohun.'

'You are not bound to say anything,' said the cobbler

in officious excitement. 'They've got to prove every-thing. They haven't proved yet that it is Colonel Bohun with the head all smashed up like that.'

'That won't wash,' said the doctor aside to the priest. 'That's out of detective stories. I was the colonel's medical man, and I knew his body better than he did. He had very fine hands, but quite peculiar ones. The second and third fingers were the same in length. Oh, that's the colonel right enough.'

As he glanced at the brained corpse upon the ground the iron eyes of the motionless blacksmith followed them and rested there also.

'Is Colonel Bohun dead?' said the smith quite calmly. 'Then he's damned.'

'Don't say anything! Oh, don't say anything,' cried the atheist cobbler, dancing about in an ecstasy of admiration of the English legal system. For no man is such a legalist as the good Secularist.

The blacksmith turned on him over his shoulder the august face of a fanatic.

'It is well for you infidels to dodge like foxes because the world's law favours you,' he said; 'but God guards His own in His pocket, as you shall see this day.'

Then he pointed to the colonel and said: 'When did this dog die in his sins?'

'Moderate your language,' said the doctor.

'Moderate the Bible's language, and I'll moderate mine. When did he die?'

'I saw him alive at six o'clock this morning,' stammered Wilfred Bohun.

'God is good,' said the smith. 'Mr Inspector, I have not the slightest objection to being arrested. It is you who may object to arresting me. I don't mind leaving the court without a stain on my character. You do mind, perhaps, leaving the court with a bad setback in your career.'

The solid inspector for the first time looked at the blacksmith with a lively eye – as did everybody else, except the short, strange priest, who was still looking down at the little hammer that had dealt the dreadful blow.

'There are two men standing outside this shop,' went on the blacksmith with ponderous lucidity, 'good tradesmen in Greenford whom you all know, who will swear that they saw me from before midnight till daybreak and long after in the committee room of our Revival Mission, which sits all night, we save souls so fast. In Greenford itself twenty people could swear to me for all that time. If I were a heathen, Mr Inspector, I would let you walk on to your downfall; but, as a Christian man, I feel bound to give you your chance and ask you whether you will hear my alibi now or in court.'

The inspector seemed for the first time disturbed and said: 'Of course I should be glad to clear you altogether now.'

The smith walked out of his yard with the same long and easy stride, and returned to his two friends from Greenford, who were indeed friends of nearly everyone present. Each of them said a few words which no one ever thought of disbelieving. When they had spoken the innocence of Simeon stood up as solid as the great church above them.

One of those silences struck the group which are more strange and insufferable than any speech. Madly, in order to make conversation, the curate said to the Catholic priest: 'You seem very much interested in that hammer, Father Brown.'

'Yes, I am,' said Father Brown; 'why is it such a small hammer?'

The doctor swung round on him.

'By George, that's true,' he cried; 'who would use a little hammer with ten larger hammers lying about?'

Then he lowered his voice in the curate's ear and said: 'Only the kind of person that can't lift a large hammer. It is not a question of force or courage between the sexes. It's a question of lifting power in the shoulders. A bold woman could commit ten murders with a light hammer and never turn a hair. She could not kill a beetle with a heavy one.'

Wilfred Bohun was staring at him with a sort of hypnotised horror, while Father Brown listened with his head a little on one side, really interested and attentive.

The doctor went on with more hissing emphasis: 'Why do those idiots always assume that the only person who hates the wife's lover is the wife's husband? Nine times out of ten the person who most hates the wife's lover is the wife. Who knows what insolence or treachery he had shown her – look there?'

He made a momentary gesture towards the red-haired woman on the bench. She had lifted her head at last and the tears were drying on her splendid face. But the eyes were fixed on the corpse with an electric glare that had in it something of idiocy.

The Revd William Bohun made a limp gesture as if waving away all desire to know; but Father Brown, dusting off his sleeve some ashes blown from the furnace, spoke in his indifferent way.

'You are like so many doctors,' he said; 'your mental science is really suggestive. It is your physical science that is utterly impossible. I agree that the woman wants to kill the co-respondent much more than the petitioner does. And I agree that a woman will always pick up a small hammer instead of a big one. But the difficulty is one of physical impossibility. No woman ever born could have smashed a man's skull out flat like that.' Then he added reflectively, after a pause: 'These people haven't grasped the whole of it. The man was actually wearing an iron helmet, and the blow scattered it like broken glass. Look at that woman. Look at her arms.'

Silence held them all up again, and then the doctor said rather sulkily: 'Well, I may be wrong; there are objections to everything. But I stick to the main point. No man but an idiot would pick up that little hammer if he could use a big hammer.'

With that the lean and quivering hands of Wilfred Bohun went up to his head and seemed to clutch his scanty yellow hair. After an instant they dropped, and he cried: 'That was the word I wanted; you have said the word.'

Then he continued, mastering his discomposure: 'The words you said were, "No man but an idiot would pick up the small hammer." '

'Yes,' said the doctor. 'Well?'

'Well,' said the curate, 'no man but an idiot did.' The rest stared at him with eyes arrested and riveted, and he went on in a febrile and feminine agitation.

'I am a priest,' he cried unsteadily, 'and a priest should be no shedder of blood. I – I mean that he should bring no one to the gallows. And I thank God that I see the criminal clearly now – because he is a criminal who cannot be brought to the gallows.'

'You will not denounce him?' enquired the doctor.

'He would not be hanged if I did denounce him,' answered Wilfred, with a wild but curiously happy smile. 'When I went into the church this morning I found a madman praying there – that poor Joe, who has been wrong all his life. God knows what he prayed; but with such strange folk it is not incredible to suppose that their prayers are all upside down. Very likely a lunatic would pray before killing a man. When I last saw poor Joe he was with my brother. My brother was mocking him.'

'By Jove!' cried the doctor, 'this is talking at last. But how do you explain – '

The Revd Wilfred was almost trembling with the excitement of his own glimpse of the truth. 'Don't you see; don't you see,' he cried feverishly, 'that is the only theory that covers both the queer things, that answers both the riddles. The two riddles are the little hammer and the big blow. The smith might have struck the big blow, but he would not have chosen the little hammer. His wife would have chosen the little hammer, but she could not have struck the big blow. But the madman might have done both. As for the little hammer – why, he was mad and might have picked up anything. And for the big blow, have you never heard, doctor, that a maniac in his paroxysm may have the strength of ten men?'

The doctor drew a deep breath and then said: 'By golly, I believe you've got it.'

Father Brown had fixed his eyes on the speaker so long and steadily as to prove that his large grey, ox-like eyes were not quite so insignificant as the rest of his face. When silence had fallen he said with marked respect: 'Mr Bohun, yours is the only theory yet propounded which holds water every way and is essentially unassailable. I think, therefore, that you deserve to be told, on my positive knowledge, that it is not the true one.' And with that the odd little man walked away and stared again at the hammer.

'That fellow seems to know more than he ought to,' whispered the doctor peevishly to Wilfred. 'Those popish priests are deucedly sly.'

'No, no,' said Bohun, with a sort of wild fatigue. 'It was the lunatic. It was the lunatic.'

The group of the two clerics and the doctor had fallen away from the more official group containing the inspector and the man he had arrested. Now, however, that their own party had broken up, they heard voices from the others.

The priest looked up quietly and then looked down again as he heard the blacksmith say in a loud voice: 'I hope I've convinced you, Mr Inspector. I'm a strong man, as you say, but I couldn't have flung my hammer bang here from Greenford. My hammer hasn't any wings that it should come flying half a mile over hedges and fields.'

The inspector laughed amicably and said: 'No; I think you can be considered out of it, though it's one of the rummiest coincidences I ever saw. I can only ask you to give us all the assistance you can in finding a man as big and strong as yourself. By George! you might be useful, if only to hold him! I suppose you yourself have no guess at the man?'

'I may have a guess,' said the pale smith, 'but it is not at a man.' Then, seeing the sacred eyes turn towards his wife on the bench, he put his huge hand on her shoulder and said: 'Nor a woman either.'

'What do you mean?' asked the inspector jocularly. 'You don't think cows use hammers, do you?'

'I think no thing of flesh held that hammer,' said the blacksmith in a stifled voice; 'mortally speaking, I think the man died alone.'

Wilfred made a sudden forward movement and peered at him with burning eyes.

'Do you mean to say, Barnes,' came the sharp voice of the cobbler, 'that the hammer jumped up of itself and knocked the man down?'

'Oh, you gentlemen may stare and snigger,' cried Simeon; 'you clergymen who tell us on Sunday in what a stillness the Lord smote Sennacherib. I believe that One who walks invisible in every house defended the honour of mine, and laid the defiler dead before the door of it. I believe the force in that blow was just the force there is in earthquakes, and no force less.'

Wilfred said, with a voice utterly indescribable: 'I told Norman myself to beware of the thunderbolt.'

'That agent is outside my jurisdiction,' said the inspector with a slight smile.

'You are not outside His,' answered the smith; 'see you to it.' And, turning his broad back, he went into the house.

The shaken Wilfred was led away by Father Brown, who had an easy and friendly way with him. 'Let us get out of this horrid place, Mr Bohun,' he said. 'May I look inside your church? I hear it's one of the oldest in England. We take some interest, you know,' he added with a comical grimace, 'in old English churches.'

Wilfred Bohun did not smile, for humour was never his strong point. But he nodded rather eagerly, being only too ready to explain the Gothic splendours to someone more likely to be sympathetic than the Presbyterian blacksmith or the atheist cobbler.

'By all means,' he said; 'let us go in at this side.' And he led the way into the high side entrance at the top of the flight of steps. Father Brown was mounting the first step to follow him when he felt a hand on his shoulder, and turned to behold the dark, thin figure of the doctor, his face darker yet with suspicion.

'Sir,' said the physician harshly, 'you appear to know some secrets in this black business. May I ask if you are going to keep them to yourself?'

'Why, doctor,' answered the priest, smiling quite pleasantly, 'there is one very good reason why a man of my trade would keep things to himself when he is not sure of them, and that is that it is so constantly his duty to keep them to himself when he is sure of them. But if you think I have been discourteously reticent with you or anyone, I will go to the extreme limit of my custom. I will give you two very large hints.'

'Well, sir?' said the doctor gloomily.

'First,' said Father Brown quietly, 'the thing is quite in your own province. It is a matter of physical science. The blacksmith is mistaken, not perhaps in saying that the blow was divine, but certainly in saying that it came by a miracle. It was no miracle, doctor, except in so far as man is himself a miracle, with his strange and wicked and yet half-heroic heart. The force that smashed that skull was a force well known to scientists – one of the most frequently debated of the laws of nature.'

The doctor, who was looking at him with frowning intentness, only said: 'And the other hint?'

'The other hint is this,' said the priest: 'Do you remember the blacksmith, though he believes in miracles, talking scornfully of the impossible fairy tale that his hammer had wings and flew half a mile across country?'

'Yes,' said the doctor, 'I remember that.'

'Well,' added Father Brown, with a broad smile, 'that fairy tale was the nearest thing to the real truth that has been said today.' And with that he turned his back and stumped up the steps after the curate.

The Revd Wilfred, who had been waiting for him, pale and impatient, as if this little delay were the last straw for his nerves, led him immediately to his favourite corner of the church, that part of the gallery closest to the carved roof and lit by the wonderful window with the angel. The little Latin priest explored and admired everything exhaustively, talking cheerfully but in a low voice all the time. When in the course of his investigation he found the side exit and the winding stair down which Wilfred had rushed to find his brother dead, Father Brown ran not down but up, with the agility of a monkey, and his clear voice came from an outer platform above.

'Come up here, Mr Bohun,' he called. 'The air will do you good.'

Bohun followed him, and came out on a kind of stone gallery or balcony outside the building, from which one could see the illimitable plain in which their small hill stood, wooded away to the purple horizon and dotted with villages and farms. Clear and square, but quite small beneath them, was the blacksmith's yard, where the inspector still stood taking notes and the corpse still lay like a smashed fly.

'Might be the map of the world, mightn't it?' said Father Brown.

'Yes,' said Bohun very gravely, and nodded his head.

Immediately beneath and about them the lines of the Gothic building plunged outwards into the void with a sickening swiftness akin to suicide. There is that element of Titan energy in the architecture of the Middle Ages that, from whatever aspect it be seen, it always seems to be rushing away, like the strong back of some maddened horse. This church was hewn out of ancient and silent stone, bearded with old fungoids and stained with the nests of birds. And yet, when they saw it from below, it sprang like a fountain at the stars; and when they saw it, as now, from above, it poured like a cataract into a voiceless pit. For these two men on the tower were left alone with the most terrible aspect of the Gothic: the monstrous foreshortening and disproportion, the dizzy perspectives, the glimpses of great things small and small things great; a topsy-turvydom of stone in the midair. Details of stone, enormous by their proximity, were relieved against a pattern of fields and farms, pygmy in their distance. A carved bird or beast at a corner seemed like some vast walking or flying dragon wasting the pastures and villages below. The whole atmosphere was dizzy and dangerous, as if men were upheld in air amid the gyrating wings of colossal genii; and the whole of that old church, as tall and rich as a cathedral, seemed to sit upon the sunlit country like a cloudburst.

'I think there is something rather dangerous about standing on these high places even to pray,' said Father Brown. 'Heights were made to be looked at, not to be looked from.'

'Do you mean that one may fall over,' asked Wilfred.

'I mean that one's soul may fall if one's body doesn't,' said the other priest.

'I scarcely understand you,' remarked Bohun indistinctly.

'Look at that blacksmith, for instance,' went on Father Brown calmly; 'a good man, but not a Christian – hard, imperious, unforgiving. Well, his Scotch religion was made up by men who prayed on hills and high crags, and learnt to look down on the world more than to look up at heaven. Humility is the mother of giants. One sees great things from the valley; only small things from the peak.'

'But he – he didn't do it,' said Bohun tremulously.

'No,' said the other in an odd voice; 'we know he didn't do it.'

After a moment he resumed, looking tranquilly out over the plain with his pale grey eyes. 'I knew a man,' he said, 'who began by worshipping with others before the altar, but who grew fond of high and lonely places to pray from, corners or niches in the belfry or the spire. And once in one of those dizzy places, where the whole world seemed to turn under him like a wheel, his brain turned also, and he fancied he was God. So that though he was a good man, he committed a great crime.'

Wilfred's face was turned away, but his bony hands turned blue and white as they tightened on the parapet of stone.

'He thought it was given to *him* to judge the world and strike down the sinner. He would never have had such a thought if he had been kneeling with other men upon a floor. But he saw all men walking about like insects. He saw one especially strutting just below him, insolent and evident by a bright green hat – a poisonous insect.'

Rooks cawed round the corners of the belfry; but

there was no other sound till Father Brown went on.

'This also tempted him, that he had in his hand one of the most awful engines of nature; I mean gravitation, that mad and quickening rush by which all earth's creatures fly back to her heart when released. See, the inspector is strutting just below us in the smithy. If I were to toss a pebble over this parapet it would be something like a bullet by the time it struck him. If I were to drop a hammer – even a small hammer – '

Wilfred Bohun threw one leg over the parapet, and Father Brown had him in a minute by the collar.

'Not by that door,' he said quite gently; 'that door leads to hell.'

Bohun staggered back against the wall, and stared at him with frightful eyes.

'How do you know all this?' he cried. 'Are you a devil?'

'I am a man,' answered Father Brown gravely; 'and therefore have all devils in my heart. Listen to me,' he said after a short pause. 'I know what you did – at least, I can guess the great part of it. When you left your brother you were racked with no unrighteous rage to the extent even that you snatched up the small hammer, half inclined to kill him with his foulness on his mouth. Recoiling, you thrust it under your buttoned coat instead, and rushed into the church. You pray wildly in many places, under the angel window, upon the platform above, and on a higher platform still, from which you could see the colonel's Eastern hat like the back of a green beetle crawling about. Then something snapped in your soul, and you let God's thunderbolt fall.'

Wilfred put a weak hand to his head, and asked in a

low voice: 'How did you know that his hat looked like a green beetle?'

'Oh, that,' said the other with the shadow of a smile, 'that was common sense. But hear me further. I say I know all this; but no one else shall know it. The next step is for you; I shall take no more steps; I will seal this with the seal of confession. If you ask me why, there are many reasons, and only one that concerns you. I leave things to you because you have not yet gone very far wrong, as assassins go. You did not help to fix the crime on the smith when it was easy; or on his wife, when that was easy. You tried to fix it on the imbecile, because you knew that he could not suffer. That was one of the gleams that it is my business to find in assassins. And now come down into the village, and go your own way as free as the wind; for I have said my last word.'

They went down the winding stairs in utter silence, and came out into the sunlight by the smithy. Wilfred Bohun carefully unlatched the wooden gate of the yard, and going up to the inspector, said: 'I wish to give myself up; I have killed my brother.'

The Well

W. W. JACOBS

I

Two men stood in the billiard-room of an old country house, talking. Play, which had been of a half-hearted nature, was over, and they sat at the open window, looking out over the park stretching away beneath them, conversing idly.

'Your time's nearly up, Jem,' said one at length, 'this time six weeks you'll be yawning out the honeymoon and cursing the man – woman I mean – who invented them.'

Jem Benson stretched his long limbs in the chair and grunted in dissent.

'I've never understood it,' continued Wilfred Carr, yawning. 'It's not in my line at all; I never had enough money for my own wants, let alone for two. Perhaps if I were as rich as you or Croesus I might regard it differently.'

There was just sufficient meaning in the latter part of the remark for his cousin to forbear to reply to it. He continued to gaze out of the window and to smoke slowly.

'Not being as rich as Croesus – or you,' resumed Carr, regarding him from beneath lowered lids, 'I paddle my own canoe down the stream of Time, and, tying it to my friends' doorposts, go in to eat their dinners.'

'Quite Venetian,' said Jem Benson, still looking out of the window. 'It's not a bad thing for you, Wilfred, that you have the doorposts and dinners – and friends.'

Carr grunted in his turn. 'Seriously though, Jem,' he said, slowly, 'you're a lucky fellow, a very lucky fellow. If there is a better girl above ground than Olive, I should like to see her.'

'Yes,' said the other, quietly.

'She's such an exceptional girl,' continued Carr, staring out of the window. 'She's so good and gentle. She thinks you are a bundle of all the virtues.'

He laughed frankly and joyously, but the other man did not join him. 'Strong sense of right and wrong, though,' continued Carr, musingly. 'Do you know, I believe that if she found out that you were not – '

'Not what?' demanded Benson, turning upon him fiercely, 'Not what?'

'Everything that you are,' returned his cousin, with a grin that belied his words, 'I believe she'd drop you.'

'Talk about something else,' said Benson, slowly; 'your pleasantries are not always in the best taste.'

Wilfred Carr rose and taking a cue from the rack, bent over the board and practised one or two favourite shots. 'The only other subject I can talk about just at present is my own financial affairs,' he said slowly, as he walked round the table.

'Talk about something else,' said Benson again, bluntly.

'And the two things are connected,' said Carr, and dropping his cue he half sat on the table and eyed his cousin.

There was a long silence. Benson pitched the end of his cigar out of the window, and leaning back closed his eyes.

'Do you follow me?' enquired Carr at length.

Benson opened his eyes and nodded at the window.

'Do you want to follow my cigar?' he demanded.

'I should prefer to depart by the usual way for your sake,' returned the other, unabashed. 'If I left by the window all sorts of questions would be asked, and you know what a talkative chap I am.'

'So long as you don't talk about my affairs,' returned the other, restraining himself by an obvious effort, 'you can talk yourself hoarse.'

'I'm in a mess,' said Carr, slowly, 'a devil of a mess. If I don't raise fifteen hundred by this day fortnight, I may be getting my board and lodging free.'

'Would that be any change?' questioned Benson.

'The quality would,' retorted the other. 'The address also would not be good. Seriously, Jem, will you let me have the fifteen hundred?'

'No,' said the other, simply.

Carr went white. 'It's to save me from ruin,' he said, thickly.

'I've helped you till I'm tired,' said Benson, turning and regarding him, 'and it is all to no good. If you've got into a mess, get out of it. You should not be so fond of giving autographs away.'

'It's foolish, I admit,' said Carr, deliberately. 'I won't do so any more. By the way, I've got some to sell. You needn't sneer. They're not my own.'

'Whose are they?' enquired the other.

'Yours.'

Benson got up from his chair and crossed over to him. 'What is this?' he asked, quietly. 'Blackmail?'

'Call it what you like,' said Carr. 'I've got some letters for sale, price fifteen hundred. And I know a man who would buy them at that price for the mere chance of getting Olive from you. I'll give you first offer.'

'If you have got any letters bearing my signature, you will be good enough to give them to me,' said Benson, very slowly.

'They're mine,' said Carr, lightly; 'given to me by the lady you wrote them to. I must say that they are not all in the best possible taste.'

His cousin reached forward suddenly, and catching him by the collar of his coat pinned him down on the table.

'Give me those letters,' he breathed, sticking his face close to Carr's.

'They're not here,' said Carr, struggling. 'I'm not a fool. Let me go, or I'll raise the price.'

The other man raised him from the table in his powerful hands, apparently with the intention of dashing his head against it. Then suddenly his hold relaxed as an astonished-looking maidservant entered the room with letters. Carr sat up hastily.

'That's how it was done,' said Benson, for the girl's benefit as he took the letters.

'I don't wonder at the other man making him pay for it, then,' said Carr, blandly.

'You will give me those letters?' said Benson, suggestively, as the girl left the room.

'At the price I mentioned, yes,' said Carr; 'but so sure as I am a living man, if you lay your clumsy hands on me again, I'll double it. Now, I'll leave you for a time while you think it over.'

He took a cigar from the box and lighting it carefully quitted the room. His cousin waited until the door had closed behind him, and then turning to the window sat there in a fit of fury as silent as it was terrible.

The air was fresh and sweet from the park, heavy with the scent of new-mown grass. The fragrance of a cigar was now added to it, and glancing out he saw his cousin pacing slowly by. He rose and went to the door, and then, apparently altering his mind, he returned to the window and watched the figure of his cousin as it moved slowly away into the moonlight. Then he rose again, and, for a long time, the room was empty.

*   *   *

It was empty when Mrs Benson came in some time later to say good-night to her son on her way to bed. She walked slowly round the table, and pausing at the window gazed from it in idle thought, until she saw the figure of her son advancing with rapid strides toward the house. He looked up at the window.

'Good-night,' said she.

'Good-night,' said Benson, in a deep voice.

'Where is Wilfred?'

'Oh, he has gone,' said Benson.

'Gone?'

'We had a few words; he was wanting money again, and I gave him a piece of my mind. I don't think we shall see him again.'

'Poor Wilfred!' sighed Mrs Benson. 'He is always in trouble of some sort. I hope that you were not too hard upon him.'

'No more than he deserved,' said her son, sternly. 'Good-night.'

2

The well, which had long ago fallen into disuse, was almost hidden by the thick tangle of undergrowth which ran riot at that corner of the old park. It was partly covered by the shrunken half of a lid, above which a rusty windlass creaked in company with the music of the pines when the wind blew strongly. The full light of the sun never reached it, and the ground surrounding it was moist and green when other parts of the park were gaping with the heat.

Two people walking slowly round the park in the fragrant stillness of a summer evening strayed in the direction of the well.

'No use going through this wilderness, Olive,' said Benson, pausing on the outskirts of the pines and eyeing with some disfavour the gloom beyond.

'Best part of the park,' said the girl briskly; 'you know it's my favourite spot.'

'I know you're very fond of sitting on the coping,' said the man slowly, 'and I wish you wouldn't. One day you will lean back too far and fall in.'

'And make the acquaintance of Truth,' said Olive lightly. 'Come along.'

She ran from him and was lost in the shadow of the pines, the bracken crackling beneath her feet as she ran. Her companion followed slowly, and emerging from the gloom saw her poised daintily on the edge of the well with her feet hidden in the rank grass and nettles which surrounded it. She motioned her companion to take a seat by her side, and smiled softly as she felt a strong arm passed about her waist.

'I like this place,' said she, breaking a long silence,

'it is so dismal – so uncanny. Do you know I wouldn't dare to sit here alone, Jem. I should imagine that all sorts of dreadful things were hidden behind the bushes and trees, waiting to spring out on me. Ugh!'

'You'd better let me take you in,' said her companion tenderly; 'the well isn't always wholesome, especially in the hot weather.

'Let's make a move.'

The girl gave an obstinate little shake, and settled herself more securely on her seat.

'Smoke your cigar in peace,' she said quietly. 'I am settled here for a quiet talk. Has anything been heard of Wilfred yet?'

'Nothing.'

'Quite a dramatic disappearance, isn't it?' she continued. 'Another scrape, I suppose, and another letter for you in the same old strain: "Dear Jem, help me out." '

Jem Benson blew a cloud of fragrant smoke into the air, and holding his cigar between his teeth brushed away the ash from his coat sleeves.

'I wonder what he would have done without you,' said the girl, pressing his arm affectionately. 'Gone under long ago, I suppose. When we are married, Jem, I shall presume upon the relationship to lecture him. He is very wild, but he has his good points, poor fellow.'

'I never saw them,' said Benson, with startling bitterness. 'God knows I never saw them.'

'He is nobody's enemy but his own,' said the girl, startled by this outburst.

'You don't know much about him,' said the other, sharply. 'He was not above blackmail; not above ruining the life of a friend to do himself a benefit. A loafer, a cur, and a liar!'

The girl looked up at him soberly but timidly and took his arm without a word, and they both sat silent while evening deepened into night and the beams of the moon, filtering through the branches, surrounded them with a silver network. Her head sank upon his shoulder, till suddenly with a sharp cry she sprang to her feet.

'What was that?' she cried breathlessly.

'What was what?' demanded Benson, springing up and clutching her fast by the arm.

She caught her breath and tried to laugh.

'You're hurting me, Jem.'

His hold relaxed.

'What is the matter?' he asked gently. 'What was it startled you?'

'I was startled,' she said, slowly, putting her hands on his shoulder. 'I suppose the words I used just now are ringing in my ears, but I fancied that somebody behind us whispered "Jem, help me out." '

'Fancy,' repeated Benson, and his voice shook; 'but these fancies are not good for you. You are frightened at the dark and the gloom of these trees. Let me take you back to the house.'

'No, I'm not frightened,' said the girl, reseating herself. 'I should never be really frightened of anything when you were with me, Jem. I'm surprised at myself for being so silly.'

The man made no reply but stood, a strong, dark figure, a yard or two from the well, as though waiting for her to join him.

'Come and sit down, sir,' cried Olive, patting the brickwork with her small, white hand, 'one would think that you did not like your company.'

He obeyed slowly and took a seat by her side,

drawing so hard at his cigar that the light of it shone upon his face at every breath. He passed his arm, firm and rigid as steel, behind her, with his hand resting on the brickwork beyond.

'Are you warm enough?' he asked tenderly, as she made a little movement.

'Pretty fair,' she shivered; 'one oughtn't to be cold at this time of the year, but there's a cold, damp air comes up from the well.'

As she spoke a faint splash sounded from the depths below, and for the second time that evening, she sprang from the well with a little cry of dismay.

'What is it now?' he asked in a fearful voice. He stood by her side and gazed at the well, as though half expecting to see the cause of her alarm emerge from it.

'Oh, my bracelet,' she cried in distress, 'my poor mother's bracelet. I've dropped it down the well.'

'Your bracelet!' repeated Benson, dully. 'Your bracelet? The diamond one?'

'The one that was my mother's,' said Olive. 'Oh, we can get it back surely. We must have the water drained off.'

'Your bracelet!' repeated Benson, stupidly.

'Jem,' said the girl in terrified tones, 'dear Jem, what is the matter?'

For the man she loved was standing regarding her with horror. The moon which touched it was not responsible for all the whiteness of the distorted face, and she shrank back in fear to the edge of the well. He saw her fear and by a mighty effort regained his composure and took her hand.

'Poor little girl,' he murmured, 'you frightened me. I was not looking when you cried, and I thought that you were slipping from my arms, down – down – '

His voice broke, and the girl throwing herself into his arms clung to him convulsively.

'There, there,' said Benson, fondly, 'don't cry, don't cry.'

'Tomorrow,' said Olive, half-laughing, half-crying, 'we will all come round the well with hook and line and fish for it. It will be quite a new sport.'

'No, we must try some other way,' said Benson. 'You shall have it back.'

'How?' asked the girl.

'You shall see,' said Benson. 'Tomorrow morning at latest you shall have it back. Till then promise me that you will not mention your loss to anyone. Promise.'

'I promise,' said Olive, wonderingly. 'But why not?'

'It is of great value, for one thing, and – But there – there are many reasons. For one thing it is my duty to get it for you.'

'Wouldn't you like to jump down for it?' she asked mischievously. 'Listen.'

She stooped for a stone and dropped it down.

'Fancy being where that is now,' she said, peering into the blackness; 'fancy going round and round like a mouse in a pail, clutching at the slimy sides, with the water filling your mouth, and looking up to the little patch of sky above.'

'You had better come in,' said Benson, very quietly. 'You are developing a taste for the morbid and horrible.'

The girl turned, and taking his arm walked slowly in the direction of the house; Mrs Benson, who was sitting in the porch, rose to receive them.

'You shouldn't have kept her out so long,' she said chidingly. 'Where have you been?'

'Sitting on the well,' said Olive, smiling, 'discussing our future.'

'I don't believe that place is healthy,' said Mrs Benson, emphatically. 'I really think it might be filled in, Jem.'

'All right,' said her son, slowly. 'Pity it wasn't filled in long ago.'

He took the chair vacated by his mother as she entered the house with Olive, and with his hands hanging limply over the sides sat in deep thought. After a time he rose, and going upstairs to a room which was set apart for sporting requisites selected a sea fishing line and some hooks and stole softly downstairs again. He walked swiftly across the park in the direction of the well, turning before he entered the shadow of the trees to look back at the lighted windows of the house. Then having arranged his line he sat on the edge of the well and cautiously lowered it.

He sat with his lips compressed, occasionally looking about him in a startled fashion, as though he half expected to see something peering at him from the belt of trees. Time after time he lowered his line until at length in pulling it up he heard a little metallic tinkle against the side of the well.

He held his breath then, and forgetting his fears drew the line in inch by inch, so as not to lose its precious burden. His pulse beat rapidly, and his eyes were bright. As the line came slowly in he saw the catch hanging to the hook, and with a steady hand drew the last few feet in. Then he saw that instead of the bracelet he had hooked a bunch of keys.

With a faint cry he shook them from the hook into the water below, and stood breathing heavily. Not a

sound broke the stillness of the night. He walked up
and down a bit and stretched his great muscles; then
he came back to the well and resumed his task.

For an hour or more the line was lowered without
result. In his eagerness he forgot his fears, and with
eyes bent down the well fished slowly and carefully.
Twice the hook became entangled in something, and
was with difficulty released. It caught a third time,
and all his efforts failed to free it. Then he dropped
the line down the well, and with head bent walked
toward the house.

He went first to the stables at the rear, and then
retiring to his room for some time paced restlessly up
and down. Then without removing his clothes he
flung himself upon the bed and fell into a troubled
sleep.

3

Long before anybody else was astir he arose and
stole softly downstairs. The sunlight was stealing in
at every crevice, and flashing in long streaks across
the darkened rooms. The dining-room into which he
looked struck chill and cheerless in the dark yellow
light which came through the lowered blinds. He
remembered that it had the same appearance when
his father lay dead in the house; now, as then, everything seemed ghastly and unreal; the very chairs
standing as their occupants had left them the night
before seemed to be indulging in some dark communication of ideas.

Slowly and noiselessly he opened the hall door and
passed into the fragrant air beyond. The sun was
shining on the drenched grass and trees, and a slowly

vanishing white mist rolled like smoke about the grounds. For a moment he stood, breathing deeply the sweet air of the morning, and then walked slowly in the direction of the stables.

The rusty creaking of a pump-handle and a spatter of water upon the red-tiled courtyard showed that somebody else was astir, and a few steps farther he beheld a brawny, sandy-haired man gasping wildly under severe self-infliction at the pump.

'Everything ready, George?' he asked quietly.

'Yes, sir,' said the man, straightening up suddenly and touching his forehead. 'Bob's just finishing the arrangements inside. It's a lovely morning for a dip. The water in that well must be just icy.'

'Be as quick as you can,' said Benson, impatiently.

'Very good, sir,' said George, burnishing his face harshly with a very small towel which had been hanging over the top of the pump. 'Hurry up, Bob.'

In answer to his summons a man appeared at the door of the stable with a coil of stout rope over his arm and a large metal candlestick in his hand.

'Just to try the air, sir,' said George, following his master's glance. 'A well gets rather foul sometimes, but if a candle can live down it, a man can.'

His master nodded, and the man, hastily pulling up the neck of his shirt and thrusting his arms into his coat, followed him as he led the way slowly to the well.

'Beg pardon, sir,' said George, drawing up to his side, 'but you are not looking over and above well this morning. If you'll let me go down I'd enjoy the bath.'

'No, no,' said Benson, peremptorily.

'You ain't fit to go down, sir,' persisted his follower. 'I've never seen you look so before. Now if – '

'Mind your business,' said his master curtly.

George became silent and the three walked with swinging strides through the long wet grass to the well. Bob flung the rope on the ground and at a sign from his master handed him the candlestick.

'Here's the line for it, sir,' said Bob, fumbling in his pockets.

Benson took it from him and slowly tied it to the candlestick. Then he placed it on the edge of the well, and striking a match, lit the candle and began slowly to lower it.

'Hold hard, sir,' said George, quickly, laying his hand on his arm, 'you must tilt it or the string'll burn through.'

Even as he spoke the string parted and the candle-stick fell into the water below.

Benson swore quietly.

'I'll soon get another,' said George, starting up.

'Never mind, the well's all right,' said Benson.

'It won't take a moment, sir,' said the other over his shoulder.

'Are you master here, or am I?' said Benson hoarsely.

George came back slowly, a glance at his master's face stopping the protest upon his tongue, and he stood by watching him sulkily as he sat on the well and removed his outer garments. Both men watched him curiously, as having completed his preparations he stood grim and silent with his hands by his sides.

'I wish you'd let me go, sir,' said George, plucking up courage to address him. 'You ain't fit to go, you've got a chill or something. I shouldn't wonder it's the typhoid. They've got it in the village bad.'

For a moment Benson looked at him angrily, then

his gaze softened. 'Not this time, George,' he said, quietly. He took the looped end of the rope and placed it under his arms, and sitting down threw one leg over the side of the well.

'How are you going about it, sir?' queried George, laying hold of the rope and signing to Bob to do the same.

'I'll call out when I reach the water,' said Benson; 'then pay out three yards more quickly so that I can get to the bottom.'

'Very good, sir,' answered both.

Their master threw the other leg over the coping and sat motionless. His back was turned toward the men as he sat with head bent, looking down the shaft. He sat for so long that George became uneasy.

'All right, sir?' he enquired.

'Yes,' said Benson, slowly. 'If I tug at the rope, George, pull up at once. Lower away.'

The rope passed steadily through their hands until a hollow cry from the darkness below and a faint splashing warned them that he had reached the water. They gave him three yards more and stood with relaxed grasp and strained ears, waiting.

'He's gone under,' said Bob in a low voice.

The other nodded, and moistening his huge palms took a firmer grip of the rope.

Fully a minute passed, and the men began to exchange uneasy glances. Then a sudden tremendous jerk followed by a series of feebler ones nearly tore the rope from their grasp.

'Pull!' shouted George, placing one foot on the side and hauling desperately. 'Pull! pull! He's stuck fast; he's not coming; PULL!'

In response to their terrific exertions the rope came

slowly in, inch by inch, until at length a violent splashing was heard, and at the same moment a scream of unutterable horror came echoing up the shaft.

'What a weight he is !' panted Bob. 'He's stuck fast or something. Keep still, sir; for heaven's sake, keep still.'

For the taut rope was being jerked violently by the struggles of the weight at the end of it. Both men with grunts and sighs hauled it in foot by foot.

'All right, sir,' cried George, cheerfully.

He had one foot against the well, and was pulling manfully; the burden was nearing the top. A long pull and a strong pull, and the face of a dead man with mud in the eyes and nostrils came peering over the edge. Behind it was the ghastly face of his master; but this he saw too late, for with a great cry he let go his hold of the rope and stepped back. The suddenness overthrew his assistant, and the rope tore through his hands. There was a frightful splash.

'You fool!' stammered Bob, and ran to the well helplessly.

'Run!' cried George. 'Run for another line.'

He bent over the coping and called eagerly down as his assistant sped back to the stables shouting wildly. His voice re-echoed down the shaft, but all else was silence.

The Lady with the Hatchet

MAURICE LEBLANC

One of the most incomprehensible incidents that preceded the great war was certainly the one which was known as the episode of the lady with the hatchet. The solution of the mystery was unknown and would never have been known, had not circumstances in the cruellest fashion obliged Prince Rénine – or should I say, Arsène Lupin? – to take up the matter and had I not been able today to tell the true story from the details supplied by him.

Let me recite the facts. In a space of eighteen months, five women disappeared, five women of different stations in life, all between twenty and thirty years of age and living in Paris or the Paris district.

I will give their names: Madame Ladoue, the wife of a doctor; Mlle Ardant, the daughter of a banker; Mlle Covereau, a washer-woman of Courbevoie; Mlle Honorine Vernisset, a dressmaker; and Madame Grollinger, an artist. These five women disappeared without the possibility of discovering a single particular to explain why they had left their homes, why they did not return to them, who had enticed them away, and where and how they were detained.

Each of these women, a week after her departure, was found somewhere or other in the western outskirts of Paris; and each time it was a dead body that was found, the dead body of a woman who had been

145

killed by a blow on the head from a hatchet. And each time, not far from the woman, who was firmly bound, her face covered with blood and her body emaciated by lack of food, the marks of carriage-wheels proved that the corpse had been driven to the spot.

The five murders were so much alike that there was only a single investigation, embracing all the five enquiries and, for that matter, leading to no result. A woman disappeared; a week later, to a day, her body was discovered; and that was all. The bonds that fastened her were similar in each case; so were the tracks left by the wheels; so were the blows of the hatchet, all of which were struck vertically at the top and right in the middle of the forehead.

The motive of the crime? The five women had been completely stripped of their jewels, purses and other objects of value. But the robberies might well have been attributed to marauders or any passers-by, since the bodies were lying in deserted spots. Were the authorities to believe in the execution of a plan of revenge or of a plan intended to do away with the series of persons mutually connected, persons, for instance, likely to benefit by a future inheritance? Here again the same obscurity prevailed. Theories were built up, only to be demolished forthwith by an examination of the facts. Trails were followed and at once abandoned.

And suddenly there was a sensation. A woman engaged in sweeping the roads picked up on the pavement a little notebook which she brought to the local police-station. The leaves of this notebook were all blank, excepting one, on which was written a list of the murdered women, with their names set down in order of date and accompanied by three figures: Ladoue, 132; Vernisset, 118; and so on.

Certainly no importance would have been attached to these entries, which anybody might have written, since everyone was acquainted with the sinister list. But, instead of five names, it included six! Yes, below the words 'Grollinger, 128', there appeared 'Williamson, 114'. Did this indicate a sixth murder?

The obviously English origin of the name limited the field of the investigations, which did not in fact take long. It was ascertained that, a fortnight ago, a Miss Hermione Williamson, a governess in a family at Auteuil, had left her place to go back to England and that, since then, her sisters, though she had written to tell them that she was coming over, had heard no more of her.

A fresh enquiry was instituted. A postman found the body in the Meudon woods. Miss Williamson's skull was split down the middle.

I need not describe the public excitement at this stage nor the shudder of horror which passed through the crowd when it read this list, written without a doubt in the murderer's own hand. What could be more frightful than such a record, kept up to date like a careful tradesman's ledger: 'On such a day, I killed so-and-so; on such a day so-and-so!'

And the sum total was six dead bodies.

Against all expectation, the experts in handwriting had no difficulty in agreeing and unanimously declared that the writing was 'that of a woman, an educated woman, possessing artistic tastes, imagination and an extremely sensitive nature'. The 'lady with the hatchet', as the journalists christened her, was decidedly no ordinary person; and scores of news-paper-articles made a special study of her case, exposing her mental condition and losing themselves in far-fetched explanations.

Nevertheless it was the writer of one of these articles, a young journalist whose chance discovery made him the centre of public attention, who supplied the one element of truth and shed upon the darkness the only ray of light that was to penetrate it. In casting about for the meaning of the figures which followed the six names, he had come to ask himself whether those figures did not simply represent the number of the days separating one crime from the next. All that he had to do was to check the dates. He at once found that his theory was correct. Mlle Vernisset had been carried off one hundred and thirty-two days after Madame Ladoue; Mlle Covereau one hundred and eighteen days after Honorine Vernisset; and so on.

There was therefore no room for doubt; and the police had no choice but to accept a solution which so precisely fitted the circumstances: the figures corresponded with the intervals. There was no mistake in the records of the lady with the hatchet.

But then one deduction became inevitable. Miss Williamson, the latest victim, had been carried off on the 26th of June last, and her name was followed by the figures 114: was it not to be presumed that a fresh crime would be committed a hundred and fourteen days later, that is to say, on the 18th of October? Was it not probable that the horrible business would be repeated in accordance with the murderer's secret intentions? Were they not bound to pursue to its logical conclusion the argument which ascribed to the figures – to all the figures, to the last as well as to the others – their value as eventual dates?

Now it was precisely this deduction which was drawn and was being weighed and discussed during the few days that preceded the 18th of October, when logic demanded the performance of yet another act of the abominable tragedy. And it was only natural that, on the morning of that day, Prince Rénine and Hortense, when making an appointment by telephone for the evening, should allude to the newspaper-articles which they had both been reading:

'Look out!' said Rénine, laughing. 'If you meet the lady with the hatchet, take the other side of the road!'

'And, if the good lady carries me off, what am I to do?'

'Strew your path with little white pebbles and say, until the very moment when the hatchet flashes in the air, "I have nothing to fear; *he* will save me." *He* is myself . . . and I kiss your hands. Till this evening, my dear.'

That afternoon, Rénine had an appointment with Rose Andrée and Dalbrèque to arrange for their departure for the States. Before four and seven o'clock, he bought the different editions of the evening papers. None of them reported an abduction.

At nine o'clock he went to the Gymnase, where he had taken a private box.

At half-past nine, as Hortense had not arrived, he rang her up, though without thought of anxiety. The maid replied that Madame Daniel had not come in yet.

Seized with a sudden fear, Rénine hurried to the furnished flat which Hortense was occupying for the time being, near the Parc Monceau, and questioned the maid, whom he had engaged for her and who was completely devoted to him. The woman said that her mistress had gone out at two o'clock, with a stamped letter in her hand, saying that she was going to the post and that she would come back to dress. This was the last that had been seen of her.

'To whom was the letter addressed?'

'To you, sir. I saw the writing on the envelope: Prince Serge Rénine.'

He waited until midnight, but in vain. Hortense did not return; nor did she return next day.

'Not a word to anyone,' said Rénine to the maid. 'Say that your mistress is in the country and that you are going to join her.'

For his own part, he had not a doubt: Hortense's disappearance was explained by the very fact of the date, the 18th of October. She was the seventh victim of the lady with the hatchet.

*   *   *

'The abduction,' said Rénine to himself, 'precedes the blow of the hatchet by a week. I have, therefore, at the present moment, seven full days before me. Let us say six, to avoid any surprise. This is Saturday: Hortense must be set free by midday on Friday; and, to make sure of this, I must know her hiding-place by nine o'clock on Thursday evening at latest.'

Rénine wrote, 'THURSDAY EVENING, NINE O'CLOCK', in big letters, on a card which he nailed above the mantelpiece in his study. Then at midday on Saturday, the day after the disappearance, he locked himself into the study, after telling his man not to disturb him except for meals and letters.

He spent four days there, almost without moving.

He had immediately sent for a set of all the leading newspapers which had spoken in detail of the first six crimes. When he had read and reread them, he closed the shutters, drew the curtains and lay down on the sofa in the dark, with the door bolted, thinking.

By Tuesday evening he was no further advanced than on the Saturday. The darkness was as dense as ever. He had not discovered the smallest clue for his guidance, nor could he see the slightest reason to hope.

At times, notwithstanding his immense power of self-control and his unlimited confidence in the resources at his disposal, at times he would quake with anguish. Would he arrive in time? There was no reason why he should see more clearly during the last few days than during those which had already elapsed. And this meant that Hortense Daniel would inevitably be murdered.

The thought tortured him. He was attached to Hortense by a much stronger and deeper feeling than the appearance of the relations between them would have led an onlooker to believe. The curiosity at the beginning, the first desire, the impulse to protect Hortense, to distract her, to inspire her with a relish for existence: all this had simply turned to love. Neither of them was aware of it, because they barely saw each other save at critical times when they were occupied with the adventures of others and not with their own. But, at the first onslaught of danger, Rénine realised the place which Hortense had taken in his life and he was in despair at knowing her to be a prisoner and a martyr and at being unable to save her.

He spent a feverish, agitated night, turning the case over and over from every point of view. The

Wednesday morning was also a terrible time for him. He was losing ground. Giving up his hermit-like seclusion, he threw open the windows and paced to and fro through his rooms, ran out into the street and came in again, as though fleeing before the thought that obsessed him: 'Hortense is suffering . . . Hortense is in the depths . . . She sees the hatchet . . . She is calling to me . . . She is entreating me . . . And I can do nothing . . . '

It was at five o'clock in the afternoon that, on examining the list of the six names, he received that little inward shock which is a sort of signal of the truth that is being sought for. A light shot through his mind. It was not, to be sure, that brilliant light in which every detail is made plain, but it was enough to tell him in which direction to move.

His plan of campaign was formed at once. He sent Adolphe, his chauffeur, to the principal newspapers, with a few lines which were to appear in type among the next morning's advertisements. Adolphe was also told to go to the laundry at Courbevoie, where Mlle Covereau, the second of the six victims, had been employed.

On the Thursday, Rénine did not stir out of doors. In the afternoon, he received several letters in reply to his advertisement. Then two telegrams arrived. Lastly, at three o'clock, there came a pneumatic letter, bearing the Trocadéro postmark, which seemed to be what he was expecting.

He turned up a directory, noted an address – 'M. de Lourtier-Vaneau, retired colonial governor, 47 *bis*, Avenue Kléber' – and ran down to his car: 'Adolphe, 47 *bis*, Avenue Kléber.'

* * *

He was shown into a large study furnished with magnificent bookcases containing old volumes in costly bindings. M. de Lourtier-Vaneau was a man still in the prime of life, wearing a slightly grizzled beard and, by his affable manners and genuine distinction, commanding confidence and liking.

'M. de Lourtier,' said Rénine, 'I have ventured to call on your excellency because I read in last year's newspapers that you used to know one of the victims of the lady with the hatchet, Honorine Vernisset.'

'Why, of course we knew her!' cried M. de Lourtier. 'My wife used to employ her as a dressmaker by the day. Poor girl!'

'M. de Lourtier, a lady of my acquaintance has disappeared as the other six victims disappeared.'

'What!' exclaimed M. de Lourtier, with a start. 'But I have followed the newspapers carefully. There was nothing on the 18 October.'

'Yes, a woman of whom I am very fond, Madame Hortense Daniel, was abducted on the 17 October.'

'And this is the 22nd!'

'Yes; and the murder will be committed on the 24th.'

'Horrible! Horrible! It must be prevented at all costs . . .'

'And I shall perhaps succeed in preventing it, with your excellency's assistance.'

'But have you been to the police?'

'No. We are faced by mysteries which are, so to speak, absolute and compact, which offer no gap through which the keenest eyes can see and which it is useless to hope to clear up by ordinary methods, such as inspection of the scenes of the crimes, police enquiries, searching for fingerprints and so on. As none of those proceedings served any good purpose in the previous cases, it would be a waste of time to resort to them in a seventh, similar case. An enemy who displays such skill and subtlety would not leave behind her any of those clumsy traces which are the first things that a professional detective seizes upon.'

'Then what have you done?'

'Before taking any action, I have reflected. I gave four days to thinking the matter over.'

M. de Lourtier-Vaneau examined his visitor closely and, with a touch of irony, asked: 'And the result of your meditations . . . ?'

'To begin with,' said Rénine, refusing to be put out of countenance, 'I have submitted all these cases to a comprehensive survey, which hitherto no one else had done. This enabled me to discover their general meaning, to put aside all the tangle of embarrassing theories and, since no one was able to agree as to the motives of all this filthy business, to attribute it to the only class of persons capable of it.'

'That is to say?'

'Lunatics, your excellency.'

M. de Lourtier-Vaneau started: 'Lunatics? What an idea!'

'M. de Lourtier, the woman known as the lady with the hatchet is a madwoman.'

'But she would be locked up!'

'We don't know that she's not. We don't know that she is not one of those half-mad people, apparently harmless, who are watched so slightly that they have full scope to indulge their little manias, their wild-beast instincts. Nothing could be more treacherous than these creatures. Nothing could be more crafty, more patient, more persistent, more dangerous and at the same time more absurd and more logical, more slovenly and more methodical. All these epithets, M. de Lourtier, may be applied to the doings of the lady with the hatchet. The obsession of an idea and the continual repetition of an act are characteristics of the maniac. I do not yet know the idea by which the lady with the hatchet is obsessed but I do know the act that results from it; and it is always the same. The victim is bound with precisely similar ropes. She is killed after the same number of days. She is struck by an identical blow, with the same instrument, in the same place, the middle of the forehead, producing an absolutely vertical wound. An ordinary murderer displays some variety. His trembling hand swerves aside and strikes awry. The lady with the hatchet does not tremble. It is as though she had taken measurements; and the edge of her weapon does not swerve by a hair's breadth. Need I give you any further proofs or examine all the other details with you? Surely not. You now possess the key to the riddle; and you know as I do that only a lunatic can behave in this way, stupidly, savagely, mechanically, like a striking clock or the blade of the guillotine . . .'

M. de Lourtier-Vaneau nodded his head: 'Yes, that is so. One can see the whole affair from that angle . . . and I am beginning to believe that this is how one ought to see it. But, if we admit that this madwoman has the sort of mathematical logic which governed the murders of the six victims, I see no connection between the victims themselves. She struck at random. Why this victim rather than that?'

'Ah,' said Rénine. 'Your excellency is asking me a question which I asked myself from the first moment, the question which sums up the whole problem and which cost me so much trouble to solve! Why Hortense Daniel rather than another? Among two millions of women who might have been selected, why Hortense? Why little Vernisset? Why Miss Williamson? If the affair is such as I conceived it, as a whole, that is to say, based upon the blind and fantastic logic of a madwoman, a choice was inevitably exercised. Now in what did that choice consist? What was the quality, or the defect, or the sign needed to induce the lady with the hatchet to strike? In a word, if she chose – and she must have chosen – what directed her choice?'

'Have you found the answer?'

Rénine paused and replied: 'Yes, your excellency, I have. And I could have found it at the very outset, since all that I had to do was to make a careful examination of the list of victims. But these flashes of truth are never kindled save in a brain over stimulated by effort and reflection. I stared at the list twenty times over, before that little detail took a definite shape.'

'I don't follow you,' said M. de Lourtier-Vaneau.

'M. de Lourtier, it may be noted that, if a number of persons are brought together in any transaction, or crime, or public scandal or what not, they are almost invariably described in the same way. On this occasion, the newspapers never mentioned anything more than their surnames in speaking of Madame Ladoue, Mlle Ardant or Mlle Covereau. On the other hand, Mlle Vernisset and Miss Williamson were always described by their Christian names as well: Honorine and Hermione. If the same thing had been done in the case of all the six victims, there would have been no mystery.'

'Why not?'

'Because we should at once have realised the relation existing between the six unfortunate women, as I myself suddenly realised it on comparing those two Christian names with that of Hortense Daniel. You understand now, don't you? You see the three Christian names before your eyes . . .'

M. de Lourtier-Vaneau seemed to be perturbed. Turning a little pale, he said: 'What do you mean? What do you mean?'

'I mean,' continued Rénine, in a clear voice, sounding each syllable separately, 'I mean that you see before your eyes three Christian names which all three begin with the same initial and which all three, by a remarkable coincidence, consist of the same number of letters, as you may prove. If you enquire at the Courbevoie laundry, where Mlle Covereau used to work, you will find that her name was Hilairie. Here again we have the same initial and the same number of letters. There is no need to seek any farther. We are sure, are we not, that the Christian names of all the victims offer the same peculiarities? And this gives us, with absolute certainty, the key to the problem which was set us. It explains the madwoman's choice. We now know the connection between the unfortunate victims. There can be no mistake about it. It's that and nothing else. And how this method of choosing confirms my theory! What proof of madness! Why kill these women rather than any others? Because their names begin with an H and consist of eight letters! You understand me, M. de Lourtier, do you not? The number of letters is eight. The initial letter is the eighth letter of the alphabet; and the word *huit*, eight, begins with an H. Always the letter H. *And the implement used to commit the crime was a hatchet.* Is your excellency prepared to tell me that the lady with the hatchet is not a madwoman?'

Rénine interrupted himself and went up to M. de Lourtier-Vaneau: 'What's the matter, your excellency? Are you unwell?'

'No, no,' said M. de Lourtier, with the perspiration streaming down his forehead. 'No . . . but all this story is so upsetting! Only think, I knew one of the victims! And then . . . '

Rénine took a water-bottle and tumbler from a small table, filled the glass and handed it to M. de Lourtier, who sipped a few mouthfuls from it and then, pulling himself together, continued, in a voice which he strove to make firmer than it had been: 'Very well. We'll admit your supposition. Even so, it is necessary that it should lead to tangible results. What have you done?'

'This morning I published in all the newspapers an advertisement worded as follows:

Excellent cook seeks situation. Write before 5 p.m. to Herminie, Boulevard Haussmann, etc.

You continue to follow me, don't you, M. de Lourtier? Christian names beginning with an H and consisting of eight letters are extremely rare and are all rather out of date: Herminie, Hilairie, Hermione. Well, these Christian names, for reasons which I do not understand, are essential to the madwoman. She cannot do without them. To find women bearing one of these Christian names and for this purpose only she summons up all her remaining powers of reason, discernment, reflection and intelligence. She hunts about. She asks questions. She lies in wait. She reads newspapers which she hardly understands, but in which certain details, certain capital letters catch her eye. And consequently I did not doubt for a second that this name of Herminie, printed in large type, would attract her attention and that she would be caught today in the trap of my advertisement.'

'Did she write?' asked M. de Lourtier-Vaneau, anxiously.

'Several ladies,' Rénine continued, 'wrote the letters which are usual in such cases, to offer a home to the so-called Herminie. But I received an express letter which struck me as interesting.'

'From whom?'

'Read it, M. de Lourtier.'

M. de Lourtier-Vaneau snatched the sheet from Rénine's hands and cast a glance at the signature. His first movement was one of surprise, as though he had expected something different. Then he gave a long, loud laugh of something like joy and relief.

'Why do you laugh, M. de Lourtier? You seem pleased.'

'Pleased, no. But this letter is signed by my wife.'

'And you were afraid of finding something else?'

'Oh no! But since it's my wife . . .'

He did not finish his sentence and said to Rénine: 'Come this way.'

He led him through a passage to a little drawing-room where a fair-haired lady, with a happy and tender expression on her comely face, was sitting in the midst of three children and helping them with their lessons.

She rose. M. de Lourtier briefly presented his visitor and asked his wife: 'Suzanne, is this express message from you?'

'To Mlle Herminie, Boulevard Haussmann? Yes,'

she said, 'I sent it. As you know, our parlour-maid's leaving and I'm looking out for a new one.'

Rénine interrupted her: 'Excuse me, madame. Just one question: where did you get the woman's address?'

She flushed. Her husband insisted: 'Tell us, Suzanne. Who gave you the address?'

'I was rung up.'

'By whom?'

She hesitated and then said: 'Your old nurse.'

'Félicienne?'

'Yes.'

M. de Lourtier cut short the conversation and, without permitting Rénine to ask any more questions, took him back to the study: 'You see, monsieur, that pneumatic letter came from a quite natural source. Félicienne, my old nurse, who lives not far from Paris on an allowance which I make her, read your advertisement and told Madame de Lourtier of it. For, after all,' he added laughing, 'I don't suppose that you suspect my wife of being the lady with the hatchet.'

'No.'

'Then the incident is closed . . . at least on my side. I have done what I could, I have listened to your arguments and I am very sorry that I can be of no more use to you . . . '

He drank another glass of water and sat down. His face was distorted. Rénine looked at him for a few seconds, as a man will look at a failing adversary who has only to receive the knock-out blow, and, sitting down beside him, suddenly gripped his arm: 'Your excellency, if you do not speak, Hortense Daniel will be the seventh victim.'

'I have nothing to say, monsieur! What do you think I know?'

'The truth! My explanations have made it plain to you. Your distress, your terror are positive proofs.'

'But, after all, monsieur, if I knew, why should I be silent?'

'For fear of scandal. There is in your life, so a profound intuition assures me, something that you are constrained to hide. The truth about this monstrous tragedy, which suddenly flashed upon you, this truth, if it were known, would spell dishonour to you, disgrace . . . and you are shrinking from your duty.'

M. de Lourtier did not reply. Rénine leant over him and, looking him in the eyes, whispered: 'There will be no scandal. I shall be the only person in the world to know what has happened. And I am as much interested as yourself in not attracting attention, because I love Hortense Daniel and do not wish her name to be mixed up in your horrible story.'

They remained face to face during a long interval. Rénine's expression was harsh and unyielding. M. de Lourtier felt that nothing would bend him if the necessary words remained unspoken; but he could not bring himself to utter them: 'You are mistaken,' he said. 'You think you have seen things that don't exist.'

Rénine received a sudden and terrifying conviction that, if this man took refuge in a stolid silence, there was no hope for Hortense Daniel; and he was so much infuriated by the thought that the key to the riddle lay there, within reach of his hand, that he clutched M. de Lourtier by the throat and forced him backwards: 'I'll have no more lies! A woman's life is at stake! Speak . . . and speak at once! If not . . . !'

M. de Lourtier had no strength left in him. All resistance was impossible. It was not that Rénine's attack alarmed him, or that he was yielding to this act of violence, but he felt crushed by that indomitable will, which seemed to admit no obstacle, and he stammered: 'You are right. It is my duty to tell everything, whatever comes of it.'

'Nothing will come of it, I pledge my word, on condition that you save Hortense Daniel. A moment's hesitation may undo us all. Speak. No details, but the actual facts.'

'Madame de Lourtier is not my wife. The only woman who has the right to bear my name is one whom I married when I was a young colonial official. She was a rather eccentric woman, of feeble mentality and incredibly subject to impulses that amounted to monomania. We had two children, twins, whom she worshipped and in whose company she would no doubt have recovered her mental balance and moral health, when, by a stupid accident – a passing carriage – they were killed before her eyes. The poor thing went mad . . . with the silent, secretive madness which you imagined. Some time afterwards, when I was appointed to an Algerian station, I brought her to France and put her in the charge of a worthy creature who had nursed me and brought me up. Two years later, I made the acquaintance of the woman who was to become the joy of my life. You saw her just now. She is the mother of my children and she passes as my wife. Are we to sacrifice her? Is our whole existence to be shipwrecked in horror and must our name be coupled with this tragedy of madness and blood?'

Rénine thought for a moment and asked: 'What is the other one's name?'

'Hermance.'

'Hermance! Still that initial . . . still those eight letters!'

'That was what made me realise everything just now,' said M. de Lourtier. 'When you compared the different names, I at once reflected that my unhappy wife was called Hermance and that she was mad . . . and all the proofs leapt to my mind.'

'But, though we understand the selection of the victims, how are we to explain the murders? What are the symptoms of her madness? Does she suffer at all?'

'She does not suffer very much at present. But she has suffered in the past, the most terrible suffering that you can imagine: since the moment when her two children were run over before her eyes, night and day she had the horrible spectacle of their death before her eyes, without a moment's interruption, for she never slept for a single second. Think of the torture of it! To see her children dying through all the hours of the long day and all the hours of the interminable night!'

'Nevertheless,' Rénine objected, 'it is not to drive away that picture that she commits murder?'

'Yes, possibly,' said M. de Lourtier, thoughtfully, 'to drive it away by sleep.'

'I don't understand.'

'You don't understand, because we are talking of a madwoman . . . and because all that happens in that disordered brain is necessarily incoherent and abnormal?'

'Obviously. But, all the same, is your supposition based on facts that justify it?'

'Yes, on facts which I had, in a way, overlooked but

163

which today assume their true significance. The first of these facts dates a few years back, to a morning when my old nurse for the first time found Hermance fast asleep. Now she was holding her hands clutched around a puppy which she had strangled. And the same thing was repeated on three other occasions.'

'And she slept?'

'Yes, each time she slept a sleep which lasted for several nights.'

'And what conclusion did you draw?'

'I concluded that the relaxation of the nerves provoked by taking life exhausted her and predisposed her for sleep.'

Rénine shuddered: 'That's it! There's not a doubt of it! The taking life, the effort of killing makes her sleep. And she began with women what had served her so well with animals. All her madness has become concentrated on that one point: she kills them to rob them of their sleep! She wanted sleep; and she steals the sleep of others! That's it, isn't it? For the past two years, she has been sleeping?'

'For the past two years, she has been sleeping,' stammered M. de Lourtier.

Rénine gripped him by the shoulder: 'And it never occurred to you that her madness might go farther, that she would stop at nothing to win the blessing of sleep! Let us make haste, monsieur! All this is horrible!'

They were both making for the door, when M. de Lourtier hesitated. The telephone-bell was ringing.

'It's from there,' he said.

'From there?'

'Yes, my old nurse gives me the news at the same time every day.'

He unhooked the receivers and handed one to Rénine, who whispered in his ear the questions which he was to put.

'Is that you, Félicienne? How is she?'

'Not so bad, sir.'

'Is she sleeping well?'

'Not very well, lately. Last night, indeed, she never closed her eyes. So she's very gloomy just now.'

'What is she doing at the moment?'

'She is in her room.'

'Go to her, Félicienne, and don't leave her.'

'I can't. She's locked herself in.'

'You must, Félicienne. Break open the door. I'm coming straight on . . . Hullo! Hullo! . . . Oh, damnation, they've cut us off!'

Without a word, the two men left the flat and ran down to the avenue. Rénine hustled M. de Lourtier into the car: 'What address?'

'Ville d'Avray.'

'Of course! In the very centre of her operations . . . like a spider in the middle of her web! Oh, the shame of it!'

He was profoundly agitated. He saw the whole adventure in its monstrous reality.

'Yes, she kills them to steal their sleep, as she used to kill the animals. It is the same obsession, but complicated by a whole array of utterly incomprehensible practices and superstitions. She evidently fancies that the similarity of the Christian names to her own is indispensable and that she will not sleep unless her victim is an Hortense or an Honorine. It's a mad-woman's argument; its logic escapes us and we know nothing of its origin; but we can't get away from it. She has to hunt and has to find. And she finds and carries off her prey beforehand and watches over it for the appointed number of days, until the moment when, crazily, through the hole which she digs with a hatchet in the middle of the skull, she absorbs the sleep which stupefies her and grants her oblivion for a given period. And here again we see absurdity and madness. Why does she fix that period at so many days? Why should one victim ensure her a hundred and twenty days of sleep and another a hundred and twenty-five? What insanity! The calculation is mysterious and of course mad; but the fact remains that, at the end of a hundred or a hundred and twenty-five days, as the case may be, a fresh victim is sacrificed; and there have been six already and the seventh is awaiting her turn. Ah, monsieur, what a terrible responsibility for you! Such a monster as that! She should never have been allowed out of sight!'

M. de Lourtier-Vaneau made no protest. His air of dejection, his pallor, his trembling hands, all proved his remorse and his despair: 'She deceived me,' he murmured. 'She was outwardly so quiet, so docile! And, after all, she's in a lunatic asylum.'

'Then how can she . . . ?'

'The asylum,' explained M. de Lourtier, 'is made up of a number of separate buildings scattered over extensive grounds. The sort of cottage in which Hermance lives stands quite apart. There is first a room occupied by Félicienne, then Hermance's bedroom and two separate rooms, one of which has its windows overlooking the open country. I suppose it is there that she locks up her victims.'

'But the carriage that conveys the dead bodies?'

'The stables of the asylum are quite close to the cottage. There's a horse and carriage there for station work. Hermance no doubt gets up at night, harnesses the horse and slips the body through the window.'

'And the nurse who watches her?'

'Félicienne is very old and rather deaf.'

'But by day she sees her mistress moving to and fro, doing this and that. Must we not admit a certain complicity?'

'Never! Félicienne herself has been deceived by Hermance's hypocrisy.'

'All the same, it was she who telephoned to Madame de Lourtier first, about that advertisement . . . '

'Very naturally. Hermance, who talks now and then, who argues, who buries herself in the newspapers, which she does not understand, as you were saying just now, but reads through them attentively, must have seen the advertisement and, having heard that we were looking for a servant, must have asked Félicienne to ring me up.'

'Yes . . . yes . . . that is what I felt,' said Rénine, slowly. 'She marks down her victims . . . With Hortense dead, she would have known, once she had used up her allowance of sleep, where to find an eighth victim . . . But how did she entice the unfortunate women? How did she entice Hortense?'

The car was rushing along, but not fast enough to please Rénine, who rated the chauffeur: 'Push her along, Adolphe, can't you? . . . We're losing time, my man.'

Suddenly the fear of arriving too late began to torture him. The logic of the insane is subject to sudden changes of mood, to any perilous idea that may enter the mind. The madwoman might easily mistake the date and hasten the catastrophe, like a clock out of order which strikes an hour too soon.

On the other hand, as her sleep was once more disturbed, might she not be tempted to take action without waiting for the appointed moment? Was this not the reason why she had locked herself into her room? Heavens, what agonies her prisoner must be suffering! What shudders of terror at the executioner's least movement!

'Faster, Adolphe, or I'll take the wheel myself! Faster, hang it.'

At last they reached Ville d'Avray. There was a steep, sloping road on the right and walls interrupted by a long railing.

'Drive round the grounds, Adolphe. We mustn't give warning of our presence, must we, M. de Lourtier? Where is the cottage?'

'Just opposite,' said M. de Lourtier-Vaneau.

They got out a little farther on. Rénine began to run along a bank at the side of an ill-kept sunken road. It was almost dark. M. de Lourtier said: 'Here, this building standing a little way back . . . Look at that window on the ground-floor. It belongs to one of the separate rooms . . . and that is obviously how she slips out.'

'But the window seems to be barred.'

'Yes; and that is why no one suspected anything. But she must have found some way to get through.'

The ground-floor was built over deep cellars. Rénine quickly clambered up, finding a foothold on a projecting ledge of stone.

Sure enough, one of the bars was missing.

He pressed his face to the window-pane and looked in.

The room was dark inside. Nevertheless he was able to distinguish at the back a woman seated beside another woman, who was lying on a mattress. The woman seated was holding her forehead in her hands and gazing at the woman who was lying down.

'It's she,' whispered M. de Lourtier, who had also climbed the wall. 'The other one is bound.'

Rénine took from his pocket a glazier's diamond and cut out one of the panes without making enough noise to arouse the madwoman's attention. He next slid his hand to the window-fastening and turned it softly, while with his left hand he levelled a revolver.

'You're not going to fire, surely!' M. de Lourtier-Vaneau entreated.

'If I must, I shall.'

Rénine pushed open the window gently. But there was an obstacle of which he was not aware, a chair which toppled over and fell.

He leapt into the room and threw away his revolver in order to seize the madwoman. But she did not wait for him. She rushed to the door, opened it and fled, with a hoarse cry.

M. de Lourtier made as though to run after her.

'What's the use?' said Rénine, kneeling down. 'Let's save the victim first.'

He was instantly reassured: Hortense was alive.

The first thing that he did was to cut the cords and remove the gag that was stifling her. Attracted by the noise, the old nurse had hastened to the room with a lamp, which Rénine took from her, casting its light on Hortense.

He was astounded: though livid and exhausted, with emaciated features and eyes blazing with fever, Hortense was trying to smile. She whispered: 'I was expecting you . . . I did not despair for a moment . . . I was sure of you . . . '

She fainted.

An hour later, after much useless searching around the cottage, they found the madwoman locked into a large cupboard in the loft. She had hanged herself.

*   *   *

Hortense refused to stay another night. Besides, it was better that the cottage should be empty when the old nurse announced the madwoman's suicide. Rénine gave Félicienne minute directions as to what she should do and say; and then, assisted by the chauffeur and M. de Lourtier, carried Hortense to the car and brought her home.

She was soon convalescent. Two days later, Rénine carefully questioned her and asked her how she had come to know the madwoman.

'It was very simple,' she said. 'My husband, who is not quite sane, as I have told you, is being looked after at Ville d'Avray; and I sometimes go to see him, without telling anybody, I admit. That was how I came to speak to that poor madwoman and how, the other day, she made signs that she wanted me to visit her. We were alone. I went into the cottage. She threw herself upon me and overpowered me before I had time to cry for help. I thought it was a jest; and so it was, wasn't it: a madwoman's jest? She was quite gentle with me . . . All the same, she let me starve. But I was so sure of you!'

'And weren't you frightened?'

'Of starving? No. Besides, she gave me some food, now and then, when the fancy took her . . . And then I was sure of you!'

'Yes, but there was something else: that other peril . . . '

170

'What other peril?' she asked, ingenuously.

Rénine gave a start. He suddenly understood – it seemed strange at first, though it was quite natural – that Hortense had not for a moment suspected and did not yet suspect the terrible danger which she had run. Her mind had not connected with her own adventure the murders committed by the lady with the hatchet.

He thought that it would always be time enough to tell her the truth. For that matter, a few days later her husband, who had been locked up for years, died in the asylum at Ville d'Avray, and Hortense, who had been recommended by her doctor a short period of rest and solitude, went to stay with a relation living near the village of Bassicourt, in the centre of France.

The Treasure Hunt

EDGAR WALLACE

There is a tradition in criminal circles that even the humblest of detective officers is a man of wealth and substance, and that his secret hoard was secured by thieving, bribery and blackmail. It is the gossip of the fields, the quarries, the tailor's shop, the laundry and the bakehouse of fifty county prisons and three convict establishments, that all highly placed detectives have by nefarious means laid up for themselves sufficient earthly treasures to make work a hobby and their official pittance the most inconsiderable portion of their incomes.

Since Mr J. G. Reeder had for over twenty years dealt exclusively with bank robbers and forgers, who are the aristocrats and capitalists of the underworld, legend credited him with country houses and immense secret reserves. Not that he would have a great deal of money in the bank. It was admitted that he was too clever to risk discovery by the authorities. No, it was hidden somewhere: it was the pet dream of hundreds of unlawful men that they would some day discover the hoard and live happily ever after. The one satisfactory aspect of his affluence (they all agreed) was that, being an old man – he was over fifty – he couldn't take his money with him, for gold melts at a certain temperature and gilt-edged stock is seldom printed on asbestos paper.

The Director of Public Prosecutions was lunching one Saturday at his club with a judge of the King's Bench – Saturday being one of the two days in the week when a judge gets properly fed. And the conversation drifted to a certain Mr J. G. Reeder, the chief of the Director's sleuths.

'He's capable,' he confessed reluctantly, 'but I hate his hat. It is the sort that So-and-so used to wear,' he mentioned by name an eminent politician; 'and I loathe his black frock-coat, people who see him coming into the office think he's a coroner's officer, but he's capable. His side-whiskers are an abomination, and I have a feeling that, if I talked rough to him, he would burst into tears – a gentle soul. Almost too gentle for my kind of work. He apologises to the messenger every time he rings for him!'

The judge, who knew something about humanity, answered with a frosty smile.

'He sounds rather like a potential murderer to me,' he said cynically.

Milord, in his extravagance, did Mr J. G. Reeder an injustice, for Mr Reeder was capable of breaking the law – quite. At the same time there were many people who formed an altogether wrong conception of J. G.'s harmlessness as an individual. And one of these was a certain Lew Kohl, who mixed bank-note printing with elementary burglary.

Threatened men live long, a trite saying but, like most things trite, true. In a score of cases, when Mr J. G. Reeder had descended from the witness stand, he had met the baleful eye of the man in the dock and had listened with mild interest to divers promises as to what would happen to him in the near or the remote future. For he was a great authority on forged bank-notes and he had sent many men to penal servitude.

Mr Reeder, that inoffensive man, had seen prisoners foaming at the mouth in their rage, he had seen them white and livid, he had heard their howling execrations and he had met these men after their release from prison and had found them amiable souls half ashamed and half amused at their nearly forgotten outbursts and horrific threats.

But when, in the early part of 1914, Lew Kohl was sentenced for ten years, he neither screamed his imprecations nor registered a vow to tear Mr Reeder's heart, lungs and important organs from his frail body.

Lew just smiled and his eyes caught the detective's for the space of a second – the forger's eyes were pale blue and speculative, and they held neither hate nor fury. Instead, they said in so many words: 'At the first opportunity I will kill you.'

Mr Reeder read the message and sighed heavily, for he disliked fuss of all kinds, and resented, in so far as he could resent anything, the injustice of being made personally responsible for the performance of a public duty.

Many years had passed, and considerable changes had occurred in Mr Reeder's fortune. He had transferred from the specialised occupation of detecting the makers of forged bank-notes to the more general practice of the Public Prosecutor's bureau, but he never forgot Lew's smile.

The work in Whitehall was not heavy and it was very interesting. To Mr Reeder came most of the anonymous letters which the Director received in shoals. In the main they were self-explanatory, and it required no particular intelligence to discover their motive. Jealousy, malice, plain mischief-making, and occasionally a sordid desire to benefit financially by the information which was conveyed, were behind the majority.

But occasionally: 'Sir James is going to marry his cousin, and it's not three months since his poor wife fell overboard from the Channel steamer crossing to Calais. There's something very fishy about this business. Miss Margaret doesn't like him, for she knows he's after her money. Why was I sent away to London that night? He doesn't like driving in the dark, either. It's strange that he wanted to drive that night when it was raining like blazes.'

This particular letter was signed 'A Friend'. Justice has many such friends.

'Sir James' was Sir James Tithermite, who had been a director of some new public department during the war and had received a baronetcy for his services.

'Look it up,' said the Director when he saw the letter. 'I seem to remember that Lady Tithermite was drowned at sea.'

'On the nineteenth of December last year,' said Mr Reeder solemnly. 'She and Sir James were going to Monte Carlo, breaking their journey in Paris. Sir James, who has a house near Maidstone, drove to Dover, garaging the car at the Lord Wilson Hotel. The night was stormy and the ship had a rough crossing – they were halfway across when Sir James came to the purser and said that he had missed his wife. Her baggage was in the cabin, her passport, rail ticket and hat, but the lady was not found, indeed was never seen again.'

The Director nodded.

'I see, you've read up the case.'

'I remember it,' said Mr Reeder. 'The case is a favourite speculation of mine. Unfortunately I see evil in everything and I have often thought how easy – but I fear that I take a warped view of life. It is a horrible handicap to possess a criminal mind.'

The Director looked at him suspiciously. He was never quite sure whether Mr Reeder was serious. At that moment, his sobriety was beyond challenge.

'A discharged chauffeur wrote that letter, of course,' he began.

'Thomas Dayford, of 179 Barrack Street, Maidstone,' concluded Mr Reeder. 'He is at present in the employ of the Kent Motor-Bus Company, and has three children, two of whom are twins and bonny little rascals.'

The Chief laughed helplessly.

'I'll take it that you know!' he said. 'See what there is behind the letter. Sir James is a big fellow in Kent, a Justice of the Peace, and he has powerful political influences. There is nothing in this letter, of course. Go warily, Reeder – if any kick comes back to this office, it goes on to you – intensified!'

Mr Reeder's idea of walking warily was peculiarly his own. He travelled down to Maidstone the next morning, and, finding a bus that passed the lodge gates of Elfreda Manor, he journeyed comfortably and economically, his umbrella between his knees. He passed through the lodge gates, up a long and winding avenue of poplars, and presently came within sight of the grey manor house.

In a deep chair on the lawn he saw a girl sitting, a book on her knees, and evidently she saw him, for she rose as he crossed the lawn and came towards him eagerly.

'I'm Miss Margaret Letherby – are you from – ?' She mentioned the name of a well-known firm of lawyers, and her face fell when Mr Reeder regretfully disclaimed connection with those legal lights.

She was as pretty as a perfect complexion and a round, not too intellectual, face could, in combination, make her.

'I thought – do you wish to see Sir James? He is in the library. If you ring, one of the maids will take you to him.'

Had Mr Reeder been the sort of man who could be puzzled by anything, he would have been puzzled by the suggestion that any girl with money of her own should marry a man much older than herself against her own wishes. There was little mystery in the matter now. Miss Margaret would have married any strong-willed man who insisted.

'Even me,' said Mr Reeder to himself, with a certain melancholy pleasure.

There was no need to ring the bell. A tall, broad man in a golfing suit stood in the doorway. His fair hair was long and hung over his forehead in a thick flat strand; a heavy tawny moustache hid his mouth and swept down over a chin that was long and powerful.

'Well?' he asked aggressively.

'I'm from the Public Prosecutor's office,' murmured Mr Reeder. 'I have had an anonymous letter.'

His pale eyes did not leave the face of the other man.

'Come in,' said Sir James gruffly. As he closed the door he glanced quickly first to the girl and then to the poplar avenue. 'I'm expecting a fool of a lawyer,' he said, as he flung open the door of what was evidently the library.

His voice was steady; not by a flicker of eyelash had he betrayed the slightest degree of anxiety when Reeder had told his mission.

'Well – what about this anonymous letter? You don't take much notice of that kind of trash, do you?'

Mr Reeder deposited his umbrella and flat-crowned hat on a chair before he took a document from his pocket and handed it to the baronet, who frowned as he read. Was it Mr Reeder's vivid imagination, or did the hard light in the eyes of Sir James soften as he read?

'This is a cock and bull story of somebody having seen my wife's jewellery on sale in Paris,' he said. 'There is nothing in it. I can account for every one of my poor wife's trinkets. I brought back the jewel case after that awful night. I don't recognise the handwriting: who is the lying scoundrel who wrote this?'

Mr Reeder had never before been called a lying scoundrel, but he accepted the experience with admirable meekness.

'I thought it untrue,' he said, shaking his head. 'I followed the details of the case very thoroughly. You left here in the afternoon – '

'At night,' said the other brusquely. He was not inclined to discuss the matter, but Mr Reeder's appealing look was irresistible. 'It is only eighty minutes' run to Dover. We got to the pier at eleven o'clock, about the same time as the boat train, and we went on board at once. I got my cabin key from the purser and put her ladyship and her baggage inside.'

'Her ladyship was a good sailor?'

'Yes, a very good sailor; she was remarkably well that night. I left her in the cabin dozing, and went for a stroll on the deck – '

'Raining very heavily and a strong sea running,' nodded Reeder, as though in agreement with something the other man had said.

'Yes – I'm a pretty good sailor – anyway, that story about my poor wife's jewels is utter nonsense. You can tell the Director that, with my compliments.'

He opened the door for his visitor, and Mr Reeder was some time replacing the letter and gathering his belongings.

'You have a beautiful place here, Sir James – a lovely place. An extensive estate?'

'Three thousand acres.' This time he did not attempt to disguise his impatience. 'Good-afternoon.'

Mr Reeder went slowly down the drive, his remarkable memory at work.

He missed the bus which he could easily have caught, and pursued an apparently aimless way along the winding road which marched with the boundaries of the baronet's property. A walk of a quarter of a mile brought him to a lane shooting off at right angles from the main road, and marking, he guessed, the southern boundary. At the corner stood an old stone lodge, on the inside of a forbidding iron gate. The lodge was in a pitiable state of neglect and disrepair. Tiles had been dislodged from the roof, the windows were grimy or broken, and the little garden was overrun with docks and thistles. Beyond the gate was a narrow, weed-covered drive that trailed out of sight into a distant plantation.

Hearing the clang of a letter-box closing, he turned to see a postman mounting his bicycle.

'What place is this?' asked Mr Reeder, arresting the postman's departure.

'South Lodge – Sir James Tithermite's property.

It's never used now. Hasn't been used for years – I don't know why; it's a short cut if they happen to be coming this way.'

Mr Reeder walked with him towards the village, and he was a skilful pumper of wells, however dry; and the postman was not dry by any means.

'Yes, poor lady! She was very frail – one of those sort of invalids that last out many a healthy man.'

Mr Reeder put a question at random and scored most unexpectedly.

'Yes, her ladyship was a bad sailor. I know because every time she went abroad she used to get a bottle of that stuff people take for seasickness. I've delivered many a bottle till Raikes the chemist stocked it – "Pickers' Travellers' Friend", that's what it was called. Mr Raikes was only saying to me the other day that he'd got half a dozen bottles on hand and he didn't know what to do with them. Nobody in Climbury ever goes to sea.'

Mr Reeder went on to the village and idled his precious time in most unlikely places. At the chemist's, at the blacksmith's shop, at the modest building yard. He caught the last bus back to Maidstone, and by great good luck the last train to London.

And, in his vague way, he answered the Director's query the next day with: 'Yes, I saw Sir James: a very interesting man.'

This was on the Friday. All day Saturday he was busy. The Sabbath brought him a new interest.

On this bright Sunday morning, Mr Reeder, attired in a flowered dressing-gown, his feet encased in black velvet slippers, stood at the window of his house in Brockley Road and surveyed the deserted thoroughfare. The bell of a local church, which was accounted high, had rung for early Mass, and there was nothing living in sight except a black cat that lay asleep in a patch of sunlight on the top step of the house opposite. The hour was 7.30, and Mr Reeder had been at his desk since six, working by artificial light, the month being March towards the close.

From the half-moon of the window bay he regarded a section of the Lewisham High Road and as much of Tanners Hill as can be seen before it dips past the railway bridge into sheer Deptford.

Returning to his table, he opened a carton of the cheapest cigarettes and, lighting one, puffed in an amateurish fashion. He smoked cigarettes rather like a woman who detests them but feels that it is the correct thing to do.

'Dear me,' said Mr Reeder feebly.

He was back at the window, and he had seen a man turn out of Lewisham High Road. He had crossed the road and was coming straight to Daffodil House – which frolicsome name appeared on the doorposts of Mr Reeder's residence. A tall, straight man, with a sombre brown face, he came to the front gate, passed through and beyond the watcher's range of vision.

'Dear me!' said Mr Reeder, as he heard the tinkle of a bell.

A few minutes later his housekeeper tapped on the door.

'Will you see Mr Kohl, sir?' she asked.

Mr J. G. Reeder nodded.

Lew Kohl walked into the room to find a middle-aged man in a flamboyant dressing-gown sitting at his desk, a pair of pince-nez set crookedly on his nose.

'Good-morning, Kohl.'

Lew Kohl looked at the man who had sent him to seven and a half years of hell, and the corner of his thin lips curled.

'Morning, Mr Reeder.' His eyes flashed across the almost bare surface of the writing-desk on which Reeder's hands were lightly clasped. 'You didn't expect to see me, I guess?'

'Not so early,' said Reeder in his hushed voice, 'but I should have remembered that early rising is one of the good habits which are inculcated by penal servitude.'

He said this in the manner of one bestowing praise for good conduct.

'I suppose you've got a pretty good idea of why I have come, eh? I'm a bad forgetter, Reeder, and a man in Dartmoor has time to think.'

The older man lifted his sandy eyebrows, the steel-rimmed glasses on his nose slipped further askew.

'That phrase seems familiar,' he said, and the eyebrows lowered in a frown. 'Now let me think – it was in a melodrama, of course, but was it "Souls in Harness" or "The Marriage Vow"?'

He appeared genuinely anxious for assistance in solving this problem.

'This is going to be a different kind of play,' said the long-faced Lew through his teeth. 'I'm going to get you, Reeder – you can go along and tell your boss, the Public Prosecutor. But I'll get you sweet! There will be no evidence to swing me. And I'll get that nice little stocking of yours, Reeder!'

The legend of Reeder's fortune was accepted even by so intelligent a man as Kohl.

'You'll get my stocking! Dear me, I shall have to

go barefooted,' said Mr Reeder, with a faint show of humour.

'You know what I mean – think that over. Some hour and day you'll go out, and all Scotland Yard won't catch me for the killing! I've thought it out – '

'One has time to think in Dartmoor,' murmured Mr J. G. Reeder encouragingly. 'You're becoming one of the world's thinkers, Kohl. Do you know Rodin's masterpiece – a beautiful statue throbbing with life – '

'That's all.' Lew Kohl rose, the smile still trembling at the corner of his mouth. 'Maybe you'll turn this over in your mind, and in a day or two you won't be feeling so gay.'

Reeder's face was pathetic in its sadness. His untidy sandy-grey hair seemed to be standing on end; the large ears, that stood out at right angles to his face, gave the illusion of quivering movement.

Lew Kohl's hand was on the doorknob.

'Womp!'

It was the sound of a dull weight striking a board; something winged past his cheek, before his eyes a deep hole showed in the wall, and his face was stung by flying grains of plaster. He spun round with a whine of rage.

Mr Reeder had a long-barrelled Browning in his hand, with a barrel-shaped silencer over the muzzle, and he was staring at the weapon open-mouthed.

'Now how on earth did that happen?' he asked in wonder.

Lew Kohl stood trembling with rage and fear, his face yellow-white.

'You – you swine!' he breathed. 'You tried to shoot me!'

Mr Reeder stared at him over his glasses.

'Good gracious – you think that? Still thinking of killing me, Kohl?'

Kohl tried to speak but found no words, and, flinging open the door, he strode down the stairs and through the front entrance. His foot was on the first step when something came hurtling past him and crashed to fragments at his feet. It was a large stone vase that had decorated the window-sill of Mr Reeder's bedroom. Leaping over the debris of stone and flower mould, he glared up into the surprised face of Mr J. G. Reeder.

'I'll get you!' he spluttered.

'I hope you're not hurt?' asked the man at the window in a tone of concern. 'These things happen. Some day and some hour – '

As Lew Kohl strode down the street, the detective was still talking.

Mr Stan Bride was at his morning ablutions when his friend and sometime prison associate came into the little room that overlooked Fitzroy Square.

Stan Bride, who bore no resemblance to anything virginal, being a stout and stumpy man with a huge, red face and many chins, stopped in the act of drying himself and gazed over the edge of the towel.

'What's the matter with you?' he asked sharply. 'You look as if you'd been chased by a busy. What did you go out so early for?'

Lew told him, and the jovial countenance of his roommate grew longer and longer –

'You poor fish!' he hissed. 'To go after Reeder with that stuff! Don't you think he was waiting for you? Do you suppose he didn't know the very moment you left the Moor?'

'I've scared him, anyway,' said the other, and Mr Bride laughed.

'Good scout!' he sneered. 'Scare that old person!' (He did not say 'person'.) 'If he's as white as you, he is scared! But he's not. Of course he shot past you – if he'd wanted to shoot you, you'd have been stiff by now. But he didn't. Thinker, eh – he's given you somep'n' to think about.'

'Where that gun came from I don't – '

There was a knock at the door and the two men exchanged glances.

'Who's there?' asked Bride, and a familiar voice answered.

'It's that busy from the Yard,' whispered Bride, and opened the door.

The 'busy' was Sergeant Allford, CID, an affable and portly man and a detective of some promise.

'Morning, boys – not been to church, Stan?'

Stan grinned politely.

'How's trade, Lew?'

'Not so bad.' The forger was alert, suspicious.

'Come to see you about a gun – got an idea you're carrying one. Lew-Colt automatic R.7/94318. That's not right, Lew–guns don't belong to this country.'

'I've got no gun,' said Lew sullenly.

Bride had suddenly become an old man, for he also was a convict on licence, and the discovery might send him back to serve his unfinished sentence.

'Will you come a little walk to the station, or will you let me go over you?'

'Go over me,' said Lew, and put out his arms stiffly whilst the detective rubbed him down.

'I'll have a look round,' said the detective, and his 'look round' was very thorough.

'Must have been mistaken,' said Sergeant Allford. And then, suddenly: 'Was that what you chucked into the river as you were walking along the Embankment?'

Lew started. It was the first intimation he had received that he had been 'tailed' that morning.

Bride waited till the detective was visible from the window crossing Fitzroy Square; then he turned in a fury on his companion.

'Clever, ain't you! That old hound knew you had a gun – knew the number. And if Allford had found it you'd have been "dragged" and me too!'

'I threw it in the river,' said Lew sulkily.

'Brains – not many but some!' said Bride, breathing heavily. 'You cut out Reeder – he's hell and poison, and if you don't know it you're deaf! Scared him? You big stiff! He'd cut your throat and write a hymn about it.'

'I didn't know they were tailing me,' growled Kohl; 'but I'll get him! And his money too.'

'Get him from another lodging,' said Bride curtly. 'A crook I don't mind, being one; a murderer I don't mind, but a talking jackass makes me sick. Get his stuff if you can – I'll bet it's all invested in real estate, and you can't lift houses – but don't talk about it. I like you, Lew, up to a point; you're miles before the point and out of sight. I don't like Reeder – I don't like snakes, but I keep away from the Zoo.'

So Lew Kohl went into new diggings on the top floor of an Italian's house in Dean Street, and here he had leisure and inclination to brood upon his grievances and to plan afresh the destruction of his enemy. And new plans were needed, for the schemes which had seemed so watertight in the quietude of a Devonshire cell showed daylight through many crevices.

Lew's homicidal urge had undergone considerable modification. He had been experimented upon by a very clever psychologist – though he never regarded Mr Reeder in this light, and, indeed, had the vaguest idea as to what the word meant. But there were other ways of hurting Reeder, and his mind fell constantly back to the dream of discovering this peccant detective's hidden treasure.

It was nearly a week later that Mr Reeder invited himself into the Director's private sanctum, and that great official listened spellbound while his subordinate offered his outrageous theory about Sir James Tithermite and his dead wife. When Mr Reeder had finished, the Director pushed back his chair from the table.

'My dear man,' he said, a little irritably, 'I can't possibly give a warrant on the strength of your surmises – not even a search warrant. The story is so fantastic, so incredible, that it would be more at home in the pages of a sensational story than in a Public Prosecutor's report.'

'It was a wild night, and yet Lady Tithermite was not ill,' suggested the detective gently. 'That is a fact to remember, sir.'

The Director shook his head.

'I can't do it – not on the evidence,' he said. 'I should raise a storm that'd swing me into Whitehall. Can't you do anything – unofficially?'

Mr Reeder shook his head.

'My presence in the neighbourhood has been remarked,' he said primly. 'I think it would be impossible to – er – cover up my traces. And yet I have located the place, and could tell you within a few inches – '

Again the Director shook his head.

'No, Reeder,' he said quietly, 'the whole thing is sheer deduction on your part. Oh, yes, I know you have a criminal mind – I think you have told me that before. And that is a good reason why I should not issue a warrant. You're simply crediting this unfortunate man with your ingenuity. Nothing doing!'

Mr Reeder sighed and went back to his bureau, not entirely despondent, for there had intruded a new element into his investigations.

Mr Reeder had been to Maidstone several times during the week, and he had not gone alone; though seemingly unconscious of the fact that he had developed a shadow, for he had seen Lew Kohl on several occasions, and had spent an uncomfortable few minutes wondering whether his experiment had failed.

On the second occasion an idea had developed in the detective's mind, and if he were a laughing man he would have chuckled aloud when he slipped out of Maidstone station one evening and, in the act of hiring a cab, had seen Lew Kohl negotiating for another.

Mr Bride was engaged in the tedious but necessary practice of so cutting a pack of cards that the ace of diamonds remained at the bottom, when his former co-lodger burst in upon him, and there was a light of triumph in Lew's cold eye which brought Mr Bride's heart to his boots.

'I've got him!' said Lew.

Bride put aside the cards and stood up.

'Got who?' he asked coldly. 'And if it's killing, you needn't answer, but get out!'

'There's no killing.'

Lew sat down squarely at the table, his hands in his pockets, a real smile on his face.

'I've been trailing Reeder for a week, and that fellow wants some trailing!'

'Well?' asked the other, when he paused dramatically.

'I've found his stocking!'

Bride scratched his chin, and was half convinced.

'You never have?'

Lew nodded.

'He's been going to Maidstone a lot lately, and driving to a little village about five miles out. There I always lost him. But the other night, when he came back to the station to catch the last train, he slipped into the waiting-room and I found a place where I could watch him. What do you think he did?'

Mr Bride hazarded no suggestion.

'He opened his bag,' said Lew impressively, 'and took out a wad of notes as thick as that! He'd been drawing on his bank! I trailed him up to London. There's a restaurant on the station and he went in to get a cup of coffee, with me keeping well out of his sight. As he came out of the restaurant he took out his handkerchief and wiped his mouth. He didn't see the little book that dropped, but I did. I was scared sick that somebody else would see it, or that he'd wait long enough to find it himself. But he went out of the station and I got that book before you could say "knife". Look!'

It was a well-worn little notebook, covered with faded red morocco. Bride put out his hand to take it.

'Wait a bit,' said Lew. 'Are you in this with me fifty-fifty, because I want some help?'

Bride hesitated.

'If it's just plain thieving, I'm with you,' he said.

'Plain thieving – and sweet,' said Lew exultantly, and pushed the book across the table.

For the greater part of the night they sat together talking in low tones, discussing impartially the methodical bookkeeping of Mr J. G. Reeder and his exceeding dishonesty.

The Monday night was wet. A storm blew up from the south-west, and the air was filled with falling leaves as Lew and his companion footed the five miles which separated them from the village. Neither carried any impedimenta that was visible, yet under Lew's waterproof coat was a kit of tools of singular ingenuity, and Mr Bride's coat pockets were weighted down with the sections of a powerful jemmy.

They met nobody in their walk, and the church bell was striking eleven when Lew gripped the bars of the South Lodge gates, pulled himself up to the top and dropped lightly on the other side. He was followed by Mr Bride, who, in spite of his bulk, was a singularly agile man. The ruined lodge showed in the darkness, and they passed through the creaking gates to the door and Lew flashed his lantern upon the keyhole before he began manipulation with the implements which he had taken from his kit.

The door was opened in ten minutes and a few seconds later they stood in a low-roofed little room, the principal feature of which was a deep, grateless fireplace. Lew took off his mackintosh and stretched it over the window before he spread the light in his lamp, and, kneeling down, brushed the debris from the hearth, examining the joints of the big stone carefully.

'This work's been botched,' he said. 'Anybody could see that.'

He put the claw of the jemmy into a crack and levered up the stone, and it moved slightly. Stopping only to dig a deeper crevice with a chisel and hammer he thrust the claw of the jemmy farther down. The stone came up above the edge of the floor and Bride slipped the chisel underneath.

'Now together,' grunted Lew.

They got their fingers beneath the hearthstone and with one heave hinged it up. Lew picked up the lamp and, kneeling down, flashed a light into the dark cavity. And then: 'Oh, my God!' he shrieked.

A second later two terrified men rushed from the house into the drive. And a miracle had happened, for the gates were open and a dark figure stood squarely before them.

'Put up your hands, Kohl!' said a voice, and hateful as it was to Lew Kohl, he could have fallen on the neck of Mr Reeder.

At twelve o'clock that night Sir James Tithermite was discussing matters with his bride-to-be: the stupidity of her lawyer, who wished to safeguard her fortune, and his own cleverness and foresight in securing complete freedom of action for the girl who was to be his wife.

'These blackguards think of nothing but their fees,' he began, when his footman came in unannounced, and behind him the Chief Constable of the county and a man he remembered seeing before.

'Sir James Tithermite?' said the Chief Constable unnecessarily, for he knew Sir James very well.

'Yes, Colonel, what is it?' asked the baronet, his face twitching.

'I am taking you into custody on a charge of wilfully murdering your wife, Eleanor Mary Tithermite.'

'The whole thing turned upon the question as to whether Lady Tithermite was a good or a bad sailor,' explained J. G. Reeder to his chief. 'If she were a bad sailor, it was unlikely that she would be on the ship, even for five minutes, without calling for the stewardess. The stewardess did not see her ladyship, nor did anybody on board, for the simple reason that she was not on board! She was murdered within the grounds of the Manor; her body was buried beneath the hearthstone of the old lodge, and Sir James continued his journey by car to Dover, handing over his packages to a porter and telling him to take them to his cabin before he returned to put the car into the hotel garage. He had timed his arrival so that he passed on board with a crowd of passengers from the boat train, and nobody knew whether he was alone or whether he was accompanied, and, for the matter of that, nobody cared. The purser gave him his key, and he put the baggage, including his wife's hat, into the cabin, paid the porter and dismissed him. Officially, Lady Tithermite was on board, for he surrendered her ticket to the collector and received her landing voucher. And then he discovered she had disappeared. The ship was searched, but of course the unfortunate lady was not found. As I remarked before – '

'You have a criminal mind,' said the Director good-humouredly. 'Go on, Reeder.'

'Having this queer and objectionable trait, I saw how very simple a matter it was to give the illusion that the lady was on board, and I decided that, if the murder was committed, it must have been within a few miles of the house. And then the local builder told me that he had given Sir James a little lesson in the art of mixing mortar. And the local blacksmith told me that the gate had been damaged, presumably by Sir James's car – I had seen the broken rods and all I wanted to know was when the repairs were effected. That she was beneath the hearth in the lodge I was certain. Without a search warrant it was impossible to prove or disprove my theory, and I myself could not conduct a private investigation without risking the reputation of our department – if I may say "our",' he said apologetically.

The Director was thoughtful.

'Of course, you induced this man Kohl to dig up the hearth by pretending you had money buried there. I presume you revealed that fact in your notebook? But why on earth did he imagine that you had a hidden treasure?'

Mr Reeder smiled sadly.

'The criminal mind is a peculiar thing,' he said, with a sigh. 'It harbours illusions and fairy stories. Fortunately, I understand that mind. As I have often said – '

The Ripening Rubies

MAX PEMBERTON

'The plain fact is,' said Lady Faber, 'we are entertaining thieves. It positively makes me shudder to
look at my own guests, and to think that some of
them are criminals.'

We stood together in the conservatory of her house
in Portman Square, looking down upon a brilliant
ballroom, upon a glow of colour, and the radiance of
unnumbered gems. She had taken me aside after the
fourth waltz to tell me that her famous belt of rubies
had been shorn of one of its finest pendants; and she
showed me beyond possibility of dispute that the
loss was no accident, but another of those amazing
thefts which startled London so frequently during
the season of 1893. Nor was hers the only case.
Though I had been in her house but an hour,
complaints from other sources had reached me. The
Countess of Dunholm had lost a crescent brooch of
brilliants; Mrs Kenningham-Hardy had missed a
spray of pearls and turquoise; Lady Hallingham
made mention of an emerald locket which was gone,
as she thought, from her necklace; though, as she
confessed with a truly feminine doubt, she was not
positive that her maid had given it to her. And these
misfortunes, being capped by the abstraction of Lady
Faber's pendant, compelled me to believe that of all
the startling stories of thefts which the season had

known the story of this dance would be the most remarkable.

These things and many more came to my mind as I held the mutilated belt in my hand and examined the fracture, while my hostess stood, with an angry flush upon her face, waiting for my verdict. A moment's inspection of the bauble revealed to me at once its exceeding value, and the means whereby a pendant of it had been snatched.

'If you will look closely,' said I, 'you will see that the gold chain here has been cut with a pair of scissors. As we don't know the name of the person who used them, we may describe them as pick-pocket's scissors.'

'Which means that I am entertaining a pickpocket,' said she, flushing again at the thought.

'Or a person in possession of a pickpocket's implements,' I suggested.

'How dreadful,' she cried, 'not for myself, though the rubies are very valuable, but for the others. This is the third dance during the week at which people's jewels have been stolen. When will it end?'

'The end of it will come,' said I, 'directly that you, and others with your power to lead, call in the police. It is very evident by this time that some person is socially engaged in a campaign of wholesale robbery. While a silly delicacy forbids us to permit our guests to be suspected or in any way watched, the person we mention may consider himself in a terrestrial paradise, which is very near the seventh heaven of delight. He will continue to rob with impunity, and to offer up his thanks for that generosity of conduct which refuses us a glimpse of his hat, or even an inspection of the boots in which he may place his plunder.'

'You speak very lightly of it,' she interrupted, as I still held her belt in my hands. 'Do you know that my husband values the rubies in each of those pendants at eight hundred pounds?'

'I can quite believe it,' said I; 'some of them are white as these are, I presume; but I want you to describe it for me, and as accurately as your memory will let you.'

'How will that help to its recovery?' she asked, looking at me questioningly.

'Possibly not at all,' I replied; 'but it might be offered for sale at my place, and I should be glad if I had the means of restoring it to you. Stranger things have happened.'

'I believe,' said she sharply, 'you would like to find out the thief yourself.'

'I should not have the smallest objection,' I exclaimed frankly; 'if these robberies continue, no woman in London will wear real stones; and I shall be the loser.'

'I have thought of that,' said she; 'but, you know, you are not to make the slightest attempt to expose any guest in my house; what you do outside is no concern of mine.'

'Exactly,' said I, 'and for the matter of that I am likely to do very little in either case; we are working against clever heads; and if my judgement be correct, there is a whole gang to cope with. But tell me about the rubies.'

'Well,' said she, 'the stolen pendant is in the shape of a rose. The belt, as you know, was brought by Lord Faber from Burmah. Besides the ring of rubies, which each drop has, the missing star includes four yellow stones, which the natives declare are ripening rubies. It is only a superstition, of course; but the gems are full of fire, and as brilliant as diamonds.'

'I know the stones well,' said I; 'the Burmese will sell you rubies of all colours if you will buy them, though the blue variety is nothing more than the sapphire. And how long is it since you missed the pendant?'

'Not ten minutes ago,' she answered.

'Which means that your next partner might be the thief?' I suggested. 'Really, a dance is becoming a capital entertainment.'

'My next partner is my husband,' said she, laughing for the first time, 'and whatever you do, don't say a word to him. He would never forgive me for losing the rubies.'

When she was gone, I, who had come to her dance solely in the hope that a word or a face there would cast light upon the amazing mystery of the season's thefts, went down again where the press was, and stood while the dancers were pursuing the dreary paths of a 'square'. There before me were the hundred types one sees in a London ballroom – types of character and of want of character, of age aping youth, and of youth aping age, of well-dressed women and ill-dressed women, of dandies and of the bored, of fresh girlhood and worn maturity. Mixed in the dazzling *mêlée*, or swaying to the rhythm of a music-hall melody, you saw the lean form of boys; the robust forms of men; the pretty figures of the girls just out; the figures, not so pretty, of the matrons, who, for the sake of the picturesque, should long ago have been in. As the picture changed quickly, and fair faces succeeded to dark faces, and the coquetting eyes of pretty women passed by with a glance to give place to the uninteresting eyes of the dancing men, I asked myself what hope would the astutest spy have of getting a clue to the mysteries in such a room; how could he look for a moment to name one man or one woman who had part or lot in the astounding robberies which were the wonder of the town? Yet I knew that if nothing were done, the sale of jewels in London would come to the lowest ebb the trade had known, and that I, personally, should suffer loss to an extent which I did not care to think about.

I have said often, in jotting down from my book a few of the most interesting cases which have come to my notice, that I am no detective, nor do I pretend to the smallest gift of foresight above my fellow men. Whenever I have busied myself about some trouble it has been from a personal motive which drove me on, or in the hope of serving someone who henceforth should serve me. And never have I brought to my aid other weapon than a certain measure of common sense. In many instances the purest good chance has given to me my only clue; the merest accident has set me straight when a hundred roads lay before me. I had come to Lady Faber's house hoping that the sight of some stranger, a chance word, or even an impulse might cast light upon the darkness in which we had walked for many weeks. Yet the longer I stayed in the ballroom the more futile did the whole thing seem. Though I knew that a nimble-fingered gentleman might be at my very elbow, that half a dozen others might be dancing cheerfully about me in that way of life to which their rascality had called them, I had not so much as a hand-breadth of suspicion; saw no face that was not the face of the dancing ass, or the smart man about town; did not observe a single creature who led me to hazard a question. And so profound at last was my disgust that I elbowed my way from the ballroom in despair; and went again to the conservatory where the palms waved seductively, and the flying corks of the champagne bottles made music harmonious to hear.

There were few people in this room at the moment – old General Sharard, who was never yet known to leave a refreshment table until the supper table was set; the Revd Arthur Mellbank, the curate of St Peter's, sipping tea; a lean youth who ate an ice with the relish of a schoolboy; and the ubiquitous Sibyl Kavanagh, who has been vulgarly described as a garrison hack. She was a woman of many partialities, whom everyone saw at every dance, and then asked how she got there – a woman with sufficient personal attraction left to remind you that she was *passée*, and sufficient wit to make an interval tolerable. I, as a rule, had danced once with her, and then avoided both her programme and her chatter; but now that I came suddenly upon her, she cried out with a delicious pretence of artlessness, and ostentatiously made room for me at her side.

'*Do* get me another cup of tea,' she said; 'I've been talking for ten minutes to Colonel Harner, who has just come from the great thirst land, and I've caught it.'

'You'll ruin your nerves,' said I, as I fetched her the cup, 'and you'll miss the next dance.'

'I'll sit it out with you,' she cried gushingly; 'and as for nerves, I haven't got any; I must have shed them with my first teeth. But I want to talk to you – you've heard the news, of course! Isn't it dreadful?'

She said this with a beautiful look of sadness, and

for a moment I did not know to what she referred. Then it dawned upon my mind that she had heard of Lady Faber's loss.

'Yes,' said I, 'it's the profoundest mystery I have ever known.'

'And can't you think of any explanation at all?' she asked, as she drank her tea at a draught. 'Isn't it possible to suspect someone just to pass the time?'

'If you can suggest anyone,' said I, 'we will begin with pleasure.'

'Well, there's no one in this room to think of, is there?' she asked with her limpid laugh; 'of course you couldn't search the curate's pockets, unless sermons were missing instead of rubies?'

'This is a case of "sermons in stones",' I replied, 'and a very serious case. I wonder you have escaped with all those pretty brilliants on your sleeves.'

'But I haven't escaped,' she cried; 'why, you're not up to date. Don't you know that I lost a marquise brooch at the Hayes' dance the other evening? I have never heard the last of it from my husband, who will not believe for a minute that I did not lose it in the crowd.'

'And you yourself believe – '

'That it was stolen, of course. I pin my brooches too well to lose them – some one took it in the same cruel way that Lady Faber's rubies have been taken. Isn't it really awful to think that at every party we go to thieves go with us? It's enough to make one emigrate to the shires.'

She fell to the flippant mood again, for nothing could keep her from that; and as there was obviously nothing to be learnt from her, I listened to her chatter sufferingly.

'But we were going to suspect people,' she continued suddenly, 'and we have not done it. As we can't begin with the curate, let's take the slim young man opposite. Hasn't he what Sheridan calls – but there, I mustn't say it; you know – a something disinheriting countenance?'

'He eats too many jam tarts and drinks too much lemonade to be a criminal,' I replied; 'besides, he is not occupied, you'll have to look in the ballroom.'

'I can just see the top of the men's heads,' said she, craning her neck forward in the effort. 'Have you noticed that when a man is dancing, either he star gazes in ecstasy, as though he were in heaven, or looks down to his boots – well, as if it were the other thing?'

'Possibly,' said I; 'but you're not going to constitute yourself a *vehmgericht* from seeing the top of people's heads.'

'Indeed,' she cried, 'that shows how little you know; there is more character in the crown of an old man's head than is dreamt of in your philosophy, as what's-his-name says. Look at that shining roof bobbing up there, for instance; that is the halo of port and honesty – and a difficulty in dancing the polka. Oh! that mine enemy would dance the polka – especially if he were stout.'

'Do you really possess an enemy?' I asked, as she fell into a vulgar burst of laughter at her own humour; but she said: 'Do I possess one? Go and discuss me with the other women – that's what I tell all my partners to do; and they come back and report to me. It's as good as a play!'

'It must be,' said I, 'a complete extravaganza. But your enemy has finished his exercise, and they are going to play a waltz. Shall I take you down?'

'Yes,' she cried, 'and don't forget to discuss me. Oh, these crushes!'

She said this as we came to the press upon the corner of the stairs leading to the ballroom, a corner where she was pushed desperately against the banisters. The vigour of the polka had sent an army of dancers to the conservatory, and for some minutes we could neither descend nor go back; but when the press was somewhat relieved, and she made an effort to progress, her dress caught in a spike of the ironwork, and the top of a panel of silk which went down one side of it was ripped open and left hanging. For a minute she did not notice the mishap; but as the torn panel of silk fell away slightly from the more substantial portion of her dress, I observed, pinned to the inner side of it, a large crescent brooch of diamonds. In the same instant she turned with indescribable quickness, and made good the damage. But her face was scarlet in the flush of its colour; and she looked at me with questioning eyes.

'What a miserable accident,' she said. 'I have spoilt my gown.'

'Have you?' said I sympathetically. 'I hope it was not my clumsiness – but really there doesn't seem much damage done. Did you tear it in front?'

There was need of very great restraint in saying this. Though I stood simply palpitating with amazement, and had to make some show of examining her gown, I knew that even an ill-judged word might undo the whole good of the amazing discovery, and deprive me of that which appeared to be one of the most astounding stories of the year. To put an end to the interview, I asked her laughingly if she would not care to see one of the maids upstairs; and she jumped at the excuse, leaving me upon the landing to watch her hurriedly mounting to the bedroom storey above.

When she was gone, I went back to the conservatory and drank a cup of tea, always the best promoter of clear thought; and for some ten minutes I turned the thing over in my mind. Who was Mrs Sibyl Kavanagh, and why had she sewn a brooch of brilliants to the inside of a panel of her gown – sewn it in a place where it was as safely hid from sight as though buried in the Thames? A child could have given the answer – but a child would have overlooked many things which were vital to the development of the unavoidable conclusion of the discovery. The brooch that I had seen corresponded perfectly with the crescent of which Lady Dunholm was robbed – yet it was a brooch which a hundred women might have possessed; and if I had simply stepped down and told Lady Faber, 'the thief you are entertaining is Mrs Sibyl Kavanagh', a slander action with damages had trodden upon the heels of the folly. Yet I would have given a hundred pounds to have been allowed full inspection of the whole panel of the woman's dress – and I would have staked an equal sum that there had been found in it the pendant of the ripening rubies; a pendant which seemed to me the one certain clue that would end the series of jewel robberies, and the colossal mystery of the year. Now, however, the woman had gone upstairs to hide in another place whatever she had to hide; and for the time it was unlikely that a sudden searching of her dress would add to my knowledge.

A second cup of tea helped me still further on my path. It made quite clear to me the fact that the woman was the recipient of the stolen jewels, rather than the actual taker of them. She, clearly, could not use the scissors which had severed Lady Faber's pendant from the ruby belt. A skilful man had in all probability done that – but which man, or perhaps men? I had long felt that the season's robberies were the work of many hands. Chance had now marked for me one pair; but it was vastly more important to know the others. The punishment of the woman would scarce stop the widespread conspiracy; the arrest of her for the possession of a crescent brooch, hid suspiciously it is true, but a brooch of a pattern which abounded in every jeweller's shop from Kensington to Temple Bar, would have been consummate lunacy. Of course, I could have taken cab to Scotland Yard, and have told my tale; but with no other support, how far would that have availed me? If the history of the surpassingly strange case were to be written, I knew that I must write it, and lose no moment in the work.

I had now got a sufficient grip upon the whole situation to act decisively, and my first step was to re-enter the ballroom, and take a partner for the next waltz. We had made some turns before I discovered that Mrs Kavanagh was again in the room, dancing with her usual dash, and seemingly in no way moved by the mishap. As we passed in the press, she even smiled at me, saying, 'I've set full sail again'; and her whole bearing convinced me of her belief that I had seen nothing.

At the end of my dance my own partner, a pretty little girl in pink, left me with the remark, 'You're awfully stupid tonight! I ask you if you've seen *Manon Lescaut,* and the only thing you say is, "The panel buttons up, I thought so." ' This convinced me that it was dangerous to dance again, and I waited in the room only until the supper was ready, and Mrs Kavanagh passed me, making for the dining-room, on the arm of General Sharard. I had loitered to see what jewels she wore upon her dress; and when I had made a note of them, I slipped from the front door of the house unobserved, and took a hansom to my place in Bond Street.

At the second ring of the bell my watchman opened the door to me; and while he stood staring with profound surprise, I walked straight to one of the jewel cases in which our cheaper jewels are kept, and took therefrom a spray of diamonds, and hooked it to the inside of my coat. Then I sent the man up stairs to awaken Abel, and in five minutes my servant was with me, though he wore only his trousers and his shirt.

'Abel,' said I, 'there's good news for you. I'm on the path of the gang we're wanting.'

'Good God, sir!' cried he, 'you don't mean that!'

'Yes,' said I, 'there's a woman named Sibyl Kavanagh in it to begin with, and she's helped herself to a couple of diamond sprays, and a pendant of rubies at Lady Faber's tonight. One of the sprays I know she's got; if I could trace the pendant to her, the case would begin to look complete.'

'Whew!' he ejaculated, brightening up at the prospect of business. 'I knew there was a woman in it all along – but this one, why, she's a regular flier, ain't she, sir?'

'We'll find out her history presently. I'm going straight back to Portman Square now. Follow me in a hansom, and when you get to the house, wait inside my brougham until I come. But before you do that, run round to Marlborough Street police-station and ask them if we can have ten or a dozen men ready to mark a house in Bayswater some time between this and six o'clock tomorrow morning.'

'You're going to follow her home then?'

'Exactly, and if my wits can find a way I'm going to be her guest for ten minutes after she quits Lady Faber's. They're sure to let you have the men either at Marlborough Street or at the Harrow Road station. This business has been a disgrace to them quite long enough.'

'That's so, sir; King told me yesterday that he'd bury his head in the sand if something didn't turn up soon. You haven't given me the exact address though.'

'Because I haven't got it. I only know that the woman lives somewhere near St Stephen's Church – she sits under, or on, one of the curates there. If you can get her address from her coachman, do so. But go and dress and be in Portman Square at the earliest possible moment.'

It was now very near one o'clock, indeed the hour struck as I passed the chapel in Orchard Street; and when I came into the square I found my own coachman waiting with the brougham at the corner by Baker Street. I told him, before I entered the house, to expect Abel; and not by any chance to draw up at Lady Faber's. Then I made my way quietly to the ballroom and observed Mrs Kavanagh – I will not say dancing, but hurling herself through the last figure of the lancers. It was evident that she did not intend to quit yet awhile; and I left her to get some supper, choosing a seat near to the door of the dining-room, so that anyone passing must be seen by me. To my surprise, I had not been in the room ten minutes when she suddenly appeared in the hall, unattended, and her cloak wrapped round her; but she passed without perceiving me; and I, waiting until I heard the hall door close, went out instantly and got my wraps. Many of the guests had left already, but a few carriages and cabs were in the square, and a link-man seemed busy in the distribution of unlimited potations. It occurred to me that if Abel had not got the woman's address, this man might give it to me, and I put the plain question to him.

'That lady who just left,' said I, 'did she have a carriage or a cab?'

'Oh, you mean Mrs Kevenner,' he answered thickly, 'she's a keb, she is, allus takes a hansom, sir; 192 Westbourne Park; I don't want to ask when I see her, sir.'

'Thank you,' said I, 'she has dropped a piece of jewellery in the hall, and I thought I would drive round and return it to her.'

He looked surprised, at the notion, perhaps, of any-one returning anything found in a London ballroom; but I left him with his astonishment and entered my carriage. There I found Abel crouching down under the front seat, and he met me with a piteous plea that the woman had no coachman, and that he had failed to obtain her address.

'Never mind that,' said I, as we drove off sharply, 'what did they say at the station?'

'They wanted to bring a force of police round, and arrest everyone in the house, sir. I had trouble enough to hold them in, I'm sure. But I said that we'd sit down and watch if they made any fuss, and then they gave in. It's agreed now that a dozen men will be at the Harrow Road station at your call till morning. They've a wonderful confidence in you, sir.'

'It's a pity they haven't more confidence in themselves – but anyway, we are in luck. The woman's address is 192 Westbourne Park, and I seem to remember that it is a square.'

'I'm sure of it,' said he; 'it's a round square in the shape of an oblong, and one hundred and ninety-two is at the side near Durham something or other; we can watch it easily from the palings.'

After this, ten minutes' drive brought us to the place, and I found it as he had said, the 'square' being really a triangle. Number one hundred and ninety-two was a big house, its outer points gone much to decay, but lighted on its second and third floors; though so far as I could see, for the blinds of the drawing-room were up, no one was moving. This did not deter me, however, and, taking my stand with Abel at the corner where two great trees gave us perfect shelter, we waited silently for many minutes, to the astonishment of the constable upon the beat, with whom I soon settled; and to his satisfaction.

'Ah,' said he, 'I knew they was rum 'uns all along; they owe fourteen pounds for milk, and their butcher ain't paid; young men going in all night, too – why, there's one of them there now.'

I looked through the trees at his word, and saw that he was right. A youth in an opera hat and a black coat was upon the doorstep of the house; and as the light of a street lamp fell upon his face, I recognised him. He was the boy who had eaten of the jam tarts so plentifully at Lady Faber's – the youth with whom Sibyl Kavanagh had pretended to have no acquaintance when she talked to me in the conservatory. And at the sight of him, I knew that the moment had come.

'Abel,' I said, 'it's time you went. Tell the men to bring a short ladder with them. They'll have to come in by the balcony – but only when I make a sign. The signal will be the cracking of the glass of that lamp you can see upon the table there. Did you bring my pistol?'

'Would I forget that?' he asked; 'I brought you two, and look out! for you may want them.'

'I know that,' said I, 'but I depend upon you. Get back at the earliest possible moment, and don't act until I give the signal. It will mean that the clue is complete.'

He nodded his head, and disappeared quickly in the direction where the carriage was; but I went straight up to the house, and knocked loudly upon the door. To my surprise, it was opened at once by a thickset man in livery, who did not appear at all astonished to see me.

'They're upstairs, sir, will you go up?' said he.

'Certainly,' said I, taking him at his word. 'Lead the way.'

This request made him hesitate.

'I beg your pardon,' said he, 'I think I have made a mistake – I'll speak to Mrs Kavanagh.'

Before I could answer he had run up the stairs nimbly; but I was quick after him; and when I came upon the landing, I could see into the front drawing-room, where there sat the woman herself, a small and oldish man with long black whiskers, and the youth who had just come into the room. But the back room, which gave off from the other with folding-doors, was empty; and there was no light in it. All this I perceived

in a momentary glance, for no sooner had the serving-
man spoken to the woman, than she pushed the youth
out upon the balcony, and came hurriedly to the
landing, closing the door behind her.

'Why, Mr Sutton,' she cried, when she saw me,
'this is a surprise; I was just going to bed.'

'I was afraid you would have been already gone,'
said I with the simplest smile possible, 'but I found a
diamond spray in Lady Faber's hall just after you had
left. The footman said it must be yours, and as I am
going out of town tomorrow, I thought I would risk
leaving it tonight.'

I handed to her as I spoke the spray of diamonds I
had taken from my own showcase in Bond Street; but
while she examined it she shot up at me a quick
searching glance from her bright eyes, and her thick
sensual lips were closed hard upon each other. Yet, in
the next instant, she laughed again, and handed me
back the jewel.

'I'm indeed very grateful to you,' she exclaimed,
'but I've just put my spray in its case; you want to
give me someone else's property.'

'Then it isn't yours?' said I, affecting disappointment. 'I'm really very sorry for having troubled you.'

'It is I that should be sorry for having brought you
here,' she cried. 'Won't you have a brandy and seltzer
or something before you go?'

'Nothing whatever, thanks,' said I. 'Let me apologise
again for having disturbed you – and wish you
"Good-night".'

She held out her hand to me, seemingly much
reassured; and as I began to descend the stairs, she
re-entered the drawing-room for the purpose, I did
not doubt, of getting the man off the balcony. The

substantial lackey was then waiting in the hall to open the door for me; but I went down very slowly, for in truth the whole of my plan appeared to have failed; and at that moment I was without the veriest rag of an idea. My object in coming to the house had been to trace, and if possible to lay hands upon the woman's associates, taking her, as I hoped, somewhat by surprise; yet though I had made my chain more complete, vital links were missing; and I stood no nearer to the forging of them. That which I had to ask myself, and to answer in the space of ten seconds, was the question, 'Now, or tomorrow?' – whether I should leave the house without effort, and wait until the gang betrayed itself again; or make some bold stroke which would end the matter there and then. The latter course was the one I chose. The morrow, said I, may find these people in Paris or in Belgium; there never may be such a clue again as that of the ruby pendant – there never may be a similar opportunity of taking at least three of those for whom we had so long hunted. And with this thought a whole plan of action suddenly leaped up in my mind; and I acted upon it, silently and swiftly, and with a readiness which to this day I wonder at.

I now stood at the hall-door, which the lackey held open. One searching look at the man convinced me that my design was a sound one. He was obtuse, patronising – but probably honest. As we faced each other I suddenly took the door-handle from him, and banged the door loudly, remaining in the hall. Then I clapped my pistol to his head (though for this offence I surmise that a judge might have given me a month), and I whispered fiercely to him: 'This house is surrounded by police; if you say a word I'll give you seven years as an accomplice of the woman upstairs, whom we are going to arrest. When she calls out, answer that I'm gone, and then come back to me for instructions. If you do as I tell you, you shall not be charged – otherwise, you go to jail.'

At this speech the poor wretch paled before me, and shook so that I could feel the tremor all down the arm of his which I held.

'I – I won't speak, sir,' he gasped. 'I won't, I do assure you – to think as I should have served such folk.'

'Then hide me, and be quick about it – in this room here, it seems dark. Now run upstairs and say I'm gone.'

I had stepped into a little breakfast-room at the back of the dining-room, and there had gone un-hesitatingly under a round table. The place was absolutely dark, and was a vantage ground, since I could see therefrom the whole of the staircase; but before the footman could mount the stairs, the woman came halfway down them, and, looking over the hall, she asked him: 'Is that gentleman gone?'

'Just left, mum,' he replied.

'Then go to bed, and never let me see you admit a stranger like that again.'

She went up again at this, and he turned to me, asking: 'What shall I do now, sir? I'll do anything if you'll speak for me, sir; I've got twenty years' kerecter from Lord Walley; to think as she's a bad 'un – it's hardly creditable.'

'I shall speak for you,' said I, 'if you do exactly what I tell you. Are any more men expected now?'

'Yes, there's two more; the capting and the clergy-min, pretty clergymin he must be, too.'

'Never mind that; wait and let them in. Then go upstairs and turn the light out on the staircase as if by accident. After that you can go to bed.'

'Did you say the police was 'ere?' he asked in his hoarse whisper; and I said: 'Yes, they're everywhere, on the roof, and in the street, and on the balcony. If there's the least resistance, the house will swarm with them.'

What he would have said to this I cannot tell, for at that moment there was another knock upon the front door, and he opened it instantly. Two men, one in clerical dress, and one, a very powerful man, in a Newmarket coat, went quickly upstairs, and the butler followed them. A moment later the gas went out on the stairs; and there was no sound but the echo of the talk in the front drawing-room.

The critical moment in my night's work had now come. Taking off my boots, and putting my revolver at the half-cock, I crawled up the stairs with the step of a cat, and entered the back drawing-room. One of the folding-doors of this was ajar, so that a false step would probably have cost me my life – and I could not possibly tell if the police were really in the street, or only upon their way. But it was my good luck that the men talked loudly, and seemed actually to be disputing. The first thing I observed on looking through the open door was that the woman had left the four to themselves. Three of them stood about the table whereon the lamp was; the dumpy man with the black whiskers sat in his armchair. But the most pleasing sight of all was that of a large piece of cotton-wool spread upon the table and almost covered with brooches, lockets, and sprays of diamonds; and to my infinite satisfaction I saw Lady Faber's pendant of rubies lying conspicuous even amongst the wealth of jewels which the light showed.

There then was the clue; but how was it to be used? It came to me suddenly that four consummate rogues such as these would not be unarmed. Did I step into the room, they might shoot me at the first sound; and if the police had not come, there would be the end of it. Had opportunity been permitted to me, I would, undoubtedly, have waited five or ten minutes to assure myself that Abel was in the street without. But this was not to be. Even as I debated the point, a candle's light shone upon the staircase; and in another moment Mrs Kavanagh herself stood in the doorway watching me. For one instant she stood, but it served my purpose; and as a scream rose upon her lips, and I felt my heart thudding against my ribs, I threw open the folding-doors, and deliberately shot down the glass of the lamp which had cast the aureola of light upon the stolen jewels.

As the glass flew, for my reputation as a pistol shot was not belied in this critical moment, Mrs Kavanagh ran in a wild fit of hysterical screaming to her bed-room above – but the four men turned with loud cries to the door where they had seen me; and as I saw them coming, I prayed that Abel might be there. This thought need not have occurred to me. Scarce had the men taken two steps when the glass of the balcony windows was burst in with a crash, and the whole room seemed to fill with police.

*   *   *

I cannot now remember precisely the sentences which were passed upon the great gang (known to police history as the Westbourne Park gang) of jewel thieves;

but the history of that case is curious enough to be worthy of mention. The husband of the woman Kavanagh – he of the black whiskers – was a man of the name of Whyte, formerly a manager in the house of James Thorndike, the Universal Provider near the Tottenham Court Road. Whyte's business had been to provide all things needful for dances; and, though it astonishes me to write it, he had even found dancing men for ladies whose range of acquaintance was narrow. In the course of business, he set up for himself eventually; and as he worked, the bright idea came to him, why not find as guests men who may snap up, in the heat and the security of the dance, such unconsidered trifles as sprays, pendants, and lockets. To this end he married, and his wife being a clever woman who fell in with his idea, she – under the name of Kavanagh – made the acquaintance of a number of youths whose business it was to dance; and eventually wormed herself into many good houses. The trial brought to light the extraordinary fact that no less than twenty-three men and eight women were bound in this amazing conspiracy, and that Kavanagh acted as the buyer of the property they stole, giving them a third of the profits, and swindling them out-rageously. He, I believe, is now taking the air at Portland; and the other young men are finding in the exemplary exercise of picking oakum, work for idle hands to do.

As for Mrs Kavanagh, she was dramatic to the end of it; and, as I learnt from King, she insisted on being arrested in bed.

The Purple Death

WILLIAM LE QUEUX

Around the big round table in the upper room of the Café de l'Univers the Crimes Club was holding its usual monthly meeting. All of the ten members, each of a different profession and each expert in his own walk of life, were present.

The *café noir* and liqueurs had been set, and the door locked, for no one was allowed at their secret deliberations, and no new member was admitted until death created a vacancy.

The secretary, the stout Madame Léontine van Hecke, suddenly addressed her companions in French, saying: 'Gentlemen, M. Dubosq wishes to consult you. I ask your attention, if you please.'

Lucien Dubosq, smart in his dinner-jacket and wearing the coveted red rosette of the Legion of Honour in his lapel, rose, and after apologising for troubling the club, explained a problem which the English and French detective service had both failed to solve.

He said that in the interests of justice a very strange and mysterious affair was being hushed up by both Scotland Yard and the French police, a mystery upon which no light could be thrown, therefore he would briefly place the facts before the members for discussion, decision, and action.

On September 22nd, at four o'clock in the

afternoon, two well-dressed men, one dark, half-bald and clean-shaven, about fifty-five years of age, and the other, a younger man in his early thirties, with fair, well-brushed hair and of a somewhat effeminate type, strolled along the beach road leading from the cinema to the fish market in the old town of Hastings, where the brown-sailed fishing smacks were lying ready to go out. There were still many London trippers about, and at a beach stall the two men bought some bananas, and, throwing themselves upon the shingle, ate them and smoked cigarettes. They conversed in low tones, evidently holding a consultation, the younger man differing from his companion.

Presently the younger man, having grown calm, drew his wallet from his pocket and, taking out something, handed it to his friend, who examined it. Then the other clapped his knee in satisfaction and returned it to his friend, who carefully replaced it in his pocket-book. Both laughed heartily, then rose, and walking back to the town, entered the Bodega, where a young, fair-haired girl of twenty-two awaited them, and they had a drink together. The girl was extremely well-dressed and had shingled hair. She wore a dark kid glove on her left hand, which apparently had some deformity.

All this was witnessed by Henry Hayes, an employee of the Hastings Corporation, whose duty was surveillance upon the beach fronting the old town, with its broken sea wall and fishing harbour. He had noticed the rather unusual movements of the two well-dressed men, for such men did not usually eat bananas upon the beach. For that reason he noted their clothes. The elder man wore in his dark knotted cravat a beautiful cornflower-blue sapphire pin which had attracted Hayes as being very pretty.

When the men had entered the Bodega just as it had opened for its evening trade, Hayes relaxed his surveillance, for he had little to do, the trippers being orderly at that end of the town, which was the reverse to that stretch of beach between the Queen's Hotel and Hastings Pier.

That was the last seen of the two visitors to Hastings alive.

Thirty-four hours later, at three o'clock in the morning, the cross-Channel mail steamer, *Isle of Thanet*, when halfway between Dover and Calais, sounded her siren against a big sailing boat not showing the regulation lights. There was half a gale blowing, and the sails being set, she came straight across the bows of the *Isle of Thanet*, much to the anger of Captain Evans, who sounded his siren again and was compelled to alter his course sharply, avoiding a collision only by a few yards.

In the darkness he saw that it was a fishing smack, but there was no light nor any sign of life aboard. He drew up at risk of trouble at Calais Maritime over his delay, and so manoeuvred his steamer as to follow the derelict.

Coming up alongside of her, he took up his megaphone and shouted to her skipper, first in French, then in Spanish, English, and Italian. But the fishing smack, tossing upon the heaving waters, made no sign.

'Ahoy, there!' he shouted. 'Where the devil are you going?' But again there was no response.

Realising that such a vessel adrift in the Channel without lights was a great danger to shipping, he at once sent off a boat's crew to board her, and stood by awaiting his men's report. The boat's crew had a difficult time in getting aboard in such a sea, but they managed to scramble up while Captain Evans turned on his searchlight to watch.

Most of the passengers were below because of the heavy gale blowing. Presently the second officer, named Richard Hardwick, who had gone with the party, came up and, waving his arms just as a heavy sea struck the smack, yelled to the captain: 'There's something wrong here, sir! We'll sail her into Calais and see you there.'

'What's wrong?' enquired Evans deeply through his megaphone.

'We can't tell yet, sir,' was his officer's reply. Then Captain Evans waved farewell and continued on his course, knowing that he would delay the Paris mail by half an hour or even more.

Meanwhile Hardwick, the officer of the *Isle of Thanet*, had ordered the lights to be relit, the sails altered, and a course set for Calais, he having the flashing harbour light to steer by.

'Funny, ain't it, sir!' remarked Williams, the man at the helm, obeying Hardwick's orders as they followed in the wake of the brilliantly lit cross-Channel steamer. 'Can you make it out?'

'No, I can't, Williams,' was the officer's reply. 'Keep her a point more westward.' And then as the steersman altered the smack's course, another big sea struck her and she rose proudly from the trough. The night was not over-dark, but the moon was obscured by swift drifting clouds as it so often is in the Channel. Ever and anon, the stormy clouds parted and the moon shone in a long silver streak upon the wind-swept waters.

'The fellow for'ard looks like a gentleman,' Williams remarked, just as another of his fellow-sailors passed along, a ghostly figure in the half light. ' 'E's been done in, no doubt. I wonder 'ow?'

'Who knows? There will be an inquiry into the derelict when we get into Calais,' replied Hardwick. 'The man's dead and we can't bring him to life. The only thing is to leave everything as it was – as I have given strict orders – and let the police solve the mystery of tonight's affair. It's beyond me, I admit, and – well – it gets on one's nerves. It is all so uncanny – three of them!'

'Yes, sir, I agree. But where is the crew? They've disappeared. They'll know something of 'em in Hastings, no doubt.'

'Of course they will. But, as you say – where is the crew? Three dead men aboard – and nobody else!'

The fishing boat marked 'CH. 38' upon her sails, which had sailed the Channel for fifteen years, and was well known to every fisherman between the North Foreland and Portland Bill, rose and fell, labouring heavily in the gale, the angry seas breaking over her every now and then, while the mail boat quickly outdistanced her in making for Calais harbour.

Two or three times the *Isle of Thanet* signalled dot-and-dash lights to the derelict, giving orders as to what Hardwick should do when entering the port.

Meanwhile Hardwick, who had spent his life on the Channel ferry, had all he could do to keep the brown-sailed old boat upon her course. The trawl was up – recently up, for fish, seaweed, and débris from it lay scattered about the swimming deck. But who had hauled it? Certainly not the three men now aboard. The fishing crew had apparently suddenly disappeared, leaving the vessel to drift without lights, a serious menace to shipping. Indeed, as showing the strict watch kept upon the Channel waters, two tramp steamers, which had passed it an hour before, had reported it to the wireless station at Niton, in the Isle of Wight, as a dangerous derelict. This notice to mariners had, in turn, been transmitted to the Admiralty, who, a quarter of an hour later, had sent out a CQ message – which is the code-signal asking everyone to listen as all ships were warned of their danger.

Through the stormy waters the battered old fishing smack laboured on for a further two hours, until at last they were under the green and red lights which marked the entrance to Calais harbour, and a dexterous turn of the wheel from Williams brought her into calm water where, after much manoeuvring, the boat was at last brought into the fishing port and tied up to the quay.

At once two French police agents, in hooded cloaks, boarded her, the Prefect of Police having already been notified by Captain Evans on the arrival of the *Isle of Thanet*. Evans and a plain-clothes policeman accompanied them.

'Well, Hardwick, what's wrong here?' asked the captain in his sharp, brusque way.

'I can't tell, sir. But you can see for yourself,' was his officer's reply.

Examination of the dirty, dismal little vessel showed an amazing state of things.

In the bows lay the body of a fair-haired young man in a cheap tweed suit. He lay curled up, his features distorted, his eyes bulging, and his countenance a curious bright purple; while down below in the small cabin lit by a single swinging oil lamp there were the remains of a rough supper upon the table, and dregs of red wine in enamelled cups. Lying on the floor were two other men, dead from no apparent cause. None of the trio were seafaring men, but the faces of all three were horribly distorted, their hands open instead of being clenched, and their faces bright purple. Yet there was no trace of the crew of four or five which such a vessel would carry.

In the cabin were signs of a violent quarrel. Some broken plates lay upon the floor, but they might have been swept off the table by the pitching of the boat when the trawl was down.

The police began a thorough search of the dead men's clothing, finding absolutely nothing to serve as a clue. But their investigations proved that the young man who was found in the bows of the boat was not a man at all, but a girl of about twenty-two or -three with fair, close-cropped hair!

The curious discovery was at once reported by telephone to the Chief of Police of Calais, who, with his chief inspector, a well-known detective named Dufour, arrived on board. The bodies of all three were searched. The elder man, who was half-bald, wore in his cravat a cornflower sapphire pin set with four diamonds, and had in his pocket the return half of a first-class ticket from London Bridge to Hastings. The inside pocket of his jacket had been torn almost out, and his face had been bruised on the left jaw either through somebody striking him with their fist, or, perhaps, in falling.

The girl attired as a man seemed a lady. Upon her arm was a solid gold slave-bangle worth at least fifty pounds, while around her neck, beneath her man's shirt, she wore a thin gold chain from which was suspended a circle of emerald-green stone which was afterwards identified as chrysoprase. In her trousers pocket was a twenty-franc gold piece, evidently a souvenir. But upon her was no mark of violence except a slight discoloration of the thumbnail on the right hand. The glove, on being removed from the left hand, showed it to be withered and looking almost like the hand of a skeleton, the thin skin upon the bones being white as marble.

The third man appeared to be aged about thirty. He wore sea-boots like his two companions, but upon his dead countenance was a look of inexpressible horror, as though he had faced some terrible shock at the moment of his death. His clothes were well-made, and upon him was found two pounds in Treasury notes and fifty francs in French bank notes. The palm of his open right hand was cut and had bled.

Beyond that all was mystery. Where was the crew of the fishing boat 'CH. 38'?

The French police at once became active and telephoned a brief report of the discovery to Scotland Yard, and they, in turn, telephoned to the Hastings police asking them to at once make enquiry as to the owner of the 'CH. 38', and what had become of the missing crew.

Soon a strange state of affairs became revealed. The boat belonged to a fishing company which had its headquarters at Grimsby and owned boats sailing from Brixham, Yarmouth and elsewhere. The skipper's name was Ben Benham, a man recently from Grimsby, as were the three hands. The original crew of the vessel had been transferred to Grimsby, Benham and his men taking their place. They had only been out on four previous trips, but what had happened to them that night was a complete mystery.

The Hastings police, assisted by two expert officers from Scotland Yard, made every enquiry, but all fruitless. The Calais police had done the same, and enquiries had been made at all the ports of the Pas-de-Calais, but without avail.

Thus the problem put before the club by Monsieur Dubosq was an extremely complex one. Who were the two men and the girl dressed as a man? Why were they on board the fishing boat? Where were the crew? What was the motive of their journey? What had occurred during the fatal voyage?

'Have photographs of the dead persons been taken?' asked Maurice Jacquinot.

'Yes. I have the photographs here,' replied the Chef de la Sûreté. And he handed round three unmounted photographs which had been taken of the dead persons in the position in which they were found.

Each member gazed at them in turn as they were passed round the table. But the member most interested was the elderly, white-bearded Dr Henri Plaud. He examined and re-examined them very minutely through his large round spectacles, and pursing his lips slightly, passed them to the podgy Baron d'Antenac, who sat at his right hand.

A discussion followed lasting over two hours, in which Gustave Delcros, Gordon Latimer, and the pretty dark-haired Parisienne, Fernande Buysse, took part. The latter, who had been so successful in the case of 'The Golden Grasshopper', was eager and enthusiastic. She suggested that the members of the club should unite at once and make independent enquiries.

This course was adopted, and it was decided that the direction of the investigation should be left in the hands of the white-bearded Dr Plaud, while Gordon Latimer, spruce and active, being English, should go to Hastings at once, accompanied by Mlle Fernande and the young journalist Maurice Jacquinot.

The judicial inquiry held by the French authorities at Calais revealed nothing, so it was decided that the affair should be kept out of the newspapers in order not to alarm anyone who held secret knowledge of what had happened. The bodies of the unknown victims were duly buried, and the case left in the hands of the Crimes Club.

On the 20th December, Gordon Latimer and Fernande Buysse, who, with others, had been pursuing active enquiries in Hastings, Folkestone, Calais, London, Paris, and elsewhere for nearly three months, were sitting together in a low-pitched, under-ground room where dancing and drinking were being indulged in, a den in Greek Street, Soho, which was one of the most disreputable spots in London's under-world. Gordon had gone there alone and had stood drinks to two or three girls of the usual type which haunt such places. Then he had pretended to 'pick up' Fernande, the smart young French girl with whom he was now seated, and who had in the past few weeks become a nightly habituée there.

They were drinking Russian tea, and as she raised her glass, she whispered in French: 'That's the girl – in the cinnamon frock, with reddish hair!'

The girl she indicated was about twenty-five, rather refined, delicate-looking and well-dressed. By her free manner, her painted lips, and her careless laughter it was plain that she was one of similar type to the other girls who frequented the place, some of them of the worst character. The fair-haired young man she was dancing with at the moment was known as 'Jimmy the Painter', and was, indeed, one of the several cat burglars who, from time to time, arouse great alarm among London householders.

Latimer looked at the girl, and asked: 'Are you quite sure?'

'I'm never sure of anything,' laughed the chic French girl. 'Only from what she's let out, I feel sure she knows something about the stuff. Shall I ask her across to sit with us?'

'No. I'll come here alone tomorrow night,' he said, and they sat drinking their tea, smoking cigarettes, and afterwards danced together.

Molly was the name by which the girl whom Fernande had pointed out was known. Such girls have no surnames. They change them too often when the police are following them. She laughed across to Fernande with whom she had become acquainted, and then glanced inquisitively at her companion, as though summing him up, perhaps, as a pigeon to be plucked – which was exactly what Latimer desired.

By their combined efforts, the five members of the Crimes Club had, in a way, been successful. They had discovered Henry Hayes, the employee of the Hastings Corporation, who had identified the photographs of the two men and the girl found upon the fishing boat as the pair whom he had seen eating bananas on the beach and afterwards meeting the girl in the Bodega. That was all. How they came to be on board the boat, or how or for what reason the girl had been transformed into a man, was an absolute enigma.

Old Dr Plaud, as director of the investigations, had, by his unerring instinct, transferred his sphere of enquiry to London, and there Latimer and Fernande, with the astute journalist, Jacquinot, and M. Delcros had gone to work in a careful, methodical and scientific manner, always keeping in mind that whenever a great crime is committed, there is always a woman in the case.

But what was the crime? What had happened in mid-Channel on that fateful September night? The foreigner can always learn more in London's cosmopolitan underworld than the Englishman, as every London detective will tell you. The cosmopolitan criminal looks upon every Englishman as a 'nark', or policeman's 'nose' or informer. Hence the foreign detective in London always has an easier task if he knows the haunts of crooks and becomes a habitué.

This is what Plaud had pointed out, and his suggestion had been at once adopted.

Indeed, the sprightly Fernande and her dancing had become quite a feature of that den known to the West End criminal as 'Old Jacob's'. To that cellar, or series of cellars, with their boarded, white-painted walls, with crude Futuristic designs upon them, many visitors to London were enticed to spend a 'merry evening', and left there minus their wallet, or doped and taken to some den even more foul. The police knew 'Old Jacob's' well, and Jacob himself, once a solicitor but now a wily old criminal who had spent some years in Dartmoor for appropriating his clients' money, always took ample precautions, and when raided, the place was found to belong to somebody else who was duly fined, and 'Old Jacob' next day removed to another underground den.

At 'The Yard' it was always declared that at 'Jacob's' there congregated the most dangerous crowd of criminals in London.

All efforts of Plaud and his companions had failed to establish the identity of the two strangers who had arrived on that September evening in Hastings, who had met the girl and given her a glass of wine, and who later had been discovered dead upon the derelict in mid-Channel.

The Crimes Club had held three meetings in Paris at which progress had been reported and the matter had been discussed, but it seemed after three months that the whole organisation of experts was up against a blank wall. On the other hand, it was argued that the crew of four men of the fishing boat could not have all disappeared – unless they had been drowned, which was not likely. Besides, the ship's lights had been deliberately extinguished, which gave colour to the theory that the three had been murdered and the boat abandoned. In addition, one of the small boats was missing, though it had not been sighted. It might have escaped to either the French or English coast in the darkness.

The clue which the shrewd young French lady journalist was following – the public being in ignorance of the highly sensational discovery – was only a slender one. In the course of the long investigations in which Jacquinot had been most active, it was found that a person somewhat resembling the man who wore the sapphire in his cravat, was known in the dregs of the London underworld as an expert thief named Orlando Martin, who had a dozen or so *aliases*. He had never been in trouble apparently, neither had his companion, for the fingerprints of the dead hands taken by the

Calais police did not correspond with any of the hundreds of thousands of records filed at Scotland Yard.

In such circumstances, with failure after failure to record, and with Dr Plaud openly pessimistic as regards finding any solution to the mystery, Gordon Latimer, dressed in a dinner-jacket, lounged into 'Jacob's' on the following night, and was soon in conversation with the neat-ankled girl, Molly. They sat together, drank coffee and Cointreau, and watched the dancing, he pretending to live in Cornwall, and up from Truro on a holiday. He told her that he was a motor dealer, and having unexpectedly sold half a dozen cars he had determined to take a holiday in London.

The girl soon saw that he was an easy victim to her charms. Indeed, he promised to meet her and take her out to lunch next day, which he did. For the following three days he was mostly in her company and constantly spending money upon her, but at night they always danced at 'Old Jacob's', where twice they met Fernande alone, and she joined them.

One evening, in consequence of a telegram he had received from Paris regarding yet another discovery, Gordon resolved to make a bold endeavour to learn something, for if what Fernande suspected were true, then Molly might be able to supply the key to the enigma.

They left 'Jacob's' at three o'clock in the morning, and he had offered to see her in a taxi as far as her flat at Baron's Court, out by West Kensington.

While in the taxi he suddenly took her hand, and said: 'Molly, you are dense. Haven't you recognised me?'

'Recognised you?' she cried, starting suddenly. 'What do you mean?'

'You take me for a mug. You don't recognise Bert Davies – Sugar's friend!'

'Bert Davies!' gasped the girl. 'Are you really Bert – his best pal?'

'I am. I came out of the Scrubs a month ago and went over to Paris to find Maisie. But I can't find Sugar anywhere. Where is he? I know he was deeply in love with you. He told me so lots of times. I hope he isn't doing time?'

The shrewd girl, whose wits were sharpened by the criminal life she led, was silent for a few moments. Teddy Candy, known in the London underworld by the sobriquet of 'Sugar', and with whom she was in love, had often spoken of his intimate friend, an expert blackmailer named Bertie Davies who was in prison owing to a little slip he had made.

'You aren't a nark, are you?' asked the girl cautiously.

'Certainly not. Maisie knows me. So does Dick Dale. Sugar used to wear a blue sapphire tiepin that he pinched from a young Italian prince one night, didn't he?'

'Dick is doing time – shot at a copper in Kingsland and got it in the neck from the Recorder.'

'I'm sorry. Dickie's one of the best. Recollect the Humber Street affair – a nasty business – but Dickie helped Teddy, didn't he?'

'Yes. It was a narrow shave for all of us. I don't like guns. But we got nearly two thousand apiece.'

'But what about Sugar? Where can I find him?' asked her good-looking companion.

'I don't know – and that's a fact,' she replied, with

a regretful air. 'I haven't seen him or heard of him since September.'

'Perhaps he's doing time?'

'Oh, no. He's disappeared.'

'How?'

'I don't know,' the girl replied. 'He and Tony Donald had a big thing on hand – a bit of bank business, he told me. One day in September he left me after lunching at the Trocadero, and I haven't seen him since. Tony's missing, too!'

'Was Sugar ever about with a big, thickset man with a beard, a rough, rather deep-voiced, unkempt fellow, who looked like a sailor?'

'The man who came up from Hastings, you mean – eh? Sugar told me he was one of us, and they were doing business together.'

'Is that all he told you?' asked Latimer.

'What are you so inquisitive for, young man?' asked the girl pertly. 'What business is it of yours – eh? I took you for a mug, but you certainly aren't one,' she laughed. The cab had stopped outside her door, and seeing this, she said: 'Come in and have a drink before you go back.'

Latimer, delighted with the information he had obtained, accepted the girl's invitation and ascended to the third floor, to a little three-roomed flat cosily furnished, where he sat down and took the whisky and soda she poured out for him.

Ten minutes later she went below and paid the taxi driver, telling him that her friend was remaining, but the actual fact was that Gordon Latimer was at that moment lying senseless upon the floor heavily drugged.

'You're a nark, you damned swine!' she cried on

returning, kicking his inanimate body savagely. 'And you'll be sorry for your inquisitiveness. You are no friend of Sugar's or of Ben Benham's either!'

She went to the telephone and rang up somebody named Joe, urging him to come at once.

Half an hour later an ill-dressed, ill-conditioned man of forty with a sinister, criminal face arrived, and to him she told the story.

The man knit his heavy brows and was silent for a few moments. Then he said: 'If he really knows something about Sugar he might possibly help us. Don't do anything rash. It may be better for us if he is alive, than if he died. We'll let him recover and loosen his tongue,' added the ex-convict. 'There's certain to be somebody with him, and he may have been watched here. So there's no time to lose. Give him the stuff that brings them round,' he urged.

She passed into an adjoining room, and returned with a small phial bottle from which she poured about twenty drops into water, and held it to his lips. Unconsciously he drank it, and ten minutes later he was again fully conscious, and amazed at finding himself face to face with the stranger.

'Well, sonny?' asked the sinister man who had served many years of penal servitude, 'what's all this you know about Sugar? If you can tell me where he is you'll get out of this alive. But if you don't, well, you'll be found dead by the police tomorrow,' he said fiercely, drawing a revolver and holding it close to his brow. 'Now, let's talk business. What do you know about Sugar?'

Gordon Latimer, realising that he was in a tight corner, decided that the best course was to tell the truth.

'I only know that he is dead.'

'Dead!' cried the girl hysterically. 'How do you know that?'

'Before I answer I want to ask a question. Is Ben Benham alive?'

'Certainly,' was Molly's reply.

'Then I may tell you that Sugar is dead, and here is his photograph taken by the French police,' said Latimer boldly, taking the three pictures from his pocketbook.

On sight of the first the girl Molly shrieked, and almost fainted.

'Yes, it is Sugar – poor, dear Sugar! Dead, and he loved me! Do forgive me – forgive us – and tell us all that you know. What happened to Sugar and to Tony Donald?'

'They are both dead – and this girl too – dressed as a man.' And he showed them the other pictures.

'Gwen!' gasped Molly. 'It's Gwen! She's dead also! Tell us what happened. Where were they found?'

Both stood open-mouthed and aghast as Latimer described the finding of the bodies on the derelict ship.

'How did your little French friend find out that we knew these people?' asked the old criminal whose name was Joe Hawker, an expert forger.

'If I tell you I shall expect you to tell me all that you know regarding the affair,' said Latimer.

'That's agreed,' replied Molly. 'We have a lot to tell you – more curious than you can possibly imagine. How did she suspect that I knew anything?'

For a few seconds Latimer reflected, then he decided that straightforwardness was best.

'The fact is, Miss Molly,' he said, 'Professor Plaud,

the French medico-legist, on seeing the photographs, at once suspected, from the position and appearance of the bodies, the fact of the palms being outstretched and the purple colour of the countenances, that death was due to an almost unknown but very subtle and deadly narcotic poison called enconine. From only one person in London, whose name is known to the professor, can the poison be obtained in secret, and a very high price is charged for it. That fact led us to search the underworld of London thoroughly for persons who had purchased it. There were six of them known to us, but our enquiries were narrowed down to yourself. You bought the poison for your friend Candy, and you kept some for yourself. It was that which you gave me in my drink just now. You can't deny it!'

The girl stood aghast at the allegation, unable to utter a word.

'I do not seek to harm you,' he at once assured her. 'I only want to solve the mystery. We have ascertained the truth up to a certain point – that you obtained the drug which cost Candy, Donald, and the girl Gwen, their lives.'

'But what happened to them?' the girl asked breathlessly. 'They wouldn't all commit suicide.'

'Before I tell you I want to know the nature of the bank business in which Candy and Donald were "interested".'

'Well – you, no doubt, saw in the papers last August how the strongroom of Carron's, the big private bank in the City, had been blown open after the night watchman had been gassed, and how nearly a quarter of a million had been carried away in a blue motor car.'

'Yes, I remember,' Latimer answered.

'Well, Sugar and Tony did the trick, while Gwen gassed the watchman. They hid the money in a house down by the sea at Pevensey Bay, but one day they were all three missing as well as old Ben Benham, and we've had no word of any of them till now you've shown us that they're dead.'

'What actually occurred becomes quite plain,' Latimer replied. 'Candy and your other two friends no doubt feared the police and were anxious to get the loot in secret across the Channel, where the securities could be disposed of. They arranged with the skipper Benham, whom they had found to be a clever smuggler, to take them and their treasure over to France on that night. They went on board after dark and steered a course presumably to fish as usual, when Benham, who had evidently stolen the drug from Candy without his knowledge, offered all three a drink, which they took with fatal results. He then seized the money and securities, paid the crew well for their silence, lowered a boat, and having extinguished the vessel's lights, they rowed forward to the French coast, where he and the crew, whom he had sworn to silence and to remain in France, separated. Three hours later the vessel was sighted by the cross-Channel steamer, and the bodies discovered in the position in which you see them.'

'Then Benham killed them!' cried the girl hysterically. 'We'll kill him!'

'There is no necessity,' was Latimer's reply. 'This afternoon I received a telegram from the Paris police to the effect that a man much resembling the skipper Benham, though he had shaved off his grey beard and moustache, was discovered at a small hotel in

Rouen. When the police went to arrest him, however, he shot himself. In the room nearly seventeen
thousand pounds in cash and nearly the whole of the
securities were found.'

My Adventure at Chislehurst

Towards the end of last September I went to the
Radio A Exhibition at Olympia, and very fine it was,
too. I drifted about, and after I'd, so to speak, 'done'
the ground floor and was going up the stairs to the
gallery, I ran into a man I knew. Just at the moment it
wouldn't do at all for me to mention his name, so I'll
merely call him James, but there's no harm in saying
that he was a retired stockbroker and he lived near
Chislehurst.

Anyhow, there he was, and he hailed me with glee
and insisted on our walking round together. I was
rather sorry about this because it's so much more fun
wandering about exhibitions by oneself, and not only
that, he was evidently starting a bad cold which didn't
attract me particularly, but there was no getting out
of it without offending him, so I didn't try.

After all, he was by way of being a friend of mine
and I'd known him for ages, but we hadn't come
across each other for some months, and during this
time he'd gone and got married again, unexpected-
like. I mean, everyone had come to look on him as a
chronic widower, and he'd have probably stopped so
if the daughter who kept house for him hadn't got
married herself and gone to live in Birmingham. You
must excuse these details, but I want you to understand exactly what the position was. As things were,

he hadn't seen the catch of running an enormous great house all by himself, so Mrs James the Second had come to the throne as a matter of course. I had never actually met her, but from all accounts she was a great success.

James was so keen on telling me about how happy he was, and so on, that it was quite a job to make him take any interest in the show, but whenever he did deign to look at or listen to anything he merely said it wasn't a patch on some rotten super-het he'd brought back from the United States. (They'd spent their honeymoon there for some unknown reason.) I naturally wasn't going to stand this sort of thing for long, so I upped and made a few remarks about American super-hets which were very well received by adjacent stall-holders. The remarks themselves weren't, perhaps, of general interest, but they landed me with a challenge. This was to dine with him that evening, hear his set, and incidentally, meet his new wife. I hadn't got an excuse ready, so I said that I should be charmed to meet his wife and, incidentally, hear his new set.

It so happened that my car was in dock for two days and James said he'd call for me at home and run me down. The question then arose as to whether I should dress first or take a bag down with me. That doesn't sound important, I know, but it had a good deal to do with something that happened afterwards. As a matter of fact I decided to change at home. I left James at the Exhibition during the afternoon, he duly picked me up at my place at half-past six or there-abouts, and we got down to Chislehurst just before seven.

We were met by the news that Mrs James wasn't

in. She'd apparently taken out her own car during the morning and gone off to see her mother who lived at Worthing and was a bit of an invalid. As this was a thing she'd been in the habit of doing every two or three weeks it was nothing out of the way, but she usually got back earlier.

At all events, pending her return, we went through the hall into the lounge, where people generally sat, and James began mixing cocktails. While he was doing this I had a look round to see how much had been altered under the new management, as one would. The only unfamiliar object in the room seemed to be a large picture hanging over the mantelpiece. I was just strolling across to get a better view (it was getting a bit dark by this time), when James said: 'Half a sec,' and he switched on some specially arranged lights round the frame which showed it up, properly. Then he said: 'What do you think of my wife?'

Well, I looked at it and said: 'Gosh! If that's at all like her she must be one of the most beautiful women I've ever seen,' and that's saying a lot. The portrait was by quite a well-known man and he'd painted her exactly full face and looking straight at you. You don't often see that because so few people can stand it. The general effect was so realistic that one almost felt one was being introduced and ought to say something. She was fair rather than dark, a little bit Scandinavian in appearance, and I put her down as a shade over thirty.

James finished mixing the cocktails and gave me mine, and then he took his up with him to dress, leaving me sitting in an armchair facing the fireplace – and the picture.

He couldn't have got further than the top of the

stairs when the telephone bell in the hall rang and he came running down to answer it. It was evidently his wife at the other end, and judging from what he said, she was explaining that she was stuck at Worthing for the night owing to some trouble with the car. Nothing serious.

(He told me afterwards that she'd first of all had a bad puncture and then found that the inner tube of the spare wheel was perished. The delay would have meant her driving part of the way home in the dark, which she didn't like.)

After that the question of his cold cropped up. She must have asked after it because I heard him say it wasn't any better. They talked about it for a bit and then lapsed into the sloppy type of conversation which one sort of expects between newly married people, but which is none the less averagely dull for anyone else to listen to.

It may have been more than averagely dull in this case because it almost sent me off to sleep. It didn't quite, but I got as far as the moment when the sub-conscious side of the brain begins to take control and you sometimes get entirely fantastic ideas. (Either that or you try to hoof the end of the bed off.) Any-how, if you remember, I was sitting looking at this brightly illuminated picture of Mrs James. Well, for an incredibly short space of time, I mean, you've no idea how short, the whole character of it seemed to change. Instead of an oil painting in rather vivid colours it suddenly looked like a photograph, or, to be strictly accurate, a photograph as reproduced in a newspaper. Try looking at one through a magnifying glass (not now – sometime), and imagine it to be four feet by three, and you will get the same effect that I did. There was a name printed under this photograph and my eyes certainly read it, but before my mind could take in what it was the illusion was gone and I was wide-awake again.

It was all over so quickly that I just said: 'Um, that's funny,' and didn't pay much attention to it.

When James came in after a lengthy and idiotic goodbye on the telephone I didn't even tell him. He'd have only made some fatuous joke about the strength of his cocktails.

He was full of apologies about his wife not being able to get home and so forth, and he explained what had happened with yards of detail. I'd gathered most of it already but I had to pretend to listen with interest so as to make him think I hadn't heard some of the other things that had been said. He then went up finally to dress and again left me alone with the picture, but although I tried from every angle, both with and without the lights, I couldn't manage to recapture the peculiar 'halftone' effect, neither was I able to remember the name which had appeared underneath. By the way, it is worth noting that if I'd decided to dress at Chislehurst instead of at home I probably shouldn't have been left alone with the picture at all, and got the jim-jams about it.

James came down in due course and we had a most elaborate dinner. He always did things very well and there was no reason why he shouldn't. People with five thousand a year often do.

At the end of dinner we carted our coffee and old brandy into the lounge, and then he introduced me to his unspeakable wireless set. I hadn't spotted it earlier because it was housed in a tallboy which had always been there.

A. J. ALAN

Needless to say, the tallboy was far and away the best thing about it. When he switched it on the volume of distorted noise was so appalling that I can't think why the ceiling didn't come down.

There was a long and terrible period during which we could only converse by means of signs, and then to my great relief one of his transformers caught fire and we had to put it out with a soda-water syphon.

By then it was getting on for eleven and I said it was time to go. That, of course, meant a final whisky, and he was just starting on his, which he'd mixed with milk, by the way, when he put it down and said: 'My word! I shall hear about it if I don't take my aspirin,' and he went upstairs to fetch some. He was gone three or four minutes, and when he came down he said he'd had the devil's own hunt, as he couldn't find any of his own and he'd been obliged to bag his wife's last three. These he proceeded to take, and then I really had to go as there was only just time to catch my train, and that was that.

Next morning, during breakfast, there was a ring at the bell, and they came and told me that Inspector Soames of Chislehurst wanted to see me, so I went out and interviewed him.

He seemed quite a decent fellow, and he led off by enquiring how I was. I thanked him and said I was very well indeed. He next wanted to know if I'd slept well, and I told him that I had, but even then he wasn't happy. Was I sure I'd felt no discomfort of any kind during the night? I said: 'None whatever, but why this sudden solicitude about my health?'

He then said: 'Well, you see, sir, it's like this. Last night you dined with Mr – er – (well – James, in fact). You left him round about 11 p.m., and he presumably

244

went straight to bed. However, at three o'clock this morning groans were heard coming from his room, and when the servants went in they found him lying half in and half out of bed, writhing with pain and partially unconscious. Doctors were immediately called in and they did all they could, but by six o'clock he was dead.' Well, this was naturally a great shock to me. It always is when you hear of people whom you know going out suddenly like that, especially when you've seen them alive and well such a little time before.

I asked the Inspector what James had died of, and he said: 'Oh, probably some acute form of food poisoning,' but it wouldn't be known for certain until after the postmortem. In the meantime, would I mind telling him everything we had had to eat and drink the night before? Which I did. Actually it was only a check, because he'd already got it all down in his notebook. I dare say he'd been talking to the cook and the maids who'd waited on us. He even knew that I hadn't had any fish, whereas James had, but there was nothing wrong with that as it had all been finished downstairs. I was able to be more helpful in the matter of drinks afterwards, and I didn't forget to mention the final whisky and milk and the three aspirins, all of which he carefully wrote down.

I next enquired after Mrs James. It had apparently been rather distressing about her. They'd telephoned to Worthing as soon as they'd found how gravely ill James was, and she'd arrived home just as he was dying. No one had had the nous to be on the look-out for her at the front door, and she'd got right up into the room and seen how things were before they could stop her. She had then completely collapsed, which was only natural, and they'd had to carry her to her room and put her to bed. Things were so bad with her that there was talk of a nurse being sent for.

My inspector friend then went away, but he warned me that I should have to appear at the inquest, which would probably be three days later.

I duly turned up but wasn't called. They only took evidence of identification and the proceedings were adjourned for three weeks to await the result of the postmortem.

I wrote to Mrs James soon afterwards asking if there was anything I could do, but she sent back a rather vague note about being too ill to see anyone, so we didn't meet.

I had another interview with the police after that, but they didn't ask me any more questions about food, and when the adjourned inquest came on it was perfectly obvious why. The cause of James's death wasn't food poisoning at all. It was fifty grains of perchloride of mercury. In case you don't know, perchloride of mercury is also called corrosive sublimate (it's used in surgical dressings), and fifty grains taken internally is a pretty hopeless proposition. In fact, according to what the very eminent pathologist person said in the witness-box, it must be about as good for your tummy as molten lead. This great man went on to give it as his opinion that the poison must have been administered not more than eight hours before death had taken place. This was allowing for the milk which would have a retarding influence. As James had died at six in the morning it meant that he must have taken his dose sometime after ten o'clock the previous night. As I had been the last person to see him alive, or at any rate conscious, it made my evidence rather important, especially as it covered the first hour of the material eight.

When my turn came I told the Court almost word for word what I'd told the Inspector, right down to the three aspirins.

The Coroner asked me a whole lot of questions about James's manner and health, and I could only say that he had seemed normal, cheerful, and, bar his cold, healthy.

When they'd done with me, Mrs James was called, and I was able to see her properly for the first time. She was even better looking than her portrait, and black suited her. One could tell that she had the sympathy of everyone. She would. She was popular in the district, and the court was packed with her friends. The Coroner treated her with the utmost consideration. She said that her relations with her husband had always been of the very best and there had never been the ghost of a disagreement. She also stated that as far as she knew he had no worries, either financial or otherwise, and that he could have had no possible reason for taking his life.

After that the Coroner became even more considerate than ever. One could see what he was after; he clearly had the fact in mind that when a rich man dies in mysterious circumstances there are always plenty of people who seem to think that his widow ought to be hanged 'on spec', so, although their evidence was hardly – what shall I say? – germane to the enquiry, witnesses were called who proved, in effect, that she had been at Worthing from lunchtime on the one day right up to four in the morning on the next, and there was no getting away from it. Even the mechanic from the Worthing garage was roped in (in his Sunday clothes). He described the trouble with her tyres and the discussion as to whether she could or could not have got home to Chislehurst before dark.

There was a good deal more evidence of the same kind, and it all went to establish that whatever else had happened, Mrs James couldn't possibly have murdered her husband, and as it seemed unlikely that he had committed suicide the jury returned an open verdict.

Now what was I to do? On the face of it, and knowing what I did, it was my duty to get up and say something like this: 'You'll pardon me, but that woman did murder her husband and, if you like, I'll tell you roughly how: She waits till he has a cold coming on and then decides to pay one of her periodical visits to her mother at Worthing. She arranges to get hung up there for the night, but she telephones at dinner-time and, I suggest, makes him promise to take some aspirin and whisky before he goes to bed – a perfectly normal remedy. She naturally takes jolly good care before starting in the morning that there are only three tablets of aspirin that he can get at and these are the – er – ones. The bottle they have been in is certainly a danger if the police get hold of it, but they don't get hold of it because she arrives home in plenty of time to change it for another.

'If things had gone entirely right for her, and I hadn't happened to be dining there that evening, no one would have known about James's dose of aspirin at all, but her technique is so sound that I'm able to watch him take it, and talk about it afterwards without it mattering. I don't suppose she liked it, but it didn't do her any appreciable harm. Then again, even if he forgets to take his tablets she runs no risk. She merely has to wait till he gets another cold. In fact the whole thing is cast iron.'

Now supposing, for the sake of argument, that I'd got up, and been allowed to say all this, what would have happened?

I should have had to admit straight off that I couldn't produce a scrap of evidence to support any of it, at least not the kind of evidence that would wash with a jury.

There certainly was James's remark: 'I shall hear about it if I don't take my aspirin.' That satisfied me who he expected to hear about it from, but there was only my bare word for it that he'd put it that way, and you know what lawyers are. They mightn't have believed me.

Then again, the Coroner was a doctor. He would have asked me how it was possible to fake up per-chloride of mercury to look like aspirin, and I should have had to agree that it wouldn't be at all easy. It happens to be a poison which the general public practically can't get, and even if they could, the tablets in which it is sold are carefully dyed blue. Besides which they aren't the right shape. If you walked into a chemist's and asked him to bleach some of them white and make them to look like aspirin he might easily think it fishy, and I doubt whether you would set his mind at rest by saying that you only wanted them for a joke, or private theatricals.

All of this I knew quite well, having taken the trouble to enquire, but there was another fact which I didn't get to know till afterwards which might have made a difference. It was rather strange. For a certain time during the War the French Army medical people

249

had put up their perchloride of mercury in white tablets, not blue, and these did in fact closely resemble the present-day aspirin. Moreover, each tablet contained seventeen grains. Now three seventeens are fifty-one, or almost exactly what James was reckoned to have taken. But all this would have gone for precisely nothing (even if I'd known it and said it), unless any of these convenient tablets could be traced to Mrs James, and they most definitely couldn't.

The police had searched the house as a matter of routine and analysed every bottle whether empty or full. One might also safely conclude that they had made enquiries at all the chemists where the lady might have dealt. I know they went to mine.

Then there was another thing which made it difficult to accuse Mrs James, and that was the absence of motive, because the obvious one, money, was practically ruled out. It transpired that she had twelve hundred a year of her own, and the average woman with as much as that isn't likely to marry and then murder some wretched man for the sake of another five thousand. She wouldn't take the trouble. In fact, what with one thing and another, my theory didn't stand a hope, so I thought I'd let it stew a little longer.

The lady left the court without a stain on her character and later on went to live in the Isle of Wight. For all I know she is still there, enjoying her twelve hundred plus five thousand a year, but whether she will go on doing it is quite another thing, because a short time ago I was just finishing a pipe before going to bed, when suddenly, apropos of nothing, there came into my head the name I had seen under her picture at the instant it had looked like a photograph.

It was a somewhat peculiar name and not the one under which she had married James.

All the same, one doesn't imagine a name for no reason at all, so I worked it out that at some time or other I must have actually seen a published photograph of Mrs James, and that staring at the picture down at Chislehurst had brought it back to me.

Anyhow, the following day I got my literary agent to send round to all the newspaper offices in Fleet Street and enquire whether a photograph of anyone of this name had appeared during the last few years. They all said 'No'.

However, my agent is of a persevering nature (he has to be). He went on and tackled the illustrated weekly papers and he struck oil almost at once. About eight years ago one of them had apparently brought out what it called a 'Riviera Supplement', and in it was the photograph. I went along and recognised it immediately, but what interested me most of all was the paragraph that referred to it. It said that this Miss What's-her-name had been acting as companion to an old lady who had a villa at Cannes. One day she, the companion, had gone across into Italy to see her mother who lived at Bordighera and was a bit of an invalid.

For some reason or other she missed the last train back and had to spend the night at Bordighera, but when she did arrive back at Cannes next day she was shocked to find that her employer had poisoned herself during the night.

The paper didn't say what poison the old lady took or how much money she left her companion, but I've found out since and I'll give you two guesses.

The Wrong Problem

JOHN DICKSON CARR

At the Detectives' Club it is still told how Dr Fell
went down into the valley in Somerset that evening
and of the man with whom he talked in the twilight
by the lake, and of murder that came up as though
from the lake itself. The truth about the crime has
long been known, but one question must always be
asked at the end of it.

The village of Grayling Dene lay a mile away
towards the sunset. The rear windows of the house
looked out towards it. The house was long gabled
built of red brick, lying in a hollow of the shaggy hills,
and its bricks had darkened like an old painting. No
lights showed inside, although the lawns were in good
order and the hedges trimmed.

Behind the house there was a long gleam of water
in the sunset, for the ornamental lake – some fifty
yards across – stretched almost to the windows. In
the middle of the lake, on an artificial island, stood a
summerhouse. A faint breeze had begun to stir,
despite the heat, and the valley was alive with a
conference of leaves.

The last light showed that all the windows of the
house, except one, had little lozenge-shaped panes.
The one exception was a window high up in a gable,
the highest in the house, looking out over the road to
Grayling Dene. It was barred.

Dusk had almost become darkness when two men came down over the crest of the hill. One was large and lean. The other, who wore a shovel-hat, was large and immensely stout, and he loomed even more vast against the skyline by reason of the great dark cloak billowing out behind him. Even at a distance you might hear the chuckles that animated his several chins and ran down the ridges of his waistcoat. The two travellers were engaged (as usual) in a violent argument. At intervals the larger one would stop and hold forth oratorically for some minutes, flourishing his cane. But, as they came down past the lake and the blind house, both of them stopped.

'There's an example,' said Superintendent Hadley. 'Say what you like, it's a bit too lonely for me. Give me the town – '

'We are not alone,' said Dr Fell.

The whole place had seemed so deserted that Hadley felt a slight start when he saw a man standing at the edge of the lake. Against the reddish glow on the water they could make out that it was a small man in neat dark clothes and a white linen hat. He seemed to be stooping forward, peering out across the water. The wind went rustling again, and the man turned round.

'I don't see any swans,' he said. 'Can you see any swans?' The quiet water was empty.

'No,' said Dr Fell, with the same gravity. 'Should there be any?'

'There should be one,' answered the little man, nodding. 'Dead. With blood on its neck. Floating there.'

'Killed?' asked Dr Fell, after a pause. He has said afterwards that it seemed a foolish thing to say; but that it seemed appropriate to that time between the lights of the day and the brain.

'Oh, yes,' replied the little man, nodding again. 'Killed, like others – human beings. Eye, ear and throat. Or perhaps I should say ear, eye and throat, to get them in order.'

Hadley spoke with some sharpness.

'I hope we're not trespassing. We knew the land was enclosed, of course, but they told us that the owners were away and wouldn't mind if we took a short cut. Fell, don't you think we'd better – ?'

'I beg your pardon,' said the little man, in a voice of such cool sanity that Hadley turned round again. From what they could see in the gloom, he had a good face, a quiet face, a somewhat ascetic face; and he was smiling. 'I beg your pardon,' he repeated in a curiously apologetic tone. 'I should not have said that. You see, I have been far too long with it. I have been trying to find the real answer for thirty years. As for the trespassing myself, I do not own this land, although I lived here once. There is, or used to be, a bench here somewhere. Can I detain you for a little while?'

Hadley never quite realised afterwards how it came about. But such was the spell of the hour, or of the place, or of the sincere, serious little man in the white linen hat, that it seemed no time at all before the little man was sitting on a rusty iron chair beside the darkening lake, speaking as though to his fingers.

'I am Joseph Lessing,' he said in the same apologetic tone. 'If you have not heard of me, I don't suppose you will have heard of my stepfather. But at one time he was rather famous as an eye, ear and throat specialist. Dr Harvey Lessing, his name was.

'In those days we – I mean the family – always

came down here to spend our summer holidays. It is rather difficult to make biographical details clear. Perhaps I had better do it with dates: as though the matter were really important, like a history book. There were four children. Three of them were Dr Lessing's children by his first wife, who died in 1899. I was the stepson. He married my mother when I was seventeen, in 1901. I regret to say that *she* died three years later. Dr Lessing was a kindly man, but he was very unfortunate in the choice of his wives.'

The little man appeared to be smiling sadly.

'We were an ordinary, contented and happy group, in spite of Brownrigg's cynicism. Brownrigg was the eldest. Eye, ear and throat pursued us: he was a dentist. I think he is dead now. He was a stout man, smiling a good deal, and his face had a shine like pale butter. He was an athlete run to seed; he used to claim that he could draw teeth with his fingers. By the way, he was very fond of walnuts. I always seem to remember him sitting between two silver candlesticks at the table, smiling, with a heap of shells in front of him and a little sharp nut-pick in his hand.

'Harvey Junior was the next. They were right to call him Junior; he was of the striding sort, brisk and high-coloured and likeable. He never sat down in a chair without first turning it the wrong way round. He always said "Ho, my lads!" when he came into a room, and he never went out of it without leaving the door open so that he could come back in again. Above everything, he was nearly always on the water. We had a skiff and a punt for our little lake – would you believe that it is ten feet deep? Junior always dressed for the part as solemnly as though he had been on the Thames, wearing a red-and-white striped blazer and a straw hat of the sort that used to be called a boater. I say he was nearly always on the water: but not, of course, after tea. That was when Dr Lessing went to take his afternoon nap in the summerhouse.'

The summerhouse, in its sheath of vines, was almost invisible now. But they all looked at it, very suggestive in the middle of the lake.

'The third child was the girl, Martha. She was almost my own age, and I was very fond of her.'

Joseph Lessing pressed his hands together.

'I am not going to introduce an unnecessary love story, gentlemen,' he said. 'As a matter of fact, Martha was engaged to a young man who had a commission in a line regiment, and she was expecting him down here any day when – the things happened. Arthur Somers, his name was. I knew him well; I was his confidant in the family.

'I want to emphasise what a hot, pleasant summer it was. The place looked then much as it does now, except that I think it was greener then. I was glad to get away from the city. In accordance with Dr Lessing's passion for "useful employment", I had been put to work in the optical department of a jeweller's. I was always skilful with my hands. I dare say I was a spindly, snappish, suspicious lad, but they were all very good to me after my mother died: except butter-faced Brownrigg, perhaps. But for me that summer centres round Martha, with her brown hair piled up on the top of her head, in a white dress with puffed shoulders, playing croquet on a green lawn and laughing. I told you it was a long while ago.

'On the afternoon of the fifteenth of August we had all intended to be out. Even Brownrigg had intended to go out after a sort of lunch-tea that we had at two o'clock in the afternoon. Look to your right, gentlemen. You see that bow window in the middle of the house, overhanging the lake? There was where the table was set.

'Dr Lessing was the first to leave the table. He was going out early for his nap in the summerhouse. It was a very hot afternoon, as drowsy as the sound of a lawn-mower. The sun baked the old bricks and made a flat blaze on the water. Junior had knocked together a sort of miniature landing-stage at the side of the lake – it was just about where we are sitting now – and the punt and the rowing-boat were lying there.

'From the open windows we could all see Dr Lessing going down to the landing-stage with the sun on his bald spot. He had a pillow in one hand and a book in the other. He took the rowing-boat; he could never manage the punt properly, and it irritated a man of his dignity to try.

'Martha was the next to leave. She laughed and ran away, as she always did. Then Junior said, "Cheerio, chaps" – or whatever the expression was then – and strode out leaving the door open. I went shortly afterwards. Junior had asked Brownrigg whether he intended to go out, and Brownrigg had said yes. But he remained, being lazy, with a pile of walnut shells in front of him. Though he moved back from the table to get out of the glare, he lounged there all afternoon in view of the lake.

'Of course, what Brownrigg said or thought might not have been important. But it happened that a gardener named Robinson had taken it into his head to trim some hedges on this side of the house. He had a full view of the lake. And all that afternoon nothing stirred. The summerhouse, as you can see, has two doors: one facing towards the house, the other in the opposite direction. These openings were closed by sun-blinds, striped red and white like Junior's blazer, so that you could not see inside. But all the afternoon the summerhouse remained dead, showing up against the fiery water and that clump of trees at the far side of the lake. No boat put out. No one went to swim. There was not so much as a ripple, any more than might have been caused by the swans (we had two of them), or by the spring that fed the lake.

'By six o'clock we were all back in the house. When there began to be a few shadows, I think something in the *emptiness* of the afternoon alarmed us. Dr Lessing should have been there, demanding something. He was not there. We halloo'd for him, but he did not answer. The rowing-boat remained tied up by the summerhouse. Then Brownrigg, in his cool fetch-and-run fashion, told me to go out and wake up the old party. I pointed out that there was only the punt, and that I was a rotten hand at punting, and that whenever I tried it I only went round in circles or upset the boat. But Junior said, "Come-along-old-chap-you-shall-improve-your-punting-I'll-give-you-a-hand."

'I have never forgotten how long it took us to get out there, while I staggered at the punt-pole, and Junior lent a hand.

'Dr Lessing lay easily on his left side, almost on his stomach, on a long wicker settee. His face was very nearly into the pillow, so that you could not see much except a wisp of sandy side-whisker. His right hand hung down to the floor, the fingers trailing into the pages of *Three Men in a Boat*.

'We first noticed that there seemed to be some –

that is, something that had come out of his ear. More we did not know, except that he was dead, and in fact the weapon has never been found. He died in his sleep. The doctor later told us that the wound had been made by some round sharp-pointed instrument, thicker than a hatpin but not so thick as a lead-pencil, which had been driven through the right ear into the brain.'

Joseph Lessing paused. A mighty swish of wind rose up in the trees beyond the lake, and their tops ruffled under clear starlight. The little man sat nodding to himself in the iron chair. They could see his white hat move.

'Yes?' prompted Dr Fell in an almost casual tone. Dr Fell was sitting back, a great bandit-shape in cloak and shovel-hat. He seemed to be blinking curiously at Lessing over his eyeglasses. 'And whom did they suspect?'

'They suspected me,' said the little man.

'You see,' he went on, in the same apologetic tone, 'I was the only one in the group who could swim. It was my one accomplishment. It is too dark to show you now, but I won a little medal by it, and I have kept it on my watch-chain ever since I received it as a boy.'

'But you said,' cried Hadley, 'that nobody – '

'I will explain,' said the other, 'if you do not interrupt me. Of course, the police believed that the motive must have been money. Dr Lessing was a wealthy man, and his money was divided almost equally among us. I told you he was always very good to me.

'First they tried to find out where everyone had been in the afternoon. Brownrigg had been sitting, or said he had been sitting, in the dining-room. But there was the gardener to prove that not he or anyone else had gone out on the lake. Martha (it was foolish, of course, but they investigated even Martha) had been with a friend of hers – I forget her name now – who came for her in the phaeton and took her away to play croquet. Junior had no alibi, since he had been for a country walk. But,' said Lessing, quite simply, 'everybody knew *he* would never do a thing like that. I was the changeling, or perhaps I mean ugly duckling, and I admit I was an unpleasant, sarcastic lad.

'This is how Inspector Deering thought I had committed the murder. First, he thought, I had made sure everybody would be away from the house that afternoon. Thus, later, when the crime was discovered, it would be assumed by everyone that the murderer had simply gone out in the punt and come back again. Everybody knew that I could not possibly manage a punt alone. You see?

'Next, the inspector thought, I had come down to the clump of trees across the lake, in line with the summerhouse and the dining-room windows. It is shallow there, and there are reeds. He thought that I had taken off my clothes over a bathing-suit. He thought that I had crept into the water under cover of the reeds, and that I had simply swum out to the summerhouse under water.

'Twenty odd yards under water, I admit, are not much to a good swimmer. They thought that Brownrigg could not see me come up out of the water, because the thickness of the summerhouse was between. Robinson had a full view of the lake, but he could not see that one part at the back of the summerhouse. Nor, on the other hand, could I see them. They thought that I had crawled under the sun-blind with the weapon in the breast of my bathing-suit. Any wetness I might have left would soon be dried by the intense heat. That, I think, was how they believed I had killed the old man who befriended me.'

The little man's voice grew petulant and dazed.

'I told them I did not do it,' he said with a hopeful air. 'Over and over again I told them I did not do it. But I do not think they believed me. That is why for all these years I have wondered –

'It was Brownrigg's idea. They had me before a sort of family council in the library, as though I had stolen jam. Martha was weeping, but I think she was weeping with plain fear. She never stood up well in a crisis, Martha didn't; she turned pettish and even looked softer. All the same, it is not pleasant to think of a murderer coming up to you as you doze in the afternoon heat. Junior, the good fellow, attempted to take my side and call for fair play; but I could see the idea in his face. Brownrigg presided, silkily, and smiled down his nose.

' "We have either got to believe you killed him," Brownrigg said, "or believe in the supernatural. Is the lake haunted? No; I think we may safely discard that." He pointed his finger at me. "You damned young snake, you are lazy and you wanted that money."

'But, you see, I had one very strong hold over them – and I used it. I admit it was unscrupulous, but I was trying to demonstrate my innocence and we are told that the devil must be fought with fire. At mention of his hold, even Brownrigg's jowls shook. Brownrigg was a dentist, Harvey was studying medicine. What hold? That is the whole point. Nevertheless, it was not what the family thought I had to fear: it was what Inspector Deering thought.

'They did not arrest me yet, because there was not enough evidence, but every night I feared it would come the next day. Those days after the funeral were too warm; and suspicion acted like woollen underwear under the heat. Martha's tantrums got on even Junior's nerves. Once I thought Brownrigg was going to hit her. She very badly needed her fiancé, Arthur Somers; but, though he wrote that he might be there any day, he still could not get leave of absence from his colonel.

'And then the lake got more food.

'Look at the house, gentlemen. I wonder if the light is strong enough for you to see it from here? Look at the house – the highest window there – under the gable. You see?'

There was a pause, filled with the tumult of the leaves.

'It's got bars,' said Hadley.

'Yes,' assented the little man. 'I must describe the room. It is a little square room. It has one door and one window. At the time I speak of, there was no furniture at all in it. The furniture had been taken out some years before, because it was rather a special kind of furniture. Since then it had been locked up. The key was kept in a box in Dr Lessing's room; but, of course, nobody ever went up there. One of Dr Lessing's wives had died there, in a certain condition. I told you he had bad luck with his wives. They had not even dared to have a glass window.'

Sharply, the little man struck a match. The brief flame seemed to bring his face up towards them out of the dark. They saw that he had a pipe in his left hand. But the flame showed little except the gentle upward turn of his eyes, and the fact that his whitish hair (of such coarse texture that it seemed white-washed) was worn rather long.

'On the afternoon of the twenty-second of August, we had an unexpected visit from the family solicitor. There was no one to receive him except myself. Brownrigg had locked himself up in his room at the front with a bottle of whisky; he was drunk, or said he was drunk. Junior was out. We had been trying to occupy our minds for the past week, but Junior could not have his boating or I my workshop: this was thought not decent. I believe it was thought that the most decent thing was to get drunk. For some days Martha had been ailing. She was not ill enough to go to bed, but she was lying on a long chair in her bedroom.

'I looked into the room just before I went down-stairs to see the solicitor. The room was muffled up with shutters and velvet curtains, as all the rooms decently were. You may imagine that it was very hot in there. Martha was lying back in the chair with a smelling-bottle, and there was a white-globed lamp burning on a little round table beside her. I remember that her white dress looked starchy; her hair was piled up on top of her head and she wore a little gold watch on her breast. Also, her eyelids were so puffed that they seemed almost oriental. When I asked her how she was, she began to cry and concluded by throwing a book at me.

'So I went on downstairs. I was talking to the solicitor when it took place. We were in the library, which is at the front of the house, and in consequence we could not hear distinctly. But we heard something. That was why we went upstairs – and even the solicitor ran. Martha was not in her own bedroom. We found out where she was from the fact that the door to the garret-stairs was open.

'It was even more intolerably hot up under the roof. The door to the barred room stood halfway open. Just outside stood a housemaid (her name, I think, was Jane Dawson) leaning against the jamb and shaking like the ribbons on her cap. All sound had dried up in her throat, but she pointed inside.

'I told you it was a little, bare, dirty brown room. The low sun made a blaze through the window, and made shadows of the bars across Martha's white dress. Martha lay nearly in the middle of the room, with her heel twisted under her as though she had turned round before she fell. I lifted her up and tried to talk to her; but a rounded sharp-pointed thing, somewhat thicker than a hatpin, had been driven through the right eye into the brain.

'Yet there was nobody else in the room.

'The maid told a straight story. She had seen Martha come out of Dr Lessing's bedroom downstairs. Martha was running, running as well as she could in those skirts; once she stumbled, and the maid thought that she was sobbing. Jane Dawson said that Martha made for the garret door as though the devil were after her. Jane Dawson, wishing anything rather than to be alone in the dark hall, followed her. She saw Martha come up here and unlock the door of the little brown room. When Martha ran inside, the maid thought that she did not attempt to close the door; but that it appeared to swing shut after her. You see?

'Whatever had frightened Martha, Jane Dawson did not dare follow her in – for a few seconds, at least, and afterwards it was too late. The maid could never afterwards describe exactly the sort of sound Martha made. It was something that startled the birds out of the vines and set the swans flapping on the lake. But the maid presently saw straight enough to push the door with one finger and peep round the edge.

'Except for Martha, the room was empty.

'Hence the three of us now looked at each other. The maid's story was not to be shaken in any way, and we all knew she was a truthful witness. Even the police did not doubt her. She said she had seen Martha go into that room, but that she had seen nobody come out of it. She never took her eyes off the door – it was not likely that she would. But when she peeped in to see what had happened, there was nobody except Martha in the room. That was easily established, because there was no place where anyone could have been. Could she have been blinded by the light? No. Could anyone have slipped past her? No. She almost shook her hair loose by her vehemence on this point.

'The window, I need scarcely tell you, was in-accessible. Its bars were firmly set, no farther apart than the breadth of your hand, and in any case the window could not have been reached. There was no way out of the room except the door or the window; and no – what is the word I want? – no mechanical device in it. Our friend Inspector Deering made certain of that. One thing I suppose I should mention. Despite the condition of the walls and ceiling, the floor of the room was swept clean. Martha's white dress with the puffed shoulders had scarcely any dirt when she lay there; it was as white as her face.

'This murder was incredible. I do not mean merely that it was incredible with regard to its physical circumstances, but also that there was Martha dead – on a holiday. Possibly she seemed all the more dead because we had never known her well when she was alive. She was (to me, at least) a laugh, a few coquetries, a pair of brown eyes. You felt her absence more than you would have felt that of a more vital person. And – on a holiday, with that warm sun, and the tennis-net ready to be put up.

'That evening I walked with Junior here in the dusk by the lake. He was trying to express some of this. He appeared dazed. He did not know why. Martha had gone up to that little brown room, and he kept endlessly asking why. He could not even seem to accustom himself to the idea that our holidays were interrupted, much less interrupted by the murders of his father and his sister.

'There was a reddish light on the lake; the trees stood up against it like black lace, and we were walking near that clump by the reeds. The thing I remember most vividly is Junior's face. He had his hat on the back of his head, as he usually did. He was staring down past the reeds, where the water lapped faintly, as though the lake itself were the evil genius and kept its secrets. When he spoke I hardly recognised his voice.

' "God," he said, "but it's in the air!"

'There was something white floating by the reeds, very slowly turning round, with a snaky discoloured talon coming out from it along the water. The talon was the head of a swan, and the swan was dead of a gash across the neck that had very nearly severed it.

'We fished it out with a boathook,' explained the little man, as though with an afterthought. And then he was silent.

On the long iron bench Dr Fell's cape shifted a little; Hadley could hear him wheezing with quiet anger, like a boiling kettle.

'I thought so,' rumbled Dr Fell. He added more sharply: 'Look here, this tomfoolery has got to stop.'

'I beg your pardon?' said Joseph Lessing, evidently startled.

'With your kind permission,' said Dr Fell, and Hadley has later said that he was never more glad to see that cane flourished or hear that common-sense voice grow fiery with controversy: 'with your kind permission, I should like to ask you a question. Will you swear to me by anything you hold sacred (if you have anything, which I rather doubt) that you do not know the real answer?'

'Yes,' replied the other seriously, and nodded.

For a little space Dr Fell was silent. Then he spoke argumentatively. 'I will ask you another question, then. Did you ever shoot an arrow into the air?'

Hadley turned round. 'I hear the call of mumbo-jumbo,' said Hadley with grim feeling. 'Hold on, now! You don't think that girl was killed by somebody shooting an arrow into the air, do you?'

'Oh, no,' said Dr Fell in a more meditative tone. He looked at Lessing. 'I mean it figuratively – like the boy in the verse. Did you ever throw a stone when you were a boy? Did you ever throw a stone, not to hit anything, but for the sheer joy of firing it? Did you ever climb trees? Did you ever like to play pirate and dress up and wave a sword? I don't think so. That's why you live in a dreary, rarefied light; that's why you dislike romance and sentiment and good whisky and all the noblest things of this world; and it is also why you do not see the unreasonableness of several things in this case.

'To begin with, birds do not commonly rise up in a great cloud from the vines because someone cries out. With the hopping and always-whooping Junior about the premises, I should imagine the birds were used to it. Still less do swans leap up out of the water and flap their wings because of a cry from far away; swans are not so sensitive. But did you ever see a boy throw a stone at a wall? Did you ever see a boy throw a stone at the water? Birds and swans would have been outraged only if something had *struck* both the wall and the water: something, in short, which fell from that barred window.

'Now, frightened women do not in their terror rush up to a garret, especially a garret with such associations. They go downstairs, where there is protection. Martha Lessing was not frightened. She went up to that room for some purpose. What purpose? She could not have been going to get anything, for there was nothing in the room to be got. What could have been on her mind? The only thing we know to have been on her mind was a frantic wish for her fiancé to get there. She had been expecting him for weeks. It is a singular thing about that room: but its window is the highest in the house, and commands the only good clear view of the road to the village.

'Now suppose someone had told her that he thought, he rather *thought*, he had glimpsed Arthur Somers coming up the road from the village. It was a long way off, of course, and the someone admitted he might have been mistaken in thinking so . . .

'H'm, yes. The trap was all set, you see. Martha Lessing waited only long enough to get the key out of the box in her father's room, and she sobbed with relief. But, when she got to the room, there was a strong sun pouring through the bars straight into her face: and the road to the village is a long way off. That, I believe, was the trap. For on the window-ledge of that room (which nobody ever used, and which someone has swept so that there shall be no footprints) this someone has conveniently placed a pair of – eh, Hadley?'

'Field-glasses,' said Hadley, and got up in the gloom.

'Still,' argued Dr Fell, wheezing argumentatively, 'there would be one nuisance. Take a pair of field-glasses, and try to use them in a window where the bars are set more closely than the breadth of your hand. The bars get in the way: wherever you turn you bump into them; they confuse sight and irritate you; and, in addition, there is a strong sun to complicate matters. In your impatience, I think you would turn the glasses sideways and pass them out through the bars. Then, holding them firmly against one bar with your hands through the bars on either side, you would look through the eyepieces.

'But,' said Dr Fell, with a ferocious geniality, 'these were no ordinary glasses. Martha Lessing had noticed before that the lenses were blurred. Now that they were in position, she tried to adjust the focus by turning the little wheel in the middle. And as she turned the wheel, like the trigger of a pistol it released the spring mechanism and a sharp steel point shot out from the right-hand lens into her eye. She dropped the glasses, which were outside the window. The weight of them tore the point from her eye; and it was this object, falling, which gashed and broke the neck of the swan just before it disappeared into the water below.'

He paused. He had taken out a cigar, but he did not light it.

'Busy solicitors do not usually come to a house "unexpectedly". They are summoned. Brownrigg was drunk and Junior absent; there was no one at the back of the house to see the glasses fall. For this time the murderer had to have a respectable alibi. Young Martha, the only one who could have been gulled into such a trap, had to be sacrificed – to avert the arrest which had been threatening someone ever since the police found out how Dr Lessing really had been murdered.

'There was only one man who admittedly did speak with Martha Lessing only a few minutes before she was murdered. There was only one man who was employed as optician at a jeweller's, and admits he had his "workshop" here. There was only one man skilful enough with his hands – ' Dr Fell paused, wheezing, and turned to Lessing. 'I wonder they didn't arrest you.'

'They did,' said the little man, nodding. 'You see, I was released from Broadmoor only a month ago.'

There was a sudden rasp and crackle as he struck another match. The tiny flame curled up; and, as he held it out politely for Dr Fell's cigar, they saw that the ascetic face wore a gentle smile against the dark.

'You – ' bellowed Hadley, and stopped. 'So it was your mother who died in that room? Then what the hell do you mean by keeping us here with this pack of nightmares?'

'No,' said the other peevishly, and with a sort of

271

pounce. He seemed distressed. 'No, no, no, no, no! That's what you don't understand. I never wanted to know who killed Dr Lessing or poor Martha. You have got hold of the wrong problem. And yet I tried to tell you what the problem was.

'You see, it was not *my* mother who died mad. It was theirs – Brownrigg's and Harvey's and Martha's. That was why they were so desperately anxious to think I was guilty, for they could not face the alternative. Didn't I tell you I had a hold over them, a hold that made even Brownrigg shake, and that I used it? Do you think they wouldn't have had me clapped into gaol straightaway if it had been *my* mother who was mad? Eh?

'Of course,' he explained apologetically, 'at the trial they had to swear it was my mother who was mad; for I threatened to tell the truth in open court if they didn't. Otherwise I should have been hanged, you see. Only Brownrigg and Junior were left. Brownrigg was a dentist, Junior was to be a doctor, and if it had been known – But that is not the point. That is not the problem. Their mother was mad, but they were harmless. I killed Dr Lessing. I killed Martha. Yet I am quite sane. Why did I do it, all those years ago? Why? Is there no rational pattern in the scheme of things, and no answer to the bedevilled of the earth?'

The match curled to a red ember, winked and went out. Clearest of all they remembered the coarse hair that was like whitewash on the black, the eyes, and the curiously suggestive hands. Then Joseph Lessing got up from the chair. The last they saw of him was his white hat bobbing and flickering across the lawn under the blowing trees.

Markheim

ROBERT LOUIS STEVENSON

'Yes,' said the dealer, 'our windfalls are of various kinds. Some customers are ignorant, and then I touch a dividend on my superior knowledge. Some are dishonest,' and here he held up the candle, so that the light fell strongly on his visitor, 'and in that case,' he continued, 'I profit by my virtue.'

Markheim had but just entered from the daylight streets, and his eyes had not yet grown familiar with the mingled shine and darkness in the shop. At these pointed words, and before the near presence of the flame, he blinked painfully and looked aside.

The dealer chuckled. 'You come to me on Christmas Day,' he resumed, 'when you know that I am alone in my house, put up my shutters, and make a point of refusing business. Well, you will have to pay for that; you will have to pay for my loss of time, when I should be balancing my books; you will have to pay, besides, for a kind of manner that I remark in you today very strongly. I am the essence of discretion, and ask no awkward questions; but when a customer cannot look me in the eye, he has to pay for it.' The dealer once more chuckled; and then, changing to his usual business voice, though still with a note of irony, 'You can give, as usual, a clear account of how you came into the possession of the object?' he continued. 'Still your uncle's cabinet? A remarkable collector, sir!'

And the little pale, round-shouldered dealer stood almost on tiptoe, looking over the top of his gold spectacles, and nodding his head with every mark of disbelief. Markheim returned his gaze with one of infinite pity, and a touch of horror.

'This time,' said he, 'you are in error. I have not come to sell, but to buy. I have no curios to dispose of; my uncle's cabinet is bare to the wainscot; even were it still intact, I have done well on the Stock Exchange, and should more likely add to it than otherwise, and my errand today is simplicity itself. I seek a Christmas present for a lady,' he continued, waxing more fluent as he struck into the speech he had prepared; 'and certainly I owe you every excuse for thus disturbing you upon so small a matter. But the thing was neglected yesterday; I must produce my little compliment at dinner; and, as you very well know, a rich marriage is not a thing to be neglected.'

There followed a pause, during which the dealer seemed to weigh this statement incredulously. The ticking of many clocks among the curious lumber of the shop, and the faint rushing of the cabs in a near thoroughfare, filled up the interval of silence.

'Well, sir,' said the dealer, 'be it so. You are an old customer after all; and if, as you say, you have the chance of a good marriage, far be it from me to be an obstacle. Here is a nice thing for a lady now,' he went on, 'this hand-glass – fifteenth century, warranted; comes from a good collection, too; but I reserve the name, in the interests of my customer, who was just like yourself, my dear sir, the nephew and sole heir of a remarkable collector.'

The dealer, while he thus ran on in his dry and biting voice, had stooped to take the object from its place;

and, as he had done so, a shock had passed through Markheim, a start both of hand and foot, a sudden leap of many tumultuous passions to the face. It passed as swiftly as it came, and left no trace beyond a certain trembling of the hand that now received the glass.

'A glass,' he said hoarsely, and then paused, and repeated it more clearly. 'A glass? For Christmas? Surely not?'

'And why not?' cried the dealer. 'Why not a glass?'

Markheim was looking upon him with an indefinable expression. 'You ask me why not?' he said. 'Why, look here – look in it – look at yourself! Do you like to see it? No! nor I – nor any man.'

The little man had jumped back when Markheim had so suddenly confronted him with the mirror; but now, perceiving there was nothing worse on hand, he chuckled. 'Your future lady, sir, must be pretty hard favoured,' said he.

'I ask you,' said Markheim, 'for a Christmas present, and you give me this – this damned reminder of years, and sins and follies – this hand-conscience! Did you mean it? Had you a thought in your mind? Tell me. It will be better for you if you do. Come, tell me about yourself. I hazard a guess now, that you are in secret a very charitable man.'

The dealer looked closely at his companion. It was very odd, Markheim did not appear to be laughing; there was something in his face like an eager sparkle of hope, but nothing of mirth.

'What are you driving at?' the dealer asked.

'Not charitable?' returned the other, gloomily. 'Not charitable; not pious; not scrupulous; unloving, unbeloved; a hand to get money, a safe to keep it. Is that all? Dear God, man, is that all?'

'I will tell you what it is,' began the dealer, with some sharpness, and then broke off again into a chuckle. 'But I see this is a love match of yours, and you have been drinking the lady's health.'

'Ah!' cried Markheim, with a strange curiosity. 'Ah, have you been in love? Tell me about that.'

'I,' cried the dealer. 'I in love! I never had the time, nor have I the time today for all this nonsense. Will you take the glass?'

'Where is the hurry?' returned Markheim. 'It is very pleasant to stand here talking; and life is so short and insecure that I would not hurry away from any pleasure – no, not even from so mild a one as this. We should rather cling, cling to what little we can get, like a man at a cliff's edge. Every second is a cliff, if you think upon it – a cliff a mile high – high enough, if we fall, to dash us out of every feature of humanity. Hence it is best to talk pleasantly. Let us talk of each other; why should we wear this mask? Let us be confidential. Who knows? we might become friends.'

'I have just one word to say to you,' said the dealer. 'Either make your purchase, or walk out of my shop.'

'True, true,' said Markheim. 'Enough fooling. To business. Show me something else.'

The dealer stooped once more, this time to replace the glass upon the shelf, his thin blond hair falling over his eyes as he did so. Markheim moved a little nearer, with one hand in the pocket of his greatcoat; he drew himself up and filled his lungs; at the same time many different emotions were depicted together on his face – terror, horror, and resolve, fascination and a physical repulsion; and through a haggard lift of his upper lip, his teeth looked out.

'This, perhaps, may suit,' observed the dealer. And

then, as he began to re-arise, Markheim bounded from behind upon his victim. The long, skewer-like dagger flashed and fell. The dealer struggled like a hen, striking his temple on the shelf, and then tumbled on the floor in a heap.

Time had some score of small voices in that shop – some stately and slow as was becoming to their great age; others garrulous and hurried. All these told out the seconds in an intricate chorus of tickings. Then the passage of a lad's feet, heavily running on the pavement, broke in upon these smaller voices and startled Markheim into the consciousness of his surroundings. He looked about him awfully. The candle stood on the counter, its flame solemnly wagging in a draught; and by that inconsiderable movement the whole room was filled with noiseless bustle and kept heaving like a sea: the tall shadows nodding, the gross blots of darkness swelling and dwindling as with respiration, the faces of the portraits and the china gods changing and wavering like images in water. The inner door stood ajar, and peered into that leaguer of shadows with a long slit of daylight like a pointing finger.

From these fear-stricken rovings, Markheim's eyes returned to the body of his victim, where it lay, both humped and sprawling, incredibly small and strangely meaner than in life. In these poor, miserly clothes, in that ungainly attitude, the dealer lay like so much sawdust. Markheim had feared to see it, and, lo! it was nothing. And yet, as he gazed, this bundle of old clothes and pool of blood began to find eloquent voices. There it must lie; there was none to work the cunning hinges or direct the miracle of locomotion; there it must lie till it was found. Found! ay, and then? Then would this dead flesh lift up a cry that would ring over England, and fill the world with the echoes of pursuit. Ay, dead or not, this was still the enemy. 'Time was that when the brains were out,' he thought; and the first word struck into his mind. Time, now that the deed was accomplished – time, which had closed for the victim, had become instant and momentous for the slayer.

The thought was yet in his mind, when, first one and then another, with every variety of pace and voice – one deep as the bell from a cathedral turret, another ringing on its treble notes the prelude of a waltz – the clocks began to strike the hour of three in the afternoon.

The sudden outbreak of so many tongues in that dumb chamber staggered him. He began to bestir himself, going to and fro with the candle, beleaguered by moving shadows, and startled to the soul by chance reflections. In many rich mirrors, some of home design, some from Venice or Amsterdam, he saw his face repeated and repeated, as it were an army of spies; his own eyes met and detected him; and the sound of his own steps, lightly as they fell, vexed the surrounding quiet. And still, as he continued to fill his pockets, his mind accused him with a sickening iteration, of the thousand faults of his design. He should have chosen a more quiet hour; he should have prepared an alibi; he should not have used a knife; he should have been more cautious, and only bound and gagged the dealer, and not killed him; he should have been more bold, and killed the servant also; he should have done all things otherwise. Poignant regrets, weary, incessant toiling of the mind to change what was unchangeable, to plan what was now useless, to be the architect of the irrevocable past. Meanwhile, and behind all this activity, brute terrors, like the scurrying of rats in a deserted attic, filled the more remote chambers of his brain with riot; the hand of the constable would fall heavy on his shoulder, and his nerves would jerk like a hooked fish; or he beheld, in galloping defile, the dock, the prison, the gallows, and the black coffin.

Terror of the people in the street sat down before his mind like a besieging army. It was impossible, he thought, but that some rumour of the struggle must have reached their ears and set on edge their curiosity; and now, in all the neighbouring houses, he divined them sitting motionless and with uplifted ear – solitary people, condemned to spend Christmas dwelling alone on memories of the past, and now startingly recalled from that tender exercise; happy family parties struck into silence round the table, the mother still with raised finger – every degree and age and humour, but all, by their own hearths, prying and hearkening and weaving the rope that was to hang him. Sometimes it seemed to him he could not move too softly; the clink of the tall Bohemian goblets rang out loudly like a bell; and alarmed by the bigness of the ticking, he was tempted to stop the clocks. And then, again, with a swift transition of his terrors, the very silence of the place appeared a source of peril, and a thing to strike and freeze the passer-by; and he would step more boldly, and bustle aloud among the contents of the shop, and imitate, with elaborate bravado, the movements of a busy man at ease in his own house.

But he was now so pulled about by different alarms that, while one portion of his mind was still alert and cunning, another trembled on the brink of lunacy.

One hallucination in particular took a strong hold on his credulity. The neighbour hearkening with white face beside his window, the passer-by arrested by a horrible surmise on the pavement – these could at worst suspect, they could not know; through the brick walls and shuttered windows only sounds could penetrate. But here, within the house, was he alone? He knew he was; he had watched the servant set forth sweet-hearting, in her poor best, 'out for the day' written in every ribbon and smile. Yes, he was alone, of course; and yet, in the bulk of empty house above him, he could surely hear a stir of delicate footing; he was surely conscious, inexplicably conscious of some presence. Ay, surely; to every room and corner of the house his imagination followed it; and now it was a faceless thing, and yet had eyes to see with; and again it was a shadow of himself; and yet again behold the image of the dead dealer, re-inspired with cunning and hatred.

At times, with a strong effort, he would glance at the open door which still seemed to repel his eyes. The house was tall, the skylight small and dirty, the day blind with fog; and the light that filtered down to the ground storey was exceedingly faint, and showed dimly on the threshold of the shop. And yet, in that strip of doubtful brightness, did there not hang wavering a shadow?

Suddenly, from the street outside, a very jovial gentleman began to beat with a staff on the shop door, accompanying his blows with shouts and railleries in which the dealer was continually called upon by name. Markheim, smitten into ice, glanced at the dead man. But no! he lay quite still; he was fled away far beyond earshot of these blows and shoutings;

he was sunk beneath seas of silence; and his name, which would once have caught his notice above the howling of a storm, had become an empty sound. And presently the jovial gentleman desisted from his knocking and departed.

Here was a broad hint to hurry what remained to be done, to get forth from this accusing neighbour- hood, to plunge into a bath of London multitudes, and to reach, on the other side of day, that haven of safety and apparent innocence – his bed. One visitor had come; at any moment another might follow and be more obstinate. To have done the deed, and yet not to reap the profit, would be too abhorrent a failure. The money – that was now Markheim's concern; and as a means to that, the keys.

He glanced over his shoulder at the open door, where the shadow was still lingering and shivering; and with no conscious repugnance of the mind, yet with a tremor of the belly, he drew near the body of his victim. The human character had quite departed. Like a suit half stuffed with bran, the limbs lay scattered, the trunk doubled, on the floor; and yet the thing repelled him. Although so dingy and in- considerable to the eye, he feared it might have more significance to the touch. He took the body by the shoulders, and turned it on its back. It was strangely light and supple, and the limbs, as if they had been broken, fell into the oddest postures. The face was robbed of all expression; but it was as pale as wax, and shockingly smeared with blood about one temple. That was, for Markheim, the one displeasing circum- stance. It carried him back, upon the instant, to a certain fair-day in a fishers' village: a grey day, a piping wind, a crowd upon the street, the blare of brasses, the booming of drums, the nasal voice of a ballad singer; and a boy going to and fro, buried overhead in the crowd and divided between interest and fear, until, coming out upon the chief place of concourse, he beheld a booth and a great screen with pictures, dismally designed, garishly coloured – Brownrigg with her apprentice, the Mannings with their murdered guest, Weare in the death-grip of Thurtell, and a score besides of famous crimes. The thing was as clear as an illusion; he was once again that little boy; he was looking once again, and with the same sense of physical revolt, at these vile pictures; he was still stunned by the thumping of the drums. A bar of that day's music returned upon his memory; and at that, for the first time, a qualm came over him, a breath of nausea, a sudden weakness of the joints, which he must instantly resist and conquer.

He judged it more prudent to confront than to flee from these considerations, looking the more hardily in the dead face, bending his mind to realise the nature and greatness of his crime. So little a while ago that face had moved with every change of sentiment, that pale mouth had spoken, that body had been all on fire with governable energies; and now, and by his act, that piece of life had been arrested, as the horologist, with interjected finger, arrests the beating of the clock. So he reasoned in vain; he could rise to no more remorseful consciousness; the same heart which had shuddered before the painted effigies of crime, looked on its reality unmoved. At best, he felt a gleam of pity for one who had been endowed in vain with all those faculties that can make the world a garden of enchantment, one who had never lived and who was now dead. But of penitence, no, not a tremor.

With that, shaking himself clear of these considerations, he found the keys and advanced toward the open door of the shop. Outside, it had begun to rain smartly, and the sound of the shower upon the roof had banished silence. Like some dripping cavern, the chambers of the house were haunted by an incessant echoing, which filled the ear and mingled with the ticking of the clocks. And, as Markheim approached the door, he seemed to hear, in answer to his own cautious tread, the steps of another foot withdrawing up the stair. The shadow still palpitated loosely on the threshold. He threw a ton's weight of resolve upon his muscles, and drew back the door.

The faint, foggy daylight glimmered dimly on the bare floor and stairs; on the bright suit of armour posted, halbert in hand, upon the landing; and on the dark wood-carvings, and framed pictures that hung against the yellow panels of the wainscot. So loud was the beating of the rain through all the house that, in Markheim's ears, it began to be distinguished into many different sounds. Footsteps and sighs, the tread of regiments marching in the distance, the chink of money in the counting, and the creaking of doors held stealthily ajar, appeared to mingle with the patter of the drops upon the cupola and the gushing of the water in the pipes. The sense that he was not alone grew upon him to the verge of madness. On every side he was haunted and begirt by presences. He heard them moving in the upper chambers; from the shop, he heard the dead man getting to his legs; and as he began with a great effort to mount the stairs, feet fled quietly before him and followed stealthily behind. If he were but deaf, he thought, how tranquilly he would possess his soul! And then again, and hearkening with ever fresh attention, he blessed himself for that unresting sense which held the outposts and stood a trusty sentinel upon his life. His head turned continually on his neck; his eyes, which seemed starting from their orbits, scouted on every side, and on every side were half rewarded as with the tail of something nameless vanishing. The four and twenty steps to the first floor were four and twenty agonies.

On that first storey, the doors stood ajar – three of them, like three ambushes, shaking his nerves like the throats of cannon. He could never again, he felt, be sufficiently immured and fortified from men's observing eyes; he longed to be home, girt in by walls, buried among bedclothes, and invisible to all but God. And at that thought he wondered a little, recollecting tales of other murderers and the fear they were said to entertain of heavenly avengers. It was not so, at least, with him. He feared the laws of nature, lest, in their callous and immutable procedure, they should preserve some damning evidence of his crime. He feared tenfold more, with a slavish, superstitious terror, some scission in the continuity of man's experience, some wilful illegality of nature. He played a game of skill, depending on the rules, calculating consequence from cause; and what if nature, as the defeated tyrant overthrew the chessboard, should break the mould of their succession? The like had befallen Napoleon (so writers said) when the winter changed the time of its appearance. The like might befall Markheim: the solid walls might become transparent and reveal his doings like those of bees in a glass hive; the stout planks might yield under his foot like quicksands and detain him in their clutch. Ay, and there were soberer accidents that might destroy him; if, for instance, the house should fall and imprison him beside the body of his victim, or the house next door should fly on fire, and the firemen invade him from all sides. These things he feared; and, in a sense, these things might be called the hands of God reached forth against sin. But about God himself he was at ease; his act was doubtless exceptional, but so were his excuses, which God knew; it was there, and not among men, that he felt sure of justice.

When he had got safe into the drawing-room, and shut the door behind him, he was aware of a respite from alarms. The room was quite dismantled, uncarpeted besides, and strewn with packing-cases and incongruous furniture; several great pier-glasses, in which he beheld himself at various angles, like an actor on a stage; many pictures, framed and unframed, standing, with their faces to the wall; a fine Sheraton sideboard, a cabinet of marquetry, and a great old bed, with tapestry hangings. The windows opened to the floor; but by great good fortune the lower part of the shutters had been closed, and this concealed him from the neighbours. Here, then, Markheim drew in a packing-case before the cabinet, and began to search among the keys. It was a long business, for there were many; and it was irksome, besides; for, after all, there might be nothing in the cabinet, and time was on the wing. But the closeness of the occupation sobered him. With the tail of his eye he saw the door – even glanced at it from time to time directly, like a besieged commander pleased to verify the good estate of his defences. But in truth he was at peace. The rain falling in the street sounded natural and pleasant. Presently, on the other side, the notes of a piano were wakened to the music of a hymn, and the voices of many children took up the air and words. How stately, how comfortable was the melody! How fresh the youthful voices! Markheim gave ear to it smilingly, as he sorted out the keys; and his mind was thronged with answerable ideas and images: church-going children, and the pealing of the high organ; children afield, bathers by the brook-side, ramblers on the brambly common, kite-flyers in the windy and cloud-navigated sky; and then, at another cadence of the hymn, back again to church, and the somnolence of summer Sundays, and the high genteel voice of the parson (which he smiled a little to recall) and the painted Jacobean tombs, and the dim lettering of the Ten Commandments in the chancel.

And as he sat thus, at once busy and absent, he was startled to his feet. A flash of ice, a flash of fire, a bursting gush of blood, went over him, and then he stood transfixed and thrilling. A step mounted the stair slowly and steadily, and presently a hand was laid upon the knob, and the lock clicked, and the door opened.

Fear held Markheim in a vice. What to expect he knew not – whether the dead man walking, or the official ministers of human justice, or some chance witness blindly stumbling in to consign him to the gallows. But when a face was thrust into the aperture, glanced round the room, looked at him, nodded and smiled as if in friendly recognition, and then withdrew again, and the door closed behind it, his fear broke loose from his control in a hoarse cry. At the sound of this the visitant returned.

'Did you call me?' he asked, pleasantly, and with that he entered the room and closed the door behind him.

Markheim stood and gazed at him with all his eyes. Perhaps there was a film upon his sight, but the outlines of the newcomer seemed to change and waver like those of the idols in the wavering candlelight of the shop; and at times he thought he knew him; and at times he thought he bore a likeness to himself; and always, like a lump of living terror, there lay in his bosom the conviction that this thing was not of the earth and not of God.

And yet the creature had a strange air of the commonplace, as he stood looking on Markheim with a smile; and when he added, 'You are looking for the money, I believe?' it was in the tones of everyday politeness.

Markheim made no answer.

'I should warn you,' resumed the other, 'that the maid has left her sweetheart earlier than usual and will soon be here. If Mr Markheim be found in this house, I need not describe to him the consequences.'

'You know me?' cried the murderer.

The visitor smiled. 'You have long been a favourite of mine,' he said; 'and I have long observed and often sought to help you.'

'What are you?' cried Markheim; 'the devil?'

'What I may be,' returned the other, 'cannot affect the service I propose to render you.'

'It can,' cried Markheim; 'it does! Be helped by you? No, never; not by you! You do not know me yet; thank God, you do not know me!'

'I know you,' replied the visitant, with a sort of kind severity or rather firmness. 'I know you to the soul.'

'Know me!' cried Markheim. 'Who can do so? My life is but a travesty and slander on myself. I have lived to belie my nature. All men do; all men are better than this disguise that grows about and stifles them. You see each dragged away by life, like one whom braves have seized and muffled in a cloak. If they had their own control – if you could see their faces, they would be altogether different, they would shine out for heroes and saints! I am worse than most; myself is more overlaid; my excuse is known to me and God. But, had I the time, I could disclose myself.'

'To me?' enquired the visitant.

'To you before all,' returned the murderer. 'I supposed you were intelligent. I thought – since you exist – you would prove a reader of the heart. And yet you would propose to judge me by my acts! Think of it – my acts! I was born and I have lived in a land of giants; giants have dragged me by the wrists since I was born out of my mother – the giants of circumstance. And you would judge me by my acts! But can you not look within? Can you not understand that evil is hateful to me? Can you not see within me the clear writing of conscience, never blurred by any wilful sophistry, although too often disregarded? Can you not read me for a thing that surely must be common as humanity – the unwilling sinner?'

'All this is very feelingly expressed,' was the reply, 'but it regards me not. These points of consistency are beyond my province, and I care not in the least by what compulsion you may have been dragged away, so as you are but carried in the right direction. But time flies; the servant delays, looking in the faces of the crowd and at the pictures on the hoardings, but still she keeps moving nearer; and remember, it is as if the gallows itself was striding towards you through the Christmas streets! Shall I help you – I, who know all? Shall I tell you where to find the money?'

'For what price?' asked Markheim.

'I offer you the service for a Christmas gift,' returned the other.

Markheim could not refrain from smiling with a kind of bitter triumph. 'No,' said he, 'I will take nothing at your hands; if I were dying of thirst, and it was your hand that put the pitcher to my lips, I should find the courage to refuse. It may be credulous, but I will do nothing to commit myself to evil.'

'I have no objection to a deathbed repentance,' observed the visitant.

'Because you disbelieve their efficacy!' Markheim cried.

'I do not say so,' returned the other; 'but I look on these things from a different side, and when the life is done my interest falls. The man has lived to serve me, to spread black looks under colour of religion, or to sow tares in the wheat-field, as you do, in a course of weak compliance with desire. Now that he draws so near to his deliverance, he can add but one act of service: to repent, to die smiling, and thus to build up in confidence and hope the more timorous of my surviving followers. I am not so hard a master. Try me; accept my help. Please yourself in life as you have done hitherto; please yourself more amply, spread your elbows at the board; and when the night begins to fall and the curtains to be drawn, I tell you, for your greater comfort, that you will find it even easy to compound your quarrel with your conscience, and to make a truckling peace with God. I came but now from such a deathbed, and the room was full of sincere mourners, listening to the man's last words; and when I looked into that face, which had been set as a flint against mercy, I found it smiling with hope.'

'And do you, then, suppose me such a creature?' asked Markheim. 'Do you think I have no more generous aspirations than to sin, and sin, and sin, and at last sneak into heaven? My heart rises at the thought. Is this, then, your experience of mankind? or is it because you find me with red hands that you presume such baseness? And is this crime of murder indeed so impious as to dry up the very springs of good?'

'Murder is to me no special category,' replied the other. 'All sins are murder, even as all life is war. I behold your race, like starving mariners on a raft, plucking crusts out of the hands of famine and feeding on each other's lives. I follow sins beyond the moment of their acting; I find in all that the last consequence is death, and to my eyes, the pretty maid who thwarts her mother with such taking graces on a question of a ball, drips no less visibly with human gore than such a murderer as yourself. Do I say that I follow sins? I follow virtues also. They differ not by the thickness of a nail; they are both scythes for the reaping angel of Death. Evil, for which I live, consists not in action but in character. The bad man is dear to me, not the bad act, whose fruits, if we could follow them far enough down the hurtling cataract of the ages, might yet be found more blessed than those of the rarest virtues. And it is not because you have killed a dealer, but because you are Markheim, that I offer to forward your escape.'

'I will lay my heart open to you,' answered Markheim. 'This crime on which you find me is my last. On my way to it I have learned many lessons; itself is a lesson – a momentous lesson. Hitherto I have been driven with revolt to what I would not; I was a bondslave to poverty, driven and scourged. There are robust virtues that can stand in these temptations; mine was not so; I had a thirst of pleasure. But today, and out of this deed, I pluck both warning and riches – both the power and a fresh resolve to be myself. I become in all things a free actor in the world; I begin to see myself all changed, these hands the agents of good, this heart at peace. Something comes over me out of the past – something of what I have dreamed on Sabbath evenings to the sound of the church organ, of what I forecast when I shed tears over noble books, or talked, an innocent child, with my mother. There lies my life; I have wandered a few years, but now I see once more my city of destination.'

'You are to use this money on the Stock Exchange, I think?' remarked the visitor; 'and there, if I mistake not, you have already lost some thousands?'

'Ah,' said Markheim, 'but this time I have a sure thing.'

'This time, again, you will lose,' replied the visitor quietly.

'Ah, but I keep back the half!' cried Markheim.

'That also you will lose,' said the other.

The sweat started upon Markheim's brow. 'Well then, what matter?' he exclaimed. 'Say it be lost, say I am plunged again in poverty, shall one part of me, and that the worse, continue until the end to override the better? Evil and good run strong in me, hailing me both ways. I do not love the one thing; I love all. I can conceive great deeds, renunciations, martyrdoms; and though I be fallen to such a crime as murder, pity is no stranger to my thoughts. I pity the poor; who knows their trials better than myself? I pity and help them. I prize love; I love honest laughter; there is no good thing nor true thing on earth but I love it from my heart. And are my vices only to direct my life, and my virtues to lie without effect, like some passive lumber of the mind? Not so; good, also, is a spring of acts.'

But the visitant raised his finger. 'For six and thirty years that you have been in this world,' said he, 'through many changes of fortune and varieties of humour, I have watched you steadily fall. Fifteen years ago you would have started at a theft. Three years back you would have blenched at the name of murder. Is there any crime, is there any cruelty or meanness, from which you still recoil? Five years from now I shall detect you in the fact! Downward, downward, lies your way; nor can anything but death avail to stop you.'

'It is true,' Markheim said huskily, 'I have in some degree complied with evil. But it is so with all; the very saints, in the mere exercise of living, grow less dainty, and take on the tone of their surroundings.'

'I will propound to you one simple question,' said the other; 'and as you answer I shall read to you your moral horoscope. You have grown in many things more lax; possibly you do right to be so; and at any account, it is the same with all men. But granting that, are you in any one particular, however trifling, more difficult to please with your own conduct, or do you go in all things with a looser rein?'

'In any one?' repeated Markheim, with an anguish of consideration. 'No,' he added, with despair; 'in none! I have gone down in all.'

'Then,' said the visitor, 'content yourself with what you are, for you will never change; and the words of your part on this stage are irrevocably written down.'

Markheim stood for a long while silent, and, indeed, it was the visitor who first broke the silence. 'That being so,' he said, 'shall I show you the money?'

'And grace?' cried Markheim.

'Have you not tried it?' returned the other. 'Two or three years ago did I not see you on the platform of revival meetings, and was not your voice the loudest in the hymn?'

'It is true,' said Markheim; 'and I see clearly what remains for me by way of duty. I thank you for these lessons from my soul; my eyes are opened, and I behold myself at last for what I am.'

At this moment, the sharp note of the doorbell rang through the house; and the visitant, as though this were some concerted signal for which he had been waiting, changed at once in his demeanour.

'The maid!' he cried. 'She has returned, as I fore-warned you, and there is now before you one more difficult passage. Her master, you must say, is ill; you must let her in, with an assured but rather serious countenance; no smiles, no overacting, and I promise you success! Once the girl is within, and the door closed, the same dexterity that has already rid you of the dealer will relieve you of this last danger in your path. Thenceforward you have the whole evening – the whole night, if needful – to ransack the treasures of the house and to make good your safety. This is help that comes to you with the mask of danger. Up!'

he cried; 'up, friend. Your life hangs trembling in the scales; up, and act!'

Markheim steadily regarded his counsellor. 'If I be condemned to evil acts,' he said, 'there is still one door of freedom open: I can cease from action. If my life be an ill thing, I can lay it down. Though I be, as you say truly, at the beck of every small temptation, I can yet, by one decisive gesture, place myself beyond the reach of all. My love of good is damned to barrenness; it may, and let it be! But I have still my hatred of evil; and from that, to your galling disappointment, you shall see that I can draw both energy and courage.'

The features of the visitor began to undergo a wonderful and lovely change: they brightened and softened with a tender triumph, and, even as they brightened, faded and dislimned. But Markheim did not pause to watch or understand the transformation. He opened the door and went downstairs very slowly, thinking to himself. His past went soberly before him; he beheld it as it was, ugly and strenuous like a dream, random as chance medley – a scene of defeat. Life, as he thus reviewed it, tempted him no longer; but on the further side he perceived a quiet haven for his bark. He paused in the passage, and looked into the shop, where the candle still burned by the dead body. It was strangely silent. Thoughts of the dealer swarmed into his mind, as he stood gazing. And then the bell once more broke out into impatient clamour.

He confronted the maid upon the threshold with something like a smile.

'You had better go for the police,' said he; 'I have killed your master.'

Bournemouth, 1884

The Man with the Twisted Lip

SIR ARTHUR CONAN DOYLE

Isa Whitney, brother of the late Elias Whitney, DD, Principal of the Theological College of St George's, was much addicted to opium. The habit grew upon him, as I understand, from some foolish freak when he was at college; for having read De Quincey's description of his dreams and sensations, he had drenched his tobacco with laudanum in an attempt to produce the same effects. He found, as so many more have done, that the practice is easier to attain than to get rid of, and for many years he continued to be a slave to the drug, an object of mingled horror and pity to his friends and relatives. I can see him now, with yellow, pasty face, drooping lids and pin-point pupils, all huddled in a chair, the wreck and ruin of a noble man.

One night – it was in June 1889 – there came a ring to my bell, about the hour when a man gives his first yawn and glances at the clock. I sat up in my chair, and my wife laid her needlework down in her lap and made a little face of disappointment.

'A patient!' said she. 'You'll have to go out.'

I groaned, for I was newly come back from a weary day.

We heard the door open, a few hurried words, and then quick steps upon the linoleum. Our own door flew open, and a lady, clad in some dark-coloured stuff, with a black veil, entered the room.

'You will excuse my calling so late,' she began, and then, suddenly losing her self-control, she ran forward, threw her arms about my wife's neck, and sobbed upon her shoulder. 'Oh, I'm in such trouble!' she cried; 'I do so want a little help.'

'Why,' said my wife, pulling up her veil, 'it is Kate Whitney. How you startled me, Kate! I had not an idea who you were when you came in.'

'I didn't know what to do, so I came straight to you.' That was always the way. Folk who were in grief came to my wife like birds to a lighthouse.

'It was very sweet of you to come. Now, you must have some wine and water, and sit here comfortably and tell us all about it. Or should you rather that I sent James off to bed?'

'Oh, no, no! I want the doctor's advice and help, too. It's about Isa. He has not been home for two days. I am so frightened about him!'

It was not the first time that she had spoken to us of her husband's trouble, to me as a doctor, to my wife as an old friend and school companion. We soothed and comforted her by such words as we could find. Did she know where her husband was? Was it possible that we could bring him back to her?

It seems that it was. She had the surest information that of late he had, when the fit was on him, made use of an opium den in the farthest east of the City. Hitherto his orgies had always been confined to one day, and he had come back, twitching and shattered, in the evening. But now the spell had been upon him eight-and-forty hours, and he lay there, doubtless among the dregs of the docks, breathing in the poison or sleeping off the effects. There he was to be found, she was sure of it, at the Bar of Gold in Upper

Swandam Lane. But what was she to do? How could she, a young and timid woman, make her way into such a place and pluck her husband out from among the ruffians who surrounded him?

There was the case, and of course there was but one way out of it. Might I not escort her to this place? And then, as a second thought, why should she come at all? I was Isa Whitney's medical adviser, and as such I had influence over him. I could manage it better if I were alone. I promised her on my word that I would send him home in a cab within two hours if he were indeed at the address which she had given me. And so in ten minutes I had left my armchair and cheery sitting-room behind me, and was speeding eastward in a hansom on a strange errand, as it seemed to me at the time, though the future only could show how strange it was to be.

But there was no great difficulty in the first stage of my adventure. Upper Swandam Lane is a vile alley lurking behind the high wharves which line the north side of the river to the east of London Bridge. Between a slop-shop and a gin-shop, approached by a steep flight of steps leading down to a black gap like the mouth of a cave, I found the den of which I was in search. Ordering my cab to wait, I passed down the steps, worn hollow in the centre by the ceaseless tread of drunken feet, and by the light of a flickering oil-lamp above the door I found the latch and made my way into a long, low room, thick and heavy with the brown opium smoke and terraced with wooden berths, like the forecastle of an emigrant ship.

Through the gloom one could dimly catch a glimpse of bodies lying in strange fantastic poses, bowed shoulders, bent knees, heads thrown back, and chins pointing upward, with here and there a dark, lack-lustre eye turned upon the newcomer. Out of the black shadows there glimmered little red circles of light, now bright, now faint, as the burning poison waxed or waned in the bowls of the metal pipes. The most lay silent, but some muttered to themselves, and others talked together in strange, low, monotonous voices, their conversation coming in gushes and then suddenly tailing off into silence, each mumbling out his own thoughts and paying little heed to the words of his neighbour. At the farther end was a small brazier of burning charcoal, beside which on a three-legged wooden stool there sat a tall, thin old man, with his jaw resting upon his two fists and his elbows upon his knees, staring into the fire.

As I entered, a sallow Malay attendant had hurried up with a pipe for me and a supply of the drug, beckoning me to an empty berth.

'Thank you. I have not come to stay,' said I. 'There is a friend of mine here, Mr Isa Whitney, and I wish to speak with him.'

There was a movement and an exclamation from my right, and peering through the gloom, I saw Whitney, pale, haggard and unkempt, staring out at me.

'My God! It's Watson,' said he. He was in a pitiable state of reaction, with every nerve in a twitter. 'I say, Watson, what o'clock is it?'

'Nearly eleven.'

'Of what day?'

'Of Friday, June 19th.'

'Good heavens! I thought it was Wednesday. It *is* Wednesday. What d'you want to frighten a chap for?' He sank his face on to his arms and began to sob in a high treble key.

'I tell you that it is Friday, man. Your wife has been waiting these two days for you. You should be ashamed of yourself!'

'So I am. But you've got mixed, Watson, for I have only been here a few hours, three pipes, four pipes – I forget how many. But I'll go home with you. I wouldn't frighten Kate – poor little Kate. Give me your hand! Have you a cab?'

'Yes, I have one waiting.'

'Then I shall go in it. But I must owe something. Find what I owe, Watson. I am all off colour. I can do nothing for myself.'

I walked down the narrow passage between the double row of sleepers, holding my breath to keep out the vile, stupefying fumes of the drug, and looking about for the manager. As I passed the tall man who sat by the brazier I felt a sudden pluck at my skirt, and a low voice whispered, 'Walk past me, and then look back at me.' The words fell quite distinctly upon my ear. I glanced down. They could only have come from the old man at my side, and yet he sat now as absorbed as ever, very thin, very wrinkled, bent with age, an opium pipe dangling down from between his knees, as though it had dropped in sheer lassitude from his fingers. I took two steps forward and looked back. It took all my self-control to prevent me from breaking out into a cry of astonishment. He had turned his back so that none could see him but I. His form had filled out, his wrinkles were gone, the dull eyes had regained their fire, and there, sitting by the fire and grinning at my surprise, was none other than Sherlock Holmes. He made a slight motion to me to approach him, and instantly, as he turned his face half round to the company once more, subsided into a doddering, loose-lipped senility.

'Holmes!' I whispered, 'what on earth are you doing in this den?'

'As low as you can,' he answered; 'I have excellent ears. If you would have the great kindness to get rid of that sottish friend of yours, I should be exceedingly glad to have a little talk with you.'

'I have a cab outside.'

'Then pray send him home in it. You may safely trust him, for he appears to be too limp to get into any mischief. I should recommend you also to send a note by the cabman to your wife to say that you have thrown in your lot with me. If you will wait outside, I shall be with you in five minutes.'

It was difficult to refuse any of Sherlock Holmes's requests, for they were always so exceedingly definite and put forward with such a quiet air of mastery. I felt, however, that when Whitney was once confined in the cab my mission was practically accomplished; and for the rest, I could not wish anything better than to be associated with my friend in one of those singular adventures which were the normal condition of his existence. In a few minutes I had written my note, paid Whitney's bill, led him out to the cab and seen him driven through the darkness. In a very short time a decrepit figure had emerged from the opium den and I was walking down the street with Sherlock Holmes. For two streets he shuffled along with a bent back and an uncertain foot. Then, glancing quickly round, he straightened himself out and burst into a hearty fit of laughter.

'I suppose, Watson,' said he, 'that you imagine that I have added opium-smoking to cocaine injections and all the other little weaknesses on which you have favoured me with your medical views.'

'I was certainly surprised to find you there.'

'But not more so than I to find you.'

'I came to find a friend.'

'And I to find an enemy.'

'An enemy?'

'Yes; one of my natural enemies, or, shall I say, my natural prey. Briefly, Watson, I am in the midst of a very remarkable inquiry, and I had hoped to find a clue in the incoherent ramblings of these sots, as I have done before now. Had I been recognised in that den my life would not have been worth an hour's purchase, for I have used it before now for my own purposes, and the rascally Lascar who runs it has sworn to have vengeance upon me. There is a trap-door at the back of that building, near the corner of Paul's Wharf, which could tell some strange tales of what has passed through it upon moonless nights.'

'What! You do not mean bodies?'

'Ay, bodies, Watson. We should be rich men if we had a thousand pounds for every poor devil who has been done to death in that den. It is the vilest murder-trap on the whole riverside, and I fear that Neville St Clair has entered it never to leave it more. But our trap should be here.' He put his two forefingers between his teeth and whistled shrilly – a signal which was answered by a similar whistle from the distance, followed shortly by the rattle of wheels and the clink of horses' hoofs.

'Now, Watson,' said Holmes, as a tall dogcart dashed up through the gloom, throwing out two golden tunnels of yellow light from its side lanterns, 'you'll come with me, won't you?'

'If I can be of use.'

'Oh, a trusty comrade is always of use; and a chronicler still more so. My room at The Cedars is a double-bedded one.'

'The Cedars?'

'Yes; that is Mr St Clair's house. I am staying there while I conduct the inquiry.'

'Where is it, then?'

'Near Lee, in Kent. We have a seven-mile drive before us.'

'But I am all in the dark.'

'Of course you are. You'll know all about it presently. Jump up here. All right, John; we shall not need you. Here's half a crown. Look out for me tomorrow, about eleven. Give her her head. So long, then!'

He flicked the horse with his whip, and we dashed away through the endless succession of sombre and deserted streets which widened gradually until we were flying across a broad balustraded bridge, with the murky river flowing sluggishly beneath us. Beyond lay another dull wilderness of bricks and mortar, its silence broken only by the heavy, regular footfall of the policeman or the songs and shouts of some belated party of revellers. A dull wrack was drifting slowly across the sky, and a star or two twinkled dimly here and there through the rifts of the clouds. Holmes drove in silence, with his head sunk upon his breast, and the air of a man who is lost in thought, while I sat beside him, curious to learn what this new quest might be which seemed to tax his powers so sorely and yet afraid to break in upon the current of his thoughts. We had driven several miles, and were beginning to get to the fringe of the belt of suburban villas, when he shook himself, shrugged his shoulders and lit up his pipe with the air of a man who has satisfied himself that he is acting for the best.

'You have a grand gift of silence, Watson,' said he. 'It makes you quite invaluable as a companion. 'Pon my word, it is a great thing for me to have someone to talk to, for my own thoughts are not over-pleasant. I was wondering what I should say to this dear little woman tonight when she meets me at the door.'

'You forget that I know nothing about it.'

'I shall just have time to tell you the facts of the case before we get to Lee. It seems absurdly simple, and yet somehow I can get nothing to go upon. There's plenty of thread, no doubt, but I can't get the end of it in my hand. Now, I'll state the case clearly and concisely to you, Watson, and maybe you can see a spark where all is dark to me.'

'Proceed, then.'

'Some years ago – to be definite, in May 1884 – there came to Lee a gentleman, Neville St Clair by name, who appeared to have plenty of money. He took a large villa, laid out the grounds very nicely, and lived generally in good style. By degrees he made friends in the neighbourhood, and in 1887 he married the daughter of a local brewer, by whom he now has two children. He had no occupation, but was interested in several companies and went into town as a rule in the morning, returning by the 5.14 from Cannon Street every night. Mr St Clair, who is now thirty-seven years of age, is a man of temperate habits, a good husband, a very affectionate father and a man who is popular with all who know him. I may add that his whole debts at the present moment, as far as we have been able to ascertain, amount to £88 10s., while he has £220 standing to his credit in the Capital and Counties Bank. There is no reason, therefore, to think that money troubles have been weighing upon his mind.

'Last Monday, Mr Neville St Clair went into town rather earlier than usual, remarking before he started that he had two important commissions to perform, and that he would bring his little boy home a box of bricks. Now, by the merest chance, his wife received a telegram upon this same Monday, very shortly after his departure, to the effect that a small parcel of considerable value which she had been expecting was waiting for her at the offices of the Aberdeen Shipping Company. Now, if you are well up in your London, you will know that the office of the company is in Fresno Street, which branches out of Upper Swandam Lane, where you found me tonight. Mrs St Clair had her lunch, started for the City, did some shopping, proceeded to the company's office, got her packet, and found herself at exactly 4.35 walking through Swandam Lane on her way back to the station. Have you followed me so far?'

'It is very clear.'

'If you remember, Monday was an exceedingly hot day, and Mrs St Clair walked slowly, glancing about in the hope of seeing a cab, as she did not like the neighbourhood in which she found herself. While she was walking in this way down Swandam Lane, she suddenly heard an ejaculation or cry, and was struck cold to see her husband looking down at her and, as it seemed to her, beckoning to her from a second-floor window. The window was open, and she distinctly saw his face, which she describes as being terribly agitated. He waved his hands frantically to her, and then vanished from the window so suddenly that it seemed to her that he had been plucked back by some irresistible force from behind. One singular point which struck her quick feminine eye was that although he wore some dark coat, such as he had started to town in, he had on neither collar nor necktie.

'Convinced that something was amiss with him, she rushed down the steps – for the house was none other than the opium den in which you found me tonight – and running through the front room she attempted to ascend the stairs which led to the first floor. At the foot of the stairs, however, she met this Lascar scoundrel of whom I have spoken, who thrust her back and, aided by a Dane, who acts as assistant there, pushed her out into the street. Filled with the most maddening doubts and fears, she rushed down the lane and, by rare good-fortune, met in Fresno Street a number of constables with an inspector, all on their way to their beat. The inspector and two men accompanied her back, and in spite of the continued resistance of the proprietor, they made their way to the room in which Mr St Clair had last been seen. There was no sign of him there. In fact, in the whole of that floor there was no one to be found save a crippled wretch of hideous aspect, who, it seems, made his home there. Both he and the Lascar stoutly swore that no one else had been in the front room during the afternoon. So determined was their denial that the inspector was staggered, and had almost come to believe that Mrs St Clair had been deluded when, with a cry, she sprang at a small deal box which lay upon the table and tore the lid from it. Out there fell a cascade of children's bricks. It was the toy which he had promised to bring home.

'This discovery, and the evident confusion which

the cripple showed, made the inspector realise that the matter was serious. The rooms were carefully examined, and results all pointed to an abominable crime. The front room was plainly furnished as a sitting-room, and led into a small bedroom, which looked out upon the back of one of the wharves. Between the wharf and the bedroom window is a narrow strip, which is dry at low tide but is covered at high tide with at least four and a half feet of water. The bedroom window was a broad one and opened from below. On examination traces of blood were to be seen upon the windowsill, and several scattered drops were visible upon the wooden floor of the bedroom. Thrust away behind a curtain in the front room were all the clothes of Mr Neville St Clair, with the exception of his coat. His boots, his socks, his hat, and his watch – all were there. There were no signs of violence upon any of these garments, and there were no other traces of Mr Neville St Clair. Out of the window he must apparently have gone for no other exit could be discovered, and the ominous bloodstains upon the sill gave little promise that he could save himself by swimming, for the tide was at its very highest at the moment of the tragedy.

'And now as to the villains who seemed to be immediately implicated in the matter. The Lascar was known to be a man of the vilest antecedents, but as, by Mrs St Clair's story, he was known to have been at the foot of the stairs within a very few seconds of her husband's appearance at the window, he could hardly have been more than an accessory to the crime. His defence was one of absolute ignorance, and he protested that he had no knowledge as to the doings of Hugh Boone, his lodger, and that he could not account in any way for the presence of the missing gentleman's clothes.

'So much for the Lascar manager. Now for the sinister cripple who lives upon the second floor of the opium den, and who was certainly the last human being whose eyes rested upon Neville St Clair. His name is Hugh Boone, and his hideous face is one which is familiar to every man who goes much to the City. He is a professional beggar, though in order to avoid the police regulations he pretends to a small trade in wax vestas. Some little distance down Threadneedle Street, upon the left-hand side, there is, as you may have remarked, a small angle in the wall. Here it is that this creature takes his daily seat, cross-legged with his tiny stock of matches on his lap, and as he is a piteous spectacle a small rain of charity descends into the greasy leather cap which lies upon the pavement beside him. I have watched the fellow more than once before ever I thought of making his professional acquaintance, and I have been surprised at the harvest which he has reaped in a short time. His appearance, you see, is so remarkable that no one can pass him without observing him. A shock of orange hair, a pale face disfigured by a horrible scar, which, by its contraction, has turned up the outer edge of his upper lip, a bulldog chin and a pair of very penetrating dark eyes, which present a singular contrast to the colour of his hair, all mark him out from amid the common crowd of mendicants and so, too, does his wit, for he is ever ready with a reply to any piece of chaff which may be thrown at him by the passers-by. This is the man whom we now learn to have been the lodger at the opium den and to have been the last man to see the gentleman of whom we are in quest.'

'But a cripple!' said I. 'What could he have done single-handed against a man in the prime of life?'

'He is a cripple in the sense that he walks with a limp; but in other respects he appears to be a powerful and well-nurtured man. Surely your medical experience would tell you, Watson, that weakness in one limb is often compensated for by exceptional strength in the others.'

'Pray continue your narrative.'

'Mrs St Clair had fainted at the sight of the blood upon the window, and she was escorted home in a cab by the police, as her presence could be of no help to them in their investigations. Inspector Barton, who had charge of the case, made a very careful examination of the premises, but without finding anything which threw any light upon the matter. One mistake had been made in not arresting Boone instantly, as he was allowed some few minutes during which he might have communicated with his friend the Lascar, but this fault was soon remedied, and he was seized and searched, without anything being found which could incriminate him. There were, it is true, some bloodstains upon his right shirt-sleeve, but he pointed to his ring-finger, which had been cut near the nail, and explained that the bleeding came from there, adding that he had been to the window not long before, and that the stains which had been observed there came doubtless from the same source. He denied strenuously having ever seen Mr Neville St Clair and swore that the presence of the clothes in his room was as much a mystery to him as to the police. As to Mrs St Clair's assertion that she had actually seen her husband at the window, he declared that she must have been either mad or dreaming. He was removed, loudly protesting, to the police-station, while the inspector remained upon the premises in the hope that the ebbing tide might afford some fresh clue.

'And it did, though they hardly found upon the mudbank what they had feared to find. It was Neville St Clair's coat, and not Neville St Clair, which lay uncovered as the tide receded. And what do you think they found in the pockets?'

'I cannot imagine.'

'No, I don't think you would guess. Every pocket was stuffed with pennies and halfpennies – four hundred and twenty-one pennies and two hundred and seventy halfpennies. It was no wonder that it had not been swept away by the tide. But a human body is a different matter. There is a fierce eddy between the wharf and the house. It seemed likely enough that the weighted coat had remained when the stripped body had been sucked away into the river.'

'But I understand that all the other clothes were found in the room. Would the body be dressed in a coat alone?'

'No, sir, but the facts might be met speciously enough. Suppose that this man Boone had thrust Neville St Clair through the window, there is no human eye which could have seen the deed. What would he do then? It would of course instantly strike him that he must get rid of the telltale garments. He would seize the coat, then, and be in the act of throwing it out, when it would occur to him that it would swim and not sink. He has little time, for he has heard the scuffle downstairs when the wife tried to force her way up, and perhaps he has already heard from his Lascar confederate that the police are hurrying up the street. There is not an instant to be lost. He rushes to some secret hoard, where he has accumulated the fruits of his beggary, and he stuffs all the coins upon which he can lay his hands into the pockets to make sure of the coat's sinking. He throws it out, and would have done the same with the other garments had he not heard the rush of steps below and only just had time to close the window when the police appeared.'

'It certainly sounds feasible.'

'Well, we will take it as a working hypothesis for want of a better. Boone, as I have told you, was arrested and taken to the station, but it could not be shown that there had ever before been anything against him. He had for years been known as a professional beggar, but his life appeared to have been a very quiet and innocent one. There the matter stands at present, and the questions which have to be solved – what Neville St Clair was doing in the opium den, what happened to him when there, where is he now, and what Hugh Boone had to do with his disappearance – are all as far from a solution as ever. I confess that I cannot recall any case within my experience which looked at the first glance so simple and yet which presented such difficulties.'

While Sherlock Holmes had been detailing this singular series of events we had been whirling through the outskirts of the great town until the last straggling houses had been left behind and we rattled along with a country hedge upon either side of us. Just as he finished, however, we drove through two scattered villages, where a few lights still glimmered in the windows.

'We are on the outskirts of Lee,' said my companion. 'We have touched on three English counties in our short drive, starting in Middlesex, passing over an angle of Surrey and ending in Kent. See that light among the trees? That is The Cedars, and beside that lamp sits a woman whose anxious ears have already, I have little doubt, caught the clink of our horse's feet.'

'But why are you not conducting the case from Baker Street?' I asked.

'Because there are many enquiries which must be made out here. Mrs St Clair has most kindly put two rooms at my disposal, and you may rest assured that she will have nothing but a welcome for my friend and colleague. I hate to meet her, Watson, when I have no news of her husband. Here we are. Whoa, there, whoa!'

We had pulled up in front of a large villa which stood within its own grounds. A stable-boy had run out to the horse's head, and springing down, I followed Holmes up the small, winding gravel drive which led to the house. As we approached, the door flew open, and a little blonde woman stood in the opening, clad in some sort of light *mousseline-de-soie*, with a touch of fluffy pink chiffon at her neck and wrists. She stood with her figure outlined against the flood of light, one hand upon the door, one half-raised in her eagerness, her body slightly bent, her head and face protruded, with eager eyes and parted lips, a standing question mark.

'Well?' she cried, 'well?' And then, seeing that there were two of us, she gave a cry of hope which sank into a groan as she saw that my companion shook his head and shrugged his shoulders.

'No good news?'

'None.'

'No bad?'

'No.'

'Thank God for that. But come in. You must be weary, for you have had a long day.'

'This is my friend, Dr Watson. He has been of most vital use to me in several of my cases, and a lucky chance has made it possible for me to bring him out and associate him with this investigation.'

'I am delighted to see you,' said she, pressing my hand warmly. 'You will, I am sure, forgive anything that may be wanting in our arrangements when you consider the blow which has come so suddenly upon us.'

'My dear madam,' said I, 'I am an old campaigner, and if I were not I can very well see that no apology is needed. If I can be of any assistance, either to you or to my friend here, I shall be indeed happy.'

'Now, Mr Sherlock Holmes,' said the lady as we entered a well-lit dining-room, upon the table of which a cold supper had been laid out, 'I should very much like to ask you one or two plain questions, to which I beg that you will give a plain answer.'

'Certainly, madam.'

'Do not trouble about my feelings. I am not hysterical, nor given to fainting. I simply wish to hear your real, real opinion.'

'Upon what point?'

'In your heart of hearts, do you think that Neville is alive?'

Sherlock Holmes seemed to be embarrassed by the question.

'Frankly, now!' she repeated, standing upon the rug and looking keenly down at him as he leaned back in a basket-chair.

'Frankly, then, madam, I do not.'

'You think that he is dead?'

'I do.'

'Murdered?'

'I don't say that. Perhaps.'

'And on what day did he meet his death?'

'On Monday.'

'Then perhaps, Mr Holmes, you will be good enough to explain how it is that I have received a letter from him today.'

Sherlock Holmes sprang out of his chair as if he had been galvanised.

'What!' he roared.

'Yes, today.' She stood smiling, holding up a little slip of paper in the air.

'May I see it?'

'Certainly.'

He snatched it from her in his eagerness, and smoothing it out upon the table he drew over the lamp and examined it intently. I had left my chair and was gazing at it over his shoulder. The envelope was a very coarse one and was stamped with the Gravesend postmark and with the date of that very day, or rather of the day before, for it was considerably after midnight.

'Coarse writing,' murmured Holmes. 'Surely this is not your husband's writing, madam.'

'No, but the enclosure is.'

'I perceive also that whoever addressed the envelope had to go and enquire as to the address.'

'How can you tell that?'

'The name, you see, is in perfectly black ink, which has dried itself. The rest is of the greyish colour which shows that blotting-paper has been used. If it had been written straight off, and then blotted, none would be of a deep black shade. This man has written the name, and there has then been a pause before he has written the address, which can only mean that he was not familiar with it. It is, of course, a trifle, but there is nothing so important as trifles. Let us now see the letter. Ha! there has been an enclosure here!'

'Yes, there was a ring. His signet-ring.'

'And you are sure that this is your husband's hand?'

'One of his hands.'

'One?'

'His hand when he wrote hurriedly. It is very unlike his usual writing, and yet I know it well.'

' "Dearest, do not be frightened. All will come well. There is a huge error which it may take some little time to rectify. Wait in patience – Neville." Written in pencil upon the flyleaf of a book, octavo size, no watermark. Hum! Posted today in Gravesend by a man with a dirty thumb. Ha! And the flap has been gummed, if I am not very much in error, by a person who had been chewing tobacco. And you have no doubt that it is your husband's hand, madam?'

'None. Neville wrote those words.'

'And they were posted today at Gravesend. Well, Mrs St Clair, the clouds lighten, though I should not venture to say that the danger is over.'

'But he must be alive, Mr Holmes.'

'Unless this is a clever forgery to put us on the wrong scent. The ring, after all, proves nothing. It may have been taken from him.'

'No, no; it is, it is his very own writing!'

'Very well. It may, however, have been written on Monday and only posted today.'

'That is possible.'

'If so, much may have happened between.'

'Oh, you must not discourage me, Mr Holmes. I know that all is well with him. There is so keen a sympathy between us that I should know if evil came upon him. On the very day that I saw him last he cut himself in the bedroom, and yet I in the dining-room rushed upstairs instantly with the utmost certainty that something had happened. Do you think that I would respond to such a trifle and yet be ignorant of his death?'

'I have seen too much not to know that the impression of a woman may be more valuable than the conclusion of an analytical reasoner. And in this letter you certainly have a very strong piece of evidence to corroborate your view. But if your husband is alive and able to write letters, why should he remain away from you?'

'I cannot imagine. It is unthinkable.'

'And on Monday he made no remarks before leaving you?'

'No.'

'And you were surprised to see him in Swandam Lane?'

'Very much so.'

'Was the window open?'

'Yes.'

'Then he might have called to you?'

'He might.'

'He only, as I understand, gave an inarticulate cry?'

'Yes.'

'A call for help, you thought?'

'Yes. He waved his hands.'

'But it might have been a cry of surprise. Astonishment at the unexpected sight of you might have caused him to throw up his hands?'

'It is possible.'

'And you thought he was pulled back?'

'He disappeared so suddenly.'

'He might have leaped back. You did not see any-one else in the room?'

'No, but this horrible man confessed to having been there, and the Lascar was at the foot of the stairs.'

'Quite so. Your husband, as far as you could see, had his ordinary clothes on?'

'But without his collar or tie. I distinctly saw his bare throat.'

'Had he ever spoken of Swandam Lane?'

'Never.'

'Had he ever shown any signs of having taken opium?'

'Never.'

'Thank you, Mrs St Clair. Those are the principal points about which I wished to be absolutely clear. We shall now have a little supper and then retire, for we may have a very busy day tomorrow.'

A large and comfortable double-bedded room had been placed at our disposal, and I was quickly between the sheets, for I was weary after my night of adventure. Sherlock Holmes was a man, however, who, when he had an unsolved problem upon his mind, would go for days, and even for a week, without rest, turning it over, rearranging his facts, looking at it from every point of view until he had either fathomed it or con-vinced himself that his data were insufficient. It was soon evident to me that he was now preparing for an all-night sitting. He took off his coat and waistcoat, put on a large blue dressing-gown, and then wandered about the room collecting pillows from the bed and cushions from the sofa and armchairs. With these he constructed a sort of Eastern divan, upon which he perched himself cross-legged, with an ounce of shag tobacco and a box of matches laid out in front of him. In the dim light of the lamp I saw him sitting there, an old briar pipe between his lips, his eyes fixed vacantly upon the corner of the ceiling, the blue smoke curling up from him, silent, motionless, with the light shining upon his strong-set aquiline features. So he sat as I dropped off to sleep, and so he sat when a sudden ejaculation caused me to wake up and I found the summer sun shining into the apartment. The pipe was still between his lips, the smoke still curled upwards, and the room was full of a dense tobacco haze, but nothing remained of the heap of shag which I had seen upon the previous night.

'Awake, Watson?' he asked.

'Yes.'

'Game for a morning drive?'

'Certainly.'

'Then dress. No one is stirring yet, but I know where the stable-boy sleeps, and we shall soon have the trap out.' He chuckled to himself as he spoke, his eyes twinkled, and he seemed a different man from the sombre thinker of the previous night.

As I dressed I glanced at my watch. It was no wonder that no one was stirring. It was twenty-five minutes past four. I had hardly finished when Holmes returned with the news that the boy was putting in the horse.

'I want to test a little theory of mine,' said he, pulling on his boots. 'I think, Watson, that you are now standing in the presence of one of the most absolute fools in Europe. I deserve to be kicked from here to Charing Cross. But I think I have the key of the affair now.'

'And where is it?' I asked, smiling.

'It was in the bathroom,' he answered. 'Oh, yes, I am not joking,' he continued, seeing my look of incredulity. 'I have just been there, and I have taken it out, and I have got it in this Gladstone bag. Come on, my boy, and we shall see whether it will not fit the lock.'

We made our way downstairs as quietly as possible and out into the bright morning sunshine. In the road stood our horse and trap, with the half-clad stable-boy waiting at the head. We both sprang in, and away we dashed down the London Road. A few country carts were stirring, bearing in vegetables to the metropolis, but the lines of villas on either side were as silent and lifeless as some city in a dream.

'It has been in some points a singular case,' said Holmes, flicking the horse on into a gallop. 'I confess that I have been as blind as a mole, but it is better to learn wisdom late than never to learn it at all.'

In town the earliest risers were just beginning to look sleepily from their windows as we drove through the streets of the Surrey side. Passing down the Waterloo Bridge Road we crossed over the river, and dashing up Wellington Street wheeled sharply to the right and found ourselves in Bow Street. Sherlock Holmes was well known to the force, and the two constables at the door saluted him. One of them held the horse's head while the other led us in.

'Who is on duty?' asked Holmes.

'Inspector Bradstreet, sir.'

'Ah, Bradstreet, how are you?' A tall, stout official, in a peaked cap and frogged jacket, had come down the stone-flagged passage. 'I wish to have a quiet word with you, Bradstreet.'

'Certainly, Mr Holmes. Step into my room here.' It was a small, office-like room, with a huge ledger upon the table and a telephone projecting from the wall. The inspector sat down at his desk. 'What can I do for you, Mr Holmes?'

'I called about that beggarman, Boone – the one who was charged with being concerned in the disappearance of Mr Neville St Clair of Lee.'

'Yes. He was brought up and remanded for further enquiries.'

'So I heard. You have him here?'

'In the cells.'

'Is he quiet?'

'Oh, he gives no trouble. But he is a dirty scoundrel.'

'Dirty?'

'Yes, it is all we can do to make him wash his hands, and his face is as black as a tinker's. Well, when once his case has been settled, he will have a regular prison bath; and I think, if you saw him, you would agree with me that he needed it.'

'I should like to see him very much.'

'Would you? That is easily done. Come this way. You can leave your bag.'

'No, I think that I'll take it.'

'Very good. Come this way, if you please.' He led us down a passage, opened a barred door, passed down a winding stair and brought us to a whitewashed corridor with a line of doors on each side.

'The third on the right is his,' said the inspector. 'Here it is!' He quietly shot back a panel in the upper part of the door and glanced through.

'He is asleep,' said he. 'You can see him very well.'

We both put our eyes to the grating. The prisoner lay with his face towards us in a very deep sleep, breathing slowly and heavily. He was a middle-sized man, coarsely clad as became his calling, with a coloured shirt protruding through the rent in his tattered coat. He was, as the inspector had said, extremely dirty, but the grime which covered his face could not conceal its repulsive ugliness. A broad wheal from an old scar ran right across it from eye to chin, and by its contraction had turned up one side of the upper lip, so that three teeth were exposed in a perpetual snarl. A shock of very bright red hair grew low over his eyes and forehead.

'He's a beauty, isn't he?' said the inspector.

'He certainly needs a wash,' remarked Holmes. 'I had an idea that he might, and I took the liberty of bringing the tools with me.' He opened the Gladstone bag as he spoke, and took out, to my astonishment, a very large bath-sponge.

'He! he! You are a funny one,' chuckled the inspector.

'Now, if you will have the great goodness to open that door very quietly, we will soon make him cut a much more respectable figure.'

'Well, I don't know why not,' said the inspector. 'He doesn't look a credit to the Bow Street cells, does he?' He slipped his key into the lock, and we all very quietly entered the cell. The sleeper half turned, and then settled down once more into a deep slumber. Holmes stooped to the water-jug, moistened his sponge, and then rubbed it twice vigorously across and down the prisoner's face.

'Let me introduce you,' he shouted, 'to Mr Neville St Clair, of Lee, in the county of Kent.'

Never in my life have I seen such a sight. The

man's face peeled off under the sponge like the bark from a tree. Gone was the coarse brown tint! Gone, too, was the horrid scar which had seamed it across and the twisted lip which had given the repulsive sneer to the face! A twitch brought away the tangled red hair, and there, sitting up in his bed, was a pale, sad-faced, refined-looking man, black-haired and smooth-skinned, rubbing his eyes and staring about him with sleepy bewilderment. Then suddenly realising the exposure, he broke into a scream and threw himself down with his face to the pillow.

'Great heavens!' cried the inspector, 'it is, indeed, the missing man. I know him from the photograph.'

The prisoner turned with the reckless air of a man who abandons himself to his destiny. 'Be it so,' said he. 'And pray what am I charged with?'

'With making away with Mr Neville St – Oh, come, you can't be charged with that unless they make a case of attempted suicide of it,' said the inspector with a grin. 'Well, I have been twenty-seven years in the force, but this really takes the cake.'

'If I am Mr Neville St Clair, then it is obvious that no crime has been committed, and that, therefore, I am illegally detained.'

'No crime, but a very great error has been committed,' said Holmes. 'You would have done better to have trusted your wife.'

'It was not my wife, it was the children,' groaned the prisoner. 'God help me, I would not have them ashamed of their father. My God! What an exposure! What can I do?'

Sherlock Holmes sat down beside him on the couch and patted him kindly on the shoulder.

'If you leave it to a court of law to clear the matter

up,' said he, 'of course you can hardly avoid publicity. On the other hand, if you convince the police authorities that there is no possible case against you, I do not know that there is any reason that the details should find their way into the papers. Inspector Bradstreet would, I am sure, make notes upon anything you might tell us and submit them to the proper authorities. The case would then never go into court at all.'

'God bless you!' cried the prisoner passionately. 'I would have endured imprisonment, ay, even execution, rather than have left my miserable secret as a family blot to my children.

'You are the first who have ever heard my story. My father was a schoolmaster in Chesterfield, where I received an excellent education. I travelled in my youth, took to the stage, and finally became a reporter on an evening paper in London. One day my editor wished to have a series of articles upon begging in the metropolis, and I volunteered to supply them. There was the point from which all my adventures started. It was only by trying begging as an amateur that I could get the facts upon which to base my articles. When an actor I had, of course, learned all the secrets of making up, and had been famous in the green-room for my skill. I took advantage now of my attainments. I painted my face, and to make myself as pitiable as possible I made a good scar and fixed one side of my lip in a twist by the aid of a small slip of flesh-coloured plaster. Then with a red head of hair, and an appropriate dress, I took my station in the business part of the city, ostensibly as a matchseller but really as a beggar. For seven hours I plied my trade, and when I returned home in the evening I found to my surprise that I had received no less than twenty-six shillings and fourpence.

'I wrote my articles and thought little more of the matter until, some time later, I backed a bill for a friend and had a writ served upon me for twenty-five pounds. I was at my wit's end where to get the money, but a sudden idea came to me. I begged a fortnight's grace from the creditor, asked for a holiday from my employers, and spent the time in begging in the City under my disguise. In ten days I had the money and had paid the debt.

'Well, you can imagine how hard it was to settle down to arduous work at two pounds a week when I knew that I could earn as much in a day by smearing my face with a little paint, laying my cap on the ground and sitting still. It was a long fight between my pride and the money, but the dollars won at last, and I threw up reporting and sat day after day in the corner which I had first chosen, inspiring pity by my ghastly face and filling my pockets with coppers. Only one man knew my secret. He was the keeper of a low den in which I used to lodge in Swandam Lane; every morning I could emerge as a squalid beggar and in the evening return to transform myself into a well-dressed man about town. This fellow, a Lascar, was well paid by me for his rooms, so that I knew that my secret was safe in his possession.

'Well, very soon I found that I was saving considerable sums of money. I do not mean that any beggar in the streets of London could earn £700 a year – which is less than my average takings – but I had exceptional advantages in my power of making up, and also in a facility of repartee, which improved by practice and made me quite a recognised character in the City. All day a stream of pennies, varied by silver, poured in upon me, and it was a very bad day in which I failed to take two pounds.

'As I grew richer I grew more ambitious, took a house in the country, and eventually married, without anyone having a suspicion as to my real occupation. My dear wife knew that I had business in the City. She little knew what.

'Last Monday I had finished for the day and was dressing in my room above the opium den when I looked out of my window and saw, to my horror and astonishment, that my wife was standing in the street with her eyes fixed full upon me. I gave a cry of surprise, threw up my arms to cover my face, and, rushing to my confidant, the Lascar, entreated him to prevent anyone from coming up to me. I heard her voice downstairs, but I knew that she could not ascend. Swiftly I threw off my clothes, pulled on those of a beggar and put on my pigments and wig. Even a wife's eyes could not pierce so complete a disguise. But then it occurred to me that there might be a search in the room, and that the clothes might betray me. I threw open the window, reopening by my violence a small cut which I had inflicted upon myself in the bedroom that morning. Then I seized my coat, which was weighted by the coppers which I had just transferred to it from the leather bag in which I carried my takings. I hurled it out of the window, and it disappeared into the Thames. The other clothes would have followed, but at that moment there was a rush of constables up the stairs, and a few minutes after I found, rather, I confess, to my relief, that instead of being identified as Mr Neville St Clair, I was arrested as his murderer.

'I do not know that there is anything else for me to explain. I was determined to preserve my disguise as long as possible, and hence my preference for a dirty face. Knowing that my wife would be terribly anxious, I slipped off my ring and confided it to the Lascar at a moment when no constable was watching me, together with a hurried scrawl telling her that she had no cause to fear.'

'That note only reached her yesterday,' said Holmes.

'Good God! What a week she must have spent!'

'The police have watched this Lascar,' said Inspector Bradstreet, 'and I can quite understand that he might find it difficult to post a letter unobserved. Probably he handed it to some sailor customer of his, who forgot all about it for some days.'

'That was it,' said Holmes, nodding approvingly; 'I have no doubt of it. But have you never been prosecuted for begging?'

'Many times; but what was a fine to me?'

'It must stop here, however,' said Bradstreet. 'If the police are to hush this thing up, there must be no more of Hugh Boone.'

'I have sworn it by the most solemn oaths which a man can take.'

'In that case I think that it is probable that no further steps may be taken. But if you are found again, then all must come out. I am sure, Mr Holmes, that we are very much indebted to you for having cleared the matter up. I wish I knew how you reach your results.'

'I reached this one,' said my friend, 'by sitting upon five pillows and consuming an ounce of shag. I think, Watson, that if we drive to Baker Street we shall just be in time for breakfast.'

The Message on the Sundial

J. J. BELL

For a good many weeks the morning mail of Mr Philip Bolsover Wingard had usually contained something unpleasant, but never anything quite so unpleasant as the letter, with its enclosure, now in his hand. And the letter was from his cousin, Philip Merivale Wingard, the man to whom he owed more benefits, and whom he hated more, than any man in the world. Certainly the letter was rather a shocking one to have place in the morning mail of a gentleman; but, oddly enough, it had never occurred to Bolsover, as he was commonly called to distinguish him from the other Philip, that he had long since forfeited his last rights to the designation.

The letter was dated from the other Philip's riverside residence, and ran as follows:

COUSIN BOLSOVER – I send you herewith an appeal just received from a deeply injured woman, to whom you have apparently given my name, instead of your own. This ends our acquaintance. If you insist on a further reason, I would merely mention your forgery of my name to a bill for £500, which fact has also been brought to my notice this morning. In the face of these two crimes it does not seem worth while to remind you that for seven years I have tried to believe in you and to help you in a material way.

You will receive this in the morning, and it gives you forty-eight hours to be out of this country. Within that time there is a sailing for South Africa. My banker has received instructions to pay you £500, one half of which you shall send to the writer of the enclosed. On that condition, and so long as you remain abroad, your forgery is my secret. This is your last chance.

PHILIP PERIVALE WINGARD

Bolsover, enduring a sickness almost physical, re-read the letter. The enclosure did not trouble him, except in so far as it looked like costing him £250. But the discovery of his forgery shook him, for it was a shock against which he had been altogether unprepared. He had not dreamed of the money-lender showing the bill, which was not due for six weeks, to his cousin. What infernal luck!

Bolsover read the letter a third time, seeking some glimmer of hope, some crevice for escape. Hitherto he had regarded his cousin as a bit of a softy, a person to be gulled or persuaded; but every word of the letter seemed to indicate a heart grown hard, a mind become unyielding.

Go abroad? Why, that would simply be asking for it! The clouds of debt were truly threatening, but if he continued to walk warily at home they might gradually disperse, whereas the outcry that would surely follow his apparent flight would, like an explosion, bring down the deluge of ruin.

What a fool was Philip! It did not occur to Bolsover then that, during all those seven years, he had lived by fooling Philip. And the most maddening thought of all was that had Philip not come back from the

Great War he, Bolsover, would be in Philip's place today! That, indeed, was the root of the hatred, planted in disappointment and nourished from the beginning on envy and greed, and lately also on chagrin and jealousy, since Philip had won the girl, as wealthy as himself, whom Bolsover had coveted for his own.

Bolsover's mouth was dry. He went over to the neglected breakfast-table, poured shakily a cup of the cooled coffee and drank it off. He took out and opened his cigarette-case. His fingers fumbled a cigarette, and he noticed their trembling. This would not do. He must get command of his nerves, of his wits. Raging was of no use. He lighted the cigarette and sat down.

Somehow he must see Philip; somehow he must prevail on Philip to abate his terms – either that, or induce Philip to pay all his debts. But the total of his debts amounted to thousands, and some of them were owing to persons whom he would fain avoid naming to his strait-laced cousin. Still, he must make the appeal, in the one direction or the other. The situation was past being desperate.

He knew that his cousin was entertaining a house-party. On the mantelshelf was a dance invitation, received three weeks ago, for that very evening. He did not suppose that Philip would now expect to see him, as a guest; yet for a moment or two he dallied with the idea of presenting himself, as though nothing had happened. But there was the possibility, a big one, too, to judge from this damned letter, that Philip would simply have the servants throw him out!

He looked at his watch – 10.20 – and went over to the telephone. He ought to have phoned at the outset, he told himself. Philip might have gone out, on the river with his friends, for the day. The prospect of seven or eight hours of uncertainty appalled him.

But at the end of a couple of minutes he heard Philip's voice enquiring who was speaking.

'Philip,' said Bolsover quickly, 'bear with me for a few moments. I have your letter. I must obey it. But, as a last favour, let us have one more meeting. There are things – '

'No! I have nothing to say to you; I wish to hear nothing from you.'

'There are things I can explain.'

'No! Excuse me. My friends are waiting for me. Good – '

'Philip, let your invitation for tonight stand. Let me come, if only for an hour.'

'What! Let you come among those girls, after that letter from that unhappy woman? A thousand times, no!'

'Well, let us meet somewhere, during the evening, outside the house. I shan't keep you long. Look here, Philip! I'll be at the sundial, at ten, and wait till you come. Don't refuse the last request I'll ever make of you.'

There was a pause till Philip said coldly: 'Very well. But, I warn you, it can make not the slightest difference.'

'Thank you, Philip. Ten, or a little after?' Bolsover retained the receiver a while.

But there was no further word from his cousin.

He went back to his chair and sat there, glowering at space. Undeniably there had been a new firmness in his cousin's voice. While he did not doubt that Philip would keep the tryst, he could no longer hope that anything would come of the interview. That being so, what was left for him?

To a man like Bolsover the disgrace was secondary; the paramount dread was a life without money for personal indulgence. He had been cornered before, but never so tightly, it seemed, as now. For the first time in his unworthy career he thought of death as the way of escape, knowing all the while that were he in the very toils of despair, he could never bring himself to take the decided step in death's direction. But he toyed gloomily with the thought, till his imagination began to perceive its other side.

What if Philip were out of the world?

At first the idea was vague and misty, but gradually it became clear, and all at once his mind recoiled, as a man recoils from the brink of a precipice – recoiled, yet only to approach again, cautiously, to survey the depths, searching furtively the steep, lest haply it should provide some safe and secret downward path. And peering into his own idea, Bolsover seemed to see at the bottom of it a pleasant place where freedom was, where fear was not. For while Bolsover had no illusions of inheriting a penny in hard cash from his cousin, he knew that a small landed estate, unencumbered, was bound on his cousin's death to come to him: and on that estate he could surely raise the wherewithal to retrieve his wretched fortunes. The greatest optimist in the world is the most abandoned gambler.

A maid came in to remove the breakfast things.

'Ain't you well this morning, Mr Wingard?' she enquired. Bolsover, resident in the private hotel for a good many months, had been generous enough in his gratuities to the servants.

'Feeling the heat,' he answered, wiping his brow. 'Dreadfully sultry, isn't it?'

'It *is* 'ot for May. Guess we're going to 'ave a thunderstorm soon. Shall I fetch some fresh coffee, or would you like a cup of tea?'

'Thanks, but I have got to go out now.'

Perhaps he was thankful for the interruption.

The bank with which his cousin dealt was in the Strand. Feeling weak, he took a taxi thither. He was known at the bank, his cousin's instructions had been duly received, and the money was handed over to him, without delay. He rather overdid his amusement, as he realised afterwards, at his shaky signature on the receipt. 'Looks as if I had been having a late night,' he remarked, passing the paper back to the grave cashier.

As the door swung behind him, he called himself a fool and wiped his face.

He lunched leisurely at an unusually early hour. He preceded the meal with a couple of cocktails, accompanied it with a pint of champagne, and followed it with a liqueur. He felt much better, though annoyed by an unwonted tendency to perspire. On his leaving the restaurant, the tendency became more pronounced, so much so that he feared it must be noticeable, and once more he took a taxi, telling the man to go Kensington way. A little later, he was sitting in a shady part of Kensington Gardens. He had wanted to get away from people.

For a while he felt comfortably in body, and almost easy in mind. He was now quite hopeful that Philip would see the unreasonableness of the terms of that letter, which had obviously been written in haste. After all, his debts amounted to no more than

£6,000 – well, say, £7,000 – a sum that would scarcely trouble his cousin to disburse, especially as it would not be required all at once. No doubt, Philip would kick, to begin with, and deliver a pretty stiff lecture, but in the end he would capitulate. Oh, yes, it had been a black morning, but there would be another story to tell by midnight. Bolsover smoked a cigarette or two, surrendered himself to a pleasant drowsiness, and fell into a doze.

He awoke heavy of limb – hot in the head and parched, and with a great spiritual depression upon him. He must have a drink. He looked at his watch. Only 4.30. His hotel, however, was not far distant, and thither he went on foot.

The hall porter presented an expressed letter which had come at midday. The writing was familiar, and Bolsover was not glad to see it. In his room he helped himself to brandy before opening the letter – a curt warning that a fairly large sum must be paid by noon on the morrow. It acted as a powerful irritant and brought on the silent frenzy against things and persons which had shaken him in the morning.

He took another drink, and presently his fiery wrath at fortune gave place to the old smouldering hate against his cousin, who now seemed to block the road to salvation. He unlocked and opened a drawer, and for a long while sat glowering at the things it contained, a revolver, which he had purchased years ago on the eve of a trip abroad, and a package of cartridges, never opened.

He saw himself at the sundial in Philip's garden, the loaded weapon in his pocket. He saw Philip coming in the darkness, from the house with its lights and music. And then he began to realise that the house was not so very far away, and imagined how the report of the revolver would shatter the night. He must think of another way, he concluded, shutting the drawer, and turned to the bottle once more.

It was near to seven o'clock when he went out. He ought to have been drunk, but apparently he was quite sober when he entered the cutler's shop in the Paddington district. He was going abroad on a game-hunting expedition, he explained, and wanted something in the way of a sheath-knife. This was supplied, and with the parcel he returned to the hotel.

After dinner he dressed, not carelessly. The brandy bottle tempted, and he put off the craving with a dose much diluted. He took train to a riverside station, then a cab for the last two miles of the journey. At five minutes before ten he was in his cousin's grounds.

The ancient sundial stood in the centre of a rose garden, which was separated from the house by a broad walk, a lawn and a path, and walled round by high, thick hedges. Beyond the bottom of the rose garden was a narrow stretch of turf, and then the river.

The night was very dark; the atmosphere heavy, breathless. It seemed to Bolsover, waiting by the dial, that the storm might burst at any moment, and his anxiety was intense lest the deluge should descend and prevent the coming of Philip. Though the knife, loosened in the sheath, lay ready in the pocket of his cloak, he kept telling himself that he would never use it, save as a threat; that he had bought it only to strengthen his courage and purpose. The effects of the alcohol apart, the man was not quite sane. A brain storm was as imminent as the storm of nature.

Peering, listening, he stood by the dial, seeing above the hedge the glow from the open windows, hearing dimly the chatter and laughter of the guests. He had arrived in the garden to the sound of music, but soon it had ceased, and now the pause between the dances seemed very long. He argued that Philip, who doubtless desired secrecy as much as himself, would leave the house only when a dance was in progress, and, fingering the knife's hilt, he cursed the idle musicians and the guests resting on the verandah, or strolling on the lawn.

The minutes passed, and at last the music started again. And when Bolsover, savage with exasperation, was telling himself that another dance was nearly over, he became aware of a sound of footfalls on gravel, and a dark figure, with a glimmer of white, appeared in the gap.

Philip Merivale Wingard came quickly down to the dial and halted opposite his cousin.

'So you are here, in spite of my warning,' he said.

'Philip, I came to ask – '

'Ask nothing. Did you get the money from the bank?'

'Thank you, yes.'

'Have you sent half of it to the woman?'

'Yes,' Bolsover lied. 'Let me explain – '

'No!' the other interrupted. 'I am going to tell you why I am here. I have decided to let you have a further five hundred, which will give you a start, wherever you may settle abroad. It shall go to you as soon as I receive your address there. But I must have your signature to a promise, that for five years you will not attempt to return to this country, without my permission. Will you sign?'

No man is so infamous that he cannot feel insulted. Bolsover felt insulted, and once more the silent frenzy shook him.

'Come,' said Philip, laying a single sheet of note-paper on the smooth table of granite. 'Here is a simple promise written out by myself – I need not say that all between us is private – and here is a pen. I'll hold a match while you sign. Come, man, unless you wish us to be discovered!'

Bolsover, his right hand in his pocket, moved round till he was against his cousin's left arm.

'Take the pen,' said Philip.

'One moment,' Bolsover returned in a thick voice.

He took a step backwards, threw up his arm, and drove the knife down between Philip's shoulders. In that moment he experienced a sort of sickness of astonishment at the ease with which the blade penetrated; in the next moment he stepped back, withdrawing the knife and holding it away from him.

Philip squirmed, made a choking noise, and fell across the broad dial, one hand clutching at the far edge. The paper, dislodged, fluttered to the feet of Bolsover, who picked it up, pocketed it, and retreated up the path, backwards, yet with eyes averted from his handiwork. And having reached a distance of seven yards, he turned right round and stood with hunched shoulders, waiting for the ghastly labouring sound to cease. Had he not killed Philip after all? For a little while he knew not what he did – prayed, may be – and then the end came, a gasping, choking noise, a slithering sound, a soft thud. He turned slowly about. There was a heap, slightly moving on the path under the dial, and then – there was a heap that was very still.

Bolsover remembered his own safety. Running softly on the grass verge, he came to the gap in the lower hedge, passed through, crossed the strip of turf, and halted at the river's edge. From the river came no sound at all. The most enthusiastic of boating people had sensed the coming storm. Gingerly Bolsover fitted the knife into its sheath, and slung it far out into the darkness. He tore the paper into tiny bits, and scattered them on the black water. Slowly they drifted away.

By a roundabout route he reached the main walk leading to the house, and deliberately went forward to the door. The servant in attendance, who knew him as his master's cousin, received him as a late arriving guest; if he noticed his pallor, he was not interested.

And the pallor was not so extreme. Bolsover was playing a part now, and so intent thereon that in a measure he forgot why he was playing it.

Before long he was among the guests, greeting those whom he knew, explaining that he had just arrived and was looking for the host, his cousin. A curate, a particular friend of Philip's, whom Bolsover had always rather disliked, remarked that he thought he had seen Philip go out by the French window of the library, about ten minutes earlier.

'You appear to be feeling the heat, Mr Wingard,' he added. 'You look quite haggard.'

'Yes, I want a drink,' Bolsover answered somewhat roughly, and was going to get it, when a girl, who with her partner had strayed to the rose garden, ran into the hall, screaming that Mr Wingard was lying by the sundial, dead – murdered!

It had come sooner than Bolsover could have wished, and for the moment he was staggered – but appropriately so. He was the first to recover his wits, and, as was his natural duty, proceeded to take charge, ordering a servant to phone for doctor and police, and requesting several of the men guests to accompany him to the scene, with the elements of first aid, lest life should still be there.

'We shall want lights!' cried Mr Minn, the curate, whose company Bolsover had not requested. 'I'll get my torch from my overcoat.'

Several torches were procured, and the party hurried down to the rose garden. The young man, whose partner had brought the alarm to the house, met them with a word of warning to prepare for a dreadful sight.

'He was alive, and no more, when we found him, but he's gone now,' the young man added. 'I'm glad you've come. I've used all my matches.'

'Did he speak?' asked the curate, as the others gathered round the dial.

'Oh, no; he didn't even attempt it, poor chap. I fancied, though, that he tried to make signs.'

'How so?'

'Towards the dial above him. And then he collapsed – in my arms. Heavens, I'm all bloody – everything is bloody!'

'Go up to the house and take some whisky,' said the curate kindly. 'But stay a moment! Did you look at the dial? Was there anything unusual about it?'

'Blood – and a fountain pen.'

'A pen!'

'Lying against the pointer.'

'Did you remove it?'

'Didn't touch it. It's a gold pen with a green stone in the top.'

338

'His own,' said Mr Minn. 'What on earth – ? Well, don't wait, Mr Marshall. I think you will find the library window open, so you can slip in and ring for a servant to fetch your overcoat to cover the – the stains. This is terrible!' The curate gave way to emotion. 'Poor Philip! My good friend and the best of men!'

Presently he joined the group. Bolsover was speaking.

'I wish we could take him to the house, but dare we do so before the doctor – and the police – have seen him?'

'I'm afraid we must wait,' said a guest.

'I felt a spot of rain just now,' said another. 'We can't let him lie here if the storm breaks. What do you say, Mr Minn?'

The curate did not seem to hear. He was playing the shuddering light of his torch on the dial.

'Gentlemen,' he said unsteadily, 'please give me your attention for a moment.'

There was a catching of breaths at the sight of the dark pool and rivulets on the smooth grey stone, followed by faint exclamations as the beam caught and lingered on the gold pen.

'His own pen, gentlemen – and with it he has written something on the dial, for there is one line of ink not quite dry – and the nib of the pen has given way.'

The beam moved towards the right, and stopped.

Here was no blood; only some writing – of a sort. The guests leaned forward, peering – all save Bolsover, who shrank back, open-mouthed, the sweat of terror on his skin. Had the dying man left a message?

'Figures!' softly exclaimed a guest.

'Yes,' said Mr Minn, producing a pencil, following with the point of it the wavering, broken lines and

curves. 'A one – a three – a nought – a six – an eight –
another nought – and something that might have been
a four, had the nib not broken, or had the hand not
failed. One, three, nought, six, eight, nought – '

A big drop of rain splashed on his hand, and he
started as though it had been blood.

'If the storm breaks now, this message, which may
be a clue, will be lost!' he cried. 'Will one of you run
to the house and fetch something waterproof to cover
the dial? Hurry, please!'

A guest ran off. Another drop fell, and another, on
the dial.

Mr Minn handed the torch to his neighbour, saying:
'Kindly, all of you, direct your lights on the figures.'
He whipped out a little notebook. 'In case of accidents,
I shall make a copy as exactly as possible.'

There was a silence while he drew, rather than
wrote down, the figures.

Bolsover's panic had passed. There was nothing in
those large ill-formed figures that could in any way
draw attention to himself. He cleared his throat, and
said: 'Mr Minn, do these figures convey anything at
all to you, as a friend of poor Philip's?'

'Nothing, Mr Wingard.' Mr Minn shook his
head. 'But whatever their meaning, they must surely
represent almost the last thought – if not the very last
thought – of our cruelly murdered friend – and an
urgent message. Whether or not they may provide
the police with a clue – '

There was a blinding glare, a stunning crash, a
throbbing silence in the blackness, and the clouds
turned, as it seemed, to water.

*

The inquest was over, the jury returning an open verdict, the only verdict in keeping with the evidence, as every person in court had agreed. The fact that Philip must have had an enemy made a mystery in itself. The figures written on the dial were a mystery also; a search through Philip's papers had revealed nothing with which they could be connected. Mr Minn was, however, congratulated by the coroner on the presence of mind which he had shown in recording them.

Bolsover won the sympathy of all by his quiet, frank answers to the coroner's questions, by his tribute to the high character and generosity of his late cousin, and by his sad, pale, stricken appearance. Yes, there was a small estate to come to him, but other expectations he had none, the gifts of his cousin in the past having been almost princely.

On the fatal night, he explained, being detained in town, he had arrived at his cousin's house, shortly after ten. His enquiries for his cousin brought from Mr Minn the reply that his cousin had gone out, and immediately thereafter came the shocking news. It was possible that the crime in the rose garden was committed while he was walking up the avenue; but if so, it must have been done silently. At this point he had asked for a glass of water, and the coroner had expressed himself satisfied.

On the morrow, he attended the funeral, as chief mourner, looking a wreck of a man. But with the turning away from the grave, the worst was over. He was safe! Only one duty remained – his presence at the reading of the will.

It was not a large gathering, and Bolsover was the person least interested. The will had been made five years ago. Bolsover, his heavy lids almost closing his eyes, listened indifferently till –

'And to my cousin and friend, Philip Bolsover Wingard, the sum of fifty thousand pounds, free of legacy duty.'

He nearly fainted. It was Mr Minn, the curate, who brought him a drink.

Lunch had been provided for the mourners, but Bolsover begged to be excused. He was feeling far from well, he said, and wished to consult his doctor in town, without delay.

'I think you are wise, Mr Wingard,' said Mr Minn, kindly. 'You are looking ill, and no wonder. But before you go, I would beg for just a few minutes' talk. Let us go to the rose garden, where we shall not be disturbed.'

'Very well,' assented Bolsover. He had hoped never again to enter the rose garden, but did not see how he could reasonably refuse to do so now. Anyway, it would be the final torment.

In silence they crossed the lawn, and passed through the gap in the hedge. In silence, also, since Bolsover had not the speech for protest, they came to the sundial.

Mr Minn bared his head, and said: 'As God Almighty's rain has washed away all the signs of this tragedy, so is His infinite mercy able to wash away the sin that caused it. Amen.'

He replaced his hat and looked very gently and gravely at Bolsover.

'Mr Wingard, I wish to show you something. I wish to show you Philip's last thought before he died.' So saying he took out his notebook and a scarlet chalk pencil.

'The figures!' muttered Bolsover, wondering.

'Yes,' replied Mr Minn, and proceeded to copy them carefully from the page to the stone, thus:

'It is strange,' said Mr Minn, adding a touch to the '3', 'that the truth did not strike us at once. It did not come to me till early this morning. And yet, once we make allowance for the penmanship of a man dying quickly and in pain, struggling to write in the dark, the thing becomes as plain as day.'

'Not to me,' said Bolsover thickly; 'but, as you know, I am worn out and – '

'Only a minute more,' said Mr Minn gently. 'I want just to tell you that those marks were not figures at all.'

'Then I'm blind.'

'We were all blind, but now we see clearly. Observe that "1" and that "3"; note how they are rather close together. But bring them quite together and we have a "B".' Mr Minn drew a sprawling 'B' on the dial. 'Then the nought becomes an "O", and what we took for a six is really an "L" – see, I put them down after the "B" – and what might well pass for an eight must now be accepted as an "S" – so! Then we have another "O", and, next, the greater part of a "V" – and there the nib broke, or the hand failed. But surely – surely enough is there, Mr Wingard, to show you your cousin's last thought, or message.'

On the dial, written in scarlet by Mr Minn, appeared these two lines:

Bobsov

Bolsov(er)

Over the face of Bolsover, gazing dumbly thereon, came a greyish shadow.

Mr Minn, watching narrowly, raised his left hand as with an effort, while his own countenance paled.

Followed what seemed a long silence. Then, all at once, Bolsover lifted up his face, a dreadful, hunted look in his eyes. His gaze sought the gap in the upper hedge, then fled round to the gap in the lower. In each gap stood a burly man, a stranger.

The curate wiped his eyes.

'My friend,' he said softly, 'I will pray for you.'

Who Killed Charlie Winpole?

ERNEST BRAMAH

I

Some time during November of a recent year news-paper readers who are in the habit of being attracted by curious items of quite negligible importance might have followed the account of the tragedy of a St Abbots schoolboy which appeared in the Press under the headings, 'Fatal Dish of Mushrooms', 'Are Toad-stools Distinguishable?' or other similarly alluring titles.

The facts relating to the death of Charlie Winpole were simple and straightforward and the jury sworn to the business of investigating the cause had no hesitation in bringing in a verdict in accordance with the medical evidence. The witnesses who had any-thing really material to contribute were only two in number – Mrs Dupreen and Robert Wilberforce Slark, MD. A couple of hours would easily have disposed of every detail of an inquiry that was generally admitted to have been a pure formality, had not the contention of an interested person delayed the inevitable conclusion by forcing the necessity of an adjournment.

Irene Dupreen testified that she was the widow of a physician and lived at Hazlehurst, Chesset Avenue, St Abbots, with her brother. The deceased was their nephew, an only child and an orphan, and was aged twelve. He was a Ward of Chancery and the Court had appointed her as guardian, with an adequate provision for the expenses of his keep and education. That allowance would, of course, cease with her nephew's death.

Coming to the particulars of the case, Mrs Dupreen explained that for a few days the boy had been suffering from a rather severe cold. She had not thought it necessary to call in a doctor, recognising it as a mild form of influenza. She kept him from school and restricted him to his bedroom. On the previous Wednesday, the day before his death, he was quite convalescent, with a good pulse and a normal temperature, but as the weather was cold she decided still to keep him in bed as a measure of precaution. He had a fair appetite, but did not care for the lunch they had, and so she asked him, before going out in the afternoon, if there was anything that he would especially fancy for his dinner. He had thereupon expressed a wish for some mushrooms, of which he was always very fond.

'I laughed and pulled his ear,' continued the witness, much affected at her recollection, 'and asked him if that was his idea of a suitable dish for an invalid. But I didn't think that it really mattered in the least then, so I went to several shops about them. They all said that mushrooms were over, but finally I found a few at Lackington's, the greengrocer in Park Road. I bought only half a pound; no one but Charlie among us cared for them and I thought that they were already very dry and rather dear.'

The connection between the mushrooms and the unfortunate boy's death seemed inevitable. When Mrs Dupreen went upstairs after dinner she found Charlie apparently asleep and breathing soundly. She quietly removed the tray and without disturbing him turned out the gas and closed the door. In the middle of the night she was suddenly and startlingly awakened by something. For a moment she remained confused, listening. Then a curious sound coming from the direction of the boy's bedroom drew her there. On opening the door she was horrified to see her nephew lying on the floor in a convulsed attitude. His eyes were open and widely dilated; one hand clutched some bedclothes which he had dragged down with him, and the other still grasped the empty water-bottle that had been by his side. She called loudly for help and her brother and then the servant appeared. She sent the latter to a medicine cabinet for mustard leaves and told her brother to get in the nearest available doctor. She had already lifted Charlie on to the bed again. Before the doctor arrived, which was in about half an hour, the boy was dead.

In answer to a question the witness stated that she had not seen her nephew between the time she removed the tray and when she found him ill. The only other person who had seen him within a few hours of his death had been her brother, Philip Loudham, who had taken up Charlie's dinner. When he came down again he had made the remark: 'The youngster seems lively enough now.'

Dr Slark was the next witness. His evidence was to the effect that about three-fifteen on the Thursday morning he was hurriedly called to Hazlehurst by a gentleman whom he now knew to be Mr Philip Loudham. He understood that the case was one of convulsions and went provided for that contingency, but on his arrival he found the patient already dead.

347

From his own examination and from what he was told he had no hesitation in diagnosing the case as one of agaric poisoning. He saw no reason to suspect any of the food except the mushrooms, and all the symptoms pointed to bhurine, the deadly principle of *Amanita Bhuroides*, or the Black Cap, as it was popularly called, from its fancied resemblance to the headdress assumed by a judge in passing death sentence, coupled with its sinister and well-merited reputation. It was always fatal.

Continuing his evidence, Dr Slark explained that only after maturity did the Black Cap develop its distinctive appearance. Up to that stage it had many of the characteristics of *Agaricus campestris*, or common mushroom. It was true that the gills were paler than one would expect to find, and there were other slight differences of a technical kind, but all might easily be overlooked in the superficial glance of the gatherer. The whole subject of edible and noxious fungi was a difficult one and at present very imperfectly understood. He, personally, very much doubted if true mushrooms were ever responsible for the cases of poisoning which one occasionally saw attributed to them. Under scientific examination he was satisfied that all would resolve themselves into poisoning by one or other of the many noxious fungi that could easily be mistaken for the edible varieties. It was possible to prepare an artificial bed, plant it with proper spawn and be rewarded by a crop of mushroomlike growth of undoubted virulence. On the other hand, the injurious constituents of many poisonous fungi passed off in the process of cooking. There was no handy way of discriminating between the good and bad except by the absolute identification of species. The salt test and the silver-spoon test were all nonsense and the sooner they were forgotten the better. Apparent mushrooms that were found in woods or growing in the vicinity of trees or hedges should always be regarded with the utmost suspicion.

Dr Slark's evidence concluded the case so far as the subpoenaed witnesses were concerned, but before addressing the jury the coroner announced that another person had expressed a desire to be heard. There was no reason why they should not accept any evidence that was tendered, and as the applicant's name had been mentioned in the case it was only right that he should have the opportunity of replying publicly.

Mr Lackington thereupon entered the witness-box and was sworn. He stated that he was a fruiterer and greengrocer, carrying on a business in Park Road, St Abbots. He remembered Mrs Dupreen coming to his shop two days before. The basket of mushrooms from which she was supplied consisted of a small lot of about six pounds, brought in by a farmer from a neighbouring village, with whom he had frequent dealings. All had been disposed of and in no other case had illness resulted. It was a serious matter to him as a tradesman to have his name associated with a case of this kind. That was why he had come forward. Not only with regard to mushrooms, but as a general result, people would become shy of dealing with him if it was stated that he had sold unwholesome goods.

The coroner, intervening at this point, remarked that he might as well say that he would direct the jury that, in the event of their finding the deceased to have died from the effects of the mushrooms or anything contained among them, that there was no evidence other than that the occurrence was one of pure mischance.

Mr Lackington expressed his thanks for the assurance, but said that a bad impression would still remain. He had been in business in St Abbots for twenty-seven years and during that time he had handled some tons of mushrooms without a single complaint before. He admitted, in answer to the interrogation, that he had not actually examined every mushroom in the half-pound sold to Mrs Dupreen, but he had weighed them, and he was confident that if a toadstool had been among them he would have detected it. Might it not be a cooking utensil that was the cause?

Dr Slark shook his head and was understood to say that he could not accept the suggestion.

Continuing, Mr Lackington then asked whether it was not possible that the deceased, doubtless an enquiring adventurous boy and as mischievous as most of his kind, feeling quite well again and being confined to the house, had got up in his aunt's absence and taken something that would explain this sad affair? They had heard of a medicine cabinet. What about tablets of trional or veronal or something of that sort that might perhaps look like sweets? . . . It was all very well for Dr Slark to laugh, but this matter was a serious one for the witness.

Dr Slark apologised for smiling – he had not laughed – and gravely remarked that the matter was a serious one for all concerned in the inquiry. He admitted that the reference to trional and veronal had, for the moment, caused him to forget the surroundings. He would suggest that in the circumstances perhaps the coroner would think it desirable to order a more detailed examination of the body to be made.

After some further discussion the coroner, while remarking that in most cases an analysis was quite unnecessary, decided that in view of what had transpired it would be more satisfactory to have a complete autopsy made. The inquest was accordingly adjourned.

A week later most of those who had taken part in the first inquiry assembled again in the room of the St Abbots Town Hall which did duty for the Coroner's Court. Only one witness was heard and his evidence was brief and conclusive.

Dr Herbert Ingpenny, consulting pathologist to St Martin's Hospital, stated that he had made an examination of the contents of the stomach and viscera of the deceased. He found evidence of the presence of the poison bhurine in sufficient quantity to account for the boy's death, and the symptoms, as described by Dr Slark and Mrs Dupreen, in the course of the previous hearing, were consistent with bhurine poisoning. Bhurine did not occur naturally except as a constituent of *Amanita Bhuroides*. One-fifth of a grain would be fatal to an adult; in other words a single fungus in the dish might poison three people. A child, especially if experiencing the effects of a weakening illness, would be even more susceptible. No other harmful substance was present.

Dr Ingpenny concluded by saying that he endorsed his colleague's general remarks on the subject of mushrooms and other fungi, and the jury, after a plain direction from the coroner, forthwith brought in a verdict in accordance with the medical evidence.

It was a foregone conclusion with anyone who knew the facts or had followed the evidence. Yet five days later Philip Loudham was arrested suddenly and charged with the astounding crime of having murdered his nephew.

2

It is at this point that Max Carrados makes his first appearance in the Winpole tragedy.

A few days after the arrest, being in a particularly urbane frame of mind himself, and having several hours with no demands on them that could not be fitly transferred to his subordinates, Mr Carlyle looked round for some social entertainment, and with a benevolent condescension very opportunely remembered the existence of his niece living at Groat's Heath.

'Elsie will be delighted,' he assured himself, on evolving this suggestion. 'She is rather out of the world up there, I imagine. Now if I get across by four, put in a couple of hours . . .'

Mrs Bellmark was certainly pleased, but she appeared to be still more surprised at something, and behind that lay an effervescence of excitement that even to Mr Carlyle's complacent self-esteem seemed out of proportion to the occasion. The reason could not be long withheld.

'Did you meet anyone, Uncle Louis?' was almost her first inquiry.

'Did I meet anyone?' repeated Mr Carlyle with his usual precision. 'Um, no, I cannot say that I met anyone particular. Of course – '

'I've had a visitor and he's coming back again

for tea. Guess who it is? But you never will. Mr Carrados.'

'Max Carrados!' exclaimed her uncle in astonishment. 'You don't say so. Why, bless my soul, Elsie, I'd almost forgotten that you knew him. It seems years ago – what on earth is Max doing in Groat's Heath?'

'That is the extraordinary thing about it,' replied Mrs Bellmark. 'He said that he had come up here to look for mushrooms.'

'Mushrooms?'

'Yes; that was what he said. He asked me if I knew of any woods about here that he could go into and I told him of the one down Stonecut Lane.'

'But don't you know, my dear child,' exclaimed Mr Carlyle, 'that mushrooms growing in woods or even near trees are always to be regarded with suspicion? They may look like mushrooms, but they are probably poisonous.'

'I didn't know,' admitted Mrs Bellmark; 'but if they are, I imagine Mr Carrados will know.'

'It scarcely sounds like it – going to a wood, you know. As it happens, I have been looking up the subject lately. But, in any case, you say that he is coming back here?'

'He asked me if he might call on his way home for a cup of tea, and of course I said, "of course".'

'Of course,' also said Mr Carlyle. 'Motoring, I suppose?'

'Yes, a big grey car. He had Mr Parkinson with him.'

Mr Carlyle was slightly puzzled, as he frequently was by his friend's proceedings, but it was not his custom to dwell on any topic that involved an admission of inadequacy. The subject of Carrados and his eccentric quest was therefore dismissed until the sound of a formidable motor car dominating the atmosphere of the quiet suburban road was almost immediately followed by the entrance of the blind amateur. With a knowing look towards his niece Carlyle had taken up a position at the farther end of the room, where he remained in almost breathless silence.

Carrados acknowledged the hostess's smiling greeting and then nodded familiarly in the direction of the playful guest.

'Well, Louis,' he remarked, 'we've caught each other.'

Mrs Bellmark was perceptibly startled, but rippled musically at the failure of the conspiracy.

'Extraordinary,' admitted Mr Carlyle, coming forward.

'Not so very,' was the dry reply. 'Your friendly little maid' – to Mrs Bellmark – 'mentioned your visitor as she brought me in.'

'Is it a fact, Max,' demanded Mr Carlyle, 'that you have been to – er – Stonecut Wood to get mushrooms?'

'Mrs Bellmark told you?'

'Yes. And did you succeed?'

'Parkinson found something that he assured me looked just like mushrooms.'

Mr Carlyle bestowed a triumphant glance on his niece.

'I should very much like to see these so-called mushrooms. Do you know, it may be rather a good thing for you that I met you.'

'It is always a good thing for me to meet you,' replied Carrados. 'You shall see them. They are in the car. Perhaps I shall be able to take you back to town?'

'If you are going very soon. No, no, Elsie' – in response to Mrs Bellmark's protesting 'Oh!' – 'I don't want to influence Max, but I really must tear myself away the moment after tea. I still have to clear up some work on a rather important case I am just completing. It is quite appropriate to the occasion, too. Do you happen to know all about the Winpole business, Max?'

'No,' admitted Carrados, without any appreciable show of interest. 'Do you, Louis?'

'Yes,' responded Mr Carlyle with crisp assurance, 'yes, I think that I may claim I do. In fact it was I who obtained the evidence that induced the authorities to take up the case against Loudham.'

'Oh do tell us all about it,' exclaimed Elsie. 'I have only seen something in the *Indicator*.'

Mr Carlyle shook his head, hemmed and looked wise, and then gave in.

'But not a word of this outside, Elsie,' he stipulated. 'Some of the evidence won't be given until next week and it might be serious – '

'Not a syllable,' assented the lady. 'How exciting! Go on.'

'Well, you know, of course, that the coroner's jury – very rightly, according to the evidence before them – brought in a verdict of accidental death. In the circumstances it was a reflection on the business methods or the care or the knowledge or whatever one may decide of the man who sold the mushrooms, a greengrocer called Lackington. I have seen Lackington, and with a rather remarkable pertinacity in the face of the evidence he insists that he could not have made this fatal blunder – that in weighing so small a quantity as half a pound, at any rate, he would at once have spotted anything that wasn't quite all right.'

'But the doctor said, Uncle Louis – '

'Yes, my dear Elsie, we know what the doctor said, but, rightly or wrongly, Lackington backs his experience and practical knowledge against theoretical generalities. In ordinary circumstances nothing more would have come of it, but it happens that Lackington has for a lodger a young man on the staff of the local paper, and for a neighbour a pharmaceutical chemist. These three men talking things over more than once – Lackington restive under the damage that had been done to his reputation, the journalist stimulating and keen for a newspaper sensation, the chemist contributing his quota of practical knowledge. At the end of a few days a fabric of circumstance had been woven which might be serious or innocent according to the further development of the suggestion and the manner in which it could be met. These were the chief points of the attack: Mrs Dupreen's allowance for the care and maintenance of Charlie Winpole ceased with his death, as she had told the jury. What she did not mention was that the deceased boy would have come into an inheritance of some fifteen thousand pounds at age and that this fortune now fell in equal shares to the lot of his two nearest relatives – Mrs Dupreen and her brother Philip.

'Mrs Dupreen was by no means in easy circumstances. Philip Loudham was equally poor and had no assured income. He had tried several forms of business and now, at about thirty-five, was spending his time chiefly in writing poems and painting water-colours, none of which brought him in any money so far as one could learn.

'Philip Loudham, it was admitted, took up the food round which the tragedy centred.

'Philip Loudham was shown to be in debt and urgently in need of money. There was supposed to be a lady in the case – I hope I need say no more, Elsie.'

'Who is she?' asked Mrs Bellmark with poignant interest.

'We do not know yet. A married woman, it is rumoured, I regret to say. It scarcely matters – certainly not to you, Elsie. To continue: Mrs Dupreen got back from her shopping in the afternoon before her nephew's death at about three o'clock. In less than half an hour Loudham left the house and going to the station took a return ticket to Euston. He left by the 3.41 and was back in St Abbots at 5.43. That would give him barely an hour in town for whatever business he transacted. What was that business?

'The chemist next door supplied the information that although bhurine only occurs in nature in this one form, it can be isolated from the other constituents of the fungus and dealt with like any other liquid poison. But it was a very exceptional commodity, having no commercial uses and probably not half a dozen retail chemists in London had it on their shelves. He himself had never stocked it and never been asked for it.

'With this suggestive but by no means convincing evidence,' continued Mr Carlyle, 'the young journalist went to the editor of *The Morning Indicator*, to which he acted as St Abbots correspondent and asked him whether he cared to take up the inquiry as a "scoop". The local trio had carried it as far as they were able. The editor of the *Indicator* decided to look into it and asked me to go on with the case. This is how my connection with it arose.'

'Oh, that's how newspapers get to know things?' commented Mrs Bellmark. 'I often wondered.'

'It is one way,' assented her uncle.

'An American development,' contributed Carrados. 'It is a little overdone there.'

'It must be awful,' said the hostess. 'And the police methods! In the plays that come from the States – ' The entrance of the friendly handmaiden, bringing tea, was responsible for this platitudinous wave. The conversation, in deference to Mr Carlyle's scruples, marked time until the door closed on her departure.

'My first business,' continued the inquiry agent, after making himself useful at the table, 'was naturally to discover among the chemists in London whether a sale of bhurine coincided with Philip Loudham's hasty visit. If this line failed, the very foundation of the edifice of hypothetical guilt gave way; if it succeeded . . . Well, it did succeed. In a street off Caistor Square, Tottenham Court Road – Trenion Street – we found a man called Lightcraft who at once remembered making such a sale. As bhurine is a specified poison the transaction would have to be entered, and Lightcraft's book contained this unassailable piece of evidence. On Wednesday, the sixth of this month, a man signing his name as "J. D. Williams", and giving "25 Chalcott Place" as his address, purchased four drachms of bhurine. Lightcraft fixed the time as about half-past four. I went to 25 Chalcott Place and found it to be a small boarding-house. No one of the name of Williams was known there.'

If Mr Carlyle's tone of finality went for anything, Philip Loudham was as good as pinioned. Mrs Bellmark supplied the expected note of admiration.

'Just fancy!' was the form it took.

'Under the Act the purchaser must be known to the chemist?' suggested Carrados.

'Yes,' agreed Mr Carlyle; 'and there our friend Lightcraft may have let himself in for a little trouble. But, as he says – and we must admit that there is something in it – who is to define what "known to" actually means? A hundred people are known to him as regular or occasional customers and he has never heard their names; a score of names and addresses represent to him regular or occasional customers whom he has never seen. This "J. D. Williams" came in with an easy air and appeared at all events to know Lightcraft. The face seemed not unfamiliar and Lightcraft was perhaps a little too facile in assuming that he *did* know him. Well, well, Max, I can understand the circumstances. Competition is keen – especially against the private chemist – and one may give offence and lose a customer. We must all live.'

'Except Charlie Winpole,' occurred to Max Carrados, but he left the retort unspoken. 'Did you happen to come across any enquiry for bhurine at other shops?' he asked instead.

'No,' replied Carlyle, 'no, I did not. It would have been an indication then, of course, but after finding the actual place the others would have no significance. Why do you ask?'

'Oh, nothing. Only don't you think that he was rather lucky in getting it first shot if our St Abbots authority was right?'

'Yes, yes; perhaps he was. But this is of no interest to us now. The great thing is that a peculiarly sinister and deliberate murder is brought home to its perpetrator. When you consider the circumstances, upon

359

my soul, I don't know that I have ever unmasked a more ingenious and cold-blooded ruffian.'

'Then he has confessed, uncle?'

'Confessed, my dear Elsie,' said Mr Carlyle with a tolerant smile, 'no, he has not confessed – men of that type never do. On the contrary, he asserted his outraged innocence with a considerable show of indignation. What else was he to do? Then he was asked to account for his movements between 4.15 and 5 o'clock on that afternoon. Egad, the fellow was so cocksure of the safety of his plans that he hadn't even taken the trouble to think that out. First he denied that he had been away from St Abbots at all. Then he remembered. He had run down to town in the afternoon for a few things. – What things? – Well, chiefly stationery. – Where had he bought it? – At a shop in Oxford Street; he did not know the name. – Would he be able to point it out? – He thought so. – Could he identify the attendant? – No, he could not remember him in the least. – Had he the bill? – No, he never kept small bills. – How much was the amount? – About three or four shillings. – And the return fare to Euston was three-and-eightpence. Was it not rather an extravagant journey? – He could only say that he did so. – Three or four shillings' worth of stationery would be a moderate parcel. Did he have it sent? – No, he took it with him. – Three or four shillings' worth of stationery in his pocket? – No, it was in a parcel. – Too large to go in his pocket? – Yes. – Two independent witnesses would testify that he carried no parcel. They were townsmen of St Abbots who had travelled down in the same carriage with him. Did he still persist that he had been engaged in buying stationery? Then he declined to say anything further – about the best thing he could do.'

'And Lightcraft identifies him?'

'Um, well, not quite so positively as we might wish. You see, a fortnight has elapsed. The man who bought the poison wore a moustache – put on, of course – but Lightcraft will say that there is a resemblance and the type of the two men the same.'

'I foresee that Mr Lightcraft's accommodating memory for faces will come in for rather severe handling in cross-examination,' said Carrados, as though he rather enjoyed the prospect.

'It will balance Mr Philip Loudham's unfortunate forgetfulness for localities, Max,' rejoined Mr Carlyle, delivering the thrust with his own inimitable aplomb.

Carrados rose with smiling acquiescence to the shrewdness of the riposte.

'I will be quite generous, Mrs Bellmark,' he observed. 'I will take him away now, with the memory of that lingering in your ears – all my crushing retorts unspoken.'

'Five-thirty, egad!' exclaimed Mr Carlyle, displaying his imposing gold watch. 'We must – or, at all events, I must. You can think of them in the car, Max.'

'I do hope you won't come to blows,' murmured the lady. Then she added: 'When will the real trial come on, Uncle Louis?'

'The Sessions? Oh, early in January.'

'I must remember to look out for it.' Possibly she had some faint idea of Uncle Louis taking a leading part in the proceedings. At any rate Mr Carlyle looked pleased, but when adieux had been taken and the door was closed Mrs Bellmark was left wondering what the enigma of Max Carrados's departing smile had been.

3

It was when they were in the car that Mr Carlyle suddenly remembered the suspected mushrooms and demanded to be shown them. A very moderate collection was produced for his inspection. He turned them over sceptically.

'The gills are too pale for true mushrooms, Max,' he declared sapiently. 'Don't take any risk. Let me pitch them out of the window?'

'No.' Carrados's hand quietly arrested the threatened action. 'No; I have a use for them, Louis, but it is not culinary. You are quite right; they are rank poison. I only want to study them for . . . a case I am interested in.'

'A case! You don't mean to say that there is another mushroom poisoner going?'

'No; it is the same.'

'But – but you said – '

'That I did not know all about it? Quite true. Nor do I yet. But I know rather more than I did then.'

'Do you mean that Scotland Yard – '

'No, Louis.' Mr Carrados appeared to find something rather amusing in the situation. 'I am for the other side.'

'The other side! And you let me babble out the whole case for the prosecution! Well, really, Max!'

'But you are out of it now? The Public Prosecutor has taken it up?'

'True, true. But, for all that, I feel devilishly had.'

'Then I will give you the whole case for the defence and so we shall be quits. In fact I am relying on you to help me with it.'

'With the defence? I – after supplying the evidence that the Public Prosecutor is acting on?'

'Why not? You don't want to hang Philip Loudham – especially if he happens to be innocent – do you?'

'I don't want to hang anyone,' protested Mr Carlyle. 'At least – not as a private individual.'

'Quite so. Well, suppose you and I between ourselves find out the actual facts of the case and decide what is to be done. The more usual course is for the prosecution to exaggerate all that tells against the accused and to contradict everything in his favour; for the defence to advance fictitious evidence of innocence and to lie roundly on everything that endangers his client; while on both sides witnesses are piled up to bemuse the jury into accepting the desired version. That does not always make for impartiality or for justice . . . Now you and I are two reasonable men, Louis – '

'I hope so,' admitted Mr Carlyle. 'I think so.'

'You can give away the case for the prosecution and I will expose the weakness of the defence, so, between us, we may arrive at the truth.'

'It strikes me as a deuced irregular proceeding. But I am curious to hear the defence all the same.'

'You are welcome to all of it that there yet is. An alibi, of course.'

'Ah!' commented Mr Carlyle with expression.

'So recently as yesterday a lady came hurriedly, and with a certain amount of secrecy, to see me. She came on the strength of the introduction afforded by a mutual acquaintanceship with Fromow, the Greek professor. When we were alone she asked me – besought me, in fact – to advise her what to do. A few hours before, Mrs Dupreen had rushed across London to her with the tale of young Loudham's arrest. Then out came the whole story. This woman – well, her name is Guestling, Louis – lives a little way down in Surrey and is married. Her husband, according to her own account – and I have certainly heard a hint about it elsewhere – leads her a studiedly outrageous existence; an admired silken-mannered gentleman in society, a tolerable polecat at home, one infers. About a year ago Mrs Guestling made the acquaintance of Loudham, who was staying in that neighbourhood painting his pretty unsaleable country lanes and golden sunsets. The inevitable, or, to accept the lady's protestations, half the inevitable, followed. Guestling, who adds an insatiable jealousy to his other domestic virtues, vetoed the new acquaintance and thenceforward the two met hurriedly and furtively in town. Had either of them any money they might have snatched their destinies from the hands of Fate and gone off together, but she has nothing and he has nothing and both, I suppose, are poor mortals when it comes to doing anything courageous and outright in this censorious world. So they drifted, drifting but not yet wholly wrecked.'

'A formidable incentive for a weak and desperate man to secure a fortune by hook or crook, Max,' said Carlyle drily.

'That is the motive that I wish to make you a present of. But, as you will insist on your side, it is also a motive for a weak and foolish couple to steal every brief opportunity for a secret meeting. On Wednesday, the sixth, the lady was returning home from a visit to some friends in the Midlands. She saw in the occasion an opportunity, and on the morning of the sixth a message appeared in the personal columns of the *Daily Telegraph* – their usual channel of communication – making an assignation. That much can be established by the irrefutable evidence of the newspaper. Philip Loudham kept the appointment and for half an hour this miserably happy pair sat holding each other's hands in a dreary deserted waiting-room of Bishop's Road Station. That half-hour was from 4.15 to 4.45. Then Loudham saw Mrs Guestling into Praed Street Station for Victoria, returned to Euston and just caught the 5.7 St Abbots.'

'Can this be corroborated – especially as regards the precise time they were together?'

'Not a word of it. They chose the waiting-room at Bishop's Road for seclusion, and apparently they got it. Not a soul even looked in while they were there.'

'Then, by Jupiter, Max,' exclaimed Mr Carlyle with some emotion, 'you have hanged your client!'

Carrados could not restrain a smile at his friend's tragic note of triumph.

'Well, let us examine the rope,' he said with his usual imperturbability.

'Here it is.' It was a trivial enough shred of evidence that the inquiry agent took from his pocketbook and put into the expectant hand; in point of fact the salmon-coloured ticket of a 'London General' omnibus.

'Royal Oak – the stage nearest Paddington – to Tottenham Court Road – the point nearest Trenion Street,' he added significantly.

'Yes,' acquiesced Carrados, taking it.

'The man who bought the bhurine dropped that ticket on the floor of the shop. He left the door open and Lightcraft followed him to close it. That is how he came to pick the ticket up, and he remembers that it was not there before. Then he threw it into a wastepaper basket underneath the counter, and that is where we found it when I called on him.'

'Mr Lightcraft's memory fascinates me, Louis,' was the blind man's unruffled comment. 'Let us drop in and have a chat with him.'

'Do you really think that there is anything more to be got in that quarter?' queried Carlyle dubiously. 'I have turned him inside out, as you may be sure.'

'True; but we approach Mr Lightcraft from different angles. You were looking for evidence to prove young Loudham guilty. I am looking for evidence to prove him innocent.'

'Very well, Max,' acquiesced his companion. 'Only don't blame me if it turns out as deuced awkward for your man as Mrs G. has done. Shall I tell you what a counsel may be expected to put to the jury as the explanation of that lady's evidence?'

'No, thanks,' said Carrados half sleepily from his corner. 'Don't trouble; I know. I told her so.'

4

Mr Lightcraft made no pretence of being glad to see his visitors. For some time he declined to open his mouth at all on the subject that had brought them there, repeating with parrot-like obstinacy to every remark on their part, 'The matter is *sub judice*. I am unable to say anything further,' until Mr Carlyle longed to box his ears and bring him to his senses. For the ears happened to be unduly prominent and at that moment glowing with sensitiveness, while the chemist was otherwise a lank and pallid man, whose transparent ivory skin and well-defined moustache gave him something of the appearance of a waxwork.

'At all events,' interposed Carrados, when his friend turned from the maddening reiteration in despair, 'you don't mind telling me a few things about bhurine – apart from this particular connection?'

'I am very busy,' and Mr Lightcraft, with his back towards the shop, did something superfluous among the bottles on a shelf.

'I imagined that the time of Mr Max Carrados, of whom even you may possibly have heard, is as valuable as yours, my good sir,' put in Mr Carlyle with scandalised dignity.

'Mr Carrados?' Lightcraft turned and regarded the blind man with interest. 'I did not know. But you must recognise the unenviable position in which I am put by this gentleman's interference.'

'It is his profession, you know,' said Carrados mildly, 'and in any case it would certainly have been someone. Why not help me to get you out of the position?'

'How is that possible?'

'If the case against Philip Loudham breaks down and he is discharged at the next hearing you would not be called upon further.'

'That would certainly be a mitigation. But why should it break down?'

'Suppose you let me try the taste of bhurine,' suggested Carrados. 'You have some left?'

'Max, Max!' cried Mr Carlyle's warning voice, 'aren't you aware that the stuff is a deadly poison? One – fifth of a grain – '

'Mr Lightcraft will know how to administer it.'

Apparently Mr Lightcraft did. He filled a graduated measure with cold water, dipped a slender glass rod into a bottle that was not kept on the shelves, and with it stirred the water. Then into another vessel of water he dropped a single drop of the dilution.

'One in a hundred and twenty-five thousand, Mr Carrados,' he said, offering him the mixture.

Carrados just touched the liquid with his lips, considered the impression and then wiped his mouth.

'Now the smell.'

The unstoppered bottle was handed to him and he took in its exhalation.

'Stewed mushrooms!' was his comment. 'What is it used for, Mr Lightcraft?'

'Nothing that I know of.'

'But your customer must have stated an application?'

The pallid chemist flushed a little at the recollection of that incident.

'Yes,' he conceded. 'There is a good deal about the whole business that is still a mystery to me. The man came in shortly after I had lit up and nodded familiarly as he said: "Good-evening, Mr Lightcraft." I naturally assumed that he was someone whom I could not quite place. "I want another half-pound of nitre," he said and I served him. Had he bought nitre before, I have since tried to recall, but I cannot. It is a common enough article and I sell it, you might say, every day. I have a poor memory for faces I am willing to admit. It has hampered me in business many a time: people expect you to remember them. We chatted about nothing in particular as I did up the packet. After he had paid and turned to go he looked back again. "By the way, do you happen to have any bhurine?" he enquired. Unfortunately I had a few ounces. "Of course you know its nature?" I cautioned him. "May I ask what you require it for?" He nodded and held up the parcel of nitre he had in his hand. "The same thing," he replied, "taxidermy." Then I supplied him with half an ounce.'

'As a matter of fact, is it used in taxidermy?'

'It does not seem to be. I don't stuff birds but I have made enquiry and no one knows of it. Nitre is largely used, and some of the dangerous poisons – arsenic and mercuric chloride, for instance – but not this although it might quite reasonably have been. No, it was a subterfuge.'

'Now the poison book, if you please.'

Mr Lightcraft produced it without demur and the blind man ran his finger along the indicated line.

'Yes; this is quite in form. Is it a fact, Mr Lightcraft, that not half a dozen chemists in London stock this particular substance? We are told that.'

'I can quite believe it. I certainly don't know of another.'

'Strangely enough, your customer of the sixth seems to have come straight here. Do you issue a price-list?'

'Only a localised one of certain photographic goods. Bhurine is not included.'

'You can suggest no reason why Mr Philip Loudham should be inspired to presume that he might be able to get this unusual drug from you? You have never corresponded with him nor come across his name or address before?'

'No. As far as I can recollect, I know nothing whatever of him.'

'Then as yet we must assume that it was pure chance. By the way, Mr Lightcraft, how does it come

that *you* stock this rare poison, which has no commercial use and for which there is no demand?'

The chemist permitted himself to smile at the blunt
terms of the inquiry.

'In the ordinary way I don't stock it,' he replied.
'This is a small quantity that I had over from my
own use.'

'Your own use? Oh, then it has a use after all?'

'No, scarcely that. Some time ago it leaked out in
a corner of the photographic world that a great
revolution in colour-photography was on the point
of realisation by the use of bhurine in one of the
processes. I, among others, at once took it up. Unfortunately it was only another instance of a discovery
that is correct in theory breaking down in practice.
Nothing came of it.'

'Dear, dear me,' said Carrados softly, with
sympathetic understanding in his voice; 'what a pity.
You are interested in photography, Mr Lightcraft?'

'It is the hobby of my life, sir. Of course most
chemists dabble in it as a part of their business, but I
devote all my spare time to experimenting, colour-
photography in particular.'

'Colour-photography; yes. It has a great future.
This bhurine process – I suppose it would have been
of considerable financial value if it had worked?'

Mr Lightcraft laughed quietly and rubbed his hands
together. For the moment he had forgotten Loudham
and the annoying case and lived in his enthusiasm.

'I should rather say it would, Mr Carrados,' he
replied. 'It would have been the most epoch-marking
thing since Gaudin produced the first dry plate in '54.
Consider it – the elaborate processes of Dyndale,
Eiloff and Jupp reduced to the simplicity of a single

contact print giving the entire range of chromatic variation. Financially it – it will scarcely bear thinking about in these times.'

'Was it widely taken up?' asked Carrados.

'The bhurine idea?'

'Yes. You spoke of the secret leaking out. Were many in the know?'

'Not at all. The group of initiates was only a small one and I should imagine that, on reflection, every man kept it to himself. It certainly never became public. Then when the theory was definitely exploded of course no one took any further interest in it.'

'Were all who were working on the same lines known to you, Mr Lightcraft?'

'Well, yes; more or less I suppose they would be,' said the chemist thoughtfully. 'You see, the man who stumbled on the formula was a member of the Iris – a society of those interested in this subject, of which I am the secretary – and I don't think it ever got beyond the committee.'

'How long ago was this?'

'A year – eighteen months. It led to unpleasantness and broke up the society.'

'Suppose it happened to come to your knowledge that one of the original circle was quietly pursuing his experiments on the same lines with bhurine – what should you infer from it?'

Mr Lightcraft considered. Then he regarded Carrados with a sharp, almost a startled, glance and then he fell to biting his nails in perplexed uncertainty.

'It would depend on who it was,' he replied.

'Was there by any chance one who was unknown to you by sight but whose address you were familiar with?'

'Paulden!' exclaimed Mr Lightcraft. 'Paulden by

heaven! I do believe you're right. He was the ablest of the lot and he never came to the meetings – a corresponding member. Southem, the original man who struck the idea, knew Paulden and told him of it. Southem was an impractical genius who would never be able to make anything work. Paulden – yes, Paulden it was who finally persuaded Southem that there was nothing in it. He sent a report to the same effect to be read at one of the meetings. So Paulden is taking up bhurine again – '

'Where does he live?' enquired Carrados.

'Ivor House, Wilmington Lane, Enstead. As secretary I have written there a score of times.'

'It is on the Great Western – Paddington,' commented the blind man. 'Still, can you get out the addresses of the others, Mr Lightcraft?'

'Certainly, certainly. I have the book of membership. But I am convinced now that Paulden was the man. I believe that I did actually see him once some years ago, but he has grown a moustache since.'

'If you had been convinced of that a few days ago it would have saved us some awkwardness,' volunteered Mr Carlyle, with no little asperity.

'When you came before, Mr Carlyle, you were so convinced yourself of it being Mr Loudham that you wouldn't hear of me thinking of anyone else,' retorted the chemist. 'You will bear me out also that I never positively identified him as my customer. Now here is the book. Southem, Potter's Bar. Voynich, Islington. Crawford, Streatham Hill. Brown, Southampton Row. Vickers, Clapham Common. Tidey, Fulham. All those I knew quite well – associated with them week after week. Williams I didn't know so closely. He is dead. Bigwood has gone to Canada. I don't think anyone else was in the bhurine craze – as we called it afterwards.'

'But now? What would you call it now?' queried Carrados.

'Now? Well I hope that you will get me out of having to turn up at court and that sort of thing, Mr Carrados. If Paulden is going on experimenting with bhurine again on the sly I shall want all my spare time to do the same myself!'

5

A few hours later the two investigators rang the bell of a substantial detached house in Enstead, the little country town twenty miles out in Berkshire, and asked to see Mr Paulden.

'It is no good taking Lightcraft to identify the man,' Carrados had decided. 'If Paulden denied it, our friend's obliging record in that line would put him out of court.'

'I maintain an open mind on the subject,' Carlyle had replied. 'Lightcraft is admittedly a very bending reed, but there is no reason why he should not have been right before and wrong today.'

They were shown into a ceremonial reception-room to wait. Mr Carlyle diagnosed snug circumstances and the tastes of an indoors, comfort-loving man in the surroundings.

The door opened, but it was to admit a middle-aged, matronly lady with good-humour and domestic capability proclaimed by every detail of her smiling face and easy manner.

'You wished to see my husband?' she asked with friendly courtesy.

'Mr Paulden? Yes, we should like to,' replied Carlyle, with his most responsive urbanity. 'It is a matter that need not occupy more than a few minutes.'

'He is very busy just now. If it has anything to do with the selection' – a local contest was at its height – 'he is not interested in politics and scarcely ever votes.' Her manner was not curious, but merely reflected a businesslike desire to save trouble all round.

'Very sensible too; very sensible indeed,' almost warbled Mr Carlyle with instinctive cajolery. 'After all,' he continued, mendaciously appropriating as his own an aphorism at which he had laughed heartily a few days before in the theatre, 'after all, what does an election do but change the colour of the necktie of the man who picks our pockets? No, no, Mrs Paulden, it is merely a – um – quite personal matter.'

The lady looked from one to the other with smiling amiability.

'Some little mystery,' her expression seemed to say. 'All right; I don't mind, only perhaps I could help you if I knew.'

'Mr Paulden is in his darkroom now,' was what she actually did say. 'I am afraid, I am really afraid that I shan't be able to persuade him to come out unless I can take a definite message.'

'One understands the difficulty of tempting an enthusiast from his work,' suggested Carrados, speaking for the first time. 'Would it be permissible to take us to the door of the darkroom, Mrs Paulden, and let us speak to your husband through it?'

'We can try that way,' she acquiesced readily, 'if it is really so important.'

'I think so,' he replied.

The darkroom lay across the hall. Mrs Paulden conducted them to the door, waited a moment, and then knocked quietly.

'Yes?' sang out a voice, rather irritably one might judge, from inside.

'Two gentlemen have called to see you about something, Lance – '

'I cannot see anyone when I am in here,' interrupted the voice with rising sharpness. 'You know that, Clara – '

'Yes, dear,' she said soothingly, 'but listen. They are at the door here and if you can spare the time just to come and speak you will know without much trouble if their business is as important as they think.'

'Wait a minute,' came the reply after a moment's pause, and then they heard someone approach the door from the other side.

It was a little difficult to know exactly how it happened in the obscure light of that corner of the hall. Carrados had stepped nearer to the door to speak. Possibly he trod on Mr Carlyle's toe, for there was a confused movement; certainly he put out his hand hastily to recover himself. The next moment the door of the darkroom jerked open, the light was let in and the warm odours of a mixed and vitiated atmosphere rolled out. Secure in the well-ordered discipline of his excellent household, Mr Paulden had neglected the precaution of locking himself in.

'Confound it all!' shouted the incensed experimenter in a towering rage; 'confound it all, you've spoiled the whole thing now!'

'Dear me,' apologised Carrados penitently, 'I am so sorry. I think it must have been my fault, do you know. Does it really matter?'

'Matter!' stormed Mr Paulden, recklessly flinging open the door fully now to come face to face with his disturbers – 'matter letting a flood of light into a darkroom in the middle of a delicate experiment!'

'Surely it was very little,' persisted Carrados.

'Pshaw,' snarled the angry photographer, 'it was enough. You know the difference between light and dark, I suppose?'

Mr Carlyle suddenly found himself holding his breath, wondering how on earth Max had conjured that opportune challenge to the surface.

'No,' was the mild and deprecating reply – the appeal *ad misericordiam* that had never failed him yet – 'no, unfortunately I don't, for I am blind. That is why I am so awkward.'

Out of the shocked silence Mrs Paulden gave a little croon of pity. The moment before she had been speechless with indignation on her husband's behalf. Paulden felt as though he had struck a suffering animal. He stammered an apology and turned away to close the unfortunate door. Then he began to walk slowly down the hall.

'You wished to see me about something?' he remarked, with matter-of-fact civility. 'Perhaps we had better go in here.' He indicated the reception-room where they had waited and followed them in. The admirable Mrs Paulden gave no indication of wishing to join the party.

Carrados came to the point at once.

'Mr Carlyle,' he said, indicating his friend, 'has recently been acting for the prosecution in a case of alleged poisoning that the Public Prosecutor has now taken up. I am interested in the defence. Both sides are thus before you, Mr Paulden.'

'How does this concern me?' asked Paulden with obvious surprise.

'You are experimenting with bhurine. The victim of this alleged crime undoubtedly lost his life by bhurine poisoning. Do you mind telling us when and where you acquired your stock of this scarce substance?'

'I have had – '

'No – a moment, Mr Paulden, before you reply,' struck in Carrados with a warning gesture. 'You must understand that nothing so grotesque as to connect you with a crime is contemplated. But a man is under arrest and the chief point against him is the half-ounce of bhurine that Lightcraft of Trenion Street sold to someone at half-past five last Wednesday fortnight. Before you commit yourself to any statement that it may possibly be difficult to recede from, you should realise that this inquiry will be pushed to the very end.'

'How do you know that I am using bhurine?'

'That,' parried Carrados, 'is a blind man's secret.'

'Oh, well. And you say that someone has been arrested through this fact?'

'Yes. Possibly you have read something of the St Abbots mushroom poisoning case?'

'I have no interest in the sensational ephemera of the Press. Very well; it was I who bought the bhurine from Lightcraft that Wednesday afternoon. I gave a false name and address, I must admit. I had a sufficient private reason for so doing.'

'This knocks what is vulgarly termed "the stuffing" out of the case for the prosecution,' observed Carlyle, who had been taking a note. 'It may also involve you in some trouble yourself, Mr Paulden.'

'I don't think that he need regard that very seriously in the circumstances,' said Carrados reassuringly.

'They must find some scapegoat, you know,' persisted Mr Carlyle. 'Loudham will raise Cain over it.'

'I don't think so. Loudham, as the prosecution will roundly tell him, has only himself to thank for not giving a satisfactory account of his movements. Loudham will be lectured, Lightcraft will be fined the minimum, and Mr Paulden will, I imagine, be virtuously told not to do it again.'

The man before them laughed bitterly.

'There will be no occasion to do it again,' he said. 'Do you know anything of the circumstances?'

'Lightcraft told us something connected with colour-photography. You distrust Mr Lightcraft, I infer?'

Mr Paulden came down to the heart-easing medium of the street.

'I've had some once, thanks,' was what he said with terse expression. 'Let me tell you. About eighteen months ago I was on the edge of a great discovery in colour-photography. It was my discovery, whatever you may have heard. Bhurine was the medium, and not being then so cautious or so suspicious as I have reason to be now, and finding it difficult – really impossible – to procure this substance casually, I sent in an order to Lightcraft to procure me a stock. Unfortunately, in a moment of enthusiasm I had hinted at the anticipated results to a man who was then my friend – a weakling called Southem. Comparing notes with Lightcraft they put two and two together and in a trice most of the secret boiled over.

'If you have ever been within an ace of a monumental discovery you will understand the torment of

WHO KILLED CHARLIE WINPOLE?

anxiety and self-reproach that possessed me. For months the result must have trembled in the balance, but even as it evaded me so it evaded the others. And at last I was able to spread conviction that the bhurine process was a failure. I breathed again.

'You don't want to hear of the various things that conspired to baffle me. I proceeded with extreme caution and therefore slowly. About two weeks ago I had another foretaste of success and immediately on it a veritable disaster. By some diabolical mischance I contrived to upset my stock bottle of bhurine. It rolled down, smashed to atoms on a developing dish filled with another chemical, and the precious lot was irretrievably lost. To arrest the experiments at that stage even for a day was to waste a month. In one place and one alone could I hope to replenish the stock temporarily at such short notice and to do it openly after my last experience filled me with dismay . . . Well, you know what happened, and now, I suppose, it will all come out.'

6

A week after his arrest Philip Loudham and his sister were sitting in the drawing-room at Hazlehurst, nervous and expectant. Loudham had been discharged scarcely six hours before, with such vindication of his character as the frigid intimation that there was no evidence against him afforded. On his arrival home he had found a letter from Max Carrados – a name with which he was now familiar – awaiting him. There had been other notes and telegrams – messages of sympathy and congratulation, but the man who had brought about his liberation did not include these conventionalities. He merely stated that he purposed calling upon Mr Loudham at nine o'clock that evening and that he hoped it would be convenient for him and all other members of the household to be at home.

'He can scarcely be coming to be thanked,' speculated Loudham, breaking the silence that had fallen on them as the hour approached. 'I should have called on him myself tomorrow.'

Mrs Dupreen assented absent-mindedly. Both were dressed in black, and both at that moment had the same thought: that they were dreaming this.

'I suppose you won't go on living here, Irene?' continued the brother, speaking to make the minutes seem tolerable.

This at least had the effect of bringing Mrs Dupreen back into the present with a rush.

'Of course not,' she replied almost sharply and looking at him direct. 'Why should I, now?'

'Oh, all right,' he agreed. 'I didn't suppose you would.' Then, as the front-door bell was heard to ring: 'Thank heaven!'

'Won't you go to meet him in the hall and bring him in?' suggested Mrs Dupreen. 'He is blind, you know.'

Carrados was carrying a small leather case which he allowed Loudham to relieve him of, together with his hat and gloves. The introduction to Mrs Dupreen was made, the blind man put in touch with a chair, and then Philip Loudham began to rattle off the acknowledgement of gratitude of which he had been framing and rejecting openings for the last half-hour.

'I'm afraid it's no good attempting to thank you

WHO KILLED CHARLIE WINPOLE?

for the extraordinary service that you've rendered me, Mr Carrados,' he began, 'and, above all I appreciate the fact that, owing to you, it has been possible to keep Mrs Guestling's name entirely out of the case. Of course you know all about that, and my sister knows, so it isn't worth while beating about the bush. Well, now that I shall have something like a decent income of my own, I shall urge Kitty – Mrs Guestling – to apply for the divorce that she is richly entitled to, and when that is all settled we shall marry at once and try to forget the experience on both sides that has led up to it. I hope,' he added tamely, 'that you don't consider us really much to blame?'

Carrados shook his head in mild deprecation.

'That is an ethical point that has lain outside the scope of my inquiry,' he replied. 'You would hardly imagine that I should disturb you at such a time merely to claim your thanks. Has it occurred to you why I should have come?'

Brother and sister exchanged looks and by their silence gave reply.

'We have still to find who poisoned Charlie Winpole.'

Loudham stared at their guest in frank bewilderment, Mrs Dupreen almost closed her eyes. When she spoke it was in a pained whisper.

'Is there anything more to be gained by pursuing that idea, Mr Carrados?' she asked pleadingly. 'We have passed through a week of anguish, coming on a week of grief and great distress. Surely all has been done that can be done?'

'But you would have justice for your nephew if there has been foul play?'

Mrs Dupreen made a weary gesture of resignation. It was Loudham who took up the question.

'Do you really mean, Mr Carrados, that there is any doubt about the cause?'

'Will you give me my case please? Thank you.' He opened it and produced a small paper bag. 'Now a newspaper, if you will.' He opened the bag and poured out the contents. 'You remember stating at the inquest, Mrs Dupreen, that the mushrooms you bought looked rather dry? They were dry, there is no doubt, for they had been gathered four days. Here are some more under precisely the same conditions. They looked, in point of fact, like these?'

'Yes,' admitted the lady, beginning to regard Carrados with a new and curious interest.

'Dr Slark further stated that the only fungus containing the poison bhurine – the *Amanita* called the Black Cap, and also by the country folk the Devil's Scent Bottle – did not assume its forbidding appearance until maturity. He was wrong in one sense there, for experiment proves that if the Black Cap is gathered in its young and deceptive stage and kept, it assumes precisely the same appearance as it withers as if it was ripening naturally. You observe.' He opened a second bag and, shaking out the contents, displayed another little heap by the side of the first. 'Gathered four days ago,' he explained.

'Why, they are as black as ink,' commented Loudham. 'And the, phew! aroma!'

'One would hardly have got through without you seeing it, Mrs Dupreen?'

'I certainly hardly think so,' she admitted.

'With due allowance for Lackington's biased opinion I also think that his claim might be allowed. Finally, it is incredible that whoever peeled the mushrooms should have passed one of these. Who was the cook on that occasion, Mrs Dupreen?'

'My maid Hilda. She does all the cooking.'

'The one who admitted me?'

'Yes; she is the only servant I have, Mr Carrados.'

'I should like to have her in, if you don't mind.'

'Certainly, if you wish it. She is' – Mrs Dupreen felt that she must put in a favourable word before this inexorable man pronounced judgment – 'she is a very good, straightforward girl.'

'So much the better.'

'I will – ' Mrs Dupreen rose and began to cross the room.

'Ring for her? Thank you,' and whatever her intention had been the lady rang the bell.

'Yes, ma'am?'

A neat, modest-mannered girl, simple and nervous, with a face as full, as clear and as honest as an English apple. 'A pity,' thought Mrs Dupreen, 'that this confident, suspicious man cannot see her now.'

'Come in, Hilda. This gentleman wants to ask you something.'

'Yes, ma'am.' The round, blue eyes went appealingly to Carrados, fell upon the fungi spread out before her, and then circled the room with an instinct of escape.

'You remember the night poor Charlie died, Hilda,' said Carrados in his suavest tone, 'you cooked some mushrooms for his supper, didn't you?'

'No, sir,' came the glib reply.

' "No", Hilda!' exclaimed Mrs Dupreen in wonderment. 'You mean "yes", surely, child. Of course you cooked them. Don't you remember?'

'Yes, ma'am,' dutifully replied Hilda.

'That is all right,' said the blind man reassuringly. 'Nervous witnesses very often answer at random at first. You have nothing to be afraid of, my good girl, if you will tell the truth. I suppose you know a mushroom when you see it?'

'Yes, sir,' was the rather hesitating reply.

'There was nothing like this among them?' He held up one of the poisonous sort.

'No, sir; indeed there wasn't, sir. I should have known then.'

'You would have known *then*? You were not called at the inquest, Hilda?'

'No, sir.'

'If you had been, what would you have told them about these mushrooms that you cooked?'

'I – I don't know, sir.'

'Come, come, Hilda. What could you have told them – something that we do not know? The truth, girl, if you want to save yourself!' Then with a sudden, terrible directness the question cleft her trembling, guilt-stricken little brain: 'Where did you get the other mushrooms from that you put with those that your mistress brought?'

The eyes that had been mostly riveted to the floor leapt to Carrados for a single frightened glance, from Carrados to her mistress, to Philip Loudham, and to the floor again. In a moment her face changed and she was in a burst of sobbing.

'Oho, oho, oho!' she wailed. 'I didn't know; I didn't know. I meant no harm. Indeed, I didn't, ma'am.'

'Hilda! Hilda!' exclaimed Mrs Dupreen in bewilderment. 'What is it you're saying? What have you done?'

'It was his own fault. Oho, oho, oho!' Every word

was punctuated by a gasp. 'He always was a little pig and making himself ill with food. You know he was, ma'am, although you were so fond of him. I'm sure I'm not to blame.'

'But *what* was it? What *have* you done?' besought her mistress.

'It was after you went out that afternoon. He put on his things and slipped down into the kitchen without the master knowing. He said what you were getting for his dinner, ma'am, and that you never got enough of them. Then he asked me not to tell about his being down, because he'd seen some white things from his bedroom window growing by the hedge at the bottom of the garden and he was going to get them. He brought in four or five and said they were mushrooms all right and would I cook them with the others and not say anything because you'd only say too many weren't good for him if you knew. And I didn't know any difference. Indeed I'm telling you the truth, ma'am.'

'Oh, Hilda, Hilda!' was torn reproachfully from Mrs Dupreen. 'You know what we've gone through. Why didn't you tell us this before?'

'I was afraid. I was afraid of what they'd do. And no one ever guessed until I thought I was safe. Indeed I meant no harm to anyone, but I was afraid that they'd punish me instead.'

Carrados had risen and was picking up his things.

'Yes,' he said, half musing to himself, 'I knew it must exist: the one explanation that accounts for everything and cannot be assailed. We have reached the bedrock of truth at last.'

The Murder of the Mandarin

ARNOLD BENNETT

I

'What's that you're saying about murder?' asked Mrs Cheswardine as she came into the large drawing-room, carrying the supper-tray.

'Put it down here,' said her husband, referring to the supper-tray, and pointing to a little table which stood two legs off and two legs on the hearthrug.

'That apron suits you immensely,' murmured Woodruff, the friend of the family, as he stretched his long limbs into the fender towards the fire, farther even than the long limbs of Cheswardine. Each man occupied an easy-chair on either side of the hearth; each was very tall, and each was forty.

Mrs Cheswardine, with a whisk infinitely graceful, set the tray on the table, took a seat behind it on a chair that looked like a toddling grandnephew of the arm-chairs, and nervously smoothed out the apron.

As a matter of fact, the apron did suit her immensely. It is astounding, delicious, adorable, the effect of a natty little domestic apron suddenly put on over an elaborate and costly frock, especially when you can hear the rustle of a silk petticoat beneath, and more especially when the apron is smoothed out by jewelled fingers. Every man knows this. Every woman knows it. Mrs Cheswardine knew it. In such matters Mrs Cheswardine knew exactly what she was about. She delighted, when her husband brought Woodruff in late of a night, as he frequently did after a turn at the club, to prepare with her own hands – the servants being in bed – a little snack of supper for them. Tomato sandwiches, for instance, miraculously thin, together with champagne or Bass. The men preferred Bass, naturally, but if Mrs Cheswardine had a fancy for a sip of champagne out of her husband's tumbler, Bass was not forthcoming.

Tonight it was champagne.

Woodruff opened it, as he always did, and involuntarily poured out a libation on the hearth, as he almost always did. Good-natured, ungainly, long-suffering men seldom achieve the art of opening champagne.

Mrs Cheswardine tapped her pink-slippered foot impatiently.

'You're all nerves tonight,' Woodruff laughed, 'and you've made me nervous.' And at length he got some of the champagne into a tumbler.

'No, I'm not,' Mrs Cheswardine contradicted him.

'Yes, you are, Vera,' Woodruff insisted calmly.

She smiled. The use of that elegant Christian name, with its faint suggestion of Russian archduchesses, had a strange effect on her, particularly from the lips of Woodruff. She was proud of it, and of her surname too – one of the oldest surnames in the Five Towns. The syllables of 'Vera' invariably soothed her, like a charm. Woodruff, and Cheswardine also, had called her Vera during the whole of her life; and she was thirty. They had all three lived in different houses at the top end of Trafalgar Road, Bursley. Woodruff fell in love with her first, when she was eighteen, but with no practical result. He was a brown-haired man, personable despite his ungainliness, but he failed to perceive that to worship from afar off is not the best way to capture a young woman with large eyes and an emotional disposition. Cheswardine, who had a black beard, simply came along and married the little thing. She fluttered down on to his shoulders like a pigeon. She adored him, feared him, cooed to him, worried him, and knew that there were depths of his mind which she would never plumb. Woodruff, after being best man, went on loving, meekly and yet philosophically, and found his chief joy in just these suppers. The arrangement suited Vera; and as for the husband and the hopeless admirer, they had always been fast friends.

'I asked you what you were saying about murder,' said Vera sharply, 'but it seems – '

'Oh! did you?' Woodruff apologised. 'I was saying that murder isn't such an impossible thing as it appears. Anyone might commit a murder.'

'Then you want to defend Harrisford? Do you hear what he says, Stephen?'

The notorious and terrible Harrisford murders were agitating the Five Towns that November. People read, talked, and dreamt murder; for several weeks they took murder to all their meals.

'He doesn't want to defend Harrisford at all,' said Cheswardine, with a superior masculine air, 'and of course anyone might commit a murder. I might.'

'Stephen! How horrid you are!'

'You might, even!' said Woodruff, gazing at Vera.

'Charlie! Why, the blood alone – '

'There isn't always blood,' said the oracular husband.

'Listen here,' proceeded Woodruff, who read variously and enjoyed philosophical speculation.

'Supposing that by just taking thought, by just wishing it, an Englishman could kill a mandarin in China and make himself rich for life, without anybody knowing anything about it! How many mandarins do you suppose there would be left in China at the end of a week!'

'At the end of twenty-four hours, rather,' said Cheswardine grimly.

'Not one,' said Woodruff.

'But that's absurd,' Vera objected, disturbed. When these two men began their philosophical discussions they always succeeded in disturbing her. She hated to see life in a queer light. She hated to think.

'It isn't absurd,' Woodruff replied. 'It simply shows that what prevents wholesale murder is not the wickedness of it, but the fear of being found out, and the general mess, and seeing the corpse, and so on.'

Vera shuddered.

'And I'm not sure,' Woodruff proceeded, 'that murder is so very much more wicked than lots of other things.'

'Usury, for instance,' Cheswardine put in.

'Or bigamy,' said Woodruff.

'But an Englishman *couldn't* kill a mandarin in China by just wishing it,' said Vera, looking up.

'How do we know?' said Woodruff, in his patient voice. 'How do we know? You remember what I was telling you about thought-transference last week. It was in Borderland.'

Vera felt as if there was no more solid ground to stand on, and it angered her to be plunging about in a bog.

'I think it's simply silly,' she remarked. 'No, thanks.'

She said 'No, thanks' to her husband, when he tendered his glass.

He moved the glass still closer to her lips.

'I said "No, thanks," ' she repeated dryly.

'Just a mouthful,' he urged.

'I'm not thirsty.'

'Then you'd better go to bed,' said he.

He had a habit of sending her to bed abruptly. She did not dislike it. But she had various ways of going. Tonight it was the way of an archduchess.

2

Woodruff, in stating that Vera was all nerves that evening, was quite right. She was. And neither her husband nor Woodruff knew the reason.

The reason had to do most intimately with frocks.

Vera had been married ten years. But no one would have guessed it, to watch her girlish figure and her birdlike ways. You see, she was the only child in the house. She often bitterly regretted the absence of offspring to the name and honour of Cheswardine. She envied other wives their babies. She doted on babies. She said continually that in her deliberate opinion the proper mission of women was babies. She was the sort of woman that regards a cathedral as a place built especially to sit in and dream soft domestic dreams; the sort of woman that adores music simply because it makes her dream. And Vera's brown studies, which were frequent, consisted chiefly of babies. But as babies amused themselves by coming down the chimneys of all the other houses in Bursley, and avoiding her house, she sought comfort in frocks. She made the best of

ARNOLD BENNETT

herself. And it was a good best. Her figure was as
near perfect as a woman's can be, and then there
were those fine emotional eyes, and that flutteringness
of the pigeon, and an ever-changing charm of gesture.
Vera had become the best-dressed woman in Bursley.
And that is saying something. Her husband was
wealthy, with an increasing income, though, of course,
as an earthenware manufacturer, and the son and
grandson of an earthenware manufacturer, he joined
heartily in the general Five Towns lamentation that
there was no longer any money to be made out of
'pots'. He liked to have a well-dressed woman about
the house, and he allowed her an incredible allowance,
the amount of which was breathed with awe among
Vera's friends; a hundred a year, in fact. He paid it
to her quarterly, by cheque. Such was his method.

Now a ball was to be given by the members of the
Ladies' Hockey Club (or such of them as had not
been maimed for life in the pursuit of this noble
pastime) on the very night after the conversation
about murder. Vera belonged to the Hockey Club (in
a purely ornamental sense), and she had procured a
frock for the ball which was calculated to crown her
reputation as a mirror of elegance. The skirt had –
but no (see the columns of the *Staffordshire Signal* for
the 9th November, 1901). The mischief was that the
gown lacked, for its final perfection, one particular
thing, and that particular thing was separated from
Vera by the glass front of Brunt's celebrated shop at
Hanbridge. Vera could have managed without it. The
gown would still have been brilliant without it. But
Vera had seen it, and she *wanted* it.

Its cost was a guinea. Well, you will say, what is a
guinea to a dainty creature with a hundred a year?

392

Let her go and buy the article. The point is that she couldn't, because she had only six and sevenpence left in the wide world. (And six weeks to Christmas!) She had squandered – oh, soul above money! – twenty-five pounds, and more than twenty-five pounds, since the 29th of September. Well, you will say, credit, in other words, tick? No, no, no! The giant Stephen absolutely and utterly forbade her to procure anything whatever on credit. She was afraid of him. She knew just how far she could go with Stephen. He was great and terrible. Well, you will say, why couldn't she blandish and cajole Stephen for a sovereign or so? Impossible! She had a hundred a year on the clear understanding that it was never exceeded nor anticipated. Well, you will discreetly hint, there are certain devices known to housewives . . . Hush! Vera had already employed them. Six and sevenpence was not merely all that remained to her of her dress allowance; it was all that remained to her of her household allowance till the next Monday.

Hence her nerves.

There that poor unfortunate woman lay, with her unconscious tyrant of a husband snoring beside her, desolately wakeful under the night-light in the large, luxurious bedroom – three servants sleeping over-head, champagne in the cellar, furs in the wardrobe, valuable lace round her neck at that very instant, grand piano in the drawing-room, horses in the stable, stuffed bear in the hall – and her life was made a blank for want of fourteen and fivepence! And she had nobody to confide in. How true it is that the human soul is solitary, that content is the only true riches, and that to be happy we must be good!

It was at that juncture of despair that she thought of mandarins. Or rather – I may as well be frank – she had been thinking of mandarins all the time since retiring to rest. There *might* be something in Charlie's mandarin theory . . . According to Charlie, so many queer, inexplicable things happened in the world. Occult – subliminal – astral – thought waves. These expressions and many more occurred to her as she recollected Charlie's disconcerting conversations. There *might* . . . One never knew.

Suddenly she thought of her husband's pockets, bulging with silver, with gold, and with bank-notes. Tantalising vision! No! She could not steal. Besides, he might wake up.

And she returned to mandarins. She got herself into a very morbid and two-o'clock-in-the-morning state of mind. Suppose it was a dodge that *did* work. (Of course, she was extremely superstitious; we all are.) She began to reflect seriously upon China. She remembered having heard that Chinese mandarins were very corrupt; that they ground the faces of the poor, and put innocent victims to the torture; in short, that they were sinful and horrid persons, scoundrels unfit for mercy. Then she pondered upon the remotest parts of China, regions where Europeans never could penetrate. No doubt there was some unimportant mandarin, somewhere in these regions, to whose district his death would be a decided blessing, to kill whom would indeed be an act of humanity. Probably a mandarin without wife or family; a bachelor mandarin whom no relative would regret; or, in the alternative, a mandarin with many wives, whose disgusting polygamy merited severe punishment! An old mandarin already pretty nearly dead; or, in the alternative, a young one just commencing a career of infamy!

'I'm awfully silly,' she whispered to herself. 'But still, if there *should* be anything in it. And I must, I must, I must have that thing for my dress!'

She looked again at the dim forms of her husband's clothes, pitched anyhow on an ottoman. No! She could not stoop to theft!

So she murdered a mandarin; lying in bed there; not any particular mandarin, a vague mandarin, the mandarin most convenient and suitable under all the circumstances. She deliberately wished him dead, on the off-chance of acquiring riches, or, more accurately, because she was short of fourteen and fivepence in order to look perfectly splendid at a ball.

In the morning when she woke up – her husband had already departed to the works – she thought how foolish she had been in the night. She did not feel sorry for having desired the death of a fellow-creature. Not at all. She felt sorry because she was convinced, in the cold light of day, that the charm would not work. Charlie's notions were really too ridiculous, too preposterous. No! She must reconcile herself to wearing a ball dress which was less than perfection, and all for the want of fourteen and fivepence. And she had more nerves than ever!

She had nerves to such an extent that when she went to unlock the drawer of her own private toilet-table, in which her prudent and fussy husband forced her to lock up her rings and brooches every night, she attacked the wrong drawer – an empty unfastened drawer that she never used. And lo! the empty drawer was not empty. There was a sovereign lying in it!

This gave her a start, connecting the discovery, as naturally at the first blush she did, with the mandarin.

Surely it couldn't be, after all.

Then she came to her senses. What absurdity! A coincidence, of course, nothing else? Besides, a mere sovereign! It wasn't enough. Charlie had said 'rich for life'. The sovereign must have lain there for months and months, forgotten.

However, it was none the less a sovereign. She picked it up, thanked Providence, ordered the dog-cart, and drove straight to Brunt's. The particular thing that she acquired was an exceedingly thin, slim, and fetching silver belt – a marvel for the money, and the ideal waist decoration for her wonderful white muslin gown. She bought it, and left the shop.

And as she came out of the shop, she saw a street urchin holding out the poster of the early edition of the *Signal*. And she read on the poster, in large letters:

DEATH OF LI HUNG CHANG

It is no exaggeration to say that she nearly fainted. Only by the exercise of that hard self-control, of which women alone are capable, did she refrain from tumbling against the blue-clad breast of Adams, the Cheswardine coachman.

She purchased the *Signal* with well-feigned calm, opened it and read: 'Stop-press news. Pekin. Li Hung Chang, the celebrated Chinese statesman, died at two o'clock this morning. – Reuter.'

3

Vera reclined on the sofa that afternoon, and the sofa was drawn round in front of the drawing-room fire. And she wore her fluffiest and languidest peignoir. And there was a perfume of eau de Cologne in the apartment. Vera was having a headache; she was having it in her grand, her official manner. Stephen had had to lunch alone. He had been told that in all probability his suffering wife would not be well enough to go to the ball. Whereupon he had grunted. As a fact, Vera's headache was extremely real, and she was very upset indeed.

The death of Li Hung Chang was heavy on her soul. Occultism was justified of itself. The affair lay beyond coincidence. She had always *known* that there was something in occultism, supernaturalism, so-called superstitions, what not. But she had never expected to prove the faith that was in her by such a homicidal act on her own part. It was detestable of Charlie to have mentioned the thing at all. He had no right to play with fire. And as for her husband, words could give but the merest rough outline of her resentment against Stephen. A pretty state of things that a woman with a position such as she had to keep up should be reduced to six and sevenpence! Stephen, no doubt, expected her to visit the pawnshop. It would serve him right if she did so – and he met her coming out under the three brass balls! Did she not dress solely and wholly to please him? Not in the least to please herself! Personally she had a mind set on higher things, impossible aspirations. But he liked fine clothes. And it was her duty to satisfy him. She strove to satisfy him

397

in all matters. She lived for him. She sacrificed herself to him completely. And what did she get in return? Nothing! Nothing! Nothing! All men were selfish. And women were their victims . . . Stephen, with his silly bullying rules against credit and so forth . . . The worst of men was that they had no sense.

She put a new dose of eau de Cologne on her forehead, and leaned on one elbow. On the mantelpiece lay the tissue parcel containing the slim silver belt, the price of Li's death. She wanted to stick it in the fire. And only the fact that it would not burn prevented her savagely doing so. There was something wrong, too, with the occultism. To receive a paltry sovereign for murdering the greatest statesman of the Eastern hemisphere was simply grotesque. Moreover, she had most distinctly not wanted to deprive China of a distinguished man. She had expressly stipulated for an inferior and insignificant mandarin, one that could be spared and that was unknown to Reuter. She supposed she ought to have looked up China at the Wedgwood Institution and selected a definite mandarin with a definite place of residence. But could she be expected to go about a murder deliberately like that?

With regard to the gross inadequacy of the fiscal return for her deed, perhaps that was her own fault. She had not wished for more. Her brain had been so occupied by the belt that she had wished only for the belt. But, perhaps, on the other hand, vast wealth was to come. Perhaps something might occur that very night. That would be better. Yet would it be better? However rich she might become, Stephen would coolly take charge of her riches, and dole them out to her, and make rules for her concerning them. And besides, Charlie would suspect her guilt. Charlie understood her, and perused her thoughts far better than Stephen did. She would never be able to conceal the truth from Charlie. The conversation, the death of Li within two hours, and then a sudden fortune accruing to her – Charlie would inevitably put two and two together and divine her shameful secret.

The outlook was thoroughly black anyway.

She then fell asleep.

When she awoke, some considerable time afterwards, Stephen was calling to her. It was his voice, indeed, that had aroused her. The room was dark.

'I say, Vera,' he demanded, in a low, slightly inimical tone, 'have you taken a sovereign out of the empty drawer in your toilet-table?'

'No,' she said quickly, without thinking.

'Ah!' he observed reflectively, 'I knew I was right.' He paused, and added, coldly, 'If you aren't better you ought to go to bed.'

Then he left her, shutting the door with a noise that showed a certain lack of sympathy with her headache.

She sprang up. Her first feeling was one of thankfulness that that brief interview had occurred in darkness. So Stephen was aware of the existence of the sovereign! The sovereign was not occult. Possibly he had put it there. And what did he know he was 'right' about?

She lighted the gas, and gazed at herself in the glass, realising that she no longer had a headache, and endeavouring to arrange her ideas.

'What's this?' said another voice at the door. She glanced round hastily, guiltily. It was Charlie.

'Steve telephoned me you were too ill to go to the dance,' explained Charlie, 'so I thought I'd come and make enquiries. I quite expected to find you in bed with a nurse and a doctor or two at least. What is it?' He smiled.

'Nothing,' she replied. 'Only a headache. It's gone now.'

She stood against the mantelpiece, so that he should not see the white parcel.

'That's good,' said Charlie.

There was a pause.

'Strange, Li Hung Chang dying last night, just after we had been talking about killing mandarins,' she said. She could not keep off the subject. It attracted her like a snake, and she approached it in spite of the fact that she fervently wished not to approach it.

'Yes,' said Charlie. 'But Li wasn't a mandarin, you know. And he didn't die after we had been talking about mandarins. He died before.'

'Oh! I thought it said in the paper he died at two o'clock this morning.'

'Two a.m. in Pekin,' Charlie answered. 'You must remember that Pekin time is many hours earlier than our time. It lies so far eastward.'

'Oh!' she said again.

Stephen hurried in, with a worried air.

'Ah! It's you, Charlie!'

'She isn't absolutely dying, I find,' said Charlie, turning to Vera: 'You are going to the dance after all – aren't you?'

'I say, Vera,' Stephen interrupted, 'either you or I must have a scene with Martha. I've always suspected that confounded housemaid. So I put a marked sovereign in a drawer this morning, and it was gone at lunchtime. She'd better hook it instantly. Of course I shan't prosecute.'

'Martha!' cried Vera. 'Stephen, what on earth are you thinking of? I wish you would leave the servants to me. If you think you can manage this house in your spare time from the works, you are welcome to try. But don't blame me for the consequences.' Glances of triumph flashed in her eyes.

'But I tell you – '

'Nonsense,' said Vera. 'I took the sovereign. I saw it there and I took it, and just to punish you, I've spent it. It's not at all nice to lay traps for servants like that.'

'Then why did you tell me just now you hadn't taken it?' Stephen demanded crossly.

'I didn't feel well enough to argue with you then,' Vera replied.

'You've recovered precious quick,' retorted Stephen with grimness.

'Of course, if you want to make a scene before strangers,' Vera whimpered (poor Charlie a stranger!), 'I'll go to bed.'

Stephen knew when he was beaten.

She went to the Hockey dance, though. She and Stephen and Charlie and his young sister, aged seventeen, all descended together to the Town Hall in a brougham. The young girl admired Vera's belt excessively, and looked forward to the moment when she too should be a bewitching and captivating wife like Vera, in short, a woman of the world, worshipped by grave, bearded men. And both the men were under the spell of Vera's incurable charm, capricious, surprising, exasperating, indefinable, indispensable to their lives.

'Stupid superstitions!' reflected Vera. 'But of course I never believed it really.'

And she cast down her eyes to gloat over the belt.

The Murdered Cousin

SHERIDAN LE FANU

And they lay wait for their own blood: they lurk
privily for their own lives. So are the ways of
every one that is greedy of gain; which taketh
away the life of the owner thereof.

This story of the Irish peerage is written, as nearly as
possible, in the very words in which it was related by
its 'heroine', the late Countess D—, and is therefore
told in the first person.

My mother died when I was an infant, and of her I
have no recollection, even the faintest. By her death
my education was left solely to the direction of my
surviving parent. He entered upon his task with a
stern appreciation of the responsibility thus cast upon
him. My religious instruction was prosecuted with an
almost exaggerated anxiety; and I had, of course, the
best masters to perfect me in all those accomplish-
ments which my station and wealth might seem to
require. My father was what is called an oddity, and
his treatment of me, though uniformly kind, was
governed less by affection and tenderness, than by a
high and unbending sense of duty. Indeed I seldom
saw or spoke to him except at meal-times, and then,
though gentle, he was usually reserved and gloomy.
His leisure hours, which were many, were passed
either in his study or in solitary walks; in short, he
seemed to take no further interest in my happiness or

improvement, than a conscientious regard to the discharge of his own duty would seem to impose.

Shortly before my birth an event occurred which had contributed much to induce and to confirm my father's unsocial habits; it was the fact that a suspicion of *murder* had fallen upon his younger brother, though not sufficiently definite to lead to any public proceedings, yet strong enough to ruin him in public opinion. This disgraceful and dreadful doubt cast upon the family name, my father felt deeply and bitterly, and not the less so that he himself was thoroughly convinced of his brother's innocence. The sincerity and strength of this conviction he shortly afterwards proved in a manner which produced the catastrophe of my story.

Before, however, I enter upon my immediate adventures, I ought to relate the circumstances which had awakened that suspicion to which I have referred, inasmuch as they are in themselves somewhat curious, and in their effects most intimately connected with my own after-history.

My uncle, Sir Arthur Tyrrell, was a gay and extravagant man, and, among other vices, was ruinously addicted to gaming. This unfortunate propensity, even after his fortune had suffered so severely as to render retrenchment imperative, nevertheless continued to engross him, nearly to the exclusion of every other pursuit. He was, however, a proud, or rather a vain man, and could not bear to make the diminution of his income a matter of triumph to those with whom he had hitherto competed; and the consequence was, that he frequented no longer the expensive haunts of his dissipation, and retired from the gay world, leaving his coterie to discover his reasons as best they might.

He did not, however, forgo his favourite vice, for though he could not worship his great divinity in those costly temples where he was formerly wont to take his place, yet he found it very possible to bring about him a sufficient number of the votaries of chance to answer all his ends. The consequence was, that Carrickleigh, which was the name of my uncle's residence, was never without one or more of such visitors as I have described. It happened that upon one occasion he was visited by one Hugh Tisdall, a gentleman of loose, and, indeed, low habits, but of considerable wealth, and who had, in early youth, travelled with my uncle upon the Continent. The period of this visit was winter, and, consequently, the house was nearly deserted excepting by its ordinary inmates; it was, therefore, highly acceptable, particularly as my uncle was aware that his visitor's tastes accorded exactly with his own.

Both parties seemed determined to avail themselves of their mutual suitability during the brief stay which Mr Tisdall had promised; the consequence was, that they shut themselves up in Sir Arthur's private room for nearly all the day and the greater part of the night, during the space of almost a week, at the end of which the servant having one morning, as usual, knocked at Mr Tisdall's bedroom door repeatedly, received no answer, and, upon attempting to enter, found that it was locked. This appeared suspicious, and the inmates of the house having been alarmed, the door was forced open, and, on proceeding to the bed, they found the body of its occupant perfectly lifeless, and hanging halfway out, the head downwards, and near the floor. One deep wound had been inflicted upon the temple, apparently with some blunt instrument, which had penetrated the brain, and another blow, less effective – probably the first aimed – had grazed his head, removing some of the scalp. The door had been double locked upon the *inside*, in evidence of which the key still lay where it had been placed in the lock. The window, though not secured on the interior, was closed; a circumstance not a little puzzling, as it afforded the only other mode of escape from the room. It looked out, too, upon a kind of courtyard, round which the old buildings stood, formerly accessible by a narrow doorway and passage lying in the oldest side of the quadrangle, but which had since been built up, so as to preclude all ingress or egress; the room was also upon the second storey, and the height of the window considerable; in addition to all which the stone window-sill was much too narrow to allow of anyone's standing upon it when the window was closed. Near the bed were found a pair of razors belonging to the murdered man, one of them upon the ground, and both of them open. The weapon which inflicted the mortal wound was not to be found in the room, nor were any footsteps or other traces of the murderer discoverable. At the suggestion of Sir Arthur himself, the coroner was instantly summoned to attend, and an inquest was held. Nothing, however, in any degree conclusive was elicited. The walls, ceiling, and floor of the room were carefully examined, in order to ascertain whether they contained a trap-door or other concealed mode of entrance, but no such thing appeared. Such was the minuteness of investigation employed, that, although the grate had contained a large fire during the night, they proceeded to examine even the very chimney, in order to discover whether escape by it were possible. But this attempt, too, was fruitless, for the chimney, built in the old fashion, rose in a perfectly perpendicular line from the hearth, to a height of nearly fourteen feet above the roof, affording in its interior scarcely the possibility of ascent, the flue being smoothly plastered, and sloping towards the top like an inverted funnel; promising, too, even if the summit were attained, owing to its great height, but a precarious descent upon the sharp and steep-ridged roof; the ashes, too, which lay in the grate, and the soot, as far as it could be seen, were undisturbed, a circumstance almost conclusive upon the point.

Sir Arthur was of course examined. His evidence was given with clearness and unreserve, which seemed calculated to silence all suspicion. He stated that, up to the day and night immediately preceding the catastrophe, he had lost to a heavy amount, but that, at their last sitting, he had not only won back his original loss, but upwards of £4,000 in addition; in evidence of which he produced an acknowledgement of debt to that amount in the handwriting of the deceased, bearing date the night of the catastrophe. He had mentioned the circumstance to Lady Tyrrell, and in presence of some of his domestics; which statement was supported by *their* respective evidence. One of the jury shrewdly observed, that the circumstance of Mr Tisdall's having sustained so heavy a loss might have suggested to some ill-minded persons, accidentally hearing it, the plan of robbing him, after having murdered him in such a manner as might make it appear that he had committed suicide; a supposition which was strongly supported by the razors having been found thus displaced and removed from their case. Two persons had probably been engaged in the attempt, one watching by the sleeping man, and ready to strike him in case of his awakening suddenly, while the other was procuring the razors and employed in inflicting the fatal gash, so as to make it appear to have been the act of the murdered man himself. It was said that while the juror was making this suggestion Sir Arthur changed colour. There was nothing, however, like legal evidence to implicate him, and the consequence was that the verdict was found against a person or persons unknown, and for some time the matter was suffered to rest, until, after about five months, my father received a letter from a person signing himself Andrew Collis, and representing himself to be the cousin of the deceased. This letter stated that his brother, Sir Arthur, was likely to incur not merely suspicion but personal risk, unless he could account for certain circumstances connected with the recent murder, and contained a copy of a letter written by the deceased, and dated the very day upon the night of which the murder had been perpetrated. Tisdall's letter contained, among a great deal of other matter, the passages which follow: 'I have had sharp work with Sir Arthur: he tried some of his stale tricks, but soon found that *I* was Yorkshire, too; it would not do – you understand me. We went to the work like good ones, head, heart, and soul; and in fact, since I came here, I have lost no time. I am rather fagged, but I am sure to be well paid for my hardship; I never want sleep so long as I can have the music of a dice-box, and wherewithal to pay the piper. As I told you, he tried some of his queer turns, but I foiled him like a man, and, in return, gave him more than he could relish of the genuine *dead knowledge*. In short, I have plucked the old baronet as never baronet was plucked before; I have scarce left him the stump of a quill. I have got promissory notes in his hand to the amount of – ; if you like round numbers, say five-and-twenty thousand pounds, safely deposited in my portable strong box, alias, double-clasped pocketbook. I leave this ruinous old rat-hole early on tomorrow, for two reasons: first, I do not want to play with Sir Arthur deeper than I think his security would warrant; and, secondly, because I am safer a hundred miles away from Sir Arthur than in the house with him. Look you, my worthy, I tell you this between ourselves – I may be wrong – but, by — , I am sure as that I am now living, that Sir A— attempted to poison me last night. So much for old friendship on both sides. When I won the last stake, a heavy one enough, my friend leant his forehead upon his hands, and you'll laugh when I tell you that his head literally smoked like a hot dumpling. I do not know whether his agitation was produced by the plan which he had against me, or by his having lost so heavily; though it must be allowed that he had reason to be a little funked, whichever way his thoughts went; but he pulled the bell, and ordered two bottles of Champagne. While the fellow was bringing them, he wrote a promissory note to the full amount, which he signed, and, as the man came in with the bottles and glasses, he desired him to be off. He filled a glass for me, and, while he thought my eyes were off, for I was putting up his note at the time, he dropped something slyly into it, no doubt to sweeten it; but I saw it all, and, when he handed it to me, I said, with an emphasis which he might easily understand, "There is some sediment in it, I'll not drink it." "Is there?" said he, and at the same time snatched it from my hand and threw it into the fire. What do you think of that? Have I not a tender bird in hand? Win or lose, I will not play beyond five thousand tonight, and tomorrow sees me safe out of the reach of Sir Arthur's Champagne.'

Of the authenticity of this document, I never heard my father express a doubt; and I am satisfied that, owing to his strong conviction in favour of his brother, he would not have admitted it without sufficient enquiry, inasmuch as it tended to confirm the suspicions which already existed to his prejudice. Now, the only point in this letter which made strongly against my uncle, was the mention of the 'double-clasped pocketbook', as the receptacle of the papers likely to involve him, for this pocketbook was not forthcoming, nor anywhere to be found, nor had any papers referring to his gaming transactions been discovered upon the dead man.

But whatever might have been the original intention of this man, Collis, neither my uncle nor my father ever heard more of him; he published the letter, however, in Faulkner's newspaper, which was shortly afterwards made the vehicle of a much more mysterious attack. The passage in that journal to which I allude, appeared about four years afterwards, and while the fatal occurrence was still fresh in public recollection. It commenced by a rambling preface, stating that 'a *certain person* whom *certain* persons thought to be dead, was not so, but living, and in full possession of his memory, and moreover, ready and able to make *great* delinquents tremble': it then went on to describe the murder, without, however, mentioning names; and in doing so, it entered into minute and circumstantial particulars of which none but an *eye-witness* could have been possessed, and by implications almost too unequivocal to be regarded in the light of insinuation, to involve the '*titled gambler*' in the guilt of the transaction.

My father at once urged Sir Arthur to proceed against the paper in an action of libel, but he would not hear of it, nor consent to my father's taking any legal steps whatever in the matter. My father, however, wrote in a threatening tone to Faulkner, demanding a surrender of the author of the obnoxious article; the answer to this application is still in my possession, and is penned in an apologetic tone: it states that the manuscript had been handed in, paid for, and inserted as an advertisement, without sufficient enquiry, or any knowledge as to whom it referred. No step, however, was taken to clear my uncle's character in the judgement of the public; and, as he immediately sold a small property, the application of the proceeds of which were known to none, he was said to have disposed of it to enable himself to buy off the threatened information; however the truth might have been, it is certain that no charges respecting the mysterious murder were afterwards publicly made against my uncle, and, as far as external disturbances were concerned, he enjoyed henceforward perfect security and quiet.

A deep and lasting impression, however, had been made upon the public mind, and Sir Arthur Tyrrell was no longer visited or noticed by the gentry of the county, whose attentions he had hitherto received. He accordingly affected to despise those courtesies which he no longer enjoyed, and shunned even that society which he might have commanded. This is all that I need recapitulate of my uncle's history, and I now recur to my own.

Although my father had never, within my recollection, visited, or been visited by my uncle, each being of unsocial, procrastinating, and indolent habits, and their respective residences being very far apart – the one lying in the county of Galway, the other in that of Cork – he was strongly attached to his brother, and evinced his affection by an active correspondence, and by deeply and proudly resenting that neglect which had branded Sir Arthur as unfit to mix in society.

When I was about eighteen years of age, my father, whose health had been gradually declining, died, leaving me in heart wretched and desolate, and, owing to his habitual seclusion, with few acquaintances, and almost no friends. The provisions of his will were curious, and when I was sufficiently come to myself to listen to, or comprehend them, surprised me not a little: all his vast property was left to me, and to the heirs of my body, for ever; and, in default of such heirs, it was to go after my death to my uncle, Sir Arthur, without any entail. At the same time, the will appointed him my guardian, desiring that I might be received within his house, and reside with his family, and under his care, during the term of my minority; and in consideration of the increased expense consequent upon such an arrangement, a handsome allowance was allotted to him during the term of my proposed residence. The object of this last provision I at once understood; my father desired, by making it the direct apparent interest of Sir Arthur that I should die without issue, while at the same time he placed my person wholly in his power, to prove to the world how great and unshaken was his confidence in his brother's innocence and honour. It was a strange, perhaps an idle scheme, but as I had been always brought up in the habit of considering my uncle as a deeply injured man, and had been taught, almost as a part of my religion, to regard him as the very soul of honour, I felt no further uneasiness respecting the arrangement than that likely to affect a shy and timid girl at the immediate prospect of taking up her abode for the first time in her life among strangers. Previous to leaving my home, which I felt I should do with a heavy heart, I received a most tender and affectionate letter from my uncle, calculated, if anything could do so, to remove the bitterness of parting from scenes familiar and dear from my earliest childhood, and in some degree to reconcile me to the measure.

It was upon a fine autumn day that I approached the old domain of Carrickleigh. I shall not soon forget the impression of sadness and of gloom which all that I saw produced upon my mind; the sunbeams were falling with a rich and melancholy lustre upon the fine old trees, which stood in lordly groups, casting their long sweeping shadows over rock and sward; there was an air of neglect and decay about the spot, which amounted almost to desolation, and mournfully increased as we approached the building itself, near which the ground had been originally more artificially and carefully cultivated than elsewhere, and where consequently neglect more immediately and strikingly betrayed itself.

As we proceeded, the road wound near the beds of what had been formerly two fishponds, which were now nothing more than stagnant swamps, overgrown with rank weeds, and here and there encroached upon by the straggling underwood; the avenue itself was much broken; and in many places the stones were almost concealed by grass and nettles; the loose stone walls which had here and there intersected the broad park, were, in many places, broken down, so as no longer to answer their original purpose as fences; piers were now and then to be seen, but the gates were gone; and to add to the general air of dilapidation, some huge trunks were lying scattered through the venerable old trees, either the work of the winter storms, or perhaps the victims of some extensive but desultory scheme of denudation, which the projector had not capital or perseverance to carry into full effect.

After the carriage had travelled a full mile of this avenue, we reached the summit of a rather abrupt eminence, one of the many which added to the picturesqueness, if not to the convenience of this rude approach; from the top of this ridge the grey walls of Carrickleigh were visible, rising at a small distance in front, and darkened by the hoary wood which crowded around them; it was a quadrangular building of considerable extent, and the front, where the great entrance was placed, lay towards us, and bore unequivocal marks of antiquity; the timeworn, solemn aspect of the old building, the ruinous and deserted appearance of the whole place, and the associations which connected it with a dark page in the history of my family, combined to depress spirits already predisposed for the reception of sombre and dejecting impressions. When the carriage drew up in the grass-grown courtyard before the hall-door, two lazy-looking men, whose appearance well accorded with that of the place which they tenanted, alarmed by the obstreperous barking of a great chained dog, ran out from some half-ruinous outhouses, and took charge of the horses; the hall-door stood open, and I entered a gloomy and imperfectly lighted apartment, and found no one within it. However, I had not long to wait in this awkward predicament, for before my luggage had been deposited in the house, indeed before I had well removed my cloak and other muffles, so as to enable me to look around, a young girl ran lightly into the hall, and kissing me heartily and somewhat boisterously exclaimed, 'My dear cousin, my dear Margaret – I am so delighted – so out of breath, we did not expect you till ten o'clock; my father is somewhere about the place, he must be close at hand. James – Corney – run out and tell your master; my brother is seldom at home, at least at any reasonable hour; you must be so tired – so fatigued – let me show you to your room; see that Lady Margaret's luggage is all brought up; you must lie down and rest yourself. Deborah, bring some coffee – up these stairs; we are so delighted to see you – you cannot think how lonely I have been; how steep these stairs are, are not they? I am so glad you are come – I could hardly bring myself to believe that you were really coming; how good of you, dear Lady Margaret.' There was real good nature and delight in my cousin's greeting, and a kind of constitutional confidence of manner which placed me at once at ease, and made me feel immediately upon terms of intimacy with her. The room into which she ushered me, although partaking in the general air of decay which pervaded the mansion and all about it, had, nevertheless, been fitted up with evident attention to comfort, and even with some dingy attempt at luxury; but what pleased me most was that it opened, by a second door, upon a lobby which communicated with my fair cousin's apartment; a circumstance which divested the room, in my eyes, of the air of solitude and sadness which would otherwise have characterised it, to a degree almost painful to one so depressed and agitated as I was.

After such arrangements as I found necessary were completed, we both went down to the parlour, a large wainscotted room, hung round with grim old portraits, and, as I was not sorry to see, containing, in its ample grate, a large and cheerful fire. Here my cousin had leisure to talk more at her ease; and from her I learned something of the manners and the habits of the two remaining members of her family, whom I had not yet seen. On my arrival I had known nothing of the family among whom I was come to reside, except that it consisted of three individuals, my uncle, and his son and daughter, Lady Tyrrell having been long dead; in addition to this very scanty stock of information, I shortly learned from my communicative companion, that my uncle was, as I had suspected, completely retired in his habits, and besides that, having been, so far back as she could well recollect, always rather strict, as reformed rakes frequently become, he had latterly been growing more gloomily and sternly religious than heretofore. Her account of her brother was far less favourable, though she did not say anything directly to his disadvantage. From all that I could gather from her, I was led to suppose that he was a specimen of the idle, coarse-mannered, profligate 'squirearchy' – a result which might naturally have followed from the circumstance of his being, as it were, outlawed from society, and driven for companionship to grades below his own – enjoying, too, the dangerous prerogative of spending a good deal of money. However, you may easily suppose that I found nothing in my cousin's communication fully to bear me out in so very decided a conclusion.

I awaited the arrival of my uncle, which was every moment to be expected, with feelings half of alarm, half of curiosity – a sensation which I have often since experienced, though to a less degree, when upon the point of standing for the first time in the presence of one of whom I have long been in the habit of hearing or thinking with interest. It was, therefore, with some little perturbation that I heard, first a slight bustle at the outer door, then a slow step traverse the hall, and finally witnessed the door open, and my uncle enter the room. He was a striking looking man; from peculiarities both of person and of dress, the whole effect of his appearance amounted to extreme singularity. He was tall, and when young his figure must have been strikingly elegant; as it was, however, its effect was marred by a very decided stoop; his dress was of a sober colour, and in fashion anterior to any thing which I could remember. It was, however, handsome, and by no means carelessly put on; but what completed the singularity of his appearance was his uncut, white hair, which hung in long, but not at all neglected curls, even so far as his shoulders, and which combined with his regularly classic features, and fine dark eyes, to bestow upon him an air of venerable dignity and pride, which I have seldom seen equalled elsewhere. I rose as he entered, and met him about the middle of the room; he kissed my cheek and both my hands, saying: 'You are most welcome, dear child, as welcome as the command of this poor place and all that it contains can make you. I am rejoiced to see you – truly rejoiced. I trust that you are not much fatigued; pray be seated again.' He led me to my chair, and continued, 'I am glad to perceive you have made acquaintance with Emily already; I see, in your being thus brought together, the foundation of a lasting friendship. You are both innocent, and both young. God bless you – God bless you, and make you all that I could wish.'

He raised his eyes, and remained for a few moments silent, as if in secret prayer. I felt that it was impossible that this man, with feelings manifestly so tender, could be the wretch that public opinion had represented him to be. I was more than ever convinced of his innocence. His manners were, or appeared to me, most fascinating. I know not how the lights of experience might have altered this estimate. But I was then very young, and I beheld in him a perfect mingling of the courtesy of polished life with the gentlest and most genial virtues of the heart. A feeling of affection and respect towards him began to spring up within me, the more earnest that I remembered how sorely he had suffered in fortune and how cruelly in fame. My uncle having given me fully to under-stand that I was most welcome, and might command whatever was his own, pressed me to take some supper; and on my refusing, he observed that, before bidding me good-night, he had one duty further to perform, one in which he was convinced I would cheerfully acquiesce. He then proceeded to read a chapter from the Bible; after which he took his leave with the same affectionate kindness with which he had greeted me, having repeated his desire that I should consider every thing in his house as altogether at my disposal. It is needless to say how much I was pleased with my uncle – it was impossible to avoid being so; and I could not help saying to myself, if such a man as this is not safe from the assaults of slander, who is? I felt much happier than I had done since my father's death, and enjoyed that night the first refreshing sleep which had visited me since that calamity. My curiosity respecting my male cousin did not long remain unsatisfied; he appeared upon the next day at dinner. His manners, though not so coarse as I had expected, were exceedingly disagreeable; there was an assurance and a forwardness for which I was not prepared; there was less of the vulgarity of manner, and almost more of that of the mind, than I had anticipated. I felt quite uncomfortable in his presence; there was just that confidence in his look and tone, which would read encouragement even in mere toleration; and I felt more disgusted and annoyed at the coarse and extravagant compliments which he was pleased from time to time to pay me, than perhaps the extent of the atrocity might fully have warranted. It was, however, one consolation that he did not often appear, being much engrossed by pursuits about which I neither knew nor cared anything; but when he did, his attentions, either with a view to his amusement, or to some more serious object, were so obviously and perseveringly directed to me, that young and inexperienced as I was, even *I* could not be ignorant of their significance. I felt more provoked by this odious persecution than I can express, and discouraged him with so much vigour, that I did not stop even at rudeness to convince him that his assiduities were unwelcome; but all in vain.

This had gone on for nearly a twelve-month, to my infinite annoyance, when one day, as I was sitting at some needlework with my companion, Emily, as was my habit, in the parlour, the door opened, and my cousin Edward entered the room. There was something, I thought, odd in his manner, a kind of struggle between shame and impudence, a kind of flurry and ambiguity, which made him appear, if possible, more than ordinarily disagreeable.

'Your servant, ladies,' he said, seating himself at the same time; 'sorry to spoil your tête-à-tête; but never mind, I'll only take Emily's place for a minute or two, and then we part for a while, fair cousin. Emily, my father wants you in the corner turret; no shilly, shally, he's in a hurry.' She hesitated. 'Be off – tramp, march, I say,' he exclaimed, in a tone which the poor girl dared not disobey.

She left the room, and Edward followed her to the door. He stood there for a minute or two, as if reflecting what he should say, perhaps satisfying himself that no one was within hearing in the hall. At length he turned about, having closed the door, as if carelessly, with his foot, and advancing slowly, in deep thought, he took his seat at the side of the table opposite to mine. There was a brief interval of silence, after which he said: 'I imagine that you have a shrewd suspicion of the object of my early visit; but I suppose I must go into particulars. Must I?'

'I have no conception,' I replied, 'what your object may be.'

'Well, well,' said he, becoming more at his ease as he proceeded, 'it may be told in a few words. You know that it is totally impossible, quite out of the question, that an off-hand young fellow like me, and a good-looking girl like yourself, could meet continually as you and I have done, without an attachment – a liking growing up on one side or other; in short, I think I have let you know as plainly as if I spoke it, that I have been in love with you, almost from the first time I saw you.' He paused, but I was too much horrified to speak. He interpreted my silence favourably. 'I can tell you,' he continued, 'I'm reckoned rather hard to please, and very hard to *hit*. I can't say when I was taken with a girl before, so you see fortune reserved me – .'

Here the odious wretch actually put his arm round my waist: the action at once restored me to utterance, and with the most indignant vehemence I released myself from his hold, and at the same time said: 'I *have*, sir, of course, perceived your most disagreeable attentions; they have long been a source of great annoyance to me; and you must be aware that I have marked my disapprobation, my disgust, as unequivocally as I possibly could, without actual indelicacy.'

I paused, almost out of breath from the rapidity with which I had spoken; and without giving him time to renew the conversation, I hastily quitted the room, leaving him in a paroxysm of rage and mortification. As I ascended the stairs, I heard him open the parlour-door with violence, and take two or three rapid strides in the direction in which I was moving. I was now much frightened, and ran the whole way until I reached my room, and having locked the door, I listened breathlessly, but heard no sound. This relieved me for the present; but so much had I been overcome by the agitation and annoyance attendant upon the scene which I had just passed through, that when my cousin Emily knocked at the door, I was weeping in great agitation. You will readily conceive my distress, when you reflect upon my strong dislike to my cousin Edward, combined with my youth and extreme inexperience. Any proposal of such a nature must have agitated me; but that it should come from the man whom, of all others, I instinctively most loathed and abhorred, and to whom I had, as clearly as manner could do it, expressed the state of my feelings, was almost too annoying to be borne; it was a calamity, too, in which I could not claim the sympathy of my cousin Emily, which had always been extended to me in my minor grievances. Still I hoped that it might not be unattended with good; for I thought that one inevitable and most welcome consequence would result from this painful *claircissement,* in the discontinuance of my cousin's odious persecution.

When I arose next morning, it was with the fervent hope that I might never again behold his face, or even hear his name; but such a consummation, though devoutedly to be wished, was hardly likely to occur. The painful impressions of yesterday were too vivid to be at once erased; and I could not help feeling some dim foreboding of coming annoyance and evil. To expect on my cousin's part anything like delicacy or consideration for me, was out of the question. I saw that he had set his heart upon my property, and that he was not likely easily to forgo such a prize, possessing what might have been considered opportunities and facilities almost to compel my compliance. I now keenly felt the unreasonableness of my father's conduct in placing me to reside with a family, with all the members of which, with one exception, he was wholly unacquainted, and I bitterly felt the helplessness of my situation. I determined, however, in the event of my cousin's persevering in his addresses, to lay all the particulars before my uncle, although he had never, in kindness or intimacy, gone a step beyond our first interview, and to throw myself upon his hospitality and his sense of honour for protection against a repetition of such annoyances.

My cousin's conduct may appear to have been an inadequate cause for such serious uneasiness; but my alarm was awakened neither by his acts nor by words, but entirely by his manner, which was strange and even intimidating. At the beginning of our yesterday's interview, there was a sort of bullying swagger in his air, which, towards the end, gave place to something bordering upon the brutal vehemence of an undisguised ruffian, a transition which had tempted me into a belief that he might seek, even forcibly, to extort from me a consent to his wishes, or by means still more horrible, of which I scarcely dared to trust myself to think, to possess himself of my property.

I was early next day summoned to attend my uncle in his private room, which lay in a corner turret of the old building; and thither I accordingly went, wondering all the way what this unusual measure might prelude. When I entered the room, he did not rise in his usual courteous way to greet me, but simply pointed to a chair opposite to his own; this boded nothing agreeable. I sat down, however, silently waiting until he should open the conversation.

'Lady Margaret,' at length he said, in a tone of greater sternness than I thought him capable of using, 'I have hitherto spoken to you as a friend, but I have not forgotten that I am also your guardian, and that

423

my authority as such gives me a right to control your conduct. I shall put a question to you, and I expect and will demand a plain, direct answer. Have I rightly been informed that you have contemptuously rejected the suit and hand of my son Edward?'

I stammered forth with a good deal of trepidation: 'I believe, that is, I have, sir, rejected my cousin's proposals; and my coldness and discouragement might have convinced him that I had determined to do so.'

'Madame,' replied he, with suppressed, but, as it appeared to me, intense anger, 'I have lived long enough to know that *coldness and discouragement*, and such terms, form the common cant of a worthless coquette. You know to the full, as well as I, that *coldness and discouragement* may be so exhibited as to convince their object that he is neither distasteful nor indifferent to the person who wears that manner. You know, too, none better, that an affected neglect, when skilfully managed, is amongst the most formidable of the allurements which artful beauty can employ. I tell you, madame, that having, without one word spoken in discouragement, permitted my son's most marked attentions for a twelve-month or more, you have no *right* to dismiss him with no further explanation than demurely telling him that you had always looked coldly upon him, and neither your wealth nor *your ladyship* (there was an emphasis of scorn on the word which would have become Sir Giles Overreach him-self) can warrant you in treating with contempt the affectionate regard of an honest heart.'

I was too much shocked at this undisguised attempt to bully me into an acquiescence in the interested and unprincipled plan for their own aggrandisement, which I now perceived my uncle and his son had deliberately formed, at once to find strength or collectedness to frame an answer to what he had said. At length I replied, with a firmness that surprised myself: 'In all that you have just now said, sir, you have grossly misstated my conduct and motives. Your information must have been most incorrect, as far as it regards my conduct towards my cousin; my manner towards him could have conveyed nothing but dislike; and if anything could have added to the strong aversion which I have long felt towards him, it would be his attempting thus to frighten me into a marriage which he knows to be revolting to me, and which is sought by him only as a means for securing to himself whatever property is mine.'

As I said this, I fixed my eyes upon those of my uncle, but he was too old in the world's ways to falter beneath the gaze of more searching eyes than mine; he simply said: 'Are you acquainted with the provisions of your father's will?'

I answered in the affirmative; and he continued: 'Then you must be aware that if my son Edward were, which God forbid, the unprincipled, reckless man, the ruffian you pretend to think him' – (here he spoke very slowly, as if he intended that every word which escaped him should be registered in my memory, while at the same time the expression of his countenance underwent a gradual but horrible change, and the eyes which he fixed upon me became so darkly vivid, that I almost lost sight of everything else) – 'if he were what you have described him, do you think, child, he would have found no shorter way than marriage to gain his ends? A single blow, an outrage not a degree worse than you insinuate, would transfer your property to us!!'

I stood staring at him for many minutes after he had ceased to speak, fascinated by the terrible, serpent-like gaze, until he continued with a welcome change of countenance: 'I will not speak again to you, upon this topic, until one month has passed. You shall have time to consider the relative advantages of the two courses which are open to you. I should be sorry to hurry you to a decision. I am satisfied with having stated my feelings upon the subject, and pointed out to you the path of duty. Remember this day month; not one word sooner.'

He then rose, and I left the room, much agitated and exhausted.

This interview, all the circumstances attending it, but most particularly the formidable expression of my uncle's countenance while he talked, though hypothetically, of *murder*, combined to arouse all my worst suspicions of him. I dreaded to look upon the face that had so recently worn the appalling livery of guilt and malignity. I regarded it with the mingled fear and loathing with which one looks upon an object which has tortured them in a nightmare.

In a few days after the interview, the particulars of which I have just detailed, I found a note upon my toilet-table, and on opening it I read as follows:

MY DEAR LADY MARGARET – You will be, perhaps, surprised to see a strange face in your room today. I have dismissed your Irish maid, and secured a French one to wait upon you; a step rendered necessary by my proposing shortly to visit the Continent with all my family.

Your faithful guardian,

ARTHUR TYRELL

On enquiry, I found that my faithful attendant was actually gone, and far on her way to the town of Galway; and in her stead there appeared a tall, raw-boned, ill-looking, elderly Frenchwoman, whose sullen and presuming manners seemed to imply that her vocation had never before been that of a lady's-maid. I could not help regarding her as a creature of my uncle's, and therefore to be dreaded, even had she been in no other way suspicious.

Days and weeks passed away without any, even a momentary doubt upon my part, as to the course to be pursued by me. The allotted period had at length elapsed; the day arrived upon which I was to communicate my decision to my uncle. Although my resolution had never for a moment wavered, I could not shake off the dread of the approaching colloquy; and my heart sank within me as I heard the expected summons. I had not seen my cousin Edward since the occurrence of the grand *claircissement*; he must have studiously avoided me; I suppose from policy, it could not have been from delicacy. I was prepared for a terrific burst of fury from my uncle, as soon as I should make known my determination; and I not unreasonably feared that some act of violence or of intimidation would next be resorted to. Filled with these dreary forebodings, I fearfully opened the study door, and the next minute I stood in my uncle's presence. He received me with a courtesy which I dreaded, as arguing a favourable anticipation respecting the answer which I was to give; and after some slight delay he began by saying: 'It will be a relief to both of us, I believe, to bring this conversation as soon as possible to an issue. You will excuse me, then, my dear niece, for speaking with a bluntness which, under other circumstances, would be unpardonable. You have, I am certain, given the subject of our last interview fair and serious consideration; and I trust that you are now prepared with candour to lay your answer before me. A few words will suffice; we perfectly understand one another.'

He paused; and I, though feeling that I stood upon a mine which might in an instant explode, nevertheless answered with perfect composure: 'I must now, sir, make the same reply which I did upon the last occasion, and I reiterate the declaration which I then made, that I never can nor will, while life and reason remain, consent to a union with my cousin Edward.'

This announcement wrought no apparent change in Sir Arthur, except that he became deadly, almost lividly pale. He seemed lost in dark thought for a minute, and then, with a slight effort, said, 'You have answered me honestly and directly; and you say your resolution is unchangeable; well, would it had been otherwise – would it had been otherwise – but be it as it is; I am satisfied.'

He gave me his hand – it was cold and damp as death; under an assumed calmness, it was evident that he was fearfully agitated. He continued to hold my hand with an almost painful pressure, while, as if unconsciously, seeming to forget my presence, he muttered, 'Strange, strange, strange, indeed! fatuity, helpless fatuity!' There was here a long pause. 'Madness *indeed* to strain a cable that is rotten to the very heart; it must break – and then – all goes.' There was again a pause of some minutes, after which, suddenly changing his voice and manner to one of wakeful alacrity, he exclaimed,

'Margaret, my son Edward shall plague you no more. He leaves this country tomorrow for France; he shall speak no more upon this subject – never, never more; whatever events depended upon your answer must now take their own course; but as for this fruitless proposal, it has been tried enough; it can be repeated no more.'

At these words he coldly suffered my hand to drop, as if to express his total abandonment of all his projected schemes of alliance; and certainly the action, with the accompanying words, produced upon my mind a more solemn and depressing effect than I believed possible to have been caused by the course which I had determined to pursue; it struck upon my heart with an awe and heaviness which *will* accompany the accomplishment of an important and irrevocable act, even though no doubt or scruple remains to make it possible that the agent should wish it undone.

'Well,' said my uncle, after a little time, 'we now cease to speak upon this topic, never to resume it again. Remember you shall have no farther uneasiness from Edward; he leaves Ireland for France tomorrow; this will be a relief to you; may I depend upon your *honour* that no word touching the subject of this interview shall ever escape you?' I gave him the desired assurance; he said, 'It is well; I am satisfied; we have nothing more, I believe, to say upon either side, and my presence must be a restraint upon you, I shall therefore bid you farewell.' I then left the apartment, scarcely knowing what to think of the strange interview which had just taken place.

On the next day my uncle took occasion to tell me that Edward had actually sailed, if his intention had not been prevented by adverse winds or weather; and two days after he actually produced a letter from his son, written, as it said, *on board*, and despatched while the ship was getting under weigh. This was a great satisfaction to me, and as being likely to prove so, it was no doubt communicated to me by Sir Arthur.

During all this trying period I had found infinite consolation in the society and sympathy of my dear cousin Emily. I never, in afterlife, formed a friendship so close, so fervent, and upon which, in all its progress, I could look back with feelings of such unalloyed pleasure, upon whose termination I must ever dwell with so deep, so yet unembittered a sorrow. In cheerful converse with her I soon recovered my spirits considerably, and passed my time agreeably enough, although still in the utmost seclusion. Matters went on smoothly enough, although I could not help sometimes feeling a momentary, but horrible uncertainty respecting my uncle's character; which was not altogether unwarranted by the circumstances of the two trying interviews, the particulars of which I have just detailed. The unpleasant impression which these conferences were calculated to leave upon my mind was fast wearing away, when there occurred a circumstance, slight indeed in itself, but calculated irrepressibly to awaken all my worst suspicions, and to overwhelm me again with anxiety and terror.

I had one day left the house with my cousin Emily, in order to take a ramble of considerable length, for the purpose of sketching some favourite views, and we had walked about half a mile when I perceived that we had forgotten our drawing materials, the absence of which would have defeated the object of our walk. Laughing at our own thoughtlessness, we returned to the house, and leaving Emily outside, I

ran upstairs to procure the drawing-books and pencils
which lay in my bedroom. As I ran up the stairs, I was
met by the tall, ill-looking Frenchwoman, evidently a
good deal flurried; '*Que veut Madame?*' said she, with
a more decided effort to be polite, than I had ever
known her make before. 'No, no – no matter,' said I,
hastily running by her in the direction of my room.
'Madame,' cried she, in a high key, '*restez ici s'il vous
plaît, votre chambre n'est pas faite.*' I continued to move
on without heeding her. She was some way behind
me, and feeling that she could not otherwise prevent
my entrance, for I was now upon the very lobby, she
made a desperate attempt to seize hold of my person;
she succeeded in grasping the end of my shawl, which
she drew from my shoulders, but slipping at the
same time upon the polished oak floor, she fell at full
length upon the boards. A little frightened as well as
angry at the rudeness of this strange woman, I hastily
pushed open the door of my room, at which I now
stood, in order to escape from her; but great was my
amazement on entering to find the apartment
preoccupied. The window was open, and beside it
stood two male figures; they appeared to be
examining the fastenings of the casement, and their
backs were turned towards the door. One of them
was my uncle; they both had turned on my entrance,
as if startled; the stranger was booted and cloaked,
and wore a heavy, broad-leafed hat over his brows; he
turned but for a moment, and averted his face; but I
had seen enough to convince me that he was no other
than my cousin Edward. My uncle had some iron
instrument in his hand, which he hastily concealed
behind his back; and coming towards me, said something as if in an explanatory tone; but I was too much

shocked and confounded to understand what it might be. He said something about '*repairs* – window-frames – cold, and safety'. I did not wait, however, to ask or to receive explanations, but hastily left the room. As I went down stairs I thought I heard the voice of the Frenchwoman in all the shrill volubility of excuse, and others uttering suppressed but vehement imprecations, or what seemed to me to be such.

I joined my cousin Emily quite out of breath. I need not say that my head was too full of other things to think much of drawing for that day. I imparted to her frankly the cause of my alarms, but, at the same time, as gently as I could; and with tears she promised vigilance, devotion, and love. I never had reason for a moment to repent the unreserved confidence which I then reposed in her. She was no less surprised than I at the unexpected appearance of Edward, whose departure for France neither of us had for a moment doubted, but which was now proved by his actual presence to be nothing more than an imposture practised, I feared, for no good end. The situation in which I had found my uncle had very nearly removed all my doubts as to his designs; I magnified suspicions into certainties, and dreaded night after night that I should be murdered in my bed. The nervousness produced by sleepless nights and days of anxious fears increased the horrors of my situation to such a degree, that I at length wrote a letter to a Mr Jefferies, an old and faithful friend of my father's, and perfectly acquainted with all his affairs, praying him, for God's sake, to relieve me from my present terrible situation, and communicating without reserve the nature and grounds of my suspicions. This letter I kept sealed and directed for two or three days always about my person, for discovery would have been ruinous, in expectation of an opportunity, which might be safely trusted, of having it placed in the post-office; as neither Emily nor I were permitted to pass beyond the precincts of the demesne itself, which was surrounded by high walls formed of dry stone, the difficulty of procuring such an opportunity was greatly enhanced.

At this time Emily had a short conversation with her father, which she reported to me instantly. After some indifferent matter, he had asked her whether she and I were upon good terms, and whether I was unreserved in my disposition. She answered in the affirmative; and he then enquired whether I had been much surprised to find him in my chamber on the other day. She answered that I had been both surprised and amused. 'And what did she think of George Wilson's appearance?' 'Who?' enquired she. 'Oh! the architect,' he answered, 'who is to contract for the repairs of the house; he is accounted a handsome fellow.' 'She could not see his face,' said Emily, 'and she was in such a hurry to escape that she scarcely observed him.' Sir Arthur appeared satisfied, and the conversation ended.

This slight conversation, repeated accurately to me by Emily, had the effect of confirming, if indeed any thing was required to do so, all that I had before believed as to Edward's actual presence; and I naturally became, if possible, more anxious than ever to despatch the letter to Mr Jefferies. An opportunity at length occurred. As Emily and I were walking one day near the gate of the demesne, a lad from the village happened to be passing down the avenue from the house; the spot was secluded, and as this person was not connected by service with those whose observation I dreaded, I committed the letter to his keeping, with strict injunctions that he should put it, without delay, into the receiver of the town post-office; at the same time I added a suitable gratuity, and the man having made many protestations of punctuality, was soon out of sight. He was hardly gone when I began to doubt my discretion in having trusted him; but I had no better or safer means of despatching the letter, and I was not warranted in suspecting him of such wanton dishonesty as a dis-position to tamper with it; but I could not be quite satisfied of its safety until I had received an answer, which could not arrive for a few days. Before I did, however, an event occurred which a little surprised me. I was sitting in my bedroom early in the day, reading by myself, when I heard a knock at the door. 'Come in,' said I, and my uncle entered the room. 'Will you excuse me,' said he, 'I sought you in the parlour, and thence I have come here. I desired to say a word to you. I trust that you have hitherto found my conduct to you such as that of a guardian towards his ward should be.' I dared not withhold my assent. 'And,' he continued, 'I trust that you have not found me harsh or unjust, and that you have perceived, my dear niece, that I have sought to make this poor place as agreeable to you as may be?' I assented again; and he put his hand in his pocket, whence he drew a folded paper, and dashing it upon the table with startling emphasis he said, 'Did you write that letter?' The sudden and fearful alteration of his voice, manner, and face, but more than all, the unexpected production of my letter to Mr Jefferies, which I at once recognised, so confounded and terrified me, that I felt almost choking. I could not utter a word. 'Did you write that letter?' he repeated, with slow and intense emphasis. 'You did, liar and hypocrite. You dared to write that foul and infamous libel; but it shall be your last. Men will universally believe you mad, if I choose to call for an inquiry. I can make you appear so. The suspicions expressed in this letter are the hallucinations and alarms of a moping lunatic. I have defeated your first attempt, madam; and by the holy God, if ever you make another, chains, darkness, and the keeper's whip shall be your portion.' With these astounding words he left the room, leaving me almost fainting.

I was now almost reduced to despair; my last cast had failed; I had no course left but that of escaping secretly from the castle, and placing myself under the protection of the nearest magistrate. I felt if this were not done, and speedily, that I should be *murdered*. No one, from mere description, can have an idea of the unmitigated horror of my situation; a helpless, weak, inexperienced girl, placed under the power, and wholly at the mercy of evil men, and feeling that I had it not in my power to escape for one moment from the malignant influences under which I was probably doomed to fall; with a consciousness, too, that if violence, if murder were designed, no human being would be near to aid me; my dying shriek would be lost in void space.

I had seen Edward but once during his visit, and as I did not meet him again, I began to think that he must have taken his departure; a conviction which was to a certain degree satisfactory, as I regarded his absence as indicating the removal of immediate danger. Emily also arrived circuitously at the same conclusion, and not without good grounds, for she managed indirectly to learn that Edward's black horse had actually been for a day and part of a night in the castle stables, just at the time of her brother's supposed visit. The horse had gone, and as she argued, the rider must have departed with it.

This point being so far settled, I felt a little less uncomfortable; when being one day alone in my bedroom, I happened to look out from the window, and to my unutterable horror, I beheld peering through an opposite casement, my cousin Edward's face. Had I seen the evil one himself in bodily shape, I could not have experienced a more sickening revulsion. I was too much appalled to move at once from the window, but I did so soon enough to avoid his eye. He was looking fixedly down into the narrow quadrangle upon which the window opened. I shrunk back unperceived, to pass the rest of the day in terror and despair. I went to my room early that night, but I was too miserable to sleep.

At about twelve o'clock, feeling very nervous, I determined to call my cousin Emily, who slept, you will remember, in the next room, which communicated with mine by a second door. By this private entrance I found my way into her chamber, and without difficulty persuaded her to return to my room and sleep with me. We accordingly lay down together, she undressed, and I with my clothes on, for I was every moment walking up and down the room, and felt too nervous and miserable to think of rest or comfort. Emily was soon fast asleep, and I lay awake, fervently longing for the first pale gleam of morning, and reckoning every stroke of the old clock with an impatience which made every hour appear like six.

It must have been about one o'clock when I thought

I heard a slight noise at the partition door between Emily's room and mine, as if caused by somebody's turning the key in the lock. I held my breath, and the same sound was repeated at the second door of my room, that which opened upon the lobby; the sound was here distinctly caused by the revolution of the bolt in the lock, and it was followed by a slight pressure upon the door itself, as if to ascertain the security of the lock. The person, whoever it might be, was probably satisfied, for I heard the old boards of the lobby creak and strain, as if under the weight of somebody moving cautiously over them. My sense of hearing became unnaturally, almost painfully acute. I suppose the imagination added distinctness to sounds vague in themselves. I thought that I could actually hear the breathing of the person who was slowly returning along the lobby.

At the head of the staircase there appeared to occur a pause; and I could distinctly hear two or three sentences hastily whispered; the steps then descended the stairs with apparently less caution. I ventured to walk quickly and lightly to the lobby door, and attempted to open it; it was indeed fast locked upon the outside, as was also the other. I now felt that the dreadful hour was come; but one desperate expedient remained – it was to awaken Emily, and by our united strength, to attempt to force the partition door, which was slighter than the other, and through this to pass to the lower part of the house, whence it might be possible to escape to the grounds, and so to the village. I returned to the bedside, and shook Emily, but in vain; nothing that I could do availed to produce from her more than a few incoherent words; it was a deathlike sleep. She had certainly drunk of some narcotic, as, probably, had I also, in spite of all the caution with which I had examined every thing presented to us to eat or drink. I now attempted, with as little noise as possible, to force first one door, then the other; but all in vain. I believe no strength could have affected my object, for both doors opened inwards. I therefore collected whatever moveables I could carry thither, and piled them against the doors, so as to assist me in whatever attempts I should make to resist the entrance of those without. I then returned to the bed and endeavoured again, but fruitlessly, to awaken my cousin. It was not sleep, it was torpor, lethargy, death. I knelt down and prayed with an agony of earnestness; and then seating myself upon the bed, I awaited my fate with a kind of terrible tranquillity.

I heard a faint clanking sound from the narrow court which I have already mentioned, as if caused by the scraping of some iron instrument against stones or rubbish. I at first determined not to disturb the calmness which I now experienced, by uselessly watching the proceedings of those who sought my life; but as the sounds continued, the horrible curiosity which I felt overcame every other emotion, and I determined, at all hazards, to gratify it. I, therefore, crawled upon my knees to the window, so as to let the smallest possible portion of my head appear above the sill.

The moon was shining with an uncertain radiance upon the antique grey buildings, and obliquely upon the narrow court beneath; one side of it was therefore clearly illuminated, while the other was lost in obscurity, the sharp outlines of the old gables, with their nodding clusters of ivy, being at first alone visible. Whoever or whatever occasioned the noise which had excited my curiosity, was concealed under the shadow of the dark side of the quadrangle. I placed my hand over my eyes to shade them from the moonlight, which was so bright as to be almost dazzling, and, peering into the darkness, I first dimly, but afterwards gradually, almost with full distinctness, beheld the form of a man engaged in digging what appeared to be a rude hole close under the wall. Some implements, probably a shovel and pickaxe, lay beside him, and to these he every now and then applied himself as the nature of the ground required. He pursued his task rapidly, and with as little noise as possible. 'So,' thought I, as shovelful after shovelful, the dislodged rubbish mounted into a heap, 'they are digging the grave in which, before two hours pass, I must lie, a cold, mangled corpse. I am *theirs* – I cannot escape.' I felt as if my reason was leaving me. I started to my feet, and in mere despair I applied myself again to each of the two doors alternately. I strained every nerve and sinew, but I might as well have attempted, with my single strength, to force the building itself from its foundations. I threw myself madly upon the ground, and clasped my hands over my eyes as if to shut out the horrible images which crowded upon me.

The paroxysm passed away. I prayed once more with the bitter, agonised fervour of one who feels that the hour of death is present and inevitable. When I arose, I went once more to the window and looked out, just in time to see a shadowy figure glide stealthily along the wall. The task was finished. The catastrophe of the tragedy must soon be accomplished. I determined now to defend my life to the last; and that I might be able to do so with some effect, I searched the room for something which might serve as a weapon;

but either through accident, or else in anticipation of such a possibility, every thing which might have been made available for such a purpose had been removed.

I must then die tamely and without an effort to defend myself. A thought suddenly struck me; might it not be possible to escape through the door, which the assassin must open in order to enter the room? I resolved to make the attempt. I felt assured that the door through which ingress to the room would be effected was that which opened upon the lobby. It was the more direct way, besides being, for obvious reasons, less liable to interruption than the other. I resolved, then, to place myself behind a projection of the wall, the shadow would serve fully to conceal me, and when the door should be opened, and before they should have discovered the identity of the occupant of the bed, to creep noiselessly from the room, and then to trust to Providence for escape. In order to facilitate this scheme, I removed all the lumber which I had heaped against the door; and I had nearly completed my arrangements, when I perceived the room suddenly darkened, by the close approach of some shadowy object to the window. On turning my eyes in that direction, I observed at the top of the casement, as if suspended from above, first the feet, then the legs, then the body, and at length the whole figure of a man present itself. It was Edward Tyrrell. He appeared to be guiding his descent so as to bring his feet upon the centre of the stone block which occupied the lower part of the window; and having secured his footing upon this, he kneeled down and began to gaze into the room. As the moon was gleaming into the chamber, and the bed-curtains were drawn, he was able to distinguish the bed itself and its contents. He appeared satisfied with his scrutiny, for he looked up and made a sign with his hand. He then applied his hands to the window-frame, which must have been ingeniously contrived for the purpose, for with apparently no resistance the whole frame, containing casement and all, slipped from its position in the wall, and was by him lowered into the room. The cold night wind waved the bed-curtains, and he paused for a moment; all was still again, and he stepped in upon the floor of the room. He held in his hand what appeared to be a steel instrument, shaped something like a long hammer. This he held rather behind him, while, with three long, *tiptoe* strides, he brought himself to the bedside. I felt that the discovery must now be made, and held my breath in momentary expectation of the execration in which he would vent his surprise and disappointment. I closed my eyes; there was a pause, but it was a short one. I heard two dull blows, given in rapid succession; a quivering sigh, and the long-drawn, heavy breathing of the sleeper was for ever suspended. I unclosed my eyes, and saw the murderer fling the quilt across the head of his victim; he then, with the instrument of death still in his hand, proceeded to the lobby-door, upon which he tapped sharply twice or thrice. A quick step was then heard approaching, and a voice whispered something from without. Edward answered, with a kind of shuddering chuckle, 'Her ladyship is past complaining; unlock the door, in the devil's name, unless you're afraid to come in, and help me to lift her out of the window.' The key was turned in the lock, the door opened, and my uncle entered the room. I have told you already that I had placed myself under the shade of a projection of the wall, close to the door. I had instinctively shrunk down cowering towards the ground on the entrance of Edward through the window. When my uncle entered the room, he and his son both stood so very close to me that his hand was every moment upon the point of touching my face. I held my breath, and remained motionless as death.

'You had no interruption from the next room?' said my uncle.

'No,' was the brief reply.

'Secure the jewels, Ned; the French harpy must not lay her claws upon them. You're a steady hand, by G—d; not much blood – eh?'

'Not twenty drops,' replied his son, 'and those on the quilt.'

'I'm glad it's over,' whispered my uncle again; 'we must lift the – the *thing* through the window, and lay the rubbish over it.'

They then turned to the bedside, and, winding the bedclothes round the body, carried it between them slowly to the window, and exchanging a few brief words with someone below, they shoved it over the window-sill, and I heard it fall heavily on the ground underneath.

'I'll take the jewels,' said my uncle; 'there are two caskets in the lower drawer.'

He proceeded, with an accuracy which, had I been more at ease, would have furnished me with matter of astonishment, to lay his hand upon the very spot where my jewels lay; and having possessed himself of them, he called to his son: 'Is the rope made fast above?'

'I'm no fool; to be sure it is,' replied he.

They then lowered themselves from the window; and I rose lightly and cautiously, scarcely daring to breathe, from my place of concealment, and was creeping towards the door, when I heard my uncle's voice, in a sharp whisper, exclaim, 'Get up again; G—d d—n you, you've forgot to lock the room door'; and I perceived, by the straining of the rope which hung from above, that the mandate was instantly obeyed. Not a second was to be lost. I passed through the door, which was only closed, and moved as rapidly as I could, consistently with stillness, along the lobby. Before I had gone many yards, I heard the door through which I had just passed roughly locked on the inside. I glided down the stairs in terror, lest, at every corner, I should meet the murderer or one of his accomplices. I reached the hall, and listened, for a moment, to ascertain whether all was silent around. No sound was audible; the parlour windows opened on the park, and through one of them I might, I thought, easily effect my escape. Accordingly, I hastily entered; but, to my consternation, a candle was burning in the room, and by its light I saw a figure seated at the dinner-table, upon which lay glasses, bottles, and the other accompaniments of a drinking party. Two or three chairs were placed about the table, irregularly, as if hastily abandoned by their occupants. A single glance satisfied me that the figure was that of my French attendant. She was fast asleep, having, probably, drunk deeply. There was something malignant and ghastly in the calmness of this bad woman's features, dimly illuminated as they were by the flickering blaze of the candle. A knife lay upon the table, and the terrible thought struck me – 'Should I kill this sleeping accomplice in the guilt of the murderer, and thus secure my retreat?' Nothing could be easier; it was but to draw the blade across her throat, the work of a second.

An instant's pause, however, corrected me. 'No,' thought I, 'the God who has conducted me thus far through the valley of the shadow of death, will not abandon me now. I will fall into their hands, or I will escape hence, but it shall be free from the stain of blood; His will be done.' I felt a confidence arising from this reflection, an assurance of protection which I cannot describe. There were no other means of escape, so I advanced, with a firm step and collected mind, to the window. I noiselessly withdrew the bars, and unclosed the shutters; I pushed open the casement, and without waiting to look behind me, I ran with my utmost speed, scarcely feeling the ground beneath me, down the avenue, taking care to keep upon the grass which bordered it. I did not for a moment slacken my speed, and I had now gained the central point between the park-gate and the mansion-house. Here the avenue made a wider circuit, and in order to avoid delay, I directed my way across the smooth sward round which the carriageway wound, intending, at the opposite side of the level, at a point which I distinguished by a group of old birch trees, to enter again upon the beaten track, which was from thence tolerably direct to the gate. I had, with my utmost speed, got about halfway across this broad flat, when the rapid tramp of a horse's hoofs struck upon my ear. My heart swelled in my bosom, as though I would smother. The clattering of galloping hoofs approached; I was pursued; they were now upon the sward on which I was running; there was not a bush or a bramble to shelter me; and, as if to render escape altogether desperate, the moon, which had hitherto been obscured, at this moment shone forth with a broad, clear light, which made every object distinctly visible. The sounds were now close behind me. I felt my knees bending under me, with the sensation which unnerves one in a dream. I reeled, I stumbled, I fell; and at the same instant the cause of my alarm wheeled past me at full gallop. It was one of the young fillies which pastured loose about the park, whose frolics had thus all but maddened me with terror. I scrambled to my feet, and rushed on with weak but rapid steps, my sportive companion still galloping round and round me with many a frisk and fling, until, at length, more dead than alive, I reached the avenue-gate, and crossed the stile, I scarce knew how. I ran through the village, in which all was silent as the grave, until my progress was arrested by the hoarse voice of a sentinel, who cried 'Who goes there?' I felt that I was now safe. I turned in the direction of the voice, and fell fainting at the soldier's feet. When I came to myself, I was sitting in a miserable hovel, surrounded by strange faces, all bespeaking curiosity and compassion. Many soldiers were in it also; indeed, as I afterwards found, it was employed as a guardroom by a detachment of troops quartered for that night in the town. In a few words I informed their officer of the circumstances which had occurred, describing also the appearance of the persons engaged in the murder; and he, without further loss of time than was necessary to procure the attendance of a magistrate, proceeded to the mansion-house of Carrickleigh, taking with him a party of his men. But the villains had discovered their mistake, and had effected their escape before the arrival of the military.

The Frenchwoman was, however, arrested in the neighbourhood upon the next day. She was tried and condemned at the ensuing assizes; and previous to her execution confessed that '*she had a hand in making Hugh Tisdall's bed*'. She had been a housekeeper in the castle at the time, and a *chère amie* of my uncle's. She was, in reality, able to speak English like a native, but had exclusively used the French language, I suppose to facilitate her designs. She died the same hardened wretch she had lived, confessing her crimes only, as she alleged, that her doing so might involve Sir Arthur Tyrrell, the great author of her guilt and misery, and whom she now regarded with unmitigated detestation.

With the particulars of Sir Arthur's and his son's escape, as far as they are known, you are acquainted. You are also in possession of their after fate; the terrible, the tremendous retribution which, after long delays of many years, finally overtook and crushed them. Wonderful and inscrutable are the dealings of God with his creatures!

Deep and fervent as must always be my gratitude to heaven for my deliverance, effected by a chain of providential occurrences, the failing of a single link of which must have ensured my destruction, it was long before I could look back upon it with other feelings than those of bitterness, almost of agony. The only being that had ever really loved me, my nearest and dearest friend, ever ready to sympathise, to counsel, and to assist; the gayest, the gentlest, the warmest heart; the only creature on earth that cared for me; *her* life had been the price of my deliverance; and I then uttered the wish, which no event of my long and sorrowful life has taught me to recall, that she had been spared, and that, in her stead, *I* were mouldering in the grave, forgotten, and at rest.

The Race of Orven

M. P. SHIEL

Never without grief and pain could I remember the fate of Prince Zaleski – victim of a too importunate, too unfortunate Love, which the fulgor of the throne itself could not abash; exile perforce from his native land, and voluntary exile from the rest of men! Having renounced the world, over which, lurid and inscrutable as a falling star, he had passed, the world quickly ceased to wonder at him; and even I, to whom, more than to another, the workings of that just and passionate mind had been revealed, half forgot him in the rush of things.

But during the time that what was called the 'Pharanx labyrinth' was exercising many of the heaviest brains in the land, my thought turned repeatedly to him; and even when the affair had passed from the general attention, a bright day in Spring, combined perhaps with a latent mistrust of the *dénouement* of that dark plot, drew me to his place of hermitage.

I reached the gloomy abode of my friend as the sun set. It was a vast palace of the older world standing lonely in the midst of woodland, and approached by a sombre avenue of poplars and cypresses, through which the sunlight hardly pierced. Up this I passed, and seeking out the deserted stables (which I found all too dilapidated to afford shelter) finally put up my *calèche* in the ruined sacristy of an old Dominican chapel, and turned my mare loose to browse for the night on a paddock behind the domain.

As I pushed back the open front door and entered the mansion, I could not but wonder at the saturnine fancy that had led this wayward man to select a brooding-place so desolate for the passage of his days. I regarded it as a vast tomb of Mausolus in which lay deep sepulchred how much genius, culture, brilliancy, power! The hall was constructed in the manner of a Roman *atrium,* and from the oblong pool of turgid water in the centre a troop of fat and otiose rats fled weakly squealing at my approach. I mounted by broken marble steps to the corridors running round the open space, and thence pursued my way through a mazeland of apartments – suite upon suite – along many a length of passage, up and down many stairs. Dust-clouds rose from the uncarpeted floors and choked me; incontinent Echo coughed answering *ricochets* to my footsteps in the gathering darkness, and added emphasis to the funereal gloom of the dwelling. Nowhere was there a vestige of furniture – nowhere a trace of human life.

After a long interval I came, in a remote tower of the building and near its utmost summit, to a richly carpeted passage, from the ceiling of which three mosaic lamps shed dim violet, scarlet and pale-rose lights around. At the end I perceived two figures standing as if in silent guard on each side of a door tapestried with the python's skin. One was a post-replica in Parian marble of the nude Aphrodite of Cnidus; in the other I recognised the gigantic form of the negro Ham, the prince's only attendant, whose fierce, and glistening, and ebon visage broadened into a grin of intelligence as I came nearer. Nodding to him, I pushed without ceremony into Zaleski's apartment.

The room was not a large one, but lofty. Even in the semi-darkness of the very faint greenish lustre radiated from an open censer-like *lampas* of fretted gold in the centre of the domed encausted roof, a certain incongruity of barbaric gorgeousness in the furnishing filled me with amazement. The air was heavy with the scented odour of this light, and the fumes of the narcotic *cannabis sativa* – the base of the *bhang* of the Mohammedans – in which I knew it to be the habit of my friend to assuage himself. The hangings were of wine-coloured velvet, heavy, gold-fringed and embroidered at Nurshedabad. All the world knew Prince Zaleski to be a consummate *cognescente* – a profound amateur – as well as a savant and a thinker, but I was, nevertheless, astounded at the mere multitudinousness of the curios he had contrived to crowd into the space around him. Side by side rested a palaeolithic implement, a Chinese 'wise man', a Gnostic gem, an amphora of Graeco-Etruscan work. The general effect was a *bizarrerie* of half-weird sheen and gloom. Flemish sepulchral brasses companied strangely with runic tablets, miniature paintings, a winged bull, Tamil scriptures on lacquered leaves of the talipot, mediaeval reliquaries richly gemmed, Brahmin gods. One whole side of the room was occupied by an organ whose thunder in that circumscribed place must have set all these relics of dead epochs clashing and jingling in fantastic dances. As I entered, the vaporous atmosphere was palpitating to the low, liquid tinkling of an invisible musical box. The prince reclined on a couch from which a draping of cloth-of-silver rolled torrent over the floor. Beside him, stretched in its open sarcophagus which rested on three brazen trestles, lay the mummy of an ancient Memphian, from the upper part of which the brown cerements had rotted or been rent, leaving the hideousness of the naked, grinning countenance exposed to view.

Discarding his gemmed chibouque and an old vellum reprint of Anacreon, Zaleski rose hastily and greeted me with warmth, muttering at the same time some commonplace about his 'pleasure' and the 'unexpectedness' of my visit. He then gave orders to Ham to prepare me a bed in one of the adjoining chambers. We passed the greater part of the night in a delightful stream of that somnolent and half-mystic talk which Prince Zaleski alone could initiate and sustain, during which he repeatedly pressed on me a concoction of Indian hemp resembling *hashish*, prepared by his own hands, and quite innocuous. It was after a simple breakfast the next morning that I entered on the subject which was partly the occasion of my visit. He lay back on his couch, volumed in a Turkish *beneesh*, and listened to me, a little wearily perhaps at first, with woven fingers, and the pale inverted eyes of old anchorites and astrologers, the moony greenish light falling on his always wan features.

'You knew Lord Pharanx?' I asked.

'I have met him in "the world". His son Lord Randolph, too, I saw once at Court at Peterhof, and once again at the Winter Palace of the Tsar. I noticed in their great stature, shaggy heads of hair, ears of a very peculiar conformation, and a certain aggressiveness of demeanour – a strong likeness between father and son.'

I had brought with me a bundle of old newspapers, and comparing these as I went on, I proceeded to lay the incidents before him.

'The father,' I said, 'held, as you know, high office in a late Administration, and was one of our big luminaries in politics; he has also been President of the Council of several learned societies, and author of a book on Modern Ethics. His son was rapidly rising to eminence in the *corps diplomatique*, and lately (though, strictly speaking, *unebenbürtig*) contracted an affiance with the Prinzessin Charlotte Mariana Natalia of Morgen-üppigen, a lady with a strain of indubitable Hohenzollern blood in her royal veins. The Orven family is a very old and distinguished one, though – especially in modern days – far from wealthy. However, some little time after Randolph had become engaged to this royal lady, the father insured his life for immense sums in various offices both in England and America, and the reproach of poverty is now swept from the race. Six months ago, almost simultaneously, both father and son resigned their various positions *en bloc*. But all this, of course, I am telling you on the assumption that you have not already read it in the papers.'

'A modern newspaper,' he said, 'being what it mostly is, is the one thing insupportable to me at present. Believe me, I never see one.'

'Well, then, Lord Pharanx, as I said, threw up his posts in the fulness of his vigour, and retired to one of his country seats. A good many years ago, he and Randolph had a terrible row over some trifle, and, with the implacability that distinguishes their race, had not since exchanged a word. But some little time after the retirement of the father, a message was

451

despatched by him to the son, who was then in India. Considered as the first step in the *rapprochement* of this proud and selfish pair of beings, it was an altogether remarkable message, and was subsequently disposed to in evidence by a telegraph official; it ran: "*Return. The beginning of the end is come.*" Whereupon Randolph did return, and in three months from the date of his landing in England, Lord Pharanx was dead.'

'*Murdered?*'

A certain something in the tone in which this word was uttered by Zaleski puzzled me. It left me uncertain whether he had addressed to me an exclamation of conviction, or a simple question. I must have looked this feeling, for he said at once: 'I could easily, from your manner, surmise as much, you know. Perhaps I might even have foretold it, years ago.'

'Foretold – what? Not the murder of Lord Pharanx?'

'Something of that kind,' he answered with a smile; 'but proceed – tell me all the facts you know.'

Word-mysteries of this sort fell frequent from the lips of the prince. I continued the narrative.

'The two, then, met, and were reconciled. But it was a reconciliation without cordiality, without affection – a shaking of hands across a barrier of brass; and even this hand-shaking was a strictly metaphorical one, for they do not seem ever to have got beyond the interchange of a frigid bow. The opportunities, however, for observation were few. Soon after Randolph's arrival at Orven Hall, his father entered on a life of the most absolute seclusion. The mansion is an old three-storeyed one, the top floor consisting for the most part of sleeping-rooms, the first of a library, drawing-room, and so on, and the ground-floor, in addition to the dining and other ordinary rooms, of another small library, looking out (at the side of the house) on a low balcony, which, in turn, looks on a lawn dotted with flower-beds. It was this smaller library on the ground-floor that was now divested of its books, and converted into a bedroom for the earl. Hither he migrated, and here he lived, scarcely ever leaving it. Randolph, on his part, moved to a room on the first floor immediately above this. Some of the retainers of the family were dismissed, and on the remaining few fell a hush of expectancy, a sense of wonder, as to what these things boded. A great enforced quiet pervaded the building, the least undue noise in any part being sure to be followed by the angry voice of the master demanding the cause. Once, as the servants were supping in the kitchen on the side of the house most remote from that which he occupied, Lord Pharanx, slippered and in dressing-gown, appeared at the doorway, purple with rage, threatening to pack the whole company of them out of doors if they did not moderate the clatter of their knives and forks. He had always been regarded with fear in his own household, and the very sound of his voice now became a terror. His food was taken to him in the room he had made his habitation, and it was remarked that, though simple before in his gustatory tastes, he now – possibly owing to the sedentary life he led – became fastidious, insisting on *recherché* bits. I mention all these details to you – as I shall mention others – not because they have the least connection with the tragedy as it subsequently occurred, but merely because I know them, and you have requested me to state all I know.'

'Yes,' he answered, with a suspicion of *ennui*, 'you are right. I may as well hear the whole – if I must hear a part.'

'Meanwhile, Randolph appears to have visited the earl at least once a day. In such retirement did he, too, live that many of his friends still supposed him to be in India. There was only one respect in which he broke through this privacy. You know, of course, that the Orvens are, and, I believe, always have been, noted as the most obstinate, the most crabbed of Conservatives in politics. Even among the past-enamoured families of England, they stand out conspicuously in this respect. Is it credible to you, then, that Randolph should offer himself to the Radical Association of the Borough of Orven as a candidate for the next election in opposition to the sitting member? It is on record, too, that he spoke at three public meetings – reported in local papers – at which he avowed his political conversion; afterwards laid the foundation-stone of a new Baptist chapel; presided at a Methodist tea-meeting; and taking an abnormal interest in the debased condition of the labourers in the villages round, fitted up as a class-room an apartment on the top floor of Orven Hall, and gathered round him on two evenings in every week a class of yokels, whom he proceeded to cram with demonstrations in elementary mechanics.'

'Mechanics!' cried Zaleski, starting upright for a moment, 'mechanics to agricultural labourers! Why not elementary chemistry? Why not elementary botany? *Why* mechanics?'

This was the first evidence of interest he had shown in the story.

I was pleased, but answered: 'The point is

unimportant; and there really is no accounting for the vagaries of such a man. He wished, I imagine, to give some idea to the young illiterates of the simple laws of motion and force. But now I come to a new character in the drama – the chief character of all. One day a woman presented herself at Orven Hall and demanded to see its owner. She spoke English with a strong French accent. Though approaching middle life she was still beautiful, having wild black eyes, and creamy-pale face. Her dress was tawdry, cheap, and loud, showing signs of wear; her hair was unkempt; her manners were not the manners of a lady. A certain vehemence, exasperation, unrepose distinguished all she said and did. The footman refused her admission; Lord Pharanx, he said, was invisible. She persisted violently, pushed past him, and had to be forcibly ejected; during all which the voice of the master was heard roaring from the passage red-eyed remonstrance at the unusual noise. She went away gesticulating wildly, and vowing vengeance on Lord Pharanx and all the world. It was afterwards found that she had taken up her abode in one of the neighbouring hamlets, called Lee.

'This person, who gave the name of Maude Cibras, subsequently called at the Hall three times in succession, and was each time refused admittance. It was now, however, thought advisable to inform Randolph of her visits. He said she might be permitted to see him, if she returned. This she did on the next day, and had a long interview in private with him. Her voice was heard raised as if in angry protest by one Hester Dyett, a servant of the house, while Randolph in low tones seemed to try to soothe her. The conversation was in French, and no word could be made out. She passed out at length, tossing her head jauntily, and smiling a vulgar triumph at the footman who had before opposed her ingress. She was never known to seek admission to the house again.

'But her connection with its inmates did not cease. The same Hester asserts that one night, coming home late through the park, she saw two persons conversing on a bench beneath the trees, crept behind some bushes, and discovered that they were the strange woman and Randolph. The same servant bears evidence to tracking them to other meeting-places, and to finding in the letter-bag letters addressed to Maude Cibras in Randolph's handwriting. One of these was actually unearthed later on. Indeed, so engrossing did the intercourse become, that it seems even to have interfered with the outburst of radical zeal in the new political convert. The *rendezvous* – always held under cover of darkness, but naked and open to the eye of the watchful Hester – sometimes clashed with the science lectures, when these latter would be put off, so that they became gradually fewer, and then almost ceased.'

'Your narrative becomes unexpectedly interesting,' said Zaleski; 'but this unearthed letter of Randolph's – what was in it?'

I read as follows:

' "DEAR MLLE CIBRAS – I am exerting my utmost influence for you with my father. But he shows no signs of coming round as yet. If I could only induce him to see you! But he is, as you know, a person of unrelenting will, and meanwhile you must confide in my loyal efforts on your behalf. At the same time, I admit that the situation is a precarious one:

you are, I am sure, well provided for in the present will of Lord Pharanx, but he is on the point – within, say, three or four days – of making another; and exasperated as he is at your appearance in England, I know there is no chance of your receiving a *centime* under the new will. Before then, however, we must hope that something favourable to you may happen; and in the meantime, let me implore you not to let your only too just resentment pass beyond the bounds of reason.

' "Sincerely yours,

' "RANDOLPH" '

'I like the letter!' cried Zaleski. 'You notice the tone of manly candour. But the *facts* – were they true? *Did* the earl make a new will in the time specified?'

'No – but that may have been because his death intervened.'

'And in the old will, *was* Mlle Cibras provided for?'

'Yes, – that at least was correct.'

A shadow of pain passed over his face.

'And now,' I went on, 'I come to the closing scene, in which one of England's foremost men perished by the act of an obscure assassin. The letter I have read was written to Maude Cibras on the 5th of January. The next thing that happens is on the 6th, when Lord Pharanx left his room for another during the whole day, and a skilled mechanic was introduced into it for the purpose of effecting some alterations. Asked by Hester Dyett, as he was leaving the house, what was the nature of his operations, the man replied that he had been applying a patent arrangement to the window looking out on the balcony, for the better protection of the room against burglars, several robberies having

457

recently been committed in the neighbourhood. The sudden death of this man, however, before the occurrence of the tragedy, prevented his evidence being heard. On the next day – the 7th – Hester, entering the room with Lord Pharanx's dinner, fancies, though she cannot tell why (inasmuch as his back is towards her, he sitting in an armchair by the fire), that Lord Pharanx has been "drinking heavily".

'On the 8th a singular thing befell. The earl was at last induced to see Maude Cibras, and during the morning of that day, with his own hand, wrote a note informing her of his decision, Randolph handing the note to a messenger. That note also has been made public. It reads as follows:

' "MAUDE CIBRAS – You may come here tonight after dark. Walk to the south side of the house, come up the steps to the balcony, and pass in through the open window to my room. Remember, however, that you have nothing to expect from me, and that from tonight I blot you eternally from my mind: but I will hear your story, which I know beforehand to be false. Destroy this note.

' "PHARANX" '

As I progressed with my tale, I came to notice that over the countenance of Prince Zaleski there grew little by little a singular fixed aspect. His small, keen features distorted themselves into an expression of what I can only describe as an abnormal *inquisitiveness* – an inquisitiveness most impatient, arrogant, in its intensity. His pupils, contracted each to a dot, became the central *puncta* of two rings of fiery light; his little sharp teeth seemed to gnash. Once before I had seen him look thus greedily, when,

458

grasping a Troglodyte tablet covered with half-effaced hieroglyphics – his fingers livid with the fixity of his grip – he bent on it that strenuous inquisition, that ardent questioning gaze, till, by a species of mesmeric dominancy, he seemed to wrench from it the arcanum it hid from other eyes; then he lay back, pale and faint from the too arduous victory.

When I had read Lord Pharanx's letter, he took the paper eagerly from my hand, and ran his eyes over the passage.

'Tell me – the end,' he said.

'Maude Cibras,' I went on, 'thus invited to a meeting with the earl, failed to make her appearance at the appointed time. It happened that she had left her lodgings in the village early that very morning, and, for some purpose or other, had travelled to the town of Bath. Randolph, too, went away the same day in the opposite direction to Plymouth. He returned on the following morning, the 9th; soon after walked over to Lee; and entered into conversation with the keeper of the inn where Cibras lodged; asked if she was at home, and on being told that she had gone away, asked further if she had taken her luggage with her; was informed that she had, and had also announced her intention of at once leaving England. He then walked away in the direction of the Hall. On this day Hester Dyett noticed that there were many articles of value scattered about the earl's room, notably a tiara of old Brazilian brilliants, sometimes worn by the late Lady Pharanx. Randolph – who was present at the time – further drew her attention to these by telling her that Lord Pharanx had chosen to bring together in his apartment many of the family jewels; and she was instructed to tell the other servants of this fact, in case they should notice any suspicious-looking loafers about the estate.

'On the 10th, both father and son remained in their rooms all day, except when the latter came down to meals; at which times he would lock his door behind him, and with his own hands take in the earl's food, giving as his reason that his father was writing a very important document, and did not wish to be disturbed by the presence of a servant. During the forenoon, Hester Dyett, hearing loud noises in Randolph's room, as if furniture was being removed from place to place, found some pretext for knocking at his door, when he ordered her on no account to interrupt him again, as he was busy packing his clothes in view of a journey to London on the next day. The subsequent conduct of the woman shows that her curiosity must have been excited to the utmost by the undoubtedly strange spectacle of Randolph packing his own clothes. During the afternoon a lad from the village was instructed to collect his companions for a science lecture the same evening at eight o'clock. And so the eventful day wore on.

'We arrive now at this hour of eight p.m. on this 10th day of January. The night is dark and windy; some snow has been falling, but has now ceased. In an upper room is Randolph engaged in expounding the elements of dynamics; in the room under that is Hester Dyett – for Hester has somehow obtained a key that opens the door of Randolph's room, and takes advantage of his absence upstairs to explore it. Under her is Lord Pharanx, certainly in bed, probably asleep. Hester, trembling all over in a fever of fear and excitement, holds a lighted taper in one hand, which she religiously shades with the other; for the storm is gusty, and the gusts, tearing through the crevices of the rattling old casements, toss great flickering shadows on the hangings, which frighten her to death. She has just time to see that the whole room is in the wildest confusion, when suddenly a rougher puff blows out the flame, and she is left in what to her, standing as she was on that forbidden ground, must have been a horror of darkness. At the same moment, clear and sharp from right beneath her, a pistol-shot rings out on her ear. For an instant she stands in stone, incapable of motion. Then on her dazed senses there supervenes – so she swore – the consciousness that some object is moving in the room – moving apparently of its own accord – moving in direct opposition to all the laws of nature as she knows them. She imagines that she perceives a phantasm – a strange something – globular-white – looking, as she says, "like a good-sized ball of cotton" – rise directly from the floor before her, ascending slowly upward, as if driven aloft by some invisible force. A sharp shock of the sense of the supernatural deprives her of ordered reason. Throwing forward her arms, and uttering a shrill scream, she rushes towards the door. But she never reaches it: midway she falls prostrate over some object, and knows no more; and when, an hour later, she is borne out of the room in the arms of Randolph himself, the blood is dripping from a fracture of her right tibia.

'Meantime, in the upper chamber the pistol-shot and the scream of the woman have been heard. All eyes turn to Randolph. He stands in the shadow of the mechanical contrivance on which he has been illustrating his points; leans for support on it. He essays to speak, the muscles of his face work, but no

sound comes. Only after a time is he able to gasp:
"Did you hear something – from below?" They answer
"yes" in chorus; then one of the lads takes a lighted
candle, and together they troop out, Randolph behind
them. A terrified servant rushes up with the news
that something dreadful has happened in the house.
They proceed for some distance, but there is an open
window on the stairs, and the light is blown out.
They have to wait some minutes till another is
obtained, and then the procession moves forward once
more. Arrived at Lord Pharanx's door, and finding it
locked, a lantern is procured, and Randolph leads
them through the house and out on the lawn. But
having nearly reached the balcony, a lad observes a
track of small woman's-feet in the snow; a halt is
called, and then Randolph points out another track of
feet, half obliterated by the snow, extending from a
coppice close by up to the balcony, and forming an
angle with the first track. These latter are great big
feet, made by ponderous labourer's boots. He holds
the lantern over the flower-beds, and shows how they
have been trampled down. Someone finds a common
scarf, such as workmen wear; and a ring and a locket,
dropped by the burglars in their flight, are also found
by Randolph half buried in the snow. And now the
foremost reach the window. Randolph, from behind,
calls to them to enter. They cry back that they cannot,
the window being closed. At this reply he seems to be
overcome by surprise, by terror. Someone hears
him murmur the words, "My God, what can have
happened now?" His horror is increased when one of
the lads bears to him a revolting trophy, which has
been found just outside the window; it is the front
phalanges of three fingers of a human hand. Again

he utters the agonised moan, "My God!" and then, mastering his agitation, makes for the window; he finds that the catch of the sash has been roughly wrenched off, and that the sash can be opened by merely pushing it up: does so, and enters. The room is in darkness: on the floor under the window is found the insensible body of the woman Cibras. She is alive, but has fainted. Her right fingers are closed round the handle of a large bowie-knife, which is covered with blood; parts of the left are missing. All the jewellery has been stolen from the room. Lord Pharanx lies on the bed, stabbed through the bedclothes to the heart. Later on a bullet is also found embedded in his brain. I should explain that a trenchant edge, running along the bottom of the sash, was the obvious means by which the fingers of Cibras had been cut off. This had been placed there a few days before by the workman I spoke of. Several secret springs had been placed on the inner side of the lower horizontal piece of the window-frame, by pressing any one of which the sash was lowered; so that no one, ignorant of the secret, could pass out from within, without resting the hand on one of these springs, and so bringing down the armed sash suddenly on the underlying hand.

'There was, of course, a trial. The poor culprit, in mortal terror of death, shrieked out a confession of the murder just as the jury had returned from their brief consultation, and before they had time to pronounce their verdict of "guilty". But she denied shooting Lord Pharanx, and she denied stealing the jewels; and indeed no pistol and no jewels were found on her, or anywhere in the room. So that many points remain mysterious. What part did the burglars play in the tragedy? Were they in collusion with Cibras? Had the strange behaviour of at least one of the inmates of Orven Hall no hidden significance? The wildest guesses were made throughout the country; theories propounded. But no theory explained *all* the points. The ferment, however, has now subsided. Tomorrow morning Maude Cibras ends her life on the gallows.'

Thus I ended my narrative.

Without a word Zaleski rose from the couch, and walked to the organ. Assisted from behind by Ham, who foreknew his master's every whim, he proceeded to render with infinite feeling an air from the *Lakmh* of Delibes; long he sat, dreamily uttering the melody, his head sunken on his breast. When at last he rose, his great expanse of brow was clear, and a smile all but solemn in its serenity was on his lips. He walked up to an ivory *escritoire*, scribbled a few words on a sheet of paper, and handed it to the negro with the order to take my trap and drive with the message in all haste to the nearest telegraph office.

'That message,' he said, resuming his place on the couch, 'is a last word on the tragedy, and will, no doubt, produce some modification in the final stage of its history. And now, Shiel, let us sit together and confer on this matter. From the manner in which you have expressed yourself, it is evident that there are points which puzzle you – you do not get a clean *coup d'oeil* of the whole regiment of facts, and their causes, and their consequences, as they occurred. Let us see if out of that confusion we cannot produce a coherence, a symmetry. A great wrong is done, and on the society in which it is done is imposed the task of making it translucent, of *seeing* it in all its relations, and of punishing it. But what happens? The society fails to rise to the occasion; on the whole, it contrives to make the opacity more opaque, does not see the crime in any human sense; is unable to punish it. Now this, you will admit, whenever it occurs, is a woeful failure: woeful I mean, not very in itself, but very in its significance: and there must be a precise cause for it. That cause is the lack of something not merely, or specially, in the investigators of the wrong, but in the world at large – shall we not boldly call it the lack of culture? Do not, however, misunderstand me: by the term I mean not so much attainment in general, as *mood* in particular. Whether or when such mood may become universal may be to you a matter of doubt. As for me, I often think that when the era of civilisation begins – as assuredly it shall some day begin – when the races of the world cease to be credulous, ovine mobs and become critical, human nations, then will be the ushering in of the ten thousand years of a *clairvoyant* culture. But nowhere, and at no time during the very few hundreds of years that man has occupied the earth, has there been one single sign of its presence. In individuals, yes – in the Greek Plato, and I think in your English Milton and Bishop Berkeley – but in humanity, never; and hardly in any individual outside those two nations. The reason, I fancy, is not so much that man is a hopeless fool, as that Time, so far as he is concerned, has, as we know, only just begun: it being, of course, conceivable that the creation of a perfect society of men, as the first requisite to a *régime* of culture, must nick to itself a longer loop of time than the making of, say, a stratum of coal. A loquacious person – he is one of your cherished "novel"-writers, by the way, if that be indeed a Novel in which there is nowhere any pretence at novelty – once assured me that he could never reflect without swelling on the greatness of the age in which he lived, an age the mighty civilisation of which he likened to the Augustan and Periclean. A certain stony gaze of anthropological interest with which I regarded his frontal bone seemed to strike the poor man dumb, and he took a hurried departure. Could he have been ignorant that ours is, in general, greater than the Periclean for the *very* reason that the Divinity is neither the devil nor a bungler; that three thousand years of human consciousness is not nothing; that a whole is greater than its part, and a butterfly than a chrysalis? But it was the assumption that it was therefore in any way great in the abstract that occasioned my profound astonishment, and indeed contempt. Civilisation, if it means anything, can only mean the art by which men live musically together – to the lutings, as it were, of Panpipes, or say perhaps, to triumphant organ bursts of martial, marching dithyrambs. Any formula defining it as "the art of lying back and getting elaborately tickled", should surely at this hour be *too* primitive – *too* Opic – to bring anything but a smile to the lips of grown white-skinned men; and the very fact that such a definition can still find undoubting acceptance in all quarters may be an indication that the true ἰδέα which this condition of being must finally assume is far indeed – far, perhaps, by ages and aeons – from becoming part of the general conception. Nowhere since the beginning has the gross problem of living ever so much as approached solution, much less the delicate and intricate one of living *together*: *àpropos* of which your body corporate not only still produces elementary organism cannot so much as catch a really athletic one as yet. Meanwhile *you* and *I* are handicapped. The individual travaileth in pain. In the struggle for quality, powers, air, he spends his strength, and yet hardly escapes asphyxiation. He can no more wriggle himself free of the psychic gravitations that invest him than the earth can shake herself loose of the sun, or he of the omnipotences that rivet him to the universe. If by chance one shoots a downy hint of wings, an instant feeling of contrast puffs him with self-consciousness: a tragedy at once: the unconscious being "the alone complete." To attain to anything, he must needs screw the head up into the atmosphere of the future, while feet and hands drip dark ichors of despair from the crucifying cross of the crude present – *a horrid strain!* Far up a nightly instigation of stars he sees: but he may not strike them with the head. If earth were a boat, and mine, I know well toward what wild azimuths I would compel her helm: but gravity, gravity – chiefest curse of Eden's sin! – is hostile. When indeed (as is ordained), the old mother swings herself into a sublimer orbit, we on her back will follow: till then we make to ourselves Icarian "organa" in vain. I mean to say that it is the plane of station which is at fault: move that upward, you move all. But meantime is it not Goethe who assures us that "further reacheth no man, make he what stretching he will"? For Man, you perceive, is not many, but One. It is absurd to suppose that England can be free while Poland is enslaved; Paris is *far* from the beginnings of civilisation whilst Toobooloo and Chicago are barbaric. Probably no ill-fated, microcephalous son of Adam ever tumbled into a mistake quite so huge, so infantile, as did Dives, if he imagined himself rich while Lazarus sat pauper at the gate. Not many, I say, but one. Even

Ham and I here in our retreat are not alone; we are embarrassed by the uninvited spirit of the present; the adamant root of the mountain on whose summit we stand is based ineradicably in the low world. Yet, thank Heaven, Goethe was not *quite* right – as, indeed, he proved in his proper person. I tell you, Shiel, I *know* whether Mary did or did not murder Darnley; I know – as clearly, as precisely, as a man can know – that Beatrice Cenci was not "guilty" as certain recently discovered documents "prove" her, but that the Shelley version of the affair, though a guess, is the correct one. It *is* possible, by taking thought, to add one cubit – or say a hand, or a dactyl – to your stature; you *may* develop powers slightly – very slightly, but distinctly, both in kind and degree – in advance of those of the mass who live in or about the same cycle of time in which you live. But it is only when the powers to which I refer are shared by the mass – when what, for want of another term, I call the age of the Cultured Mood has at length arrived – that their exercise will become easy and familiar to the individual; and who shall say what presciences, prisms, séances, what introspective craft, Genie apocalypses, shall not *then* become possible to the few who stand spiritually in the van of men.

'All this, you will understand, I say as some sort of excuse for myself, and for you, for any hesitation we may have shown in loosening the very little puzzle you have placed before me – one which we certainly must not regard as difficult of solution. Of course, looking at all the facts, the first consideration that must inevitably rivet the attention is that arising from the circumstance that Viscount Randolph has strong reasons to wish his father dead. They are avowed enemies; he is the *fiancé* of a princess whose husband he is probably too poor to become, though he will very likely be rich enough when his father dies; and so on. All that appears on the surface. On the other hand, we – you and I – know the man: he is a person of gentle blood, as moral, we suppose, as ordinary people, occupying a high station in the world. It is impossible to imagine that such a person would commit an assassination, or even countenance one, for any or all of the reasons that present themselves. In our hearts, with or without clear proof, we could hardly believe it of him. Earls' sons do not, in fact, go about murdering people. Unless, then, we can so reason as to discover other motives – strong, adequate, irresistible – and by "irresistible" I mean a motive which must be *far* stronger than even the love of life itself – we should, I think, in fairness dismiss him from our mind.

'And yet it must be admitted that his conduct is not free of blame. He contracts a sudden intimacy with the acknowledged culprit, whom he does not seem to have known before. He meets her by night, corresponds with her. Who and what is this woman? I think we could not be far wrong in guessing some very old flame of Lord Pharanx's of *Théâtre des Variétés* type, whom he has supported for years, and from whom, hearing some story to her discredit, he threatens to withdraw his supplies. However that be, Randolph writes to Cibras – a violent woman, a woman of lawless passions – assuring her that in four or five days she will be excluded from the will of his father; and in four or five days Cibras plunges a knife into his father's bosom. It is a perfectly natural sequence – though, of course, the *intention* to produce by his words the actual effect produced might have been absent; indeed, the letter of Lord Pharanx himself, had it been received, would have tended to produce that very effect; for it not only gives an excellent opportunity for converting into action those evil thoughts which Randolph (thoughtlessly or guiltily) has instilled, but it further tends to rouse her passions by cutting off from her all hopes of favour. If we presume, then, as is only natural, that there was no such intention on the part of the earl, we *may* make the same presumption in the case of the son. Cibras, however, never receives the earl's letter: on the morning of the same day she goes away to Bath, with the double object, I suppose, of purchasing a weapon, and creating an impression that she has left the country. How then does she know the exact *locale* of Lord Pharanx's room? It is in an unusual part of the mansion, she is unacquainted with any of the servants, a stranger to the district. Can it be possible that Randolph *had told her*? And here again, even in that case, you must bear in mind that Lord Pharanx also told her in his note, and you must recognise the possibility of the absence of evil intention on the part of the son. Indeed, I may go further and show you that in all but every instance in which his actions are in themselves *outré*, suspicious, they are rendered, not less *outré*, but less suspicious, by the fact that Lord Pharanx himself knew of them, shared in them. There was the cruel barbing of that balcony window; about it the crudest thinker would argue thus to himself: "Randolph practically incites Maude Cibras to murder his father on the 5th, and on the 6th he has that window so altered in order that, should she act on his suggestion, she will be caught on attempting to leave the room, while he himself, the actual culprit being discovered *en flagrant délit*, will escape every shadow of suspicion." But, on the other hand, we know that the alteration was made with Lord Pharanx's consent, most likely on his initiative – for he leaves his favoured room during a whole day for that very purpose. So with the letter to Cibras on the 8th – Randolph despatches it, but the earl writes it. So with the disposal of the jewels in the apartment on the 9th. There had been some burglaries in the neighbourhood, and the suspicion at once arises in the mind of the crude reasoner: Could Randolph – finding now that Cibras has "left the country", that, in fact, the tool he had expected to serve his ends has failed him – could he have thus brought those jewels there, and thus warned the servants of their presence, in the hope that the intelligence might so get abroad and lead to a burglary, in the course of which his father might lose his life? There are evidences, you know, tending to show that the burglary did actually at last take place, and the suspicion is, in view of that, by no means unreasonable. And yet, militating against it, is our knowledge that it was Lord Pharanx who "*chose*" to gather the jewels round him; that it was in his presence that Randolph drew the attention of the servant to them. In the matter, at least, of the little political comedy the son seems to have acted alone; but you surely cannot rid yourself of the impression that the radical speeches, the candidature, and the rest of it, formed all of them only a very elaborate, and withal clumsy, set of preliminaries to the *class*. Anything, to make the perspective, the sequence of *that* seem natural. But in the class, at any rate, we have the tacit acquiescence, or even the co-operation of Lord Pharanx. You have described the conspiracy of quiet which, for some reason or other, was imposed on the household; in that reign of silence the bang of a door, the fall of a plate, becomes a domestic tornado. But have you ever heard an agricultural labourer in clogs or heavy boots ascend a stair? The noise is terrible. The tramp of an army of them through the house and overhead, probably jabbering uncouthly together, would be insufferable. Yet Lord Pharanx seems to have made no objection; the novel institution is set up in his own mansion, in an unusual part of it, probably against his own principles; but we hear of no murmur from him. On the fatal day, too, the calm of the house is rudely broken by a considerable commotion in Randolph's room just overhead, caused by his preparation for "a journey to London". But the usual angry remonstrance is not forthcoming from the master. And do you not see how all this more than acquiescence of Lord Pharanx in the conduct of his son deprives that conduct of half its significance, its intrinsic suspiciousness?

'A hasty reasoner then would inevitably jump to the conclusion that Randolph was guilty of something – some evil intention – though of precisely what he would remain in doubt. But a more careful reasoner would pause: he would reflect that *as* the father was implicated in those acts, and *as* he was innocent of any such intention, so might possibly, even probably, be the son. This, I take it, has been the view of the officials, whose logic is probably far in advance of their imagination. But supposing we can adduce one act, undoubtedly actuated by evil intention on the part of Randolph – one act in which his father certainly did *not* participate – what follows next? Why, that we revert at once to the view of the hasty reasoner, and conclude that *all* the other acts in the same relation were actuated by the same evil motive; and having reached that point, we shall be unable longer to resist the conclusion that those of them in which his father had a share *might* have sprung from a like motive in *his* mind also; nor should the mere obvious impossibility of such a condition of things have even the very least influence on us, as thinkers, in causing us to close our mind against its logical possibility. I therefore make the inference, and pass on.

'Let us then see if we can by searching find out any absolutely certain deviation from right on the part of Randolph, in which we may be quite sure that his father was not an abettor. At eight on the night of the murder it is dark; there has been some snow, but the fall has ceased – how long before I know not, but so long that the interval becomes sufficiently appreciable to cause remark. Now the party going round the house come on two tracks of feet meeting at an angle. Of one track we are merely told that it was made by the small foot of a woman, and of it we know no more; of the other we learn that the feet were big and the boots clumsy, and, it is added, the marks were *half obliterated by the snow*. Two things then are clear: that the persons who made them came from different directions, and probably made them at different times. That, alone, by the way, may be a sufficient answer to your question as to whether Cibras was in collusion with the "burglars". But how does Randolph behave with reference to these tracks? Though he carries the lantern, he fails to perceive the first – the woman's – the discovery of which is made by a lad; but the second, half hidden in the snow, he notices

readily enough, and at once points it out. He explains
that burglars have been on the warpath. But examine
his horror of surprise when he hears that the window
is closed; when he sees the woman's bleeding fingers.
He cannot help exclaiming, "My God! what has
happened *now*?" But why "now"? The word cannot
refer to his father's death, for that he knew, or
guessed, beforehand, having heard the shot. Is it not
rather the exclamation of a man whose schemes
destiny has complicated? Besides, he should have
expected to find the window closed: no one except
himself, Lord Pharanx, and the workman, who was
now dead, knew the secret of its construction; the
burglars therefore, having entered and robbed the
room, one of them, intending to go out, would press
on the ledge, and the sash would fall on his hand with
what result we know. The others would then either
break the glass and so escape; or pass through the
house; or remain prisoners. That immoderate surprise
was therefore absurdly illogical, after seeing the
burglar-track in the snow. But how, above all, do you
account for Lord Pharanx's silence during and after
the burglars' visit – if there was a visit? He was, you
must remember, alive all that time; *they* did not kill
him; certainly they did not shoot him, for the shot is
heard after the snow has ceased to fall, – that is, after,
long after, they have left, since it was the falling snow
that had half obliterated their tracks; nor did they
stab him, for to this Cibras confesses. Why then,
being alive, and not gagged, did he give no token of
the presence of his visitors? There were in fact no
burglars at Orven Hall that night.'

'But the track!' I cried, 'the jewels found in the
snow – the neckerchief!'

Zaleski smiled. 'Burglars,' he said, 'are plain, honest folk who have a just notion of the value of jewellery when they see it. They very properly regard it as mere foolish waste to drop precious stones about in the snow, and would refuse to company with a man weak enough to let fall his neckerchief on a cold night. The whole business of the burglars was a particularly inartistic trick, unworthy of its author. The mere facility with which Randolph discovered the buried jewels by the aid of a dim lantern, should have served as a hint to an educated police not afraid of facing the improbable. The jewels had been *put* there with the object of throwing suspicion on the imaginary burglars; with the same design the catch of the window had been wrenched off, the sash purposely left open, the track made, the valuables taken from Lord Pharanx's room. All this was deliberately done by someone – would it be rash to say at once by whom?

'Our suspicions having now lost their whole character of vagueness, and begun to lead us in a perfectly definite direction, let us examine the statements of Hester Dyett. Now, it is immediately comprehensible to me that the evidence of this woman at the public examinations was looked at askance. There can be no doubt that she is a poor specimen of humanity, an undesirable servant, a peering, hysterical caricature of a woman. Her statements, if formally recorded, were not believed; or if believed, were believed with only half the mind. No attempt was made to deduce anything from them. But for my part, if I wanted specially reliable evidence as to any matter of fact, it is precisely from such a being that I would seek it. Let me draw you a picture of that class of intellect. They have a greed for information, but the information, to satisfy them, must relate to actualities; they have no sympathy with fiction; it is from their impatience of what seems to be that springs their curiosity of what *is*. Clio is their muse, and she alone. Their whole lust is to gather knowledge through a hole, their whole faculty is to *peep*. But they are destitute of imagination, and do not lie; in their passion for realities they would esteem it a sacrilege to distort history. They make straight for the substantial, the indubitable. For this reason the Peniculi and Ergasili of Plautus seem to me far more true to nature than the character of Paul Pry in Jerrold's comedy. In one instance, indeed, the evidence of Hester Dyett appears, on the surface of it, to be quite false. She declares that she sees a round white object moving upward in the room. But the night being gloomy, her taper having gone out, she must have been standing in a dense darkness. How then could she see this object? Her evidence, it was argued, must be designedly false, or else (as she was in an ecstatic condition) the result of an excited fancy. But I have stated that such persons, nervous, neurotic even as they may be, are not fanciful. I therefore accept her evidence as true. And now, mark the consequence of that acceptance. I am driven to admit that there must, from some source, have been light in the room – a light faint enough, and diffused enough, to escape the notice of Hester herself. This being so, it must have proceeded from around, from below, or from above. There are no other alternatives. Around there was nothing but the darkness of the night; the room beneath, we know, was also in darkness. The light then came from the room above – from the mechanic classroom. But there is only one possible means by which the light from an upper can diffuse a lower room. It *must* be by a hole in the intermediate boards. We are thus driven to the discovery of an aperture of some sort in the flooring of that upper chamber. Given this, the mystery of the round white object "driven" upward disappears. We at once ask, why not *drawn* upward through the newly discovered aperture by a string too small to be visible in the gloom? Assuredly it was drawn upward. And now having established a hole in the ceiling of the room in which Hester stands, is it unreasonable – even without further evidence – to suspect another in the flooring? But we actually have this further evidence. As she rushes to the door she falls, faints, and fractures the lower part of her leg. Had she fallen *over* some object, as you supposed, the result might have been a fracture also, but in a different part of the body; being where it was, it could only have been caused by placing the foot inadvertently in a hole while the rest of the body was in rapid motion. But this gives us an approximate idea of the *size* of the lower hole; it was at least big enough to admit the foot and lower leg, big enough therefore to admit that "good-sized ball of cotton" of which the woman speaks: and from the lower we are able to conjecture the size of the upper. But how comes it that these holes are nowhere mentioned in the evidence? It can only be because no one ever saw them. Yet the rooms must have been examined by the police, who, if they existed, must have seen them. They therefore did not exist: that is to say, the pieces which had been removed from the floorings had by that time been neatly replaced, and, in the case of the lower one, covered by the carpet, the removal of which had caused so much commotion in Randolph's room on the fatal day. Hester Dyett would have been able to notice and bring at least one of the apertures forward in evidence, but she fainted before she had time to find out the cause of her fall, and an hour later it was, you remember, Randolph himself who bore her from the room. But should not the aperture in the top floor have been observed by the class? Undoubtedly, if its position was in the open space in the middle of the room. But it was not observed, and therefore its position was not there, but in the only other place left – behind the apparatus used in demonstration. That then was *one* useful object which the apparatus – and with it the elaborate hypocrisy of class, and speeches, and candidature – served: it was made to act as a curtain, a screen. But had it no other purpose? That question we may answer when we know its name and its nature. And it is not beyond our powers to conjecture this with something like certainty. For the only "machines" possible to use in illustration of simple mechanics are the screw, the wedge, the scale, the lever, the wheel-and-axle, and Atwood's machine. The mathematical principles which any of these exemplify would, of course, be incomprehensible to such a class, but the first five most of all, and as there would naturally be some slight pretence of trying to make the learners understand, I therefore select the last; and this selection is justified when we remember that on the shot being heard, Randolph leans for support on the "machine", and stands in its shadow; but any of the others would be too small to throw any appreciable shadow, except one – the wheel-and-axle – and that one would hardly afford support to a tall man in the erect position. The Atwood's machine is therefore forced on us; as to its construction, it is, as you are aware, composed of two upright posts, with a crossbar fitted with pulleys and strings, and is intended to show the motion of bodies acting under a constant force – the force of gravity, to wit. But now consider all the really glorious uses to which those same pulleys may be turned in lowering and lifting unobserved that "ball of cotton" through the two apertures, while the other strings with the weights attached are dangling before the dull eyes of the peasants. I need only point out that when the whole company trooped out of the room, Randolph was the last to leave it, and it is not now difficult to conjecture why.

'Of what, then, have we convicted Randolph? For one thing, we have shown that by marks of feet in the snow preparation was made beforehand for obscuring the cause of the earl's death. That death must therefore have been at least expected, foreknown. Thus we convict him of expecting it. And then, by an independent line of deduction, we can also discover the *means* by which he expected it to occur. It is clear that he did not expect it to occur when it did by the hand of Maude Cibras – for this is proved by his knowledge that she had left the neighbourhood, by his evidently genuine astonishment at the sight of the closed window, and, above all, by his truly morbid desire to establish a substantial, an irrefutable *alibi* for himself by going to Plymouth on the day when there was every reason to suppose she would do the deed – that is, on the 8th, the day of the earl's invitation. On the fatal night, indeed, the same morbid eagerness to build up a clear *alibi* is observable, for he surrounds himself with a cloud of witnesses in the upper chamber. But that, you will admit, is not nearly so perfect a one as a journey, say, to Plymouth would have been. Why then, expecting the death, did he not take some such journey? Obviously because on *this* occasion his personal presence was necessary. When, *in conjunction* with this, we recall the fact that during the intrigues with Cibras the lectures were discontinued, and again resumed immediately on her unlooked-for departure, we arrive at the conclusion that the means by which Lord Pharanx's death was expected to occur was the personal presence of Randolph *in conjunction* with the political speeches, the candidature, the class, the apparatus.

'But though he stands condemned of foreknowing, and being in some sort connected with, his father's death, I can nowhere find any indication of his having personally accomplished it, or even of his ever having had any such intention. The evidence is evidence of complicity – and nothing more. And yet – and yet – even of *this* we began by acquitting him unless we could discover, as I said, some strong, adequate, altogether irresistible motive for such complicity. Failing this, we ought to admit that at some point our argument has played us false, and led us into conclusions wholly at variance with our certain knowledge of the principles underlying human conduct in general. Let us therefore seek for such a motive – something deeper than personal enmity, stronger than personal ambition, *than the love of life itself*! And now, tell me, at the time of the occurrence of this mystery, was the whole past history of the House of Orven fully investigated?'

'Not to my knowledge,' I answered; 'in the papers there were, of course, sketches of the earl's career, but that I think was all.'

'Yet it cannot be that their past was unknown, but only that it was ignored. Long, I tell you, long and often, have I pondered on that history, and sought to trace with what ghastly secret has been pregnant the destiny, gloomful as Erebus and the murk of black-peplosed Nux, which for centuries has hung its pall over the men of this ill-fated house. Now at last I know. Dark, dark, and red with gore and horror is that history; down the silent corridors of the ages have these blood-soaked sons of Atreus fled shrieking before the pursuing talons of the dread Eumenides. The first earl received his patent in 1535 from the eighth Henry. Two years later, though noted as a rabid "king's man", he joined the Pilgrimage of Grace against his master, and was soon after executed, with Darcy and some other lords. His age was then fifty. His son, meantime, had served in the king's army under Norfolk. It is remarkable, by the way, that females have all along been rare in the family, and that in no instance has there been more than one son. The second earl, under the sixth Edward, suddenly threw up a civil post, hastened to the army, and fell at the age of forty at the battle of Pinkie in 1547. He was accompanied by his son. The third in 1557, under Mary, renounced the Catholic faith, to which, both before and since, the family have passionately clung, and suffered (at the age of forty) the last penalty. The fourth earl died naturally, but suddenly, in his bed at the age of fifty during the winter of 1566. At midnight *of the same day* he was laid in the grave by his son. This son was later on, in 1591, seen by *his* son to fall from a lofty balcony at Orven Hall, while walking in his sleep at high noonday. Then for some time nothing happens; but the eighth earl dies mysteriously in 1651 at the age of forty-five. A fire occurring in his room, he leapt from a window to escape the flames. Some of his limbs were thereby fractured, but he was in a fair way to recovery when there was a sudden relapse, soon ending in death. He was found to have been poisoned by *radix aconiti indica*, a rare Arabian poison not known in Europe at that time except to *savants*, and first mentioned by Acosta some months before. An attendant was accused and tried, but acquitted. The then son of the House was a Fellow of the newly founded Royal Society, and author of a now-forgotten work on Toxicology, which, however, I have read. No suspicion, of course, fell on *him*.'

As Zaleski proceeded with this retrospect, I could not but ask myself with stirrings of the most genuine wonder, whether he could possess this intimate knowledge of *all* the great families of Europe! It was as if he had spent a part of his life in making special study of the history of the Orvens.

'In the same manner,' he went on, 'I could detail the annals of the family from that time to the present. But all through they have been marked by the same latent tragic elements; and I have said enough to show you that in each of the tragedies there was invariably something large, leering, something of which the mind demands explanation, but seeks in vain to find it. Now we need no longer seek. Destiny did not design that the last Lord of Orven should any more hide from the world the guilty secret of his race. It was the will of the gods – and he betrayed himself. "Return," he writes, "the beginning of the end is come." What end? *The* end – perfectly well known to Randolph, needing no explanation for *him*. The old, old end, which in the ancient dim time led the first lord, loyal still at heart, to forsake his king; and another, still devout, to renounce his cherished faith, and yet another to set fire to the home of his ancestors. You have called the two last scions of the family "a proud and selfish pair of beings"; proud they were, and selfish too, but you are in error if you think their selfishness a personal one: on the contrary, they were singularly oblivious of self in the ordinary sense of the word. Theirs was the pride and the selfishness of *race*. What consideration, think you, other than the weal of his house, could induce Lord Randolph to take on himself the shame – for as such he certainly regards it – of a conversion to radicalism? He would, I am convinced, have *died* rather than make this pretence for merely personal ends. But he does it – and the reason? It is because he has received that awful summons from home; because "the end" is daily coming nearer, and it must not find him unprepared to meet it; it is because Lord Pharanx's senses are becoming *too* acute; because the clatter of the servants' knives at the other end of the house inflames him to madness; because his excited palate can no longer endure any food but the subtlest delicacies; because Hester Dyett is able from the posture in which he sits to conjecture that he is intoxicated; because, in fact, he is on the brink of the dreadful malady which physicians call "*General Paralysis of the Insane*". You remember I took from your hands the newspaper containing the earl's letter to Cibras in order to read it with my own eyes. I had my reasons, and I was justified. That letter contains three mistakes in spelling: "here" is printed "hear", "pass" appears as "pas", and "room" as "rume". Printers' errors, you say? But not so – one might be,

two in that short paragraph could hardly be, three
would be impossible. Search the whole paper through,
and I think you will not find another. Let us reverence
the theory of probabilities: the errors were the writer's,
not the printer's. General Paralysis of the Insane is
known to have this effect on the writing. It attacks
its victims about the period of middle age – the age
at which the deaths of all the Orvens who died
mysteriously occurred. Finding then that the dire
heritage of his race – the heritage of madness – is
falling or fallen on him, he summons his son from
India. On himself he passes sentence of death: it is
the tradition of the family, the secret vow of self-
destruction handed down through ages from father to
son. But he must have aid: in these days it is difficult
for a man to commit the suicidal act without detection
– and if madness is a disgrace to the race, equally so is
suicide. Besides, the family is to be enriched by the
insurances on his life, and is thereby to be allied with
royal blood; but the money will be lost if the suicide
be detected. Randolph therefore returns and blossoms
into a popular candidate.

'For a time he is led to abandon his original plans
by the appearance of Maude Cibras; he hopes that
she may be made to destroy the earl; but when she
fails him, he recurs to it – recurs to it all suddenly, for
Lord Pharanx's condition is rapidly becoming critical,
patent to all eyes, could any eye see him – so much so
that on the last day none of the servants are allowed
to enter his room. We must therefore regard Cibras
as a mere addendum to, an extraneous element in,
the tragedy, not as an integral part of it. She did not
shoot the noble lord, for she had no pistol; nor did
Randolph, for he was at a distance from the bed of

death, surrounded by witnesses; nor did the imaginary burglars. The earl therefore shot himself; and it was the small globular silver pistol, such as this' – here Zaleski drew a little embossed Venetian weapon from a drawer near him – 'that appeared in the gloom to the excited Hester as a "ball of cotton", while it was being drawn upward by the Atwood's machine. But if the earl shot himself he could not have done so *after* being stabbed to the heart. Maude Cibras, therefore, stabbed a dead man. She would, of course, have ample time for stealing into the room and doing so after the shot was fired, and before the party reached the balcony window, on account of the delay on the stairs in procuring a second light; in going to the earl's door; in examining the tracks, and so on. But having stabbed a dead man, she is not guilty of murder. The message I just now sent by Ham was one addressed to the Home Secretary, telling him on no account to let Cibras die tomorrow. He well knows my name, and will hardly be silly enough to suppose me capable of using words without meaning. It will be perfectly easy to prove my conclusions, for the pieces removed from, and replaced in, the floorings can still be detected, if looked for; the pistol is still, no doubt, in Randolph's room, and its bore can be compared with the bullet found in Lord Pharanx's brain; above all, the jewels stolen by the "burglars" are still safe in some cabinet of the new earl, and may readily be discovered. I therefore expect that the *dénouement* will now take a somewhat different turn.'

That the *dénouement* did take a different turn, and pretty strictly in accordance with Zaleski's forecast, is now matter of history, and the incidents, therefore, need no further comment from me in this place.

From Behind the Barrier

J. S. FLETCHER

At three o'clock that morning I returned to my house in North Audley Street and went straight upstairs to my bedroom, devoutly hoping that nothing would rouse me out of bed again. I had gone to bed at half-past ten on the previous evening, only to be called up before midnight to treat a case which was not serious, and again at one to deal with another of more importance. Now, returning to bed for the third time, I hoped that it might fulfil the old proverb and pay for all, but after ten years' experiences of the nightly vicissitudes of those who practise the healing art, I felt by no means sure that my hopes would be fulfilled.

That they were not to be fulfilled that night was made evident before my head had fairly touched the pillow. The electric night-bell at my bedside suddenly burst out into a shrill whirring clamour which almost startled me, used as I was to its incursions upon my privacy at all sorts of unreasonable moments. And whoever it was that had his finger pressed upon the button in the street below was evidently absolutely determined that I should hear, for the noise never ceased for an instant until I went to the speaking-tube which hung near the bell.

'Yes, yes!' I said to the unknown clamourer. 'I hear you – don't go on ringing. What is it?'

A voice, agitated, thick of utterance, trembling in

its eagerness, came up the tube from the man waiting impatiently on my doorstep. Its accent, its words, suggested the notion of a man labouring under great excitement and distress of mind: 'For God's sake, Ralston, let me in – let me in quickly, Ralston – I – oh, be quick, I say – let me in!'

There was something familiar to me in the voice – the use of my name without any prefix showed that the man was some friend or acquaintance. And yet I did not entirely recognise my strange visitor by accent or note. I spoke again.

'Yes, yes!' I said. 'I'm coming down at once – this minute. But who is it?'

The voice came again – more agitated than ever: 'Oh, be quick! It's I – Arthur Treherbert. I want to see you, Ralston. I'm – I'm afraid. Be quick, I say.'

I slipped the stopper into the tube and hurried into some clothes and downstairs to the hall as fast as I could go. And in the couple of minutes which all this occupied I wondered whatever had brought Arthur Treherbert to my door and what he was afraid of that he should betray such evident agitation. Arthur Treherbert? – why, of course I knew him, though we had not seen much of each other for many years. He and his brother Frank – they were twins, and curiously like each other in appearance – had been classmates of mine at Bart.'s, and at that time we were on friendly terms. But their intentions of practising medicine were never carried out; when they were twenty-two years of age some kinsman died and left them, quite unexpectedly, a considerable estate in Wiltshire, which they were to share conjointly, and since that time they had scarcely ever been seen in any of their old haunts.

However, here was Arthur Treherbert back in London, and presenting himself at my door under circumstances which, to say the least, seemed unusual. I seemed to scent mystery as I undid bolts and bars, and my desire for sleep had vanished before a feeling of inquisitiveness as to what awaited me on the other side of the door.

I had paused to light the lamp in the hall, and when I opened the door its effulgence fell on Arthur Treherbert standing on the top step and holding on to the doorpost for support. I saw at once that he was mentally disturbed in no ordinary degree – his face was white, drawn, and covered with perspiration; his eyes were wild and staring, and the pupils were unusually dilated; his mouth and jaw were twitching in a fashion which showed that he was nearly on the point of losing all self-control. Without more ado I seized him by the elbow, drew him into the hall and shut the door.

'What is it, Arthur?' I asked as calmly as possible.

I felt him make a strenuous effort to assert himself. His muscles twitched in my grasp and he swallowed two or three times before he could speak.

'I – I don't know,' he said at last. 'It's – I don't know what it is – I've been – frightened. Oh!'

He lifted one hand and passed it rapidly across his eyes and forehead. The action seemed to denote two desires – one, to shut some picture away from sight; the other, to wipe some thought out of his mind.

I made no reply to what he said. I led him into my dining-room, forced him into an easy-chair, and gave him a stiff dose of brandy. His teeth chattered against the rim of the glass.

'Now then, Arthur, what is it?' I asked, after I had

watched him attentively for some minutes and seen that he was recovering his self-command. 'Drink off the rest of the brandy and tell me all about it. You're better now – pull yourself together.'

He set down the empty glass with a hand that was much steadier than it had been five minutes before, and his brows knitted in a palpable effort to think and speak clearly.

'Take your time, Arthur,' I said. 'Try to be clear.'

While he waited, evidently following my advice to get a clear notion of what he wanted to say, I looked him over very carefully, and I now perceived that he was as unceremoniously clothed as I was myself – that is to say, wherever he had suddenly sprung from, he had quitted his quarters in his nightclothes, over which he had drawn trousers and jacket. His head was uncombed, and he had come out without hat or cap; his feet had no more protection than was afforded by a pair of dress shoes. He looked, indeed, as any man might look who is called out of bed in the middle of the night by an unwonted sound and sent downstairs to search for burglars. But no man could have shown such signs of fear at the mere prospect of meeting a burglar as Arthur Treherbert was showing in his face when I admitted him to my house.

For the rest of him, I did not regard him as being greatly changed. I remembered him and Frank very well as being much more alike than twin brothers usually are – each had the same tall, slim, slightly stooping figure, the same long, thin, delicate face, the same dreamy eyes and sensitive mouth, the same air of being much more interested in the unseen and the spiritual than in the seen and the material. I had always said of them that they were dreamers, and that their kinsman's action in providing them with a competency for life was most providential, and now, as I watched Arthur carefully, I was more than ever convinced of the truth of my early belief. His eyes were the eyes of a man who sees, or thinks he sees, into the unseen.

His self-control was increasing every moment; he looked up at me at last, and smiled apologetically, and I saw that he was master of himself. He shook his head and shrugged his shoulders.

'You'll think this awfully strange, Ralston,' he said. 'I – I've been through the strangest experience – it makes me shudder yet. Will you give me a cigar? – it will soothe my nerves, I think.'

I handed him a cigar-box and took and lighted a cigar myself.

'Tell me all about it,' I said.

'It's a long story,' he answered. 'It's – queer. You'll have to follow it closely, Ralston, to make sure of it. I can't. You see, it's this way – you remember that Frank and I had an estate left to us in the old days at Bart.'s and that we gave up all idea of the medical profession and settled down at Upford Magna?'

'Of course, I remember very well,' I replied.

'We have spent most of our time there since,' he went on. 'We always got on together capitally, Frank and I – our tastes are similar. Of late we have devoted a lot of time to the study of psychology. Now and then, of course, we have come to town, but it has been very rarely – Frank has come more than I have – there have been times when it was necessary to transact business, and he is the better business man of the two. And – let me see – is this Thursday? – yes, Thursday – well, he left Upford Magna for London

on business last Monday morning, and since then I
have not heard of him.'

'When did you expect to hear?' I asked.

'His intention was to return home on Tuesday
afternoon,' answered Treherbert. 'He was only going
to stay one night in town. But he did not return on
the Tuesday. I was not alarmed, but I was uneasy,
because we have been so thoroughly identified that I
felt sure that he would make me acquainted with the
slightest alteration in his movements. I heard nothing
from him, however.'

'I take it that you came up to town yourself yesterday, Arthur,' I said, nodding significantly at his attire,
'for I see you have been sleeping somewhere. How do
you know that Frank did not cross you on the way –
you coming, he going?'

'No,' he returned, 'Frank had not returned at a late
hour last night. I wired to them for news of him –
they had none. Ralston, Frank has disappeared, and I
believe it has been through foul play.'

I regarded him earnestly – it was easy to see that he
was saying what he really felt to be true.

'Do you mean that?' I asked, almost pityingly, for I
thought it rather early times to conceive such a notion.
'Consider – you have only missed him for three days.'

He shook his head.

'Frank has met with foul play,' he reiterated, 'and it
was on Monday night. Listen: on Monday night I
went to bed as usual at Upford Magna and went to
sleep quite calmly. About midnight I woke suddenly,
with a terrible consciousness that Frank was in deadly
peril – he did not call to me with his actual voice, but
his mental self, his soul, if you so like to phrase it,
called to me insistently. It was a brief, agonising call –

then all was over. I felt nothing more and the rest was utter silence, blankness. I was so alarmed that as soon as it was possible I wired to Frank – that would be about eight o'clock on Tuesday morning – at the Hotel Metropole – we always stay there when we come to town – to ask him if all was well with him.

'Getting no reply by noon, I wired to the management to enquire if Mr Frank Treherbert was there or had been there. Their reply came at once – in the negative. He had not been there at all. Then I wired to several other places where I thought I might get news of him. Nobody could tell me anything except the manager of the Piccadilly branch of the National Provincial Bank of England – we keep our principal account there – who had seen him on Monday afternoon just before three o'clock. Of course, I knew Frank was going to cash a cheque there – that had been his principal reason for coming to town. Beyond that – '

'Wait a moment, Arthur,' I said. 'Was the cheque for a considerable amount?'

'Yes,' he answered, 'it was for three thousand pounds.'

'Continue your story,' said I. 'I am following it closely.'

'Well, beyond that,' he went on, 'I could hear nothing. But all that day, and more particularly during Tuesday night, when I did not sleep, I was conscious of a feeling that Frank was calling me. There was no outward sound – it was an inward call – a perpetual voicing of his want of me in a fashion much more forcible than words. And on Wednesday – that is, yesterday – morning the feeling was so strong that I left home for London and got to town early in the afternoon. All the way in the train I felt him calling, and I felt sure that I was going in answer to his call. But when I got out of the train at Waterloo I had a momentary sense of the almost entire hopelessness of the situation. To find one man amongst so many millions! – you see the apparent absurdity of the task, Ralston?'

'Naturally, I do,' I assented. 'But I am more concerned in what you did than in that, Arthur.'

'Well, first I went to the bank, because it was there that Frank had last been seen, so far as I was aware. There was nothing to learn there. Frank had cashed his cheque, in gold, after his usual absurd custom. He had had the parcels of gold packed in a strong leather bag which he had taken there for the purpose, and this had been carried out by a porter and placed in a passing hansom which Frank hailed. The porter had not heard Frank mention any destination to the cabman, nor had he noticed the number of the cab or its driver. So I could learn no more there.'

'The cabman might be advertised for,' I suggested.

'Yes – I thought of that,' continued Arthur, 'and I intended to send advertisements to all the principal newspapers today. But after leaving the bank in Piccadilly, a remarkable thing happened which put me on a new scent – indeed, on the direct track of Frank. As is usual in so many cases in life, I hit upon it by what is, erroneously, I think, called accident. It was this way – I had walked aimlessly along Piccadilly, in the direction of the Park, and had stopped at last to look at some pictures in a shop window. While I lingered there I became conscious that a man at my side was regarding me with considerable attention. I turned and glanced at him – a well-dressed, portly, fresh-faced man. On meeting my glance he raised his hat very politely and observed that the day was fine. I agreed that it was.

'This was somewhat extraordinary, but nothing to what followed. The man seemed to fidget about for a moment, and then said enquiringly, "Shall you be returning to the hotel tonight, Mr Treherbert?" I stared at him for a second, and then, suddenly realising the truth – that he was mistaking me for Frank – I replied, "Hotel? – what hotel? – I don't know what you mean." Then he looked surprised. "Don't you remember, sir," he said, "you engaged a room – number eighteen – in my hotel on Monday evening and went out very early on Tuesday morning? – so early indeed that none of us saw you? I was a bit anxious when you did not turn in on Tuesday night – shall we expect you tonight, sir?" Well, of course, I was now certain that I had hit upon a clue to Frank's whereabouts – the man was mistaking one twin-brother for the other. You know, Ralston, we are the same height, we are very much alike in features and figure, and we dress alike – always have done. There is not much to be wondered at in the man's mistake, is there?'

'Not a bit,' said I. 'But what a fortunate meeting!'

'I determined to take full advantage of it,' responded Arthur, 'and I told the man there and then that it was my brother Frank to whom he must be referring, and that I was in search of him. Then he told me his story – his name was Charles Burchell, and he was the proprietor of a small private hotel in Upper Brook Street, used, I fancy, a good deal by military and naval men and bachelors. He said that Frank engaged a room there on Monday evening and certainly slept there that night, as he himself saw him retiring to his room. But he had disappeared at a very early hour next morning. The chambermaid on being questioned said that the door of his room was open and the room untenanted when she went on duty. Yet no one had seen him leave the hotel. Was it possible, I asked Mr Burchell, that he could do so unobserved? Yes, he said, it was possible, but highly improbable. However, there the fact remained – Frank had disappeared.'

'That,' I said, 'is strange, but it may be accounted for in some quite natural fashion. What did you do?'

'I decided, of course, to go to the hotel with Mr Burchell. We walked there together. I saw Frank's signature in the visitors' book. There was no doubt that he had arrived there on Monday evening, at an early hour. But, even then, three hours had elapsed between his arrival at Burchell's and his departure from the bank, and he could have driven from one place to the other in a few minutes. However, we could not go into the question of what he was doing during those three hours just then – the obvious thing was to see Frank's room and examine the luggage to see if he had left any clue. So I went up to number eighteen with Mr Burchell.'

Arthur Treherbert stopped abruptly, and some of the horror which I had seen in his eyes on his first entrance came back to them. His hand began to tremble again and the signs of fear and agitation increased so rapidly that I gave him another dose of brandy and bade him pull himself together.

'Try to think of the concrete facts,' I said, 'and leave the abstract aside just now.'

'But I can't, man!' he exclaimed. 'And perhaps

what you call the abstract was more concrete to me than you think of. As soon as I got into that room, Ralston, I had a definite sense of Frank's presence, but in a quite different way from any in which I had ever realised it before. It was as if – as if his presence was making strong efforts to materialise itself to me, and could not. I put it down to the fact that Frank had lived in the room, and proceeded to examine his belongings. He had taken away with him from Upford Magna a suitcase and a dressing-case – there they were, and their various contents were in evidence; in fact, the room looked as if its occupant might be expected to step into it at any moment. And here are two or three significant things, Ralston: Frank's over-coat was hanging there – so was his hat – his walking-stick was in a corner. Is it not strange that he should have left an hotel at a presumably very early hour of the morning at this time of the year – October – without hat or coat?'

'Scarcely probable that he would do so,' I answered. 'But, Arthur, what of the bag containing the money? Was it there?'

'There was not a sign of it – I know it very well – he had carried it for similar purposes before – had had it made, indeed, for carrying money. And now, Ralston, listen to this as an illustration of how unobservant most people are. Nobody in the hotel could say positively how many bags Frank had with him on his arrival. The man who had taken them off the cab was uncertain; the man who had carried them to the room was uncertain; the chambermaid who had seen them in the room was uncertain. But Frank and that particular bag had disappeared.'

'The probability is, Arthur, that Frank never took

the bag there at all,' I said. 'He very likely placed it in some other bank's custody or in a safe deposit.'

'It may be so,' he replied, 'but I'm not so much concerned – indeed, I'm not concerned at all – about the money as about Frank. I want to tell you what happened. The proprietor, Mr Burchell, was inclined to be quite cheery about matters – he said that Frank had probably gone off on some business of his own and would return in safety. Yet he admitted that men do not usually clear out of an hotel at a very early hour on an October morning without hat or coat. However, he still persisted that Frank could not possibly have come to any harm there and that he would return – probably that evening – and he suggested that I should stay the night there and wait for him. To this I consented, and he apportioned me a room exactly opposite Frank's.'

He paused for a moment and sipped wearily at the brandy. 'Ralston, you cannot believe what I went through during that evening and in the early hours of the morning until I came to you! I purposely dined late, I purposely sat up late. It was one o'clock when I went to bed – Frank had not made his appearance then. I got into bed, but it was not likely that I should sleep, under the circumstances. Yet I did sleep – after a fashion – a light, uneasy sleep. I woke with a feeling of the utmost horror – I felt that Frank was in his room and that he was calling me – at least it was not so much a calling as a drawing, an attracting, and literal compulsion, which was forcing me to go to him. I lay there, sweating with terror, for some time – at last I was obliged to get up. I opened my door, I went across the corridor, I pushed open the door of Frank's room, I stepped within it. And – '

He showed such signs of evident horror at this stage that I had to bid him control himself again. After a moment's battling with his emotions he went on: 'Ralston, before God, I felt that he was there – there in that room – close to me – but not as he was. There – there was a difference. It was as if he was stretching out arms from behind a barrier which neither of us could surmount, as if he called to me across a vast space through which his voice could not carry. But he was there – he *is* there. I tell you he's there, Ralston – somewhere in that room – oh!'

He began to shake and groan in his agony of mind, and it was some minutes before I could bring him back to a calmer state. Then I asked him what happened next. He shook his head.

'I – I don't know,' he answered. 'I – I must have hurried on some clothes' – he paused and looked down at his garments wonderingly – 'and then I must have run downstairs. I remember now that the night-porter was in the hall and that he looked startled and astonished. Oh, yes – I remember, too, that I said, "Let me out – let me out!" several times, and that he stared queerly at me as he unlocked the door. And then I ran – I don't know where, but I suddenly saw your name on the door, and – oh, Ralston, what's to be done? I know Frank's there – in that room – I *felt* him.'

'What's to be done, Arthur, at present, is to secure some sleep for you – you'll be ill and useless if you go on like this,' I said. 'Now, listen – I'm going to take you upstairs and make you go to bed and I'll give you a composing draught. And in the morning – or, rather, after breakfast, I'll help you in every way I can.'

He shook his head as if in doubt of my policy, but I

insisted on his obeying me, and I very soon had the satisfaction of seeing him sound asleep. And that accomplished I put the matter out of my mind – I think, looking back upon it, that I did not attach very much importance to it, believing really that Arthur Treherbert had unduly excited himself about his brother's disappearance – and went to bed and to sleep myself.

But first thing in the morning I took a practical step. I had once or twice had occasion to employ the services of a private enquiry agent, one Stephen Phimister, a man who had made his name at Scotland Yard in his day and had been concerned in some big cases. No one would ever have taken Phimister for a detective – he dressed and looked like a smart groom and was never seen without a bit of straw in his mouth, at which he perpetually chewed – but no one who had ever had dealings with him could doubt his sagacity and penetration. He was a man of few words, and he heard my account of Arthur Treherbert in silence.

'What do you make of it, Phimister?' I enquired. 'Presentiment and telepathy are not much in your line, are they?'

Phimister shifted his straw from one corner of his lips to the other and gazed meditatively at his legs, which were clothed that morning in riding-breeches and Newmarket gaiters.

'There's not much that isn't in my line, Doctor,' he said, 'call it by what name you please. But I think we'll just walk round to Burchell's hotel with your friend and see if we can make anything out.'

And so, about ten o'clock that morning, the three of us set out, Phimister asking a question or two of

Arthur Treherbert as we went along. I had lent Arthur sufficient necessaries to complete his toilet, and had furnished him with a hat and an overcoat – there was nothing, therefore, in his appearance to arouse criticism or attention. Yet I could see, as soon as we entered the hotel, that the servants standing about were eyeing him over with considerable curiosity, and before we had time to ask for him Mr Burchell came out of his office and greeted Arthur in a fashion which showed that he had been in some anxiety about him. When he saw that he was accompanied he hurried us all into a private room.

'My dear sir!' he exclaimed. 'I have been much concerned about you – I understand that you quitted the house late last night in a state of great agitation, and – '

'Has my brother returned or been heard of?' enquired Arthur abruptly.

Mr Burchell spread out his hands.

'I regret to say that Mr Frank Treherbert had not yet been seen or heard of,' he answered. 'It is very strange.'

'These are friends of mine,' said Arthur. 'Dr Ralston, who was also a friend of my brother's, and Mr Phimister, who is a private enquiry agent.'

Mr Burchell favoured Mr Phimister with a sharp glance.

'I've heard of you often, Mr Phimister,' he said. 'Do you think you can suggest anything about the disappearance of this gentleman?'

Phimister chewed at his straw.

'Did anyone see Mr Frank leave the house?' he asked.

'Not a soul,' replied Mr Burchell.

'Could he have let himself out?'

'He could,' said Mr Burchell, 'but it isn't very probable that he wouldn't have been observed.'

'Let us see his room,' said Phimister.

We all went upstairs together. As we drew near the door of the room – number eighteen – Arthur Treherbert began to show signs of great emotion. I was obliged to take him by the arm, to speak firmly to him – even then he trembled with fear. Once within the room his agitation increased. He shook from head to foot, and when I forced him into a chair he rocked himself to and fro in it as if in an uncontrollable paroxysm of grief.

'He's here – here – here!' he said, repeating the phrase over and over again. 'I can feel him. And yet – oh, God, Ralston, what does it mean? – it's as if – as if he were dead!'

Phimister, straw in mouth, hands in pockets, was looking about the room. My eyes followed his. There was in reality little to look at. The furniture was good, solid, and very old-fashioned – a four-poster mahogany bedstead that must have been made in Georgian days, a big mahogany wardrobe, and the like. There was Frank's suitcase – there was a suit of clothes, neatly folded, lying upon a chair. Brushes and combs and the usual appurtenances were set out on dressing-table and washstand. An overcoat hung behind the door, on the peg above it was a hat. Nothing could have been more ordinary, less romantic than the appearance of that room.

Phimister turned to Arthur Treherbert. Without appearing to notice Arthur's emotion he enquired: 'How many suits of clothes did your brother bring to town with him, do you know?'

'Yes,' said Arthur, 'I do know. Two. A grey suit, in which he travelled, and a dark suit – also grey but very dark.'

'There's the light-grey one,' said Phimister, pointing to the neatly folded suit lying on a chair, 'and here' – he opened the suitcase – 'here is the darker one. And here is, presumably, the shirt he took off on going to bed on Monday night, for there are the collar-stud and sleeve-links left in it, and there also, presumably, are his underclothes. So then, if he did leave the hotel he left it in his nightclothes. And by the by, if he didn't, where are his nightclothes?'

But the nightclothes were not to be found.

'It's a queer business,' said Mr Burchell.

But Phimister's next operation was indeed queer. First, he walked all round the old four-poster bed, then he got down on his hands and knees and examined it. And suddenly, with a knowing look at me, he began to divest the bed of its furniture – pillows, blankets, sheets, in regular order. It was one of those very old-fashioned beds in which a layer of feather beds and mattresses are deposited as in a trough – two mattresses at the bottom, a feather bed on the top.

'Give me a hand, Mr Burchell,' said Phimister as he stripped off the last sheet and exposed the feather bed.

'You surely don't think – ' began Burchell.

'Steady,' said Phimister. 'Now, then, help me to lift that mattress. Now for it – ah!'

There lay Frank Treherbert's dead body. That it was a dead body one could see at a glance – that Frank had been murdered one saw a moment later. Nor did it take more than a glance to see how he had been murdered – he had evidently been dealt a tremendous blow which had rendered him unconscious and had then been deliberately strangled. And the rope with which he had been strangled – part of an old woollen bell-rope – remained round his neck, so tightly drawn and knotted that one turned heartsick to think of the fiendish determination with which the deed had been done.

After a first frantic outburst of grief Arthur Treherbert's manner suddenly underwent a complete transformation. He became strangely cool and collected; the only sign of his inward excitement was betrayed in the glitter of his eyes, which looked as if they were already fastened on some victim who was to be punished without mercy.

'Who did it – who did it?' he repeated. 'Who did it?'

'Ah, that's what we must get at,' said Phimister. 'For the moment, gentlemen, allow me to lock up this room and let us go downstairs and consult. Now then,' he continued when we were in Burchell's private room, 'who told you that Mr Frank Treherbert had gone out on Tuesday morning?'

Mr Burchell began to think.

'I don't know that anybody did,' he answered at last. 'I think it was noticed in the house that he was not seen about, and I believe the chambermaid finally volunteered the information that he must have gone out very early because she had found his room empty when she came on duty. I remember that the room had been tidied and put straight by nine o'clock that morning, because I happened to pass the open door and glanced within, and I couldn't help thinking that the chambermaid had been very expeditious.'

'Let me see the chambermaid,' said Phimister.

Mr Burchell, however, could not produce the chambermaid. The woman in question, Meacher, had been taken ill on Tuesday morning and had asked leave to go home for a week or two, and Mrs Burchell had given her consent.

Phimister chewed at his straw.

'What is this woman like?' he enquired.

'A strong, strapping woman,' replied Mr Burchell. 'Able to do the work of any other two in the house. She has been here three years – a quiet, respectable woman.'

'Where does she live?' asked Phimister.

But that nobody could tell him. It appeared that nobody had sufficient interest in Meacher to care whether she lived in Mayfair or Hackney, and some time elapsed before a scullery-maid was found who knew exactly where Meacher lived in Dalston, but could not remember the name of the street.

'But I could go to the house – straight,' she said.

'Let this young woman put her outdoor things on and come with us, Mr Burchell,' said Phimister. 'And don't say anything to your wife of what we've discovered till we come back.'

With the scullery-maid on the box, acting as guide, and Burchell, Phimister, Arthur Treherbert and myself inside the cab, we drove a long way before we paused at the end of a dismal little street running out of the Kingsland Road. The scullery-maid climbed down and stretched out a toil-stained forefinger.

'It's the fifth house on that side,' she said.

We four men went in a body to the house indicated – a mean, grey house with a patch of damp garden outside. Three of us waited at the gate while Phimister exchanged a word or two with a woman who answered his knock. He beckoned us to approach, to enter.

'She's out,' he said, 'but she'll be back presently. Hah! – look here!'

Within a little room into which Phimister turned as if by instinct were two large trunks, quite new, into which their owner had evidently been packing a large variety of objects. She had just as evidently interrupted the packing process to go out for a while – a considerable number of articles lay about on chairs and tables.

'I think she's going on a long journey, is Miss Meacher,' said the woman of the house. 'She ain't said nothink to me about it, but she's been that busy a-buyin' things and packin' of 'em that it looks as if somethink was up, don't it?'

'Ah!' said Phimister. 'Don't it just?'

The woman eyed us all with some curiosity and then withdrew, muttering something about attending to her own concerns. Phimister closed the door upon her and turned to Arthur.

'Now, Mr Treherbert,' he said, 'I want you to make yourself useful. This woman will let herself in with her latchkey and come straight in here. Stand there, Mr Treherbert, where you'll be the first object her eyes can fall on. If that doesn't fetch her I'm a Dutchman.'

Arthur Treherbert stood erect where Phimister placed him. His eyes were fixed on the closed door in a glare that threatened to scorch it.

Five minutes passed – ten – fifteen. Then steps in the garden, the grating of a latchkey, a heavy foot in the hall. Then the door was thrown wide open.

A big, raw-boned, masculine-looking woman with

harsh features and eyes set close together under a slanting forehead – Meacher – a murderess.

She stopped as if she had been shot, uttered one sharp cry, and fell in a heap at Arthur Treherbert's feet.

*   *   *

Before they hanged her at Newgate a few weeks later, Meacher, probably from the mere joys attendant upon reminiscences, told the chaplain 'all about it'.

'It was all his own fault,' she said; 'more his then mine. When I goes in to tidy up at night there's my lord a-countin' over all that money in gold sovereigns – playin' with it like a child. "There, chambermaid," he says, "did you ever see such a lot before – doesn't it tinkle?"

' "You'd ought to put that in the hotel safe, sir," says I, "Not I," says he. "I'll put it in the wardrobe there while I'm downstairs and take the key of the room with me." Fool! – in course, it tempted me to do for him. And I done it very easy,' concluded Meacher. 'I only had to 'it him once, and the rest was nothink at all. But I never had no luck. Oh, if they'd only been three hours later!'

Vendetta

GUY DE MAUPASSANT

Paulo Saverini's widow dwelt alone with her son in a small, mean house on the ramparts of Bonifacio. Built on a spur of the mountain and in places actually overhanging the sea, the town looks across the rock-strewn straits to the low-lying coast of Sardinia. On the other side, girdling it almost completely, there is a fissure in the cliff, like an immense corridor, which serves as a port, and down this long channel, as far as the first houses, sail the small Italian and Sardinian fishing-boats, and once a fortnight the broken-winded old steamer from Ajaccio. Clustered together on the white hillside, the houses form a patch of even more dazzling whiteness. Clinging to the rock, gazing down upon those deadly straits where scarcely a ship ventures, they look like the nests of birds of prey. The sea and the barren coast, stripped of all but a scanty covering of grass, are forever harassed by a restless wind, which sweeps along the narrow funnel, ravaging the banks on either side. In all directions the black points of innumerable rocks jut out from the water, with trails of white foam streaming from them, like torn shreds of cloth, floating and quivering on the surface of the waves.

The widow Saverini's house was planted on the very edge of the cliff and its three windows opened upon this wild and dreary prospect. She lived there with her son Antoine and their dog Sémillante, a great gaunt brute of the sheepdog variety, with a long, rough coat, whom the young man took with him when he went out shooting.

One evening, Antoine Saverini was treacherously stabbed in a quarrel by Nicolas Ravolati, who escaped that same night to Sardinia.

At the sight of the body, which was brought home by passers-by, the old mother shed no tears, but she gazed long and silently at her dead son. Then, laying her wrinkled hand upon the corpse, she promised him the vendetta. She would not allow anyone to remain with her, and shut herself up with the dead body. The dog Sémillante, who remained with her, stood at the foot of the bed and howled, with her head turned towards her master and her tail between her legs. Neither of them stirred, neither the dog nor the old mother, who was now leaning over the body, gazing at it fixedly, and silently shedding great tears. Still wearing his rough jacket, which was pierced and torn at the breast, the boy lay on his back as if asleep, but there was blood all about him – on his shirt, which had been torn open in order to expose the wound, on his waistcoat, trousers, face and hands. His beard and hair were matted with clots of blood.

The old mother began to talk to him, and at the sound of her voice the dog stopped howling.

'Never fear, never fear, you shall be avenged, my son, my little son, my poor child. You may sleep in peace. You shall be avenged, I tell you. You have your mother's word, and you know she never breaks it.'

Slowly she bent down and pressed her cold lips to the dead lips of her son. Sémillante resumed her howling, uttering a monotonous, long-drawn wail, heart-rending and terrible. And thus the two remained, the woman and the dog, till morning.

The next day Antoine Saverini was buried, and soon his name ceased to be mentioned in Bonifacio.

He had no brother, nor any near male relation. There was no man in the family who could take up the vendetta. Only his mother, his old mother, brooded over it.

From morning till night she could see, just across the straits, a white speck upon the coast. This was the little Sardinian village of Longosardo, where the Corsican bandits took refuge whenever the hunt for them grew too hot. They formed almost the entire population of the hamlet. In full view of their native shores they waited for a chance to return home and regain the bush. She knew that Nicolas Ravolati had sought shelter in that village.

All day long she sat alone at her window gazing at the opposite coast and thinking of her revenge, but what was she to do with no one to help her, and she herself so feeble and near her end? But she had promised, she had sworn by the dead body of her son, she could not forget, and she dared not delay. What was she to do? She could not sleep at night, she knew not a moment of rest or peace, but racked her brains unceasingly. Sémillante, asleep at her feet, would now and then raise her head and emit a piercing howl. Since her master had disappeared, this had become a habit; it was as if she were calling him, as if she, too, were inconsolable and preserved in her canine soul an ineffaceable memory of the dead.

One night, when Sémillante began to whine, the old mother had an inspiration of savage, vindictive ferocity. She thought about it till morning. At day-break she rose and betook herself to church. Prostrate on the stone floor, humbling herself before God, she besought Him to aid and support her, to lend to her poor, worn-out body the strength she needed to avenge her son.

Then she returned home. In the yard stood an old barrel with one end knocked in, in which was caught the rainwater from the eaves. She turned it over, emptied it, and fixed it to the ground with stakes and stones. Then she chained up Sémillante to this kennel and went into the house.

With her eyes fixed on the Sardinian coast, she walked restlessly up and down her room. He was over there, the murderer.

The dog howled all day and all night. The next morning, the old woman brought her a bowl of water, but no food. Another day passed. Sémillante was worn out and slept. The next morning her eyes were gleaming, and her coat staring, and she tugged frantically at her chain. And again the old woman gave her nothing to eat. Maddened with hunger Sémillante barked hoarsely. Another night went by.

At daybreak, the widow went to a neighbour and begged for two trusses of straw. She took some old clothes that had belonged to her husband, stuffed them with straw to represent a human figure, and made a head out of a bundle of old rags. Then, in front of Sémillante's kennel, she fixed a stake in the ground and fastened the dummy to it in an upright position.

The dog looked at the straw figure in surprise and, although she was famished, stopped howling.

The old woman went to the pork butcher and bought a long piece of black pudding. When she came home she lighted a wood fire in the yard, close to the kennel, and fried the black pudding. Sémillante bounded up and down in a frenzy, foaming at the mouth, her eyes fixed on the gridiron with its maddening smell of meat.

Her mistress took the steaming pudding and wound it like a tie round the dummy's neck. She fastened it on tightly with string as if to force it inwards. When she had finished she unchained the dog.

With one ferocious leap, Sémillante flew at the dummy's throat and with her paws on its shoulders began to tear it. She fell back with a portion of her prey between her jaws, sprang at it again, slashing at the string with her fangs, tore away some scraps of food, dropped for a moment, and hurled herself at it in renewed fury. She tore away the whole face with savage rendings and reduced the neck to shreds.

Motionless and silent, with burning eyes, the old woman looked on. Presently she chained the dog up again. She starved her another two days, and then put her through the same strange performance. For three months she accustomed her to this method of attack, and to tear her meals away with her fangs. She was no longer kept on the chain. At a sign from her mistress, the dog would fly at the dummy's throat.

She learned to tear it to pieces even when no food was concealed about its throat. Afterwards as a reward she was always given the black pudding her mistress had cooked for her.

As soon as she caught sight of the dummy, Sémillante quivered with excitement and looked at her mistress, who would raise her finger and cry in a shrill voice, 'Tear him.'

*

One Sunday morning when she thought the time had come, the widow Saverini went to confession and communion, in an ecstasy of devotion. Then she disguised herself as a tattered old beggarman, and struck a bargain with a Sardinian fisherman, who took her and her dog across to the opposite shore.

She carried a large piece of black pudding wrapped in a cloth bag. Sémillante had been starved for two days and her mistress kept exciting her by letting her smell the savoury food.

The pair entered the village of Longosardo. The old woman hobbled along to a baker and asked for the house of Nicolas Ravolati. He had resumed his former occupation, which was that of a joiner, and he was working alone in the back of his shop.

The old woman threw open the door and called: 'Nicolas! Nicolas!'

He turned round. Slipping the dog's lead, she cried: 'Tear him! Tear him!'

The maddened dog flew at his throat. The man flung out his arms, grappled with the brute and they rolled on the ground together. For some moments he struggled, kicking the floor with his feet. Then he lay still, while Sémillante tore his throat to shreds.

Two neighbours, seated at their doors, remembered having seen an old beggarman emerge from the house and, at his heels, a lean black dog, which was eating, as it went along, some brown substance that its master was giving it.

By the evening the old woman had reached home again.

That night she slept well.

The Sapient Monkey

HEADON HILL

I would advise every person whose duties take him into the field of 'private enquiry' to go steadily through the daily papers the first thing every morning. Personally I have found the practice most useful, for there are not many *causes célèbres* in which my services are not enlisted on one side or the other, and by this method I am always up in my main facts before I am summoned to assist. When I read the account of the proceedings at Bow Street against Franklin Gale in connection with the Tudways' bank robbery, I remember thinking that on the face of it there never was a clearer case against a misguided young man.

Condensed for the sake of brevity, the police-court report disclosed the following state of things:

Franklin Gale, clerk, aged twenty-three, in the employment of Messrs Tudways, the well-known private bankers of the Strand, was brought up on a warrant charged with stealing the sum of £500 – being the moneys of his employers. Mr James Spruce, assistant cashier at the bank, gave evidence to the effect that he missed the money from his till on the afternoon of July 22. On making up his cash for the day he discovered that he was short of £300 worth of notes and £200 in gold. He had no idea how the amount had been abstracted. The prisoner was an assistant bookkeeper at the bank, and had access behind the counter. Detective-sergeant Simmons said that the case had been placed in his hands for the purpose of tracing the stolen notes. He had ascertained that one of them – of the value of £5 – had been paid to Messrs Crosthwaite & Co., tailors, of New Bond Street, on July 27th, by Franklin Gale. As a result, he had applied for a warrant, and had arrested the prisoner. The latter was remanded for a week, at the end of which period it was expected that further evidence would be forthcoming.

I had hardly finished reading the report when a telegram was put into my hands demanding my immediate presence at Rosemount, Twickenham. From the address given, and from the name of 'Gale' appended to the despatch, I concluded that the affair at Tudways' Bank was the cause of the summons. I had little doubt that I was to be retained in the interests of the prisoner, and my surmise proved correct.

Rosemount was by no means the usual kind of abode from which the ordinary run of bank clerks come gaily trooping into the great City in shoals by the early trains. There was nothing of cheap gentility about the 'pleasant suburban residence standing in its own grounds of an acre', as the house-agent would say – with its lawns sloping down to the river, shaded by mulberry and chestnut trees, and plentifully garnished with the noble flower which gave it half its name. Rosemount was assuredly the home either of some prosperous merchant or of a private gentleman, and when I crossed its threshold I did so quite prepared for the fuller enlightenment which was to follow. Mr Franklin Gale was evidently not one of the struggling genus bank clerk, but must be the son of well-to-do people, and not yet flown from the parent nest. When I left my office I had thought that I was bound on a forlorn hope, but at the sight of Rosemount – my first real 'touch' of the case – my spirits revived. Why should a young man living amid such signs of wealth want to rob his employers? Of course I recognised that the youth of the prisoner precluded the probability of the place being his own. Had he been older, I should have reversed the argument. Rosemount in the actual occupation of a middle-aged bank clerk would have been prima-facie evidence of a tendency to outrun the constable.

I was shown into a well-appointed library, where I was received by a tall, silver-haired old gentleman of ruddy complexion, who had apparently been pacing the floor in a state of agitation. His warm greeting towards me – a perfect stranger – had the air of one who clutches at a straw.

'I have sent for you to prove my son's innocence, Mr Zambra,' he said. 'Franklin no more stole that money than I did. In the first place, he didn't want it; and, secondly, if he had been ever so pushed for cash, he would rather have cut off his right hand than put it into his employer's till. Besides, if these thickheaded policemen were bound to lock one of us up, it ought to have been me. The five-pound note with which Franklin paid his tailor was one – so he assures me, and I believe him – which I gave him myself.'

'Perhaps you would give me the facts in detail?' I replied.

'As to the robbery, both my son and I are as much in the dark as old Tudway himself,' Mr Gale proceeded. 'Franklin tells me that Spruce, the cashier, is accredited to be a most careful man, and the very last to leave his till to take care of itself. The facts that came out in evidence are perfectly true. Franklin's desk is close to the counter, and the note identified as one of the missing ones was certainly paid by him to Crosthwaite & Co., of New Bond Street, a few days after the robbery. It bears his endorsement, so there can be no doubt about that.

'So much for their side of the case. Ours is, I must confess, from a legal point of view, much weaker, and lies in my son's assertion of innocence, coupled with the knowledge of myself and his mother and his sisters that he is incapable of such a crime. Franklin insists that the note he paid to Crosthwaite & Co., the tailors, was one that I gave him on the morning of the 22nd. I remember perfectly well giving him a five-pound note at breakfast on that day, just before he left for town, so that he must have had it several hours before the robbery was committed. Franklin says that he had no other banknotes between the 22nd and 27th, and that he cannot, therefore, be mistaken. The note which I gave him I got fresh from my own bankers a day or two before, together with some others; and here is the most unfortunate point in the case. The solicitor whom I have engaged to defend Franklin has made the necessary enquiries at my bankers, and finds that the note paid to the tailors is *not* one of those which I drew from the bank.'

'Did not your son take notice of the number of the note you gave him?' I asked.

'Unfortunately, no. He is too much worried about

the numbers of notes at his business, he says, to note
those which are his own property. He simply sticks to
it that he knows it must be the same note because he
had no other.'

In the slang of the day, Mr Franklin Gale's story
seemed a little too thin. There was the evidence of
Tudways that the note paid to the tailor was one of
those stolen from them, and there was the evidence
of Mr Gale, senior's, bankers that it was not one of
those handed to their client. What was the use of the
prisoner protesting in the face of this that he had paid
his tailor with his father's present? The notes stolen
from Tudways were, I remembered reading, consecutive ones of a series, so that the possibility of
young Gale having at the bank changed his father's
gift for another note, which was subsequently stolen,
was knocked on the head. Besides, he maintained
that it was the *same* note.

'I should like to know something of your son's
circumstances and position,' I said, trying to divest
the question of any air of suspicion it might have
implied.

'I am glad you asked me that,' returned Mr Gale,
'for it touches the very essence of the whole case. My
son's circumstances and position are such that were
he the most unprincipled scoundrel in creation he
would have been nothing less than an idiot to have
done this thing. Franklin is not on the footing of an
ordinary bank clerk, Mr Zambra. I am a rich man,
and can afford to give him anything in reason, though
he is too good a lad ever to have taken advantage of
me. Tudway is an old friend of mine, and I got him to
take Franklin into the bank with a view to a partner-
ship. Everything was going on swimmingly towards

that end: the boy had perfected himself in his duties, and made himself valuable; I was prepared to invest a certain amount of capital on his behalf; and, lastly, Tudway, who lives next door to me here, got so fond of him that he allowed Franklin to become engaged to his daughter Maud. Would any young man in his senses go and steal a paltry £500 under such circumstances as that?'

I thought not, but I did not say so yet. 'What are Mr Tudway's views about the robbery?' I asked.

'Tudway is an old fool,' replied Mr Gale. 'He believes what the police tell him, and the police tell him that Franklin is guilty. I have no patience with him. I ordered him out of this house last night. He had the audacity to come and offer not to press the charge if the boy would confess.'

'And Miss Tudway?'

'Ah! she's a brick. Maud sticks to him like a true woman. But what is the use of our sticking to him against such evidence?' broke down poor Mr Gale, impotently. 'Can you, Mr Zambra, give us a crumb of hope?'

Before I could reply there was a knock at the library door, and a tall, graceful girl entered the room. Her face bore traces of weeping, and she looked anxious and dejected; but I could see that she was naturally quick and intelligent.

'I have just run over to see if there is any fresh news this morning,' she said, with an enquiring glance at me.

'This is Mr Zambra, my dear, come to help us,' said Mr Gale; 'and this,' he continued, turning to me, 'is Miss Maud Tudway. We are all enlisted in the same cause.'

'You will be able to prove Mr Franklin Gale's innocence, sir?' she exclaimed.

'I hope so,' I said; 'and the best way to do it will be to trace the robbery to its real author. Has Mr Franklin any suspicions on that head?'

'He is as much puzzled as we are,' said Miss Tudway. 'I went with Mr Gale here to see him in that horrible place yesterday, and he said there was absolutely no one in the bank he cared to suspect. But he *must* get off the next time he appears. My evidence ought to do that. I saw with my own eyes that he had only one £5 note in his purse on the 25th – that is two days before he paid the tailor, and three days after the robbery.'

'I am afraid that won't help us much,' I said. 'You see, he might easily have had the missing notes elsewhere. But tell me, under what circumstances did you see the £5 note?'

'There was a garden party at our house,' replied Miss Tudway, 'and Franklin was there. During the afternoon a man came to the gate with an accordion and a performing monkey, and asked permission to show the monkey's tricks. We had the man in, and after the monkey had done a lot of clever things the man said that the animal could tell a good banknote from a "flash" one. He was provided with spurious notes for the purpose; would any gentleman lend him a good note for a minute, just to show the trick? The man was quite close to Franklin, who was sitting next to me. Franklin, seeing the man's hand held out towards him, took out his purse and handed him a note, at the same time calling my attention to the fact that it was his only one, and laughingly saying that he hoped the man was honest. The sham note and the good one were placed before the monkey, who at once tore up the bad note and handed the good one back to Franklin.'

'This is more important than it seems,' I said, after a moment's review of the whole case. 'I must find that man with the monkey, but it bids fair to be difficult. There are so many of them in that line of business.'

Miss Tudway smiled for the first time during the interview.

'It is possible that I may be of use to you there,' she said. 'I go in for amateur photography, and I thought that the man and his monkey made so good a subject that I insisted on taking him before he left. Shall I fetch the photograph?'

'By all means,' I said. 'Photography is of the greatest use to me in my work. I generally arrange it myself, but if you have chanced to take the right picture for me in this case so much the better.'

Miss Tudway hurried across to her father's house and quickly returned with the photograph. It was a fair effort for an amateur, and portrayed an individual of the usual seedy stamp, equipped with a huge accordion and a small monkey secured by a string. With this in my hand it would only be a matter of time before I found the itinerant juggler who had presented himself at the Tudways' garden party, and I took my leave of old Mr Gale and Miss Maud in a much more hopeful frame of mind. Every circumstance outside the terrible array of actual evidence pointed to my client's innocence, and if this evidence had been manufactured for the purpose, I felt certain that the 'monkey man' had had a hand in it.

On arriving at my office I summoned one of my

assistants – a veteran of doubtful antecedents – who owns to no other name than 'Old Jemmy'. Old Jemmy's particular line of business is a thorough knowledge of the slums and the folk who dwell there; and I knew that after an hour or two on Saffron Hill my ferret, armed with the photograph, would bring me the information I wanted. Towards evening Old Jemmy came in with his report, to the effect that the 'party' I was after was to be found in the top attic of 7 Little Didman's Fields, Hatton Garden, just recovering from the effects of a prolonged spree.

'He's been drunk for three or four days, the land-lord told me,' Old Jemmy said. 'Had a stroke of luck, it seems, but he is expected to go on tramp tomorrow, now his coin has given out. His name is Pietro Schilizzi.'

I knew I was on the right scent now, and that the 'monkey man' had been made the instrument of *changing* the note which Franklin Gale had lent him for one of the stolen ones. A quick cab took me to Little Didman's Fields in a quarter of an hour, and I was soon standing inside the doorway of a pestilential apartment on the top floor of No. 7, which had been pointed out to me as the abode of Pietro Schilizzi. A succession of snores from a heap of rags in a corner told me the whereabouts of the occupier. I went over, and shaking him roughly by the shoulder, said in Italian: 'Pietro, I want you to tell me about that little juggle with a banknote at Twickenham the other day. You will be well rewarded.'

The fellow rubbed his eyes in half-drunken astonishment, but there certainly was no guilty fear about him as he replied: 'Certainly, signor; any-thing for money. There was nothing wrong about the note, was there? Anyhow, I acted innocently in the matter.'

'No one finds fault with you,' I said; 'but see, here is a five-pound note. It shall be yours if you will tell me exactly what happened.'

'I was with my monkey up at Highgate the other evening,' Mr Schilizzi began, 'and was showing Jacko's trick of telling a good note from a bad one. It was a small house in the Napier Road. After I had finished, the gentleman took me into a public house and stood me a drink. He wanted me to do something for him, he said. He had a young friend who was careless, and never took the number of notes, and he wanted to teach him a lesson. He had a bet about the number of a note, he said. Would I go down to Twickenham next day to a house he described, where there was to be a party, and do my trick with the monkey? I was to borrow a note from the young gentleman, and then, instead of giving him back his own note after the performance, I was to substitute one which the High-gate gentleman gave me for the purpose. He met me at Twickenham next day, and came behind the garden wall to point out the young gentleman to me. I managed it just as the Highgate gentleman wanted, and he gave me a couple of pounds for my pains. I have done no wrong; the note I gave back was a good one.'

'Yes,' I said, 'but it happens to have been stolen. Put on your hat and show me where this man lives in Highgate.'

The Napier Road was a shabby street of dingy houses, with a public house at the corner. Pietro stopped about halfway down the row and pointed out No. 21.

'That is where the gentleman lives,' he said.

We retraced our steps to the corner public house.

'Can you tell me who lives at No. 21?' I asked of the landlord, who happened to be in the bar.

'Certainly,' was the answer; 'it is Mr James Spruce – a good customer of mine, and the best billiard player hereabouts. He is a cashier at Messrs Tudways' bank, in the Strand, I believe.'

It all came out at the trial – not of Franklin Gale, but of James Spruce, the fraudulent cashier. Spruce had himself abstracted the notes and gold entrusted to him, and his guilty conscience telling him that he might be suspected, he had cast about for a means of throwing suspicion on some other person. Chancing to witness the performance of Pietro's monkey, he had grasped the opportunity for foisting one of the stolen notes on Franklin Gale, knowing that sooner or later it would be traced to him. The other notes he had intended to hold over till it was safe to send them out of the country; but the gold was the principal object of his theft.

Mr Tudway, the banker, was, I hear, so cut up about the false accusation that he had made against his favourite that he insisted on Franklin joining him as a partner at once, and the marriage is to take place before very long. I am also told that the photograph of the 'monkey man', handsomely enlarged and mounted, will form one of the mural decorations of the young couple.